The Outsider

The Outsider

by Richard Wright

PERENNIAL LIBRARY
Harper & Row, Publishers
New York, Hagerstown, San Francisco, London

The Outsider was originally published by Harper & Row, Publishers, Inc., in 1953.

First PERENNIAL LIBRARY edition published 1965

ISBN: 0-06-080022-4

82 20 19 18 17

For Rachel

my daughter who was born on alien soil

Cruelty has a Human Heart,
And Jealousy a Human Face;
Terror the Human Form Divine,
And Secrecy the Human Dress.

—WILLIAM BLAKE

Mark me, and be astonished,
And lay your hand upon your mouth.

—JOB

BOOK 1: Dread

> Dread is an alien power which lays hold
> of an individual, and yet one cannot tear
> oneself away, nor has a will to do so; for
> one fears what one desires.
>
> — KIERKEGAARD

From an invisible February sky a shimmering curtain of
snowflakes fluttered down upon Chicago. It was five
o'clock in the morning and still dark. On a South Side
street four masculine figures moved slowly forward shoulder to shoulder and the sound of their feet tramping and
sloshing in the melting snow echoed loudly. The men were
warmly dressed and wore mufflers about their throats. The
brims of their hats, encrusted with snow, were pulled down
at rakish tilts over their eyes. Behind turned-up overcoat
collars their gruff voices exploded in jokes, laughter, and
shouts. They jostled one another with rude affection and
their hot breaths projected gusts of vapor onto the chilled
morning air. One of the men threw out an arm and
grabbed a companion about the neck and crooned:
"Booker, let me rest my tired, cold body on you, hunh?"

"Hell, naw! Stand on your own two big flat feet, Cross!"
Booker, a short, black man, protested with a laugh.

The man called Cross turned and flung his arm about
the shoulders of a big, fat, black man and said, "Then how
about you, Joe?"

"Look, Crossy, I'm tired too," Joe defended himself,
shying off. "Why pick on me?"

" 'Cause you're soft as a mattress and can stand it,"
Cross explained.

"If you're cold, it's your own damn hard luck," Joe said.

1

"You don't take care of yourself. Me, I ain't never cold. I know how come you're always so cold, Cross. You drink too much. Don't eat enough. Don't sleep. But, *me* . . . ha-ha! I eat and sleep as much as I can. And my good old fat helps to keep me warm. Ain't that right, Pink?"

The man called Pink did not reply at once; he was reddish in color and older than the other three.

"Cross," Pink said seriously, "you ought to take some vitamins or something. Man, you *couldn't* be cold now. Hell, we just left that steamy Post Office twenty minutes ago."

Cross swiftly pulled the glove off his right hand and, grabbing Pink's shoulder, rammed his bare fingers down the collar of Pink's neck.

"How do they feel, Pink?" Cross demanded.

"Jeeesus! Your fingers're cold as *snakes!*" Pink gasped, his eyes lit with concern. "They ought to call you *Mr. Death!*"

"I just need some alcohol," Cross said grimly. "My old engine won't run without it."

"You better quit that bottle, Cross," Joe, the big, fat, black man warned. "When you start *living* on alcohol, you're traveling a road that ain't got no turning. You been hitting that bottle heavy for a month now. Better let up, boy."

"Man, whisky ain't never hurt nobody," Pink said; he broke into song:

> If the ocean was whisky
>> And I was a duck
> I'd dive right in
>> And never come up.

A rich, rolling laughter erupted and died away over the snow-blanketed sidewalks.

"Crossy, how come you're drinking so much these days?" Booker asked in a tone free of moral objections.

"My soul needs it," Cross mumbled.

"Makes you feel better, hunh?" Booker asked.

"No. Makes me feel *less*," Cross corrected him.

"But how about your liver?" Joe demanded.

2

"My liver's in the death house," Cross admitted.

"Say, Pinkie, remember when Crossy used to be the life of the gang?" Joe asked. "Now he just swills and every word he says is a gripe."

"We all have blue days," Pink said.

"*Pink* has *blue* days." Cross's tongue played softly with the words.

All of them laughed except Cross, whose lips shaped themselves into an ambiguous smile whose meaning might have been a jeering at or a participation in the merriment. He was tall but slightly built, with a smooth brown and yellow skin, and his body moved as though it had more nervous energy than it could contain.

"Aw, leave Cross alone," Pink said.

"Thanks, pal," Cross muttered.

Joe suddenly paused amid the flakes of dancing snow, laughing hysterically, slapping his thighs, sending blasts of steam onto the frigid air. The sheen of a street lamp sharply etched his ebony face.

"What's the matter, Joe?" Booker asked.

"Oh, God," Joe gasped, his fat cheeks trembling and tears gleaming at the corners of his eyes.

"All right; share the damn joke," Pink said.

The three men confronted Joe and waited for his mirth to subside.

"Today I heard somebody say the damnedest thing about Cross—" Joe went off into another spasm of mirth, bending over, coughing, spluttering, sending tiny flecks of spittle into the runaway snowflakes. Joe finally straightened and placed a brotherly hand upon Cross's shoulder. "Now, listen, if I tell what I heard, you won't be mad, will you?"

"I don't give a damn what you heard," Cross said.

"Well, spill it, man," Pink urged impatiently.

"Somebody said," Joe began, "that Cross was trying to imitate the United States Government. They said the trouble with Cross was his four A's. *Alcohol. Abortions. Automobiles.* And *alimony.*" Joe laughed so violently that his eyes were buried in fat. Jerking out his words, he continued: "They called C-cross the Q-q-quadruple-A Program! Said that the best thing for Cross w-was to plow h-himself under. . . ."

Cross stood aloof as the others bent double with their laughter. Cross didn't resent what had been said; it was as though they were laughing at the foibles of an absent man who was well known to him. He smiled, admitting to himself that the analogy was not badly put, that it fitted the snarled facts of his life pretty aptly, and that he couldn't have summed up his situation any better himself. The more Pink, Joe, and Booker guffawed, the longer Cross retained his nervous, ambiguous smile. Finally the laughter died and Joe, putting his arm about Cross's shoulder, promised consolingly: "Goddammit, Crossy, I'm gonna buy you a drink. Hell, I'm gonna buy you *two* drinks. You need 'em."

Still chuckling, they trudged on through the snow to a corner tavern whose neon sign dimly identified it as The Salty Dog. They pushed through the door and went in. Cross followed solemnly, his hands dug into his overcoat pockets, a cigarette stub glowing in his lips. He sat with the others in a booth and looked at them with quiet eyes and an enigmatic smile. A short, fat, brown proprietor with a bald head and a gray goatee called to them from behind the bar: "Same old thing, boys?"

"Same old thing, Doc," Joe and Pink chorused.

"Crossy, what's the trouble?" Booker asked softly.

"You *know* what's wrong with 'im," Joe insisted. "His Quadruple-A Program's got 'im down."

They laughed again. Doc set four whiskies before them and, at the sight of the little glasses of pale brown fluid, they grew sober, almost dignified; each took up his glass daintily and threw back his head and tossed the liquor down his throat.

"One of these days, Doc," Cross said, sighing and smacking his lips, "we're going to fool you. We're going to swallow the glasses too."

"Atta boy!" Joe approved.

"The spirit moved 'im at last," Booker commented.

"Crossy," Joe said, "you're losing your touch. Remember the time you used to pull them crazy stunts?" Joe turned to the others for confirmation. "When Cross first came to work in the Post Office, he was a nonstop riot, a real killer-diller. Early in the evening, when the rush hour was on, he used to—we were working on the eleventh floor

4

then——lift up the window, run his hand in his pocket and toss out every cent of silver he had. Just throw it all out of the window to the street. And then he'd lean out and watch the commotion of all them little antlike folks down there going wild, scrambling and scratching and clawing after them few pieces of money and then, when the money was all gone, they'd stand looking up to the window of the eleventh floor with their mouths hanging open like fishes out of water. And Cross'd be laughing to beat all hell. And Cross'd say that them folks was praying when their faces were turned up like that, waiting for more money to fall. Ha-ha!

"Remember when two men jumped at the same time for the same quarter that Cross had tossed out? They dived toward each other and they butted head on and knocked each other out, cold. They just lay there, like a truck had hit 'em, and all the other folks crowded round, looking and wondering what had happened. They had to send the riot cars full of cops to break up the mob and take the two dopes who had been diving for the quarter to jail. Ha-ha! Honest to God, I thought I'd die laughing. Cross said that that was the only time he ever felt like God. Ha-ha!"

They laughed musingly, their eyes resting on Cross's face, which carried a detached smile.

"Remember that wild gag he pulled at Christmastime in 19 . . . ?" Joe frowned thoughtfully and the others waited. "When the hell was that now? Oh, yes! It was in 1945. I'll never forget it. Cross bought a batch of magazines, *Harper's, Atlantic Monthly, Collier's, Ladies' Home Journal,* and clipped out those ads that say you can send your friends a year's subscription as a Christmas gift. Well, Cross signed 'em and sent 'em to his friends. But he didn't sign 'em with *his* name, see? He signed 'em with the names of friends of people he was sending the subscriptions to. He sent me one and it was signed by my wife. Ha-ha! Was she mad? But in the end, she really paid for it. Crossy sent one to James Harden and signed it with my name. Ha-ha! Christmas morning Harden calls me up and starts thanking me for the gift subscription I'd sent 'im to *Harper's*. I didn't know what the hell Harden was talking about, and I was so 'shamed I sat right down and sent

5

Harper's a check! Man, the whole South Side was in a dither that Christmas morning. Folks was thanking other folks for presents the others didn't know nothing about. And Crossy was listening and watching and saying nothing. Lord, it was a mess! Cross, how in God's name did you dream up such stuff? Any man who can do things like that is a man standing *outside* of the world! Know what I mean? Like somebody outside of your window was looking into your house and poking out his tongue at you." Joe went into a gale of laughter; then he pointed to Cross's smiling face. "Look at 'im, will you? He sits there, smiling, not saying a word, not letting on he used to pull stunts like that."

They laughed, looking at Cross with tenderness in their eyes.

"Say, remember all them big, deep books he used to read and tell us about?" Joe asked, looking from Cross to the others. "He used to use so many big words I thought he'd choke! Every time I saw 'im, he had a batch of books under his arm."

"But what I couldn't understand," Pink recalled, "was why Cross wouldn't believe anything in the books he read. One time he was all hepped-up over one writer and the next time he was through with 'im and was gone on to another."

"And the books in Cross's room!" Booker exclaimed. "I went to see 'im one day when he was sick, and I could hardly get in the door! Big books, little books, books piled everywhere! He even had books in bed with 'im."

Their heads tilted back with laughter; Cross smiled without rancor.

"I told 'im," Booker continued, " 'Crossy, you better find a gal to sleep with you, 'cause them books can't keep you warm!' Man, in the clothes closet: books. In the bathroom: books. Under the bed: books. I said, 'Crossy, you ain't got no flu germs; you got bookworms!' "

They clapped their hands with laughter; Cross smiled and looked off.

"Cross, you ain't never said how come you was reading all them books," Joe pointed out.

"I was looking for something," Cross said quietly.

6

"What?" Pink asked.

"I don't know," Cross confessed gloomily.

"Did you find it?" Joe asked.

"No."

Joe, Pink, and Booker howled with delight.

"In those days Cross's mind was like a little mouse, running every which way— Say, Cross, how many books you got in your room?"

"I don't know," Cross mumbled.

"I wished I had a dollar for every book you got," Joe sighed. "Now, honest, Crossy, how come you don't read no more?"

"I've put away childish things," Cross said.

"Aw, be yourself, man," Booker said.

"I am what I am," Cross said. "I'm sparing you guys a lot. I'm not going to bother you with my troubles."

"Can't we help you any, Cross?" Joe asked seriously.

"Lay off, guys," Cross said, frowning for the first time. "I'm all right." He turned and beckoned to Doc. "Bring me a bottle, Doc!"

"Don't drink any more, Cross," Pink begged.

"Ain't you gonna eat some breakfast?" Booker asked.

"Whisky ain't no good on an empty stomach," Joe reminded him.

"It's my stomach," Cross said.

"Aw, leave 'im alone," Booker said.

"But a man who drinks ought to eat," Joe insisted.

"Eating's all you think about, Joe," Cross growled.

"Hell, you got to eat to live!" Joe shouted with authoritative rudeness. "And you better stop drinking and eat and sleep some." Joe suddenly laughed and began a game of make-believe, imitating a baby's crying: "Awwwww—awwwww—awwww—!" He altered his tone. "Now, what the little baby wants?" He bawled out the answer: "The bottle, the bottle, the *whisky* bottle, Mama!"

Laughter seethed and Cross joined in to show his appreciation.

"Leave 'im alone," Booker said. "He knows his own mind."

"If he keeps up that drinking, he won't have no mind left," Joe said emphatically. "And it'll kill 'im."

"All right," Cross said darkly. "Do I want to live forever?"

"You're nuts," Joe said.

"It pleases me," Cross said without anger.

"Okay," Joe said.

"Sure; it's okay," Cross said, opening the bottle and taking a long swig.

"Wheeew," Joe whistled. "You can't *drink* like that, boy!"

"I *am*," Cross said calmly.

"You gonna finish that bottle today?" Booker asked softly.

"Maybe. How do I know?"

"Ain't you gonna sleep?"

"If I can."

" 'If I can,' " jeered Joe. "Stop dringing and you *can* sleep."

"I wouldn't sleep at all then," Cross said.

"What's *eating* you, Cross?" Pink implored softly. "We've been your friends for six years. Spill it. We'll help you—"

"Skip it," Cross said. "Am I complaining? You signed for my last loan and that took care of my Quadruple-A debts. That's enough."

They laughed at how Cross could laugh at himself.

"There're some things a man must do alone," Cross added.

The three men looked silently at Cross. He knew that they liked him, but he felt that they were outside of his life, that there was nothing that they could do that would make any difference. Now more than ever he knew that he was alone and that his problem was one of the relationship of himself to himself.

"We ain't your mama and your papa," Joe sighed, forcing a sad smile. "We can't hold your hand, Big Boy. And you're a big boy, you know."

"Yes, I'm a big boy," Cross smiled bitterly.

"It's between you and your Maker, your problem," Joe said.

"Lucky Joe," Cross murmured in a tone of envy.

"What do you mean?" Joe asked.

8

Cross rose, smiled widely for the first time, pointed his finger into Joe's fat, black, round face, and intoned: " 'And God made man in his own image. . . .' "

Pink and Booker yelled with laughter. Joe passed his hand caressingly and self-consciously over his black face and looked puzzled. Cross demanded in a mockingly serious voice: "Did God really make *that* face? Is He guilty of *that*? If He did, then He was walking in His sleep!" Cross shook with laughter. "To blame God for making Joe is to degrade the very concept of God!"

Pink and Booker leaped to their feet and grabbed Joe about the waist.

"Did God really make you, Joe?" Pink demanded.

"Was God absent-minded when He cooked you up, Joe?" Booker asked.

Joe forced a smile, but underneath he was a little disturbed. Then he protested: "God made me, all right. He made my soul and He made my *body* too."

"But why did He make your body so *fat*, Joe?" Cross asked.

"I just ate too much and got fat," Joe replied sheepishly.

"But *God* gave you your appetite," Pink told him.

"And the body reflects the soul," Cross clenched it.

They all rose except Cross; he still sat and smiled up at Joe.

"Go home and get some shut-eye, Cross," Joe advised him.

"God won't let me sleep," Cross said.

"God ain't got *nothing* to do with it!" Joe pronounced.

"Then who keeps me awake all day long?" Cross wanted to know.

"You, yourself," Joe said.

"Maybe you're right," Cross conceded.

"So long," Pink said.

"See you, Crossy," Joe said.

" 'Bye, now," Booker said.

"So long," Cross mumbled, not looking at them as they filed out.

"Some guys," Doc said from behind the bar.

"Yeah; *some* guys," Cross repeated, staring at the floor.

Yeah; it was time to sleep. He felt dead. How long could

9

he last like this? His eyes suddenly clouded with displeasure. He had promised to see Dot this morning, but he didn't want to talk to her, much less see her. . . . That was all he needed: seeing Dot and having one of those long, hysterical, weeping arguments. He knew what Dot wanted to ask and the answer was no and it would always be no! Oh, *damn* that Dot! But if he didn't call her, she'd soon be coming to his room and they'd argue all day long. And that was the last thing he wanted. Yes; he'd better call her; he'd tell her he was sick, feeling too bad to see her. He rose, jammed the whisky bottle into his overcoat pocket, went into the telephone booth, dropped a coin into the slot and dialed. Almost at once Dot's voice sang over the wire: "How are you, darling?"

She was waiting in the hallway by the phone, he thought.

"I feel like hell," he growled.

"Have you eaten breakfast?"

"Naw; I just left the Post Office—"

"But honey, you got off from work at *four* o'clock and now it's nearly *six*. You've had plenty of time to eat."

"I was in a bar," he told her.

"Oh, God, Cross! You must stop *drinking!*"

"Do you think I can with what I've got on my mind?"

"Come over right *now,* hunh? I'll cook your breakfast—"

"Naw."

"Why?"

"I don't want to."

"You promised you'd see me this morning—"

"But I don't feel like it. I'm exhausted."

"You mean you're too drunk!" she said savagely.

"So?"

"Oh, God, Cross! Why did I ever get mixed up with you?"

"I've told you how to get *unmixed* with me, haven't I?"

"Don't you say that to me again!"

"I *am* saying it!"

"Listen, come here now! I want to talk to you!"

"I'm tired, I tell you!"

"I don't care! You come over *now!*"

10

"You're crazy, Dot! Do you think you can make people do things they don't want to do?" he asked her earnestly.

He heard her suck in her breath and when her voice came over the wire again it was so shrill that he had to hold the receiver away from his ear.

"If you *don't* see me this morning, you'll be *sorry!* You hear? Whatever happens'll be *your* fault! You can't treat me this way! I won't *let* you! You hear? I said I won't *let* you! You made me a promise and I want you to keep it! Now, come over here. I've got something to tell you—"

"Dot—"

"No; no; let me talk—"

"Listen, Dot—"

"I said let *me* talk!"

"Oh, goddammit, Dot!"

"Don't cuss me! Oh, God, don't cuss me when I'm like this! Can't you understand? Have a little pity—" Her voice caught in her throat. "I'll *kill* myself—"

"Dot—don't go on like that—"

"You don't think I'll kill myself, but I will—"

"You're crazy!"

"I'll get you for that!" she shouted. "I *will!*"

"If you keep shouting at me, I'll hang up!"

"I *will* shout at you!"

He hesitated, then slammed the receiver onto the hook. Damn her! He was trembling. He'd known that it'd go like this and he'd be unnerved for the rest of the day. He fumbled for the bottle and took a deep swallow. Yes; he had to get some sleep or go mad. He went out of the telephone booth and waved good-by to Doc and kept on out the door and walked along the snow-piled sidewalks. He caught a trolley and rode standing on the platform, swaying as much from the rocking of the car as from the alcohol. He alighted in front of his apartment building, groped for his key, and let himself in. Fifteen minutes later he was undressed and in bed. He was so tired that he could scarcely feel the sensations of his body and he could not relax. He stared wakefully in the semidarkness and wondered what he could do about Dot. . . .

What a messy life he was living! It was crazy; it was

11

killing him; it was senseless; and he was a fool to go on living it. What a stinking botch he'd made out of everything he had touched! Why? He didn't know. I could be teaching school, he told himself. He'd dropped out of the university right after he'd married Gladys and after that nothing had gone right.

He lay still, his bloodshot eyes staring blankly before him, and drifted into dreams of his problems, compulsively living out dialogues, summoning up emotional scenes with his mother, reliving the reactions of his wife, Dot, and his friends. Repeatedly he chided himself to go to sleep, but it did no good, for he was hungry for these waking visions that depicted his dilemmas, yet he knew that such brooding did not help; in fact, he was wasting his waning strength, for into these unreal dramas he was putting the whole of his being. The long hours of the day dragged on.

He twisted on his crumpled bed, reshaped his lumpy pillow until his head nestled into it exactly right; and, for the hundredth time, he closed his eyes and lay still, trying to purge his mind of anxiety, beseeching sleep. He felt his numbed limbs slowly shedding tension and for a moment he floated toward a world of dreams, seesawing softly between sleeping and waking. Then, convulsively, his entire body jerked rigidly to stem a fearful feeling of falling through space. His rebellious nerves twanged with a terror that his mind sought desperately to deny. He shook his head, his body seething with hate against himself and the world.

He checked his watch: two o'clock. A gray day showed through the curtained window and from the snowy street rose the din of traffic. Today was like yesterday and he knew that tomorrow would be the same. And it had been like this now for months. Each morning he'd come from work and crawl wearily into bed and toss for hours, yearning for the mercy of a sleep that was not his and at last he realized that his search for surcease was hopeless. He sighed, stood, crossed to the dresser and took another pull from the bottle. At eight o'clock he'd report to work and for eight long hours he'd sway upon his feet, drugged with fatigue, straining against collapse, sorting mail like a sleepwalker. He moistened his lips with his tongue. He had not eaten all day and, as the alcohol deadened the raw nerves of his stomach, he thought: I'll do it now; I'll end this farce. . . . He hunched determinedly forward and his crinkled pajamas bagged about his gaunt body and the muscles of his neck bulged. He'd not crawl like a coward through stupid days; to act quickly was the simplest way of jumping through the jungle of problems that plagued him from within and from without. A momentary dizziness swamped him; his throat tightened; his vision blurred; his chest heaved and he was defenseless against despair. He sprang to the dresser and yanked open a drawer and pulled forth his gun. Trembling, feeling the cold blue steel touching his sweaty palm, he lifted the glinting barrel to his right temple, then paused. His feelings were like tumbling dice. . . . He wilted, cursed, his breath expiring through parted lips. Choked with self-hate, he flung himself on the bed and buried his face in his hands.

Broken thus in will, he relaxed for the first time in weeks; he could rest only when he was too drained of energy to fret further. At length he lifted his head and the fingers of his right hand pressed nervously against his lower lip, then tapped his knee as though to still the writhing of his spirit. He was despairingly aware of his body as an alien and despised object over which he had no power, a burden that was always cheating him of the fruits of his thought, mocking him with its stubborn and supine solidity.

Claimed at last by the needs of the hour, he proceeded to bathe and dress. Again he drank from the bottle and was grateful for the sense of depression caused by the alcohol which made him feel less of pleasure, pain, anxiety, and hope. Could he get through the night without collapsing? Suddenly he was filled with an idea: *He would take the gun with him!* And if the pressure from within or without became too great he would use it; his gun would be his final protection against the world as well as against himself. . . . And if he was ever so unlucky as to be found sprawled from nervous collapse upon some frozen sidewalk or upon the floor of the Post Office, it would be manfully better to let others see a bloody hole gaping in his temple than to present to the eyes of strangers a mass of

13

black flesh stricken by stupor. His decision renewed his courage; if he had not thought of the gun, he doubted if he could have gone to work.

He pulled on his overcoat and stood hesitantly by the door; but even the gun sagging in his pocket did not convince him that he was fit to work. During the past month he had been absent so often on excuses of illness that he did not dare telephone and report himself on the sick list. He would master his tricky sensations; he would force himself to carry on till he dropped. He usually found that he did not really collapse even when he had the consciousness of being about to pitch forward on his face. . . .

He yearned to talk to someone; he felt his mere telling his story would have helped. But to whom could he talk? To his mother? No; she would only assure him that he was reaping the wages of sin and his sense of dread would deepen. Could he talk to his wife with whom he was not living? God, no! She'd laugh bitterly and say, "I told you so!" There was Dot, his sweetheart; but she was not capable of understanding anything. Moreover, she was partly the cause of his present state. And there was not a single man to whom he cared to confess the nightmare that was his life. He had sharp need of a confidant, and yet he knew that if he had an ideal confidant before whom he could lay his whole story, he would have instantly regretted it, would have murdered his confidant the moment after he had confided to him his shame. How could he have gone on living knowing that someone else knew how things were with him? Cross was proud.

His hand touched the doorknob and the telephone shrilled. Now, who in hell could that be? Was it Dot? Or Gladys? He turned the doorknob and the telephone rang again. Hell! Anger flashed through him at some vague someone who was trying to snatch him from his futile wrestling with his problem, trying to pry him loose from the only thing that made his life possess meaning even though it made him suffer. Impatiently he picked up the receiver.

"Cross? Is that you?" It was his mother's quavering, high-pitched voice coming uncertainly over the wire.

"How are you, Ma?"

"Fine, Cross, I reckon," she said querulously, like those who are over sixty and who feel uncommonly well but are too superstitious to admit it. "Can I see you, Cross? Sometime today . . . ?"

He bridled, trying to slap away the clutch of his mother's wrinkled hand as it reached invisibly for him.

"Anything wrong, Ma?"

"I want to see you," she said, evading his question.

He did not want to see her, certainly not now with this mood of bleak dread in him.

"Ma, I'm trying to sleep," he lied, speaking reprovingly.

Silence. He felt he had hurt her and he grew angry. He waited for her to speak further, but only the metallic hum of the line came to his ear.

"Ma," he called softly. "You're still there?"

"Yes, Cross." A note of firm patience in her voice frightened him.

"What is it, Ma? I work nights and I've got to get some rest."

Again silence.

"Is it about money?" he asked, trying to hasten it.

Another silence; then his mother's voice came clearly: "Cross, that Dot girl was just by here to see me. . . ."

Her tone, charged and precise, was filled with a multitude of accusations that evoked a vast hot void in him. His mother was still talking, but he did not hear her. His eyes darted like those of a bayed animal. Oh, God! *Why had Dot done that?* He had not kept his promise to see her this morning and she had gotten into a panic; that was it. But she had sworn to consult him before acting on her own, and now . . . His life was a delicate bridge spanning a gaping chasm and hostile hands were heaping heavy loads upon that bridge and it was about to crack and crash downward.

"What did you say, Ma?" He pretended that he had not heard.

How much did she know? Perhaps everything! That crazy Dot! He could wring her neck for this! She had no right to tell tales to his mother! Women had no sense of . . .

"You *know* what I'm talking about, boy," his mother scolded him sternly. "That girl's in trouble—"

"*Who* are you talking about, Ma?" He still stalled for time.

"Stop acting foolish, Cross! That girl's blaming *you*—"

"Blaming me for what?" he asked. He knew that he was acting silly, but he could not easily change his attitude now.

"She's in a family way, Cross," his mother spoke boldly, a woman lodging woman's ancient complaint against man. "And she says it's *you!* She's worried sick. She had to talk to somebody, so she came to me. Son, what have you done?" There came the sound of a sob being choked back. "You're married. You've three children. What're you going to do?"

"Just a sec. Somebody's at the door," he lied for respite.

Like always, he had doubled his burdens; he heard his mother's tirades and at the same time he pretended that he was not reacting to them, and this dual set of responses made him frantic. That hare-brained Dot! Trying to save herself and ruining me, the only one who can save her. . . . He brought the phone to his mouth.

"Is she still there, Ma?" His tone of voice confessed that he knew what it was all about.

"Hunh? No; she's gone," his mother said. "She's gone to see Gladys. . . . Cross, that girl's young, a child. She can get you into serious trouble. . . ."

Dot was talking to his wife! This was the end! The void in him grew hotter. He knew Gladys would do her damnedest now; she would be merciless. Her knowing about Dot would redouble her hate for him. She would bare the details of his private blunderings before the domestic courts. . . . He had to try to stop her. But could he? Maybe it was already too late?

"I'll be right over," he said, hanging up abruptly.

He took another drink and went out the door. As he descended the stairs, his mother's scolding intensified his mood of self-loathing, a mood that had been his longer than he could recall, a mood that had been growing deeper with the increasing complexity of the events of his life. He knew himself too well not to realize the meaning of what

16

he was feeling; yet his self-knowledge, born of a habit of incessant reflection, did not enable him to escape the morass in which his feelings were bogged. His insight merely augmented his emotional conflicts. He was aware, intimately and bitterly, that his dread had been his mother's first fateful gift to him. He had been born of her not only physically but emotionally too. The only psychological difference between them was that he was aware of having received this dark gift from her at a time when he was too young to reject it, and she had given it to him in a period of her life when her intense grief over the death of her husband had rendered her incapable of realizing the full import of what she had been doing. And he could never speak to her about this difference in emotional similarity; he could only pretend that it did not exist, for not only did his deep love of her forbid it; but he did not possess enough emotional detachment from her for that to happen. As her son, he was much too far from her and at the same time much too close, much too warm toward her and much too cold. To keep her life from crushing his own, he had slain the sense of her in his heart and at the same time had clung frantically to his memory of that sense.

From the vestibule he stepped into a frozen world lit by a lemon-colored sun whose glare sparkled on mounds of ice. The snow had stopped and the sky stretched pale and blue; the air was dry and bitter cold. The sun disclosed in sharp detail the red brick buildings, glinted on the slow-moving trolleys, and cast into the windowpanes reflections that stung his eyes. His shoulders hunched forward and he shivered and clenched his teeth to keep them from chattering, his breath steaming against the freezing air.

He was conscious of himself as a frail object which had to protect itself against a pending threat of annihilation. This frigid world was suggestively like the one which his mother, without knowing it, had created for him to live in when he had been a child. Though she had loved him, she had tainted his budding feelings with a fierce devotion born of her fear of a life that had baffled and wounded her. His first coherent memories had condensed themselves into an image of a young woman whose hysterically loving presence had made his imagination conscious of an invisible

God—Whose secret grace granted him life——hovering oppressively in space above him. His adolescent fantasies had symbolically telescoped this God into an awful face shaped in the form of a huge and crushing NO, a terrifying face which had, for a reason he could never learn, created him, had given him a part of Himself, and yet had threateningly demanded that he vigilantly deny another part of himself which He too had paradoxically given him. This God's NO-face had evoked in his pliable boy's body an aching sense of pleasure by admonishing him to shun pleasure as the tempting doorway opening blackly onto hell; had too early awakened in him a sharp sense of sex by thunderingly denouncing sex as the sin leading to eternal damnation; had posited in him an unbridled hunger for the sensual by branding all sensuality as the monstrous death from which there was no resurrection; had made him instinctively choose to love himself over and against all others because he felt himself menaced by a mysterious God Whose love seemed somehow like hate. Mother love had cleaved him: a wayward sensibility that distrusted itself, a consciousness that was conscious of itself. Despite this, his sensibilities had not been repressed by God's fearful negations as represented by his mother; indeed, his sense of life had been so heightened that desire boiled in him to a degree that made him afraid. Afraid of what? Nothing exactly, precisely . . . And this constituted his sense of dread.

As he neared his mother's rooming house, he could already feel the form of her indictment, could divine the morally charged words she would hurl at him. And he knew that his reaction would be one of sullen and guilty anger. Why, then, was he going to see her? Because he really wanted her to rail at him, denounce him, and he would suffer, feel his hurt again, and, in doing so, would know intuitively that somewhere in the depths of his raw wound lay his salvation or his disaster. This obscure knowledge had stayed his finger on the trigger of the gun whose barrel had touched his temple this morning. . . .

He entered a dilapidated building, went down a dark hallway and tapped upon a door. Sounds of muffled movement came to him; the door opened and framed his

18

mother's solemnly lined face, the white hair pulled severely
back from a wide forehead, a gnarled right hand holding a
woolen shawl about stooped shoulders Her mouth was a
tight, flat slit and her eyes peered through cloudy
spectacles.

"Hi, Ma."

Without answering, she widened the door and he walked
past her into a tiny, shabby room that smelled of a sweet-
ish odor of decaying flesh that seems to cling to the aged
who are slowly dying while still living.

He noticed, as he did each time he visited her, that she
appeared to have shrunken a bit more; and he knew that it
was her chronic fretting that was whitening the hairs of her
head, deepening the lines in her face, and accentuating the
stoop of her back. His mother could no more relax than he
could. Like me, she's using up herself too fast, and she's
just a little over sixty. . . . If she cared for herself more,
judged life less severely, time would deal easier with her.
. . . Why were some people fated, like Job, to live a
never-ending debate between themselves and their sense of
what they believed life should be? Why did some hearts
feel insulted at being alive, humiliated at the terms of existence? It was as though one felt that one had been promised
something and when that promise had not been kept, one
felt a sense of loss that made life intolerable; it was as
though one was angry but did not know toward what or
whom the anger should be directed; it was as though one
felt betrayed, but could never determine the manner of the
betrayal. And this was what was making his mother old
before her time. . . .

He smoked, looked about vacantly, avoiding her accusing eyes, and was already fighting down a feeling of defensive guilt. She turned and began rummaging aimlessly in a
dresser drawer and he knew that she was deliberately making him wait before she spoke, attempting to reduce him
again to the status of a fearfully impressionable child. Before pronouncing her condemnations, she would make him
feel that she was weighing him in the scales of her drastic
judgment and was finding, to her horror, that he was self-
centered and ridden by this lust for pleasure, irresponsible
and thoughtlessly squandering his life's substance. And aft-

19

erward he would listen with a face masked in indifference and he would know that she was right; but he would also know that there was nothing that either he or she could do about it, that there was no cure for his malady, and, above all, that this dilemma was the meaning of his life.

Long ago, in his fourteenth year, while standing waiting for her preachments, he had demanded to know why she always pinioned him in solitude before handing down her moral laws, and she had replied that it was to make him develop the habit of reflecting deeply, that she knew as well as she when he had done wrong and she wanted to teach him to be his own judge. Anger now rose in him and he sought for some way to make her feel it. He grew suddenly resentful of the rickety furniture of the room. It's her own damn fault if she lives like this. . . . She could be living comfortably with Gladys. . . .

Yet, even as he thought it, he knew that he was wrong. Gladys and his mother hated each other; once, when they had lived together during the early days of his marriage, Gladys and his mother had vied for female dominance in the home and it had ended with his mother's packing and leaving, declaring that she preferred to live alone rather than with a willful daughter-in-law who didn't respect her.

"Why do you insist on living like this?" he broke the ice.

"We're not going to talk about how *I'm* living," she countered.

"No matter. But why do you live like this?" he asked again.

"And why do you live as *you're* living?" she demanded bitterly, turning to him. "You're drinking again. I can *smell* it."

"Not much," he said; his voice was clipped but controlled.

Her right hand dabbed clumsily at a tear on her wrinkled cheek. She slid into a chair and cried, her withered lips twisting, her false teeth wobbling loosely on shrunken gums.

"You've starting spoiling little girls, taking advantage of children. . . . Son, can't you *control* yourself? Where's all this leading you? Why in God's name do you lie to a little girl like Dot and seduce her?"

20

"I didn't lie—"

"You *did!*" she blazed. "You let her hope for what you couldn't do, and that's lying. I'm no fool! If you didn't lie to her, that's worse. Then she's just a little whore. And if she's a whore, why did you take up with her? Cross, it's easy to fool a young girl. If you're proud of this cheap trick, you've fallen lower than I thought you had."

She had done it; she had evoked in him that shameful mood of guilt born of desire and fear of desire. He knew that she was not lamenting for him alone, but for her own betrayed maidenhood, for how she had once been so treacherously beguiled into trusting surrender; she was blaming him somehow for its having gone wrong, confusedly seeking his masculine sympathy for her sexually blighted life! Goddamn her! Had she no sense of shame? He imagined himself rising and with a single sweep of his palm slapping her to the floor. And in the same instant a poignant pity for her seized him. Poor, lost, lonely woman clinging for salvation to a son whom she knew was as lost as she was. He was too close to her and too far from her; much too warm toward her and much too cold. If only he understood her less! But he was cut off from that; he was anchored in a knowledge that offended him. And this image of his mother's incestuously tinged longings would linger with him for days and he could curse her for it, and finally he would curse himself for living in a crazy world that he could not set right.

"Promising a child and knowing you don't mean it," she sobbed in despair. "How can men *do* that?"

He knew that now she was reliving her own experience, grieving over the thwarted hopes that had driven her into the arms of religion for the sake of her sanity. And he? Where could he be driven? Nowhere. His mother was lucky; she had a refuge, even if that refuge was an illusion. But he could only get out of this world or stay in it and bear it. And yet *she* was complaining to *him!* If she knew what he lived each day, she would be horrified. But she was convinced that he was hardhearted, that he was withholding his help out of selfish malice. An ironic smile stole across his lips.

"You can laugh!" she stormed at him. "But God'll pun-

21

ish you! He *will!* You'll see before you die! You'll weep! God is a just God. And He's a hard and jealous God! If you mock Him, He'll show you His Power!"

"I'm sorry, Ma," he sighed.

"Sorry for what?" she railed. "You can't undo what you've done. You've sinned, Cross, and it's to God you must confess with a contrite heart. Even if that girl gets rid of her child, she'll be forever hurt. She'll remember what you promised—"

"But I didn't *promise* her anything," he protested.

"Oh, stop lying," she said. "You *did!* You promised by the way you *acted.* . . ."

A hopeless silence rose between them. Through the years his mother had related to him how, when she had been a country school teacher in a tiny Southern community, she had met his father during the early days of the First World War. A Negro regiment had been camped nearby and excitement was everywhere. Her heart was ready and full of love. They first met at a church dance and he had straightaway declared his love. In her romantic eyes he was a huge boy going away to die on some distant battlefield and her heart had gone impulsively out to him, and finally her body also.

They married a month after they met and his regiment moved northward. She followed, feeling glad that she was giving him her life. But she soon learned that there were other girls foolish enough to look at him through romantic eyes and give him their hearts and bodies too. She finally upbraided him and he was cynical and defiant; then, more to avoid her than from motives of patriotism, he had, after returning from France, joined the army as a regular soldier. She trailed him dismally from army camp to army camp, begging for an understanding. Instead, the gap grew wider. Even before her son was born in 1924, she knew that she was only in his way, a worrisome wife. It was then that she took her sorrow and her infant son to God with copious tears. A year later she learned that somewhere in the reaches of Harlem, in a dirty, vacant lot at midnight, the police had found him lying wounded. He had been in a drunken street brawl, had lain unconscious in subzero weather, and had died a day later in an army hospital. . . .

With Cross in her arms, she had returned South and resumed her teaching, but her real profession was a constant rehearsal in her memory of her tiny but pathetic drama, a continuous clutching of it to her heart in a blend of complaint and accusation.

Cross looked at her; tears were still streaming on her cheeks.

"What're you going to do, Cross?"

He stood and gazed solemnly down at her.

"I don't know, Ma."

"Is it really over between you and Gladys?"

"You know it is."

"But your children? They *need* you. . . . Cross, you can lose your job. Gladys can ruin you, and so can that girl. A wronged woman is a hard woman, Cross."

On wobbly legs he waited for her to grow quiet. He was frantic to see Gladys.

"To think I named you Cross after the Cross of Jesus," she moaned.

"I got to go," he said brusquely. "You need anything, Ma?"

"I need to know that you've found God, Cross," she whispered. "For months now everything I've heard about you is bad."

"I'll—" He felt the need to be kind. "See you tomorrow, hunh?"

"And pray, son."

He went out the door quickly. He had to see Gladys and attempt to curb whatever rash moves she might be contemplating after Dot's crazy visit. But the thought of Gladys made him ill; he knew that she would grasp at his predicament and turn it against him, would try to use it to hold him at her mercy. Goddammit, if necessary, he would threaten to throw up his job. . . . That ought to make her think a little; the only thing Gladys really wanted was money.

Of all the mad things on earth, the maddest was Dot's talking to Gladys. Damn . . . He paused in the snow and stared: He ought to see Dot first and learn what had happened between her and Gladys. And he would give Dot the dressing down of her life! Didn't she know that Gladys was her enemy, that she would never befriend her, would do all in her power to humiliate her? Yes; instinct should have warned Dot not to reveal her plight to the wife of the man she said she loved. He stopped at a street corner and looked at his watch. He had three hours before reporting to work; he had to hurry.

The sun had waned and already a touch of darkness was in the sky. It was growing rapidly colder and an icy wind swept through the streets. Hunger and emotional tension had drained him; he had to eat to stave off that incessant grinding in his stomach. He saw a dingy lunch stand with a sweaty plate-glass window. He'd grab a bite to eat. . . . He turned, crossed the ice-packed pavement, pushed through a narrow doorway and saw a crowd of working-class Negroes and heard babbling voices. He perched himself atop a high stool and propped his elbows upon a greasy counter.

"A hamburger and a cup of coffee," he told the girl who came toward him.

"Right," she sang out.

The girl turned to prepare his order and his eyes, trained by habit, followed the jellylike sway of her sloping hips. At once his imagination began a reconstruction of the contour of her body, using the clues of her plump arms, her protruding breasts, the gently curving shape of her legs, and the width of her buttocks. Through the bluish haze of tobacco smoke and the hubbub of laughter coming from the rear of the café, his senses dreamily seized upon her, not as the girl standing by the steam table, but just as woman, as an image of a body, and he drifted toward a state of desire, his consciousness stirring vaguely with desire for desire, for woman as body of woman. . . . The girl came toward him now and he looked fully at her; she slid the plate with the hamburger to him and he saw her face: hard, with small reddish eyes; a full, coarsely formed mouth; huge cheekbones that slanted to a stubborn chin; sullen lips. . . . An intractable bitch, he thought. He

24

sighed as the girl's too-solid reality eroded his deepening mood of desire. . . .

He munched his hamburger and fell into a melancholy brooding. What was this thing of desire that haunted him? I desire desire, he told himself. And there's no apparent end or meaning to it. . . . And then there came to his mind the memory of the many sultry, smoky nights when he had been drunk with his friends in cheap dives and had seen girls like this. And, on those times, like today, a drive toward desire had risen imperiously in him and he had been just drunk enough for this desire for desire to hold fast to itself in spite of the girl's blatant ugliness, and he had sordidly bargained with her and had had her; and, as now, in the end he had recoiled from her in self-disgust while lying beside her in bed just as he had recoiled a moment ago from this one without ever having gone to bed with her. On those drunken occasions he had gone back alone to his empty room to reflect moodily upon the obscurity of what he had been seeking when he had wanted the girl. Surely it had not been *that* girl he had so ardently wanted. No. But, yes, it had been the girl and it had *not* been the girl; he saw clearly that he had wanted the girl because his desire impulse had pointed to her; but after having had her, desire was still not satisfied, still sought to encompass something within desire and hold it steady, to possess it, to become one with it. And that's impossible, he told himself. I'm crazy to try to do it. . . . Yet, he did try, and his trying seemed to be the essence of living. And marriage, could he build a marriage on desire? Should one give pledges, make promises, swear vows the sacredness of which depended upon such running sands as desires?

And what about his desire for Dot? Although she was carrying his child, his desire for her had already gone. . . . God in Heaven! What could he do? When he had been a child he had thought that life was a solidly organized affair, but when he had grown up he had found that it had the disorganized character of a nightmare. What crazy fool had thought up these forms of human relations? Or had men and women just drifted blindly through the centuries into such emotional arrangements? He was convinced that an idiot could have conceived better ways of establishing emotional alliances, and men must have felt uneasy about it too, for they had sought to make desire and passion stable by subjecting them to legal contracts! If human emotions fail to remain constant, then draft laws stipulating that that which will not remain constant *must* remain constant. . . . As he brooded over the meaning of desire a quiet sense of awe drenched him. Moods like these were the nearest he ever came to religious feelings.

He listened as a wave of guffaws rose from the crowd of Negroes in the rear of the café. Most of them were young and they were bent double with mirth. A tall Negro lifted his voice with loud authority over the rolling laughter.

"Where there's lots of rumors, there's bound to be some truth in 'em," he pronounced.

"You mean to tell me you believe flying saucers are *real?*" a short, brown boy demanded with indignation. "You got better sense than *that!*"

Cross had heard a hundred such arguments in bars and cafés and he was ready to relax and listen to yet another one, to see to what heights of fantasy it would soar.

"I say these white folks is hiding something," the tall Negro maintained, "and what they're hiding *scares* 'em!"

"And what're they hiding?" the waitress asked.

"Things they don't want *you* to know," the tall Negro said cryptically.

Teasing laughter full of suspense went from man to man. Cross could feel that they wanted to believe this high mystery, but they needed more fantastic facts before their beliefs could jell.

"Know what they found in one of them flying saucers?" the tall man demanded. "One of 'em was full of little men, about two feet high, with skin like peach fuzz—"

Laughter showered in the café.

"But what the white folks so scared about?" someone asked. "Little men can't hurt nobody."

Silence. All eyes were turned expectantly to the face of the tall man.

"THEM LITTLE MEN THE WHITE FOLKS FOUND IN THEM SAUCERS WAS COLORED MEN AND THEY WAS FROM MARS!" The tall man spoke in deep solemn tones. "That's why they hushed up the story. They didn't want the world to know

26

that the rest of the universe is colored! Most of the folks on this earth is colored, and if the white folks knew that the other worlds was full of colored folks who wanted to come down here, what the hell chance would the white folks have?"

Screams of approval, leaping from chairs, and clapping of hands.

"You ought to be shot to think of a thing like that!"

"It fits in with the way white folks act!"

Laughter died slowly. The men wiped their mouths with the backs of their hands, gazing at one another with sly joy.

"But it *could* be true," a man said soberly. "White folks in America, France, England, and Italy are the scaredest folks that ever lived on this earth. They're scareda Reds, Chinese, Indians, Africans, *everybody*."

"But how come you reckon they so scared?" an elderly man asked.

" 'Cause they're guilty," the tall man explained. "And guilty folks are *scared* folks! For four hundred years these white folks done made everybody on earth feel like they ain't human, like they're *outsiders*. They done kicked 'em around and called 'em names. . . . What's a Chinese to a white man? Chink-Chink Chinaman with pigtails down his back and he ain't fit for nothing but to cook and wash clothes. What's a Hindu to a white man? A nigger who's in love with ghosts and kisses cows. What's a black man to a white man? An ape made by God to cut wood and draw water, and always with a yen to rape white girls. A Mexican? A greasy, stinking rascal who ought to be worked to death and then shot. A Jew? A Christ killer, a cheat, a rat. A Japanese? A monkey with a yellow skin . . . Now our colored brothers are visiting us from Mars and Jupiter and the white folks is sweating in a panic—"

Negroes rolled in laughter, feeling that the powerful white world had been lowered to their own humble plane by the magic of comic words. One black boy danced ecstatically, then, holding his hands over his mouth as though he felt it unseemly to vent his savage mirth indoors, ran out of the café, leaving the door open. Upon the snowy sidewalk he screamed and howled and flapped his arms in the

27

icy wind. For a moment he paused, then ran back to the door and, gasping for breath, said: "Man, that's sure cool!" He lifted his eyes to the gray sky. "You colored brothers on Mars, come on down here and help us!"

Cross found himself joining in the laughter. His heart went out to these rejected men whose rebel laughter banished self-murder from his thoughts. If only he could lose himself in that kind of living! Weren't there somewhere in this world rebels with whom he could feel at home, men who were outsiders not because they had been born black and poor, but because they had thought their way through the many veils of illusion? But where were they? How could one find them?

It was time to go. Amidst the laughter he paid his check and went out, passing the black boy on the sidewalk and looking back several times to see other Negroes leave the café to join the black boy laughing in the white snow.

Yes, he had to see Dot. The thought made tension rise in him and he went into a bar and had a double whisky. When he came out a bluish mist hung in the air. The outlines of the buildings were beginning to blur. A freezing wind stung his face. He found a taxi and climbed in.

Underneath all he had felt that day, Dot had rested as a kind of uneasy undertow, a slow black tide that would not be stopped. And, now that he was going to have it out with her, he flinched at the hurt he had to inflict. It had been a year ago that she had first floated into his mind as just another image of desire, woman as body of woman; but, for reasons which he had not foreseen, she had clung to him and he had clung to her and slowly she had come to mean more to him than just a woman's body. Now that the moment of what she so melodramatically referred to as the "payoff" was at hand, he did not like it. What bothered him most was that he knew that he had to betray her, and this betrayal was not springing from any innate perversity in him, but from the very complexity of his relations with Gladys. There was no way out but to hurt her, and he was convinced that she knew it. He had helped her with money, advice, sharing with her his life; but it seemed that these gifts enraged her. She had said that they were not enough and he knew that, as a woman, she was right. Dot

28

was so close to what she wanted in life, that is, to marry him, that its impossibility drove her almost out of her mind.

In her struggle for legal possession of him, Cross knew that she was in the end counting heavily upon his weakness to carry her through. Yes, he was weak, but he knew that he was weak, and that made a difference. He also knew more about the turnings and twistings of her mind than she knew he knew, and this knowledge gave him an ironic insight into her that he did not relish. How could he ever make her know that, though he gave forth the appearance of weakness, this weakness was really a kind of strength of not wanting to hurt others. His own experience had shown him that he was cold-bloodedly brutal when trapped in situations involving his self-respect. All his life he had been plagued by being caught in relations where others had tried to take advantage of him because they had thought him weak and gullible; and when he had finally confronted them with the fact that he knew that they were playing with him, they had hated him with a redoubled fury for having deceived them! And he dreaded that happening with Dot.

He had never tried to conceal from Dot his situation; he had been transparently honest with her from the beginning; he had told her everything, and if she had any illusions they were of her own making. And what saddened him to inward tears was that he suspected that Dot had allowed herself to become impregnated in order to test the strength of their attachment, hoping that he would be so moved and harassed by her passionate appeals that he would find some way of breaking legally with Gladys and marrying her. And he knew that freedom was the last thing on earth that Gladys would ever grant him.

He had met Dot, of all the places in a teeming city, in the liquor section of the South Center Department Store one Saturday morning last spring. There had been a widely advertised sale of Jamaica rum and long lines of people had queued up to buy at the unheard-of rate of two bottles of rum for three dollars. The store had been jammed with milling crowds. He had taken his place at the end of a long queue and a moment later he had been aware that a young, willowy yellow girl had fallen in directly behind him. It

29

was warm; he was without a coat and his shirt sleeves were
rolled up past his elbows. He sniffed the perfume she wore,
then gave her a quick survey; she was uncommonly pretty
and was wearing a sheer pink print dress that showed the
shape of her body with disturbing distinctness. She looks
sweet, he thought. He glanced at her, trying to catch her
eye; but the jostling crowd so distracted him that he forgot
her until a few minutes later, when, all at once, he felt his
naked elbow touching something yieldingly soft behind
him. He looked around and she smiled shyly; a soft lump
rose in his throat. Good God, what a gal! And so *young*.
. . . Did she know that his elbow was touching her left
breast? If she did, she gave no outward sign; she still had
that vague, sweet smile that could mean anything: coyness
or just simple self-consciousness. Why, she's just a child, he
thought with a twinge of shame. He looked at her again,
feeling his elbow still touching her breast; she smiled and
looked off, yet she did not try to move away. She knows.
. . . But really, would a young girl with a face so sensitive and fine allow him to do that to her in public? Was she
alone or was that man behind her her husband? The image
of woman as body of woman filled him and his head felt
pleasantly giddy.

He was determined to know if she knew that his bare
elbow was tantalizingly touching the tip of her breast. Perhaps she's so excited about the rum that she doesn't feel it.
. . . But that was impossible. He sensed in her a quality
of quiet waiting and it made him feel that she *did* know
and did not mind, was even welcoming it. The line inched
forward. The metallic ringing of cash registers sang out
over the crowd. Traffic clanged through the streets outside.
And all around was bubbling a cacophony of voices. He
was now so near the counter that he could see the towering
rows of bottles of dark yellow rum. Slowly, so slowly that
no one could notice anything, he moved his bare elbow to
and fro across the tip of her breast, realizing with sensual
astonishment: She's not wearing a brassiere! Desire surged
softly through him. Out of the corner of his eye he could
see that she had not moved; she was staring steadily ahead,
holding her purse primly in front of her. He tried it again;
she did not move or seem aware that she was being

30

touched at all; her face was sweet, composed, solemn, angel-like in its purity and remoteness from erotic passion. Was she aware or was she not? He had to know; it obsessed him. She could, of course, abruptly leave the line to indicate her disgust; or she could, if she were the hysterical breed, yell out that he was molesting her. But he did not believe that she would. . . . Was she playing the same game that he was playing? And who was she? Again he moved his naked elbow across her left breast, caressing it, gently indenting the soft, surrendering flesh under the sheer cloth of her dress as much as he dared, and, this time, he knew that she knew, for he felt the tip of her loose breast gradually hardening, growing delicately into a pointed, taut nipple. He gazed at her directly now, but still she did not look at him; and her face was as passive and serene as a summer landscape. The line shortened and he fondled her breast with his elbow and she made no move to withdraw her body; instead, as the line snaked forward, she managed to keep her breast where his elbow could touch it. He was now certain that the man behind her was not her husband, did not know her. Finally he turned to her and smiled, still touching her breast, and said:

"It's a long time, hunh, to wait for two bottles of rum?"

"It's awful," she said, and they both laughed.

"You like rum?" he asked.

"Now, what do you think?" she countered teasingly.

"What do you make with it? Cuba libres or rum punches?"

"Both," she said.

"You live around here?"

"Naw. Up near Thirty-seventh Street."

He looked at her openly now, as a man looks at a woman he likes and wants.

"You *couldn't* be over sixteen," he ventured.

"You're wrong. I'm seventeen," she corrected him.

They had spoken in low tones, as though both were conspiring to keep secret the erotic link that was springing up between them. He noticed that she was trembling slightly and he knew that she was being claimed by a state he knew well: dread. This was perhaps the first time she had ever let herself be caressed in this manner and he must

31

not frighten her. He cast about for something to say to let her know that, though he was after her, he was also a gentleman and that she need not be afraid of him, that she could rely on him for discreetness and good sense.

They were at the counter now and he paid for his rum and stood aside, waiting for her. When she left the counter, he said: "Here. Let me help you carry that."

"Thank you," she said with a charming degree of hesitation; then she allowed him to take her bottles.

They walked out of the store together, making small talk. She told him that she had been living with her mother and a younger brother; but her mother had been a terror, depriving her of all freedom. She said that she had just run off from home and was living with Myrtle, a girl friend. . . . During the first five minutes he had let her know that he was not free, that he worked in the Post Office, that he was married but not living with his wife. They passed a movie house and he asked her if she liked movies and she said yes. He invited her to see a show with him that afternoon and she demurred modestly. She doesn't want to seem too *forward,* he thought; and he laughed out loud about it when he was alone in his room.

"But you can call me sometimes, if you want to," she said, and she gave him her telephone number.

That was how it had begun. She had known from the beginning that he was not free and she had told him that it did not really matter for the time being. In their relationship he had found her a passionate child achingly hungry for emotional experience. Of an afternoon she would come to his room with the most disconcerting directness he had ever known in a woman. He would try to talk to her and as he talked he could tell that she was not listening; she was pulling off her dress, stripping down her nylon stockings, stepping out of her nylon slip and panties. . . . And afterward he would stare at her unbelievingly as she would stomp her foot and tell him with a childlike seriousness that was all the more serious because it was so childlike: "I never want to make love with anybody but you."

"You'll live and learn," he had told her, yawning.

"Don't *say* that," she had protested with sudden fury,

32

and he realized with a sense of dismay that what had taken place was to her sacred.

But that did not prevent some nuance of perversity in him from trying to make her admit that she had been conscious of his elbow caressing her breast that warm, spring Saturday morning in the liquor store, but she would never confess it, would exhibit feelings of shame and indignation whenever he mentioned it; but beneath her ardent denials was a furtive sense of erotic pleasure. He was amused by the manner in which she balanced her moral notions with her emotional hungers. Under his questioning she would pause in her dressing and stare at him with wide, hurt eyes and exclaim: "How can you *say* that? You sure have a *filthy* imagination!"

"But, Dot, dammit, you *knew!* I swear you did—"

"Do you think I'd let anybody do *that* to me in public?" she asked, her voice ringing with genuine incredulity.

"But you *did,* Dot!"

"I *didn't!*"

Tears would roll down her cheeks and he would take her in his arms and soothe her. And until the end she would never concede that that morning was the first time that she had ever felt so keen a sensual pleasure. But Cross was certain of it and it made him marvel that she could deny it with such passionate consistency.

His bond with her grew deeper with the passing days, for it was with her that, for the first time in his life, he found himself talking freely, emptying out of his soul the dammed-up waters of reflection and brooding thought. He told her of his morbidly tangled relation with his mother; he told her how, when he had been twenty-one years of age, he had naïvely been sucked into a stupid marriage with Gladys; and he confessed to her his incurable melancholy stemming from his mulling over his emotions. He never quite knew how much of what he told her she understood, but she always listened patiently, now and then timidly venturing a detached question or two, but never commending or blaming. He came at last to believe that she accepted the kind of talk in which he indulged as a mysterious part of a man's equipment, along with his sex-

33

ual organs. But the mere fact that she listened to his analytical tirades had been a boon to him beyond his deepest hopes.

And now he had to hurt her. And what would she do? Once he had toyed with trying to find possible friends of his with whom she could fall in love; he had once even spoken to her in glowing terms of a man who worked with him on the job. And he had been amazed when she had turned to look at him and demanded:

"Are you trying to pawn me off on somebody?"

It so shamed him that he had never tried it again. Then, one Sunday evening over dinner in a crowded restaurant, she told him that she was carrying his child. His food stuck in his throat. Later, in his room, she had wildly resisted his suggestion that she abort the child. The scenes of emotional conflict that took place the following month had frayed him almost to madness.

He had just left one woman, his mother, who had hurled at him her life draped in the dark hues of complaint and accusation, who had tried futilely to rouse compassion in him by dramatizing the forlorn nature of her abandoned plight; now he was on his way to struggle with yet another woman. And after Dot there loomed the formidable figure of his wife.

"Okay, Buddy; here you are," the taxi driver told him as the cab swerved to a curb hidden by snowdrifts.

He paid, ran up the steps, pushed the bell of Dot's apartment three times, the signal they agreed upon when he was calling to see her. The buzzer was so long in answering that he thought she was not in. Where could she be? He rang again and was about to leave when the buzzer suddenly responded in a long blast of sound. He opened the vestibule door, feeling that something was wrong. He heard the buzzer still emitting its tinny throb long after he had passed the second floor. She must be upset or something. . . . When he reached the door of Dot's apartment, he saw Myrtle, Dot's girl friend, looking at him with a face as devoid of expression as she could make Myrtle was a tall, dark girl with a handsome face and sardonic eyes. Cross slowed his movements, sensing knowledge of a crisis behind Myrtle's reserved manner.

34

"Hi," he greeted her.

Without answering, she caught hold of his arm and drew him forcibly into the hallway of the apartment.

"Where's Dot?" he asked, trying to keep his voice calm.

"In bed," she said flatly.

"What's happened?"

"*You* ought to be asking. . . . All hell's broke loose, that's all."

"What do you mean? I want to see Dot."

"You can't now," she said with an air of petty satisfaction.

He started for Dot's bedroom and Myrtle held him back.

"The *doctor's* in there," she whispered fiercely.

"The doctor? Why? Tell me what's happening!"

"You *men!*" She curled her lips in scorn. "How much do you think a poor girl can stand?"

"Okay. You can can that," he told her roughly, unable to suppress hot resentment. "Dot can talk to me like that, but *you* can't!"

He had never liked her and she did not like him and she was acting now as he had known she would act if she ever had the chance. One instinct told him to ignore her, but she had cut too deeply into his feelings for him to leave off. He stood glaring at her, his fingers trembling.

"Look, I'm Dot's best friend, see?" she shot at him. "I'm taking care of her, trying to repair the damage you've done. I can say what I damn well like. . . ."

"Not to *me,*" Cross said.

"And why not?" she flipped at him.

"Because I don't sleep with you," he told her brutally, looking her straight in the eyes.

An anger so intense burned in Myrtle's face that her large eyes shrank in size.

"You dirty sonofabitch," she said in an even, low tone.

"Thanks," he said.

He opened the door of Dot's room and peered in.

"Who is it?" a loud masculine voice called out to him as he stood uncertainly.

It was the doctor who had yelled; Cross could see his

back bent over Dot's bed. Dot was lying with her face to the wall.

"It's me, honey. Cross."

"Please, please, don't come in now, Cross."

"Will you be kind enough to wait outside until I'm through here?" the doctor asked brusquely. "What happens after I'm gone is your business. . . ."

Cross shut the door and turned to see the smirk on Myrtle's face.

"What happened?"

"I ought to spit right in your face for what you said to me," she said. "What she ever saw in your sullen heart, God only knows!"

"I'm sorry," he relented to get information. "But why don't you tell me what's happened?"

"Yeah, *sorry* . . . Men are always *sorry*," she derided him openly.

"For Christ's sake!" he exploded. "Now's no time to carry on like that! Tell me what happened."

"Wait and she'll tell you," Myrtle said and went into the kitchen, closing the door behind her.

Cross sat and fumed. How crazy women could be sometimes. . . . What did she think she was gaining by throwing dramatic fits? He looked up as she came briskly out of the kitchen, opened the door of the hall closet, took out her coat and put it on. She paused, not looking directly at him. The muscles of Cross's body tightened; he could have kicked her right through the brick wall into the snowdrifts piled outside.

"I've got to go down to the drugstore and get a prescription filled," she said matter-of-factly. "I'm leaving a hypodermic needle and a syringe boiling in a pan on the gas stove. Turn out the fire under it in two or three minutes, will you?" She shot him a sidelong glance. "You ought to be able to do *that* much now."

"You can go to hell," he growled at her.

"I'd gladly go, if only I could take you along with me," she snapped, pulling the door shut behind her so violently that it sounded like a rifle shot.

His nerves twitched in protest; then he was conscious

36

that the droning murmur of the doctor's voice in the bedroom had ceased and he heard Dot's distressed voice: "Oh, Cross! What was that?"

Before he could reply the doctor had opened the door and was glaring at him.

"The girl slammed the door," Cross told the doctor sheepishly.

"This child's a nervous wreck," the doctor said, throwing up his hands in despair. "She's got to be kept quiet."

Cross huddled forward in his chair. The doctor went back into Dot's room, drawing the door shut.

Once more the masculine murmur of the doctor's voice resumed. What was he saying to her? And what had she told him? He was convinced that he was under discussion and it made him feel deprived of his humanity, converted into a condemned object, exposed to the baleful gaze of a million eyes. He crept softly to the door, cocked his head and listened, but he could not distinguish any words. Now and then he could hear Dot's silvery voice rising in a melody of complaint, of protest. Goddamn . . . Why had she called in that doctor without telling him? If she'd only trust me. . . . But he knew that her trusting him would not get her what she wanted; he was in no position to marry her. All right; suppose Dot was in trouble? Did that justify her subjecting him to shame? The South Side was a small community and if Dot had revealed their relations to this doctor, their predicament would be on the lips of a thousand gossiping men and women in a day's time. . . .

He had a hot impulse to rise and flee the apartment and disappear forever. . . . What had he to lose by throwing up this fool's game? His job? It wasn't worth a damn, he was so mortgaged with debt. He really had nothing to lose. What a stupid situation for an intelligent man to find himself in! What greater shame was there for a man than to walk the streets cringing with fear of grasping women? Somehow he would shake loose from this and never in all his life let himself be caught again. . . .

He was already supporting Dot, but she could, if she wanted to be brutal about it, compel him, through a court of law, to support the child after it was born. He knew that she would do that only if she were certain that he would never marry her. Had Gladys told her that a divorce was impossible? More than likely she had. . . .

He ought to leave *now*. . . . But he sat, hating himself. There were his small sons, Cross Junior, Peter, and Robert, whom he loved and did not want to leave. He must regain his influence over Dot. She had gone berserk because he had broken his promise to see her this morning and now he would have to be with her constantly to bring her around. Above all, he had to persuade her to abort the child for her sake, his sake. . . .

A gurgle of water sounded in the kitchen. That pot that Myrtle had told him to look after! He ran and turned out the gas just in time; there were only a few bubbles left in the pan.

The telephone rang. He entered the hallway and stood uncertainly.

"Shall I answer it, Dot?" he called through the door.

"Yes, please," Dot answered weakly.

He picked up the receiver.

"Dot? Is that you?" It was the voice of a woman speaking with breathless eagerness.

"No, it's not," he said.

"Who's speaking?" The voice was cautious now, but still urgent.

"Just a friend," Cross said, disguising his tone. He was always afraid of Gladys' trapping him in Dot's apartment.

"Is this Mr. Damon?"

"No," he lied, hoping that his voice would not carry to Dot's room. "I'm a friend of Myrtle."

"Won't you please call Dot to the phone?"

"I'm afraid she can't come. She's in bed. The doctor's with her. Who's this?"

"Mary, a friend of Dot. Listen, I have a message for her. Tell Dot I've found a lawyer. He's a whizz. She's to call me as soon as possible."

"I see." His eyes widened.

"Tell her that she'll have to act fast to tie up Damon—"

"I'll tell her." He struggled to keep his voice normal.

There was a hesitating silence.

"*Who's* this speaking?" Fear was in the voice.

"Brown's the name," he lied.

"Oh . . . For a moment I was afraid you *were* that Damon man." The voice sighed with relief.

"Oh, no. I wouldn't want to be in his shoes—"

"Tell Dot that she's *got* to hang on to her birth certificate; it's her quickest way of proving that she's under sixteen. My lawyer says that as long as she's not sixteen, Damon's guilty of rape. Now, Dot's birthday comes in June, and that gives her four months of grace."

Cross felt danger closing in about him.

"What did you say?"

"Explain this to Dot," the voice spoke distinctly. "Wait a minute."

He held his breath as a faint rustle of paper came over the wire.

"I got it." The voice was edged with satisfaction. "I copied it down the way my lawyer read it to me this morning. Here it is: '. . . Every male person of the age of seventeen years and upwards who shall have carnal knowledge of any female person under the age of sixteen years and not his wife, either with or without her consent shall be adjudged guilty of the crime of rape. . . .' You know what *carnal* means, don't you?"

"Yes," Cross breathed; he felt trapped in a nightmare.

"'. . . Every person convicted of the crime of rape shall be imprisoned in a penitentiary for a term of not less than one year and may extend to life. . . .' You got that?"

"Yes."

"Now, this Damon's married, so he *can't* marry Dot and wriggle out that way," the voice went on in a tone of hard triumph. "So if Dot doesn't get mushy, she's got Damon where she wants him."

"I see," Cross said. "But are you sure Dot's *under* sixteen?"

"I've seen her birth certificate," the voice assured him.

"I'll tell her," Cross promised heavily.

"Good."

"Good-by."

" 'By."

He hung up, swayed a bit, then sat. Dot was a minor? How was that possible? He was certain that she had told him a year ago that she was seventeen. Jesus . . . Could it be true? He had been honest with her and she had tricked him! Yet, in casting back his mind, he remembered that he had often felt that she was young for her age, a child. How in God's name had he stumbled into a situation of such deadly seriousness? He sat hunched over in the chair, too stunned to move. If ever, now was the time to act upon the impulse of flight. He had about fifty dollars in his pocket. He ought to buy a railroad ticket for as long a journey as the money would cover, and vanish. There was no doubt now but that Dot had made up her mind, and from now on he had to regard her as his enemy. Longing for a drink, he rummaged in the kitchen and found an inch of gin in a bottle and drained it.

The hall door clicked and Myrtle entered without glancing at him. Yes; she was in on this too. Her knowledge that he was a potential convict was what had made her so bold. He glared at her as she pulled off her coat and went into the kitchen for a tray; she went into Dot's room, closing the door behind her. That bitch . . . His talk with Dot would be decisive; either she called off the lawyer or he would drop her and let her do her worst. He had a last weapon, his gun, and it would change things and leave her dismayed. . . .

At last the doctor emerged, leaving Dot's door open this time. Moving methodically, the doctor placed his black bag on a chair and proceeded to get into his overcoat. He pulled on his hat and looked at Cross with cold eyes. He grabbed his bag and went abruptly out the door. Yes; Dot had identified him to the doctor. Cross felt sick and cheap.

On his tongue was a storm of reproaches he wanted to hurl at Dot, but he checked himself. To lose his temper would be playing into her hands, giving her the opportunity for an emotional scene. He walked slowly into the room and saw Dot lying with her face to the wall. Myrtle sat huddled on the side of the bed, weeping. The hypodermic needle and the syringe lay on the tray at the foot of the bed. A medicinal odor hung in the air.

"Myrtle, what the hell's eating you?" he demanded.

As he had expected, they had been waiting for his

signal; both women started to berate him at once. It was Dot's voice that won out.

"Please, Cross, in the name of God," Dot begged, without turning to look at him. "Be gentle with Myrtle. She's been waiting on me night and day. She's all I got. Don't insult her."

"I'm not insulting anybody—"

Myrtle jerked upright, her face wet with tears.

"You did! And what have I ever done to you?"

"You started slashing at me the moment I got into this apartment," he charged her.

"But can't you see what's happening?" Myrtle blazed at him. "This poor child's half out of her mind. . . . Try to be *human!*"

"That's the trouble," he almost hissed. "I'm simply too *damned* human."

"If I was Dot, I wouldn't take this off you for a single minute," Myrtle burst out. "Oh, boy, I'd have you in a way that you'd never forget!"

"Do you think I don't know that?"

"I'd get your money, your job, and throw you smack into jail!"

"Oh, Myrtle, no . . ." Dot protested.

Yes, Myrtle was going further than Dot wanted. Cross looked at the two of them. There was a note of hard irony in his voice: "Yeah, I know. I'm just a big, bad, black brute. Pushing little girls around. Taking advantage of the helpless. Spoiling innocent children. I've no feelings. I'm just having a damn grand time and making others suffer." He summed up their case for them and then sat on the edge of the bed beside Myrtle.

"You're a man and you can't dodge your responsibilities," Myrtle told him wailingly.

"I'm not responsible to *you* for anything," Cross told her. "And I don't like your meddling. Now, get the hell out of here and let me talk to Dot."

"You're a *real* bastard," Myrtle said. "You ought to marry Dot, but I pity her spending a lifetime with you."

"Don't worry," he taunted her. "I'm not going to spend a lifetime with *you*."

"Cross, for God's sake," Dot whimpered. "Don't be that way."

"That's the only way he can be," Myrtle said.

"Get out of here, Myrtle," Cross told her again.

There was silence. He stood his ground. He was determined to wreck their rehearsed appeal to him. Both of them were weeping now and he made no move.

"You're lucky that it's Dot you're dealing with instead of me," Myrtle said. Weeping, she stood and walked from the room.

Cross heard the door close behind his back. He could almost see the little wheels turning in the brains of both girls as they planned their next move. Men had to consult together for concerted action; women simply gravitated together spontaneously, motivated by their situation in life as women.

"Dot, I want to talk to you," he began. "Are you up to it, or should I come back in the morning?"

Dot lay without moving. He knew that she was debating. Finally she slowly turned over and faced him, the mass of her tumbling brown tresses framing an oval of face delicate and demure. God, but she's really beautiful. . . . Her deep brown eyes were haunted, empty. She lifted her head an inch from the damp pillow and then let it fall again, as though she was too weak to bear the strain of holding it erect. She managed a wan smile. What an actress! How do they learn it? Is it instinct?

"I'm sorry, Cross," she whispered.

And he was truly sorry too. He wanted in that instant to take her in his arms and comfort her, but he knew that she would at once take advantage of it, would exploit it, would try to wring out of a simple act of compassion a promise of marriage. Goddamn! He reined in his feelings. She was gazing toward the window and the thought shot through his mind: She's about to switch her tactics. . . . His eyes traveled along the slight outlines of her body stretching under the blanket; she was so tiny and yet somehow so strong, this girl. Woman as body of woman was not in his consciousness now, but there was rolling teasingly through his memory a memory of it. He did not really want to hurt her, but what was he to do? How could he avoid it?

42

"Dot, let's start from the beginning," he commenced. "Are you going to do what I suggested?"

"What do you mean, Cross?" she hedged, sparring for time, her eyes swimming helplessly at him.

"About the child," he told her. "I've got it all arranged." She leaped to a sitting position.

"No, no, no!" she cried hysterically. "Don't ask me *that* again! Please, Cross, if you do—"

"I *am* asking you," he said. "There's nothing else I can do."

She sprang from the bed in her nylon gown and screamed, then ran on bare, scampering feet across the room to the window. He walked toward her, calmly. The door burst open and Myrtle stood staring at them with parted lips and tense eyes.

"If you ask me that again, I'll jump out of the window! I swear I will! I swear, I swear. . . ." Dot sobbed, clawing blindly at the window latch.

"Oh, God!" Myrtle exclaimed, grabbing Dot with both arms. "Darling, don't! You don't know what you are doing!" She looked beseechingly at Cross, who stood near Dot. Cross had not budged; he regarded Dot coldly. "Please, Cross, help me to get her back to bed. . . ."

"Get back in bed, Dot," Cross said in a detached voice; he still did not touch her.

Dot sobbed brokenly, clinging convulsively to Myrtle. Then she slid heavily to the wooden floor, resting on her bare knees. The nylon gown was pulled taut across the curves of her firm, yellow thighs, and through the sheer white translucence of the tissue he could see the dark smudge of her pubic hair. She beat her knees frantically with her fists, violently shaking her head, tears streaming from her eyes. She keened: "No, no! I'll *never* kill my child! I'll die first! You can't make me *murder*. . . . ! It's my child and I'll keep it and love it like I love my own life. . . . ! Oh, God, don't let this happen to me!" She gulped for breath and fell prone to the floor, her body jerking with nervous spasms.

"Help me, Cross," Myrtle begged, struggling with Dot.

He did not move; he stood looking silently at both of them. Myrtle stood over Dot, looking from him to Dot.

Yes, she's trying to weigh how much influence this is having on me, he thought. A woman's business is emotion and her trade is carried on in cash of tears. . . . He would help to keep Dot from leaping out of the window, but that was all he'd do at the moment. And, besides, he was not convinced that she would leap.

"Come, darling," Myrtle coaxed, lifting Dot.

Dot allowed herself to be led back to the bed. Myrtle eased her upon it and Dot sat and sobbed, her hands covering her face.

"I won't kill my child," she began again. "I *won't*. . . ."

"Darling, get in bed," Myrtle said. "The doctor said you had to be careful. You know you're not well."

Cross knew that these words were aimed at him. When Dot was in bed, Myrtle turned to him.

"Why do you treat her like that?" she demanded. "The doctor said—"

"Leave me alone!" he shouted; he did not relent; he could not.

"I never dreamed anyone like you existed," Myrtle said.

"You know better now," he said tersely.

Myrtle ran from the room. Cross sat on the edge of the bed and tenderly touched Dot's shaking shoulder.

"Dot," he began, "try to listen calmly. This may be the last time I can talk to you like this—"

"Don't say that, Cross. You're going to leave me?" she asked.

"I don't know what I'm going to do," he said.

Dot lay very still. Cross heard an El train thundering past outside.

"You promised not to tell anybody about this without first telling me," he began.

"Oh, Cross, I *had* to tell the doctor," she said in a rush of words. "I was so nervous and he kept asking me what was the matter—"

"I'm not talking about *that!*"

Dot's eyes showed helpless bewilderment. He knew that her pretended naïveté was particularly dangerous, for in it was a pathetic appeal for love that his heart yearned to answer. He knew that her deception stemmed from her

44

craving for security and that she was expecting him, if he ever caught her in it, to forgive her.

"Don't you know that if you destroy me, you're hurting yourself?" he asked her. "This calling in a lawyer—"

"Oh, Cross!" she wailed. "I didn't. You don't *understand!*"

"I understand more than you think," he told her.

She flung herself into his arms and clutched him frantically. All grief and despair vanished from her face as quickly as a summer rain, and he could not help but marvel at the weapons of a woman when she fought. Her volatile emotions altered with dialectical suddenness, changing into their opposites, disappearing, hiding under new guises.

"Mary phoned and told me to tell you that she had a lawyer for you," he told her.

"That was Mary on the phone a while back?" she asked with wide eyes.

"Yes."

Dot sighed with such relief that Cross wondered if she had other plots cooking. . . .

"Oh, Mary . . . She's crazy," Dot explained it away in a childlike voice. "I don't have to obey her, Cross. The lawyer was her idea."

"Dot, how old are you?" he asked her softly.

She did not look at him; her eyes were steadily before her and yet he knew that she knew that he was staring at her and waiting for an answer.

"Dot, I'm talking to you. How old are you?" he demanded.

The knowledge of the criminal threat she held over him stood between them like an invisible wall. She still could not turn to look at him; then she bent forward suddenly, covered her face with her hands and sobbed.

"I don't know what to do," she gulped.

She had failed to answer; instead, she had let him see the emotional dilemma in which she was caught, let him glimpse the terrible weapon she held in her hand, let him surmise how reluctantly she would use it, but use it she would.

"Look, Dot, you can haul me before a court and get me convicted, but I swear to you that I'll find some way out, you hear?" he warned her. "You lied to me. You told me you were seventeen. You led me to this crime, if you call it a crime. Now, how old are you?"

"I'll be sixteen in June," she breathed, not looking at him.

Cross sighed. "Why did you lie to me?"

"I wanted you," she whispered, her eyelashes nestling against her cheeks.

"And now you want me put into jail for ten, maybe twenty years?"

Myrtle entered and lifted the tray from the bed.

"Darling, I'll never do that to you," Dot said sweetly, too sweetly.

"If you do, you'll never win," he warned her solemnly.

"Maybe Superman'll kill himself and escape everybody?" Myrtle gave a brittle laugh. "You *could* run off to South America, too."

She went briskly through the door and Cross balled his fingers in fury. He turned again to Dot.

"Look, start with Ma. Why did you go to her?"

Again Dot became too weak to talk; through tears she groped blindly for Cross's hand and gripped it.

"I was wild— Even my mother won't speak to me," she whimpered.

"Your mother? Does *she* know?" he demanded, amazed.

She gave him a look that begged forgiveness. Then her face suddenly brightened.

"Your mother's wonderful," she said.

Goddammit! Wouldn't Dot ever learn that he saw through her poses?

"I understand now why you love her so," Dot went on warmly. "She has such a *noble* face. . . . And she's *for* us, Crossy. She hates Gladys; she didn't tell me so, but I can feel it. She says your children are beautiful! Oh, Crossy, I'd love to take care of them. I *would!*"

She's out of her mind. . . . Did she think that she could take away another woman's children? Were there no limits to her vanity? Dot turned and looked yearningly at him.

"The children, yours and mine, could all be together—"

"Did Gladys tell you that?" he asked with soft irony.

Dot's eyes narrowed as she conjured up the image of Gladys. "She hates me; she hates you—God, she's *awful!*"

"Look, Dot, I'm going to tell you the lay of the land, then you must let your common sense guide you. Gladys will not let me go; her keeping me is her revenge on me for leaving her. Let's live together and ride this out. Or, get rid of the child—"

Dot sat up and looked at him; she had changed.

"Cross, you *got* to get a divorce," she pronounced.

"*Somebody* has to give way in this," he insisted.

"I won't kill the child," she said simply.

She was telling him that she would not let go of the hold she had upon him, no matter what. He stood up.

"I don't give a damn," he muttered. "I couldn't care less—"

"Then, why do you blame me for getting a lawyer?" she demanded.

"I'm not talking to you. I'm talking to myself, about myself," he said. His eyes were hot and vacant. "You're threatening me with jail to make me get a divorce my wife won't give."

"Pull off your coat, honey," she seemed to relent.

"Naw; I got to go," he said. "I've got to see Gladys and try to undo some of the harm you've done."

"Aren't you going to tell me *something?*" she begged.

"*You* tell me what to tell you!" he shouted.

Myrtle came in and stood by the bed, and asked, "What did you decide about Dot, Cross?"

"Nothing," he told her bluntly.

"Wouldn't your wife take some money?"

"Sure; if I had it."

"Can't you borrow some?"

"I'm already up to my neck in debt."

"Give her monthly payments—"

"And what'll be left for Dot, then? I'm paying for the car—"

"Sell it," Myrtle suggested.

"I haven't got the car to sell. Gladys has it and she's

hanging on to it and I've got to keep up the payments," he explained.

"Well, it's your funeral," Myrtle said. "You don't expect Dot to sit here and not defend herself, do you?"

"All right; put me in jail, if you want to."

He turned abruptly and walked out. He was so spent that he felt that he was floating down the steps. The street lamps gleamed dully through the night's mist. He tramped over snow-carpeted sidewalks without knowing it. He had to see Gladys, but he did not know what he would say to her. He paused and rubbed his hand over his eyes. If those who were pressing him knew how little like a human being he felt, they would recoil in horror; he felt unreal, scarcely alive. How long could he go on like this? Shame flooded him as he recalled his attempt with the gun. He could not even do *that*. . . .

He stopped at a street corner and waited for a southbound trolley. The snow enforced a hush over the city, muffling the sounds of traffic and the footsteps of passersby. Above him an invisible plane droned through the night sky. Icy wind flapped his overcoat and he turned his back to escape its knifelike pain on his face. His eyes caught a scrap of paper whirling uncertainly on currents of wind; he watched it rise, veer, hover, then vanish aimlessly around a corner. A clanging trolley heaved into view and he approached the tracks and sprang on the car when it slowed to a stop. He paid and sat in the rear. He closed his eyes and leaned his head against the sweaty windowpane.

Dread was deep in him now; he had to tackle Gladys and he did not know how. The tussle between them had been so long and bitter that there was not much room left for jockeying. Over the years they had hurled at each other every curse word they knew and he felt that his present visit would be by far the most grueling. He had not seen her for more than three months; he made his payments to her by sending a check through the mails every two weeks. Not seeing her had made him forgo his joy in seeing his sons and he missed them acutely. But Gladys had so adroitly managed their parting that she had extorted his not seeing the children as part of the price he had to pay for being rid of her. After the terrible scene the last time he had seen her, he had told her that he did not intend to come again, and, in his black mood, had given her the right to tell the children any damn thing she chose. And Gladys had seized literally upon his words and had written a special-delivery letter to his mother informing her that he had disowned his children, branding him an unnatural monster. His mother had summoned him, had upbraided him, wept and prayed.

His head lolled as the trolley jolted through the snowy night streets. His mind drifted back to the time he had been attending day classes at the University of Chicago, majoring in philosophy and working the night shift in the Post Office. In those days he had not had much time for fun and had been constantly hankering for relaxation. His mother had been in the South, living in the house that she had bought through her lifelong and morbid frugality, and he had been a lonely young man wanting pleasure in a big city. Her pious letters had urged him to marry, but he had ignored her naïve moralizing and had remained single. Ideas had been his only sustained passion, but he knew that his love of them had that same sensual basis that drew him achingly to the sight of a girl's body swinging in a tight skirt along a sunny street.

He had been more than ready for Gladys when she had first risen on his horizon. He had congratulated himself on having tumbled upon a naïve girl who was gratefully receiving his amorous attentions, and it was not until long afterward that he had discovered that she had waited patiently while he had gropingly strayed into her domain, and then she had quietly closed the trap door over him. If some ironic enemy had been intending to tangle him in an ill-suited marriage, his self-enforced abstinence could not have better prepared him for her. She had been living in his South Side rooming house and he had spoken to her only casually. A registered nurse, quiet, perhaps more than a little repressed and with maybe a tendency toward the hysterical, she was soft-spoken, brown-skinned, and well-made. Sometimes he had seen her in her handsome nurse's uniform and he had admitted that she looked distinctively attractive in it.

49

Early one rainy autumn afternoon five years ago he had gone down to drive his Ford to work and had found her standing in the vestibule, sheltering herself against the downpour. He could see the edges of her white uniform showing around the hem of her coat. Surmising that she was trying to get to work, he had offered her a lift. He'd started a bantering conversation which had ended with her accepting an invitation to have a drink with him at the Golden Key the next afternoon.

That was how it began. The next afternoon—the rain was still falling—he sat waiting for her in a rear booth of the tavern, hunched over an unfinished drink. She presented herself a half hour late all done up in a smart, dark blue suit with a white silk blouse. A red silk scarf was tied over her head, and flouncing over her whole body was a transparent, plastic raincoat. He helped her out of her coat and noticed the tiny drops of rain gleaming on her wide forehead and her pert nose. She smelled like lilacs and autumn leaves. . . .

As they drank they talked about themselves, their families, racial problems. He found that she had no settled tastes or convictions, and he was flattered to discover that she was curious about his notions and had the good sense to listen quietly when he told her something important. Years later Cross realized that she had had enough sagacity to clear ample psychological ground about her so that he could move in at ease and without knowing that she was luring him. Her feminine instinct placed him at once in the role of a strong and reliable man and encouraged him to play it; he found himself liking to talk to her.

He had already made up his mind to invite her to dinner when she suddenly lifted her left wrist and looked at her watch. "Oh, God! It's almost six. I've got to go."

"I thought you were going to be free," he said, disappointed.

"You didn't ask me to be," she said quickly. "I've got to go to a cocktail party. You know, the white and colored nurses' associations are merged and if a colored member doesn't show up when she's invited, they might get the notion that we don't want to belong." She frowned and

50

stared off. "Really, I feel out of place in a roomful of whites. I'm afraid I'll be the only spook there."

"Guess I'll catch up on my sleep," he yawned.

"If that's all you've got to do, come with me to the party. Then I'll have dinner with you. And I'd feel better if you were with me."

They hustled out of the bar and drove to the Loop. The party was paralyzingly dull, with Cross and Gladys standing huddled together at one end of a huge, buzzing roomful of people, holding their drinks self-consciously, watching the others. He was amazed at how uneasy Gladys was in the presence of whites.

"Look, buck up." He tried to put some backbone in her. "Don't let the mere existence of these people scare you."

"They think they're *something* and we're *nothing*," she muttered.

"It's up to us to make ourselves something," he argued. "A man creates himself. . . ."

"You are a *man*," she said simply.

He understood now; it was the helplessness of dependence that made her fret so. Men made themselves and women were made only through men.

They had been there only half an hour when Gladys whispered to him: "Let's get the goddam hell out of here. They make me sick!"

"Okay," he agreed. "But whites don't scare me."

They went straight to a bar on the South Side where Gladys brooded. He studied her, wondering what memories lay under her mood. Through gentle questioning he stumbled upon it; she had attended a racially mixed school in her adolescence and the snubs and ostracism had branded her with a deep sense of not belonging and a yearning to have her status as an outsider cleared of shame. Her consciousness of being an outcast made him feel close to her, enabled him to drape about her a net of tender compassion. Underneath sex and common interests flowed a profounder tide of identity.

After dinner they began to drink in earnest, then they danced in a far South Side night club, and it was while holding her in his arms on the dance floor that desire for her leaped in him and it carried an extra urge to bind her to him and make her feel her humanity; he hungered for her as an image of woman as body of woman, but also as a woman of his own color who was longing to conquer the shame imposed upon her by her native land because of her social and racial origin. Gladys finally said that she wanted some fresh air and they went to a little bar on Forty-seventh Street where they drank some more. They got quite drunk.

"I ought to be getting in," Gladys said. "It's late."

"Okay. I'll put the car up and we'll walk home. Is that all right?"

"Anything you do is all right," she said, her head lolling and her eyes a little glazed.

He took her arm and guided her wandering steps to the car; he kissed her when they were inside and she went limp. But when he attempted to caress her, she resisted. He put the car in the garage, then walked beside her, his arm about her waist.

"I'm drunk, really drunk," she said as though talking to herself.

"I am too," he confessed, chuckling.

It was raining and she began to stumble. Giggling, they supported each other. It was after three o'clock in the morning and they were fairly floating. The rain began to fall in broad, steady sheets and Cross, who wore no hat, let his coat flop open.

"Honey, you're getting wet," she said.

"I don't feel it," he said.

"But you'll catch cold!"

"Naw!"

He suggested another drink when they were near the rooming house and she agreed. They each had three. In the vestibule of their building, he kissed her; then, on the landing leading to their rooms, he kissed her again in the stillness and darkness.

Nestling close to him, she mumbled as out of a dream: "I hate white people."

"Why?"

"They're mean."

"Did white people ever bother you?"

52

"Hell, naw! I wouldn't let 'em," she said belligerently.

"Then why do you hate 'em?"

" 'Cause they're *different* from me. I don't like 'em even to look at me. They make me self-conscious, that's why. Ain't that enough?"

"If you say so, baby. But, listen, *I'm* not white."

"That's what's so nice about it," she said drunkenly.

He led her to his room, and when he switched on the light she had a fleeting moment of soberness and shook her head, taking an aimless step backward. He tried to kiss her again and she twisted out of reach.

He switched off the light and kissed her and she melted, letting her lips cling fully to his; he carried her to the bed and they slept together in their damp clothes, being too drunk to undress. It was the beginning of the unleashing of a mutual, silent, and intense passion.

Cross's drunken carousal in the rain gave him pneumonia and Gladys stayed home from her job to nurse him. Quietly and all the time avoiding discussing it, she took total charge of him, created a situation that spelled unconditional surrender. She straightened out his disordered room, sent his piles of soiled linen to the laundry, gave him his penicillin injections, cooked and brought up his food. He accepted it all meekly, gazing up at her in humble gratitude when his fever was over one hundred and four. He had never been so comfortably looked after in all his life.

During the following week, Cross had her in his bed, on the floor, standing up, in the bathroom. . . . She made no demands, imposed no conditions, set no limits; she simply clung to him and when she spoke at all on general topics it was about how good it was to have someone to be with when the whole world was white and she was colored; he could say nothing to her about her color consciousness because he did not know how to handle it. In time he grew to accept it along with her womanness.

The climax of their relationship came unexpectedly when the fat, black, religious landlady told Cross that, now that he was well, she could no longer permit Miss Dennis' "actually living in your room like that. You know it ain't decent. I want folks to respect my home."

He told Gladys and she wept; he held her in his arms till she quieted.

"What must people think of me?" she moaned.

"To hell with that landlady," Cross said.

"You think the others in the house feel the same way?"

"God, I don't know."

"I hope it doesn't get to my job. . . ."

He hadn't thought of that.

"I don't want to leave you," she told him.

"So; it's settled."

"But what are we going to do?" The question echoed with unvoiced meaning.

It was the first time he had thought of marriage and it frightened him. But could he abandon her like that? He felt that if he had said he was through with her, she would have accepted it humbly. And it made him feel guilty. Well, would he ever find anyone better than she? He studied her face for a moment, then said impulsively: "Let's get married."

She had wept again. They rented an apartment and were furnishing it when they were married. Gladys had definite ideas about the home and Cross, having none, deferred to her. She argued gently that the thing to do was to buy a house and they did, arranging for the payments to fall due monthly.

The birth of their first child, a son, Cross Junior, marked the beginning of protracted trouble. After safely transporting Gladys, who was in violent labor, to the hospital, Cross went out with a picked group of his Post Office cronies—Pink, Joe, and Booker—to stage a celebration which ended for his cronies after seven hours of guzzling, but which, for Cross, extended itself for two whole days and nights during which he managed to pick up—he never knew exactly where or how—a brown-skinned girl who encouraged him to continue his "bat" as long as he had money to spend.

As strenuously as he tried, he could never recall clearly how he had come to bring the girl home with him and he never saw her after that to ask. He suspected that he had drunkenly decided to do it after his money had run out; he had confused recollections of being thrown out of bars because he couldn't pay for his drinks. Before his nonstop carousal, Gladys had tried to reach him by telephoning from the hospital and, worried, she had come home with the baby and a nurse to find Cross unshaven, bleary-eyed and in bed with what she called his "whore." Gladys' reaction had been so savage and intense that she had wept for days, refusing food, living in a mood of deep depression. Finally she demanded of Cross despairingly: "Aren't you happy with me?"

"Sure," he had said lightly, not wanting to think about it.

"Where did you meet the girl?"

"In a bar, I think. . . ." he said vaguely.

"How in God's name can you pick up a girl in a bar?"

In a nervous rage he had demanded: "Do *you* want to go? Or do you want *me* to go? I told you I was *drunk*, didn't I?"

They remained together, but the naturalness and trust that had characterized their earlier relationship were gone. Cross hoped that Gladys had written off that shameful episode as an unrepeatable aberration which she would forget. But whenever he drank she would fling it at him and, in the end, a slow, mounting resentment rose in him toward her. More and more she sulked and, as he suffered her nagging, he felt increasingly walled off from her; but the more he felt it the more he sought to hide it, and finally there crept into his dealings with her a weird quality of irony. It first manifested itself in an innocent question: How could he help Gladys? And the moment he asked himself that question he knew that he did not love her and perhaps had never loved her. . . . She had become for him an object of compassion. He was now haunted by the idea of finding some way to make her hate him. Her hatred would be a way of squaring their relationship, of curing her of her love for him, of setting her free as well as himself.

One winter when Cross was ill, Gladys nursed him and tried to re-establish over him her old emotional authority. It resulted in another pregnancy from which there issued two more sons, twins, Peter and Robert. Gladys had been hopeful, but not for long. Expenses increased and Cross's salary was squeezed. Gladys now had her hands full while Cross worked extra hours to pull in more money. The house was bedlam, filled with shouting, tumbling children. Cross found it all but impossible to sleep during the day and he became so nervous that Gladys would flare at him: "What are you trying to do? Drive us all out so you can fill the house with your whores?"

Dating from this period, a wave of self-loathing began to engulf Cross. Until now he had managed to keep up his classes at the University, but he lost heart for study and dropped out of school. Each time he realized how much he had lost control of his life, his self-hatred swelled. He knew himself too well to blame Gladys and he was scrupulous enough to let her know it, which baffled and tortured her all the more. She longed for some simple definition of their troubles that she could grasp. She thought that she was losing her physical appeal for him and she went, without telling him—and submitted to an extraordinarily expensive operation to have her breasts lifted! That more than anything else had depressed Cross, filled him with a compassion mingled with disgust. He had been so stunned by it that he could never discuss it with her.

One afternoon in a bar, dawdling over a drink, he recalled how shocked Gladys had been when she had come home from the hospital with Junior and had found him in bed with the girl. That fantastic happening had now become accepted as an "accident." Well, why couldn't another "accident" happen? One so fatal and unique that it would make her remember the last one as a guide by which to interpret it! He was far from planning anything overtly criminal; it was a complicated psychological attack whose consequences would clarify Gladys' feelings about him. But what on earth could that "accident" be? It would have to be so decisive that she would tell him to go and never come back. He would support her and the children, of course. He sipped his drink idly, turning his wish carefully over in his mind. Then his self-hate, his aversion for Gladys, his perpetual toying with his own feelings resulted in a sudden, confoundingly luminous idea. He had it! By God, this was it! It would flow from him as naturally as it would be embraced by her, and it was simple. Could he

56

carry it out? It would take cool nerve, insight, timing, and ruthless execution. What decided him was a cynical question: "If I fail, I'll be no worse off than I am now, will I?"

He always finished his night shift in the Post Office at four o'clock in the morning; then, with his cronies, he went to The Salty Dog, a bar around the corner from his house, for what they jokingly called a "daycap," since they slept during the day. At five o'clock he went home for breakfast, which Gladys prepared in the kitchen in her kimono. Afterward he went directly to bed. But on *that* morning, he would not stop for his "daycap"; he would go back for his drink *after* he had done it. Such timing would make his actions seem more normal. Furthermore, his going back to have a drink with the boys would give him an alibi, in case he needed one. Above all, the children should be sound asleep when he did it; he did not want to disturb them in any way.

He decided upon a Friday morning to carry his plan into action. After he left work he detached himself unobtrusively from his friends and went directly home, arriving shortly after four o'clock. Gladys had just gone into the kitchen and was putting a pot of coffee on the gas stove. He walked in and advanced wordlessly upon her, his eyes fastened on her face.

"Oh, good morning, Cross," she said, glancing at the electric clock on the wall. "You're early, aren't you?"

He stood directly in front of her, his eyes unblinking and his face a blank mask.

"What's the matter?" she asked, backing away a step.

He reached forward and gave her a slap with his open palm, not hard, but stinging and with enough force to send her stumbling backward into a corner.

"Cross!" her voice was not loud, but charged with shock.

Then for a moment she was still as stone, staring at him, her lips parted, her hands lifted to shield her face. She lay against the wall, her open kimono showing her full breasts. The sound that came from her now coincided with her recognition of danger.

"No, no, no . . ." She spoke in low, clipped words, the inflection of her voice rising.

As he advanced toward her again, her mouth opened slowly and her chest heaved as she drew in her breath to scream. He roughly seized both of her hands in his left hand and slapped her once more, then stood leering down at her with a twisted face.

"Oh, God!" she screamed. "Don't kill me, Cross!"

As if pulled by cables of steel, he whirled and walked from the kitchen and out of the front door, hearing Gladys sobbing. He had not uttered a single syllable and the whole assault had taken no more than a minute. When he reached the door of the bar, he stood a moment to collect himself. He saw his pals sitting in the rear; he eased himself toward them and sat down.

"Where did you go, Crossy?" big, fat Joe asked carelessly.

"I was making a phone call," he said, lighting a cigarette and controlling his hand to keep it from trembling.

They began arguing politics. He spoke with composure, glancing now and then at the clock on the wall, wondering what was happening at home. He was pleased that the children had not heard him. Would she call the police? He doubted it; she would wait and talk to him first. Would she tell the children? He did not think so. Would she go to see his mother? Maybe. Her mind must be in a turmoil. . . . At five-thirty, he said casually: "Well, guys, I've got to cut out and get some shut-eye."

He rose and waved good-by. Now was the test. If his abrupt, physical attack upon Gladys provoked an immediate storm of reaction, then it would go badly for him; but if she was frantically trying to find some explanation for it, then all might go well. The main strategy was not to let her settle upon any one reason for it, to keep her judgment torturingly uncertain. Everything depended upon how much pretended incredulity he could show, how much simulated surprise he could convincingly sustain. As he turned into the walk leading to the house, he had a bad moment; a surging impulse made him want to turn about and dodge it all. He shook it off, entered the front door, walked down the hallway and went into the bathroom. That had always been his routine and he adhered to it now. As he washed he whistled a tune, not steadily, but in snatches, not like a

58

man intentionally trying to create an impression of carefree-ness, but like a man with nothing serious on his mind. There was not a sound of movement in the house. Where was Gladys? Had she funked and fled? No; she would not leave the children. . . . He emerged from the bathroom and went into the kitchen; he knew that she was not there, but he had to act as though he expected to find her frying his bacon and eggs. On the gas stove a blue flame glowed under the coffeepot and the scent of burning metal assailed his nostrils. He went to the stove and saw that the coffee had evaporated from the pot and that the metal around the bottom gleamed bright red. He shut off the gas and looked over his shoulder. That meant that Gladys had quit the kitchen the moment he had left the house. That's normal. . . .

"Gladys!" he called out quietly, questioningly.

There was no answer. He made for the bedroom, calling again: "Gladys!"

Silence. He opened the bedroom door and asked into the semigloom: "Gladys, aren't you up yet?"

Silence. He hesitated a second, then switched on the wall light. Gladys was huddled on the bed, her eyes black with fear. She was so immobile that at first he thought that maybe she was dead, had died of shock. But, no; he could see her chest slowly rising and falling.

"What's the matter?" he asked softly.

She did not answer. Tears rolled down her cheeks and her fingers writhed.

"Didn't you know you left the coffeepot on the fire? All the water boiled out and it was red hot. . . ."

She did not move.

"What's the matter? Are you ill?" he asked.

He walked toward her and she lunged violently back-ward, falling from the bed to the floor, leaving one of her bedroom slippers on the quilt. He stopped, blinked his eyes in simulated bewilderment. He advanced upon her again and Gladys shook her head wildly.

"No, no, no . . . Don't hit me, Cross! *Don't* . . . !" she whimpered convulsively, barricading her face and head with her elbows.

59

He stared at her, his mouth drooping open in mock amazement. "What's the matter with you?"

"Cross," she sobbed. "I never thought you'd *hit* me."

He stepped away from her imperceptibly, as though stunned. "*Hit* you? What in the world are you talking about?"

He went to her and she shrank, burrowing herself against the wall. He caught hold of her shoulder and she lifted her eyes and stared at him and he returned her stare with make-believe astonishment until her eyes fell.

"What's the matter, Gladys! You're shaking! Here, let me put you to bed. I'll call a doctor. . . ."

He was still holding on to her shoulder and felt a slight lessening of tension in her muscles. Trembling, she allowed him to lead her to the bed and push her gently upon it. She looked at him with eyes filled with shock.

"Lie down and keep still," he said hurriedly, feigning deep anxiety. "I'll have the doctor here in a minute. If you felt like that, why didn't you phone me at the Post Office?"

Delicately he pulled the cover over her, went to the telephone at the bedside, picked it up, dialed the first letter and then glanced at her.

"No, no, no . . . No, Cross," she begged; her eyes were pools of bewilderment. She breathed uncertainly. Her gaze fell and her fingers fluttered.

"Now, listen, you'd better have the doctor take a look at you," he said, pitching his voice to a tone of half command and half entreaty.

She began to sob again, burying her face in the pillow. He sat on the edge of the bed and patted her shoulder.

"Take it easy. Have you any pains? What's happened? Where are the children?"

She stared at him again, unable to believe the evidence of her senses. Her head rocked on its neck. Her mouth trembled and she had to move her lips several times before she could speak.

"Why did you do it?" she whimpered. Then she spoke fully, almost rising to a point of objectivity. "Do you hate me that much?"

"Do *what?*" He asked, replacing the receiver upon the

60

hook of the transmitter. "*Hate* you? What *are* you talking about?"

"Oh, God!" she cried. "You *know* what you did?"

Fear filled him for a second. She was in her crisis now; would she veer against him or would she still float in indecision?

"You're dreaming!" he shot at her. "Do you know what you are saying?"

"You hit me. . . . You beat me. . . . What *for*?" she asked insistently.

"*Beat* you?" he echoed, as though he had to repeat the word to believe in its reality. His face was the living personification of stupefied surprise. "You are out of your mind. Now, look here, be calm. Tell me what happened."

She looked distractedly about the room like a rat searching for a hole. She was a tiny child hearing a grownup tell a tale that it did not believe, but it dared not challenge that tale because it had no way of successfully disputing it, feeling that its reasoning was not acceptable.

"Cross, you came into the kitchen and knocked me down," she explained in a low voice.

"You're crazy!" He stood and pretended to look suspiciously about the room. "Who's been here?"

"You!"

"Good Lord, you're wild!" He shook his head. "I *just* left the bar; I went there directly from work and had a drink, like always. . . . Look, get hold of yourself." He aped bewilderment. "Have you been drinking?"

"Oh, Cross!"

"Listen, if you don't stop I'll call the doctor. You've got the children to look after." He copied tones of responsibility.

She stared at him, dumbfounded. Slowly, she shook her head. *Yes!* The idea was working in her mind. It was coming off much easier than he had thought. But he had to be firm and not retreat from his position.

"When do you think I hit you, Gladys?"

"I *didn't* imagine it," she whimpered.

It was working; she was beginning to wonder if what had happened had not been wiped from his memory. Silence followed. The restoration of normality must depend upon *his* initiative; what had so mysteriously occurred must seem to have been swallowed up in his mind as though it had never transpired; he must not in any way grant it one whit of objective reality.

"Look, kid," he began kindly. "I know we aren't the loving couple one reads about in books. But you mustn't let our troubles break you down. There's no sense in brooding till you start imagining things. You need a rest. . . ."

She clutched his arm. "Cross, don't you *remember* what you did?"

"Gladys, really, I hate to say it, but you're *off!*"

"I'm sane, Cross," she said, unable to restrain her tears.

She collected her senses; she was no longer physically afraid; she was fearful of something more menacingly dark than a slap.

"I don't know what's happened to you," he played his role.

"Cross, you *remember* you hit me," she moaned.

"I *didn't!*" His face grew hard. "You're mixed up. . . . Tell me, *who's* been here?"

"Nobody," she breathed.

"Who else saw me come in here?"

"Nobody," she whispered, her eyes widening with understanding.

"Look, Junior's coming," he spoke in a low, rapid voice. "Brace up. . . . You'll upset him."

"Is it possible?" she asked herself in a despairing whisper.

She pulled herself unsteadily from the bed to the dresser and began arranging her hair with palsied hands. He could see her watching his reflection in the mirror; he had to be careful. She had forgotten her bedroom slipper on the quilt; he got it and held it out to her.

"Here; you better put it on," he said in a neutral voice.

She obeyed him with movements charged with suppressed fear. But when he looked at her she glanced quickly away.

Junior, four years of age, came running in in his pajamas. "I'm hungry," he sang, lifting an earnest, brown face to his father.

Cross swept the boy up in his arms and fondled him.

Watching Cross out of the corners of her eyes, Gladys went hesitantly from the room to prepare breakfast. Cross burrowed his head playfully into Junior's stomach and the boy giggled. He was now certain that he could handle it. This was the beginning, the setup; next time would be the payoff.

During the following week, under the cover of anxious solicitude, Cross craftily urged Gladys to see a doctor and she politely refused. A few days later she timidly begged *him* to see a doctor, telling him that she was certain that what had happened was a recurrence of what he had done with the girl. In a tone of play-acting shock, looking her levelly in the eyes, he scoffed at her interpretation and assured her that he was absolutely sane. He now made it a rigorous rule never to refer to the "accident"; all mention of it had to come from her. And, as time went on, she found it more and more difficult to bring it up; but he knew that the thought of it was continually hovering in the back of her mind.

One day, touching his cheek gently as she spoke—hoping by the gesture to negate any hint that she thought him insane—she expressed concern that he might harm the children "while in one of your spells." He patted her shoulder and said soothingly: "Don't worry, darling. Everything's all right." She beseeched him to cut his drinking, his smoking, to sleep more. She strove to keep more order in the house, chiding the children lovingly not to "make noise and get on poor papa's nerves."

He chose Easter Sunday morning for his next attack. He knew that nothing would be further from Gladys' mind then, for her attention would be involved in coloring Easter eggs and arranging new clothes for the children's Easter outing. He worked the night of Easter Eve and went straight home and found Gladys alone in the kitchen; she whirled with fear as he came in, for she knew that he was early as on that other fateful morning. Again he walked slowly toward her, wordlessly, his facial expression simulating dementia.

"No, no, no . . . !"

He slapped her resoundingly and she went down like a log.

"Junior!" she yelled. "Somebody help me!"

He stooped and slapped her once more, his face contorted in an imitation of rage; then he turned and rushed out, hurried to the bar and joined Joe, Pink and Booker, who had not missed him this time. He sat coolly talking and drinking with them, but his mind was trying to picture what was happening at home. At a little past five he went back, let himself in with his key, and headed as usual to the bathroom to wash up. He lathered his hands and whistled softly. Suddenly he was still, hearing muffled footsteps moving haltingly along the hallway. What's she doing . . . ? Then all was quiet. He dried his face and hands and when he emerged he did not have to look for Gladys, for there she was at the door, confronting him with his gun, pointing it straight at his heart.

"Cross," she said heavily, struggling to manage her breathing, "I can't bear with you another minute. Pack your things and get out, now! You're crazy. You're a danger to yourself and everyone else!"

He saw such fear in her face that he was afraid that she would lose control of herself and pull the trigger.

"My God," his voice rang with sincerity. "Take it easy. . . ."

His nervousness made Gladys step quickly away from him and wave the gun threateningly.

"If you come near me, I'll shoot!" she cried. "And I'll go free, because you're crazy!"

Her arm trembled and she reached toward him, the gun barrel coming within inches of his right temple.

"Gladys," he breathed, leaning weakly against a wall. "I can't get my clothes unless you let me pass."

"You're sick, Cross," she pronounced in neutral, distant tones.

Realizing that she was blocking his path, she stepped cautiously to one side. He went into the bedroom and began to pack. She waited in the doorway, still nervously clutching the gun.

"Gladys," he started to protest.

"Get out!" she ordered in a frenzy.

He packed a suitcase and stood looking at her out of the

corners of his eyes. "I'll come back for the rest of my stuff later—"

"You let me know and I'll *send* your things," she said. "Don't ever set foot in this house without first telling me, you hear! If you do, it'll be dangerous for you."

"I'll phone you," he mumbled.

She held open the front door, still brandishing the gun in her shaking hand. He walked over the threshold, sweating, fearing that he would stumble.

"See a doctor, Cross," she said, slamming the door.

On the sidewalk he paused and saw her peering at him from behind one of the lace window curtains in the living room, still grasping the gun. He resolved to buy another gun; he felt naked without one. Walking away, he felt good.

Cross roused himself on the jolting trolley, wiped a clear spot on the sweaty windowpane and saw that he had ridden past Gladys' place. Good God . . . He rushed to the front of the car and when it slowed he swung off. As he neared the house his steps faltered. He was doubtful that Gladys would help him, but his predicament was so bad he had to try, whatever the outcome. He mounted the steps and paused; his instincts warned him away from this Gladys whom he had made hate him too well. But he had to see her. He pushed the button of the doorbell and almost in the moment of his pushing it, the door flung open and Gladys stood before him, grim, erect. Out of a tightly organized face two deep-set eyes regarded him with composed hate.

"Hello, Gladys," he mumbled.

"I've been waiting for you," she said with placid irony. "I watched you creep up the walk like a doomed man. Are you scared of your home now?"

"I want to talk to you about something important," he told her.

A twisted smile played on Gladys' rouged lips. "I suppose it's about Miss Dorothy Powers, hunh?"

Anger flashed through him. No; he had to be calm.

"That's it, Gladys," he admitted, forcing a smile.

She stepped to one side and he moved gingerly into the

hallway, feeling for the first time intimidated by Gladys. He glanced about apprehensively, his body screaming for a drink to brace him for this ordeal.

"Where're the kids?" he asked to fill the gaping silence.

"I knew you were coming," she announced, "so I sent them to a friend's house this afternoon."

He walked into the living room and sat. Gladys followed and stood at the other end of the room and regarded him with hostile eyes. He could feel that she was clamoring for an emotional scene. Well, he'd refuse her the satisfaction. He'd be polite, bantering, if possible.

"A young lady visited you this morning, I think," he said, trying to rid his voice of anxiety.

"You mean that bitch you sent—!"

"Gladys, I didn't send anybody here," he cut in quickly.

"Cross, for God's sake, why do you insist on being such a crawling coward? You *sent* her here—"

"I didn't, I tell you!"

"You're lying!"

"Gladys, I know how you feel about me—"

"You ought to," she spat at him. "Do you think you can walk over me? Well, you won't, ever! You sent that little whore here to beg me . . ."

He tried to stop listening. It was going worse than he thought. Well, if she wanted to blast Dot, let her. The main thing was the question of divorce.

"There is one thing, by God," she roared, "that you are going to do! You are going to *respect* me. You can't send a filthy, stinking little tart like that to talk to me. You can be sure I gave your bitch a hot welcome, and she won't forget it, not soon!" Gladys groped for words, her mouth open. "And while I'm on it, let me settle one more question. You'll *not* get a divorce. For a rotten slut like her, *never!* That's the way I feel and I'm not ashamed of it! If you can be dirty, then so can I! Keep on living with her, but if she asks you to make her respectable, tell her you can't! Take your Dorothy and sleep with her and let her give you a litter of bastards. That's all she's fit for, and you, too, it seems! Is that clear?"

Her hysterical tirade made him ashamed for her. The satisfaction she was deriving from it was obscene.

66

"Look, I'm not going to argue with your feelings." He clutched at words to stem the tide. "Let's arrange something. I'm supporting you and the children—"

"And by the living hell, you'll keep on!"

"Okay. I agree. But your welfare depends on my job—"

He jerked as she burst into a gale of cynical laughter. "So, you've been to the Post Office?" she asked. "They put the fear of God into you, hunh? That's why you came crawling to me. . . ."

Cross froze. Had she already told the postal officials about the possibility of his being convicted of rape? He had come to bargain with her, but if she had already talked, the game was all but lost.

"What are you talking about?" he asked quietly.

"Cross, are you stupid?" There was a mocking pity in her tone. "I must protect myself. . . . That little whore of yours wasn't gone from here an hour before my lawyer and I were at the Post Office—"

"Why?"

He knew why she had gone, but he wanted to know how far she had gone. Maybe his job was already lost!

Gladys spoke quietly, as though she were a schoolteacher explaining a complicated problem to a dullard. She came to within a few feet of Cross and sat.

"Cross, you really cannot expect me to think of you and your troubles," she said. "You're intelligent and you know what you're doing. I had to act in my own defense. I went straight to the Postmaster and told him that your Miss Powers was about to charge you with rape—"

"Did she tell you that?" Cross asked, feeling that his chair was whirling him round.

"Of course she did," Gladys informed him with a smile. "Do you think she's informing you of her moves against you? The Postmaster knows, of course, that you cannot marry the girl. . . . And if you are convicted, you're ruined. Now, the Postal Inspector has your case, see?"

Cross had no will to stop her; he knew that she was summing up his situation accurately.

"Cross, don't be naïve," she continued. "There's nothing that Miss Powers can do but charge you, unless she's willing to live with you and bear your child. . . . And I doubt if she loves you that much." She paused, lit a cigarette, eying Cross the while. "Now, there are some rather disagreeable things I must say to you.

"Number One: You're signing this house over to me at once. Number Two: You're signing over the car to me. Number Three: You're going to the Post Office tonight and borrow eight hundred dollars from the Postal Union on your salary. I've already made the arrangements with the Postal Inspector. He's okayed it. I want that money to clear the titles of both the house and the car." She stood, lifted her hand to bar his words. "I know you want to say no," she said. "But you can't. Cross, understand this: so far as I'm concerned, you're *through!* I'm squeezing you like a lemon. If you don't do what I'm asking, in the morning I shall keep an appointment with Miss Powers. She, *I*, and her lawyer will go to the Forty-ninth Street Police Station and I will help her bring charges against you. I'm not justifying my actions. I'm not apologizing, see? I'm just telling you. That's how things stand between us, Cross."

He was willing to sign over everything, but he did not want to borrow the money; it would mean debts for two years to come. And he could use that money to try to bribe Dot. . . .

"They may not let me have the money," he said.

"Mr. Dumb," she said scornfully, "if the Postal Union thought you were going to be indicted for rape, they wouldn't let you have the money, because you wouldn't have a job. I let them think the girl would abort the child, that you'd pay her off. . . . I made sure with the Postmaster that your job was safe, and the Postal Union has been told that it's all right. . . ."

"But the girl can *still* charge me," Cross protested without strength. "What game's this you're playing?"

"*My* game," Gladys said.

"The eight hundred dollars," he was pleading now, "could keep the girl and I could make payments to you—"

"I don't give a damn about that girl," she snapped. "What happens between you and her is your business!"

Gladys was using Dot to drag money from him and at

68

the same time betraying Dot. Cross wanted to close his eyes and sleep this nightmare away.

"If you get eight hundred dollars, you won't help the girl?"

"Hell, no! Why should I? Let that bitch rot!"

He was properly trapped. There was nothing more to say. This was a cold and vindictive Gladys created by him. He rose and moved toward the door.

"What's your answer?" she asked.

"Okay. I'll get the money. I'll phone you tonight."

"Oh, there's one other thing," she said, opening the door for him. "Is your life insurance paid up?"

"Hunh?" His voice sounded far away. "Yes; yes . . ."

"Have you changed the beneficiary?" she asked.

"No; why should I?"

"I just wanted to know," she said.

He felt as though he were already dead and was listening to her speak about him. He went out and did not glance back. He was not aware of trampling through the deep snow. About him were sounds that had no meaning. When he came fully to himself, his feet were like two icy stumps. I must have fever. . . . He paused and stared around him. He was tired. Oh, God, I got to get that money for Gladys. . . . He looked about for a taxi. Oh, there's the El. . . . He ran for the entrance, stumbled up the steps, fished a dime from his pocket, and rushed to the platform just as a Loopbound train slid to a stop. He found a seat, fell into it, and sat hunched over, brooding.

Seeing Gladys had compounded his problems. If he did what she wanted, he was lost; and if he didn't, he was lost. Yet, because he could not make up his mind to ditch it all, he had to follow her demands.

Before reaching Roosevelt Road the El dipped underground. Cross rose, swaying with the speed of the train, and traversed each coach until he came to the first car, whose front window looked out upon a dim stretch of tunnel. He leaned his forehead against the glass and stared at the rushing ribbons of steel rails whose glinting surfaces vanished beneath his feet.

At his station, he got off and went toward the Post Office, a mass of steel and stone with yellow windows glowing. The night air was still; it had begun to grow a little warmer. It's going to snow again, he thought idly. Yes, he'd see about the loan right now, but he'd not work tonight. He hungered for sleep. He flashed his badge to the guard at the door and went inside. Where's that Postal Union office? Yes; there on the right. . . . He pushed open the door and saw Finch, the Union secretary, sitting quietly, his hat on, chewing an unlighted cigar and holding a deck of soiled playing cards in his hands. Cross approached Finch's desk and for a moment they stared at each other. He suddenly hated Finch's whiteness, not racially, but just because Finch was white and safe and calm and he was not.

"Damon, huh?"

"Yes."

"I was waiting for you," Finch said. "Sit down."

Cross obeyed. He did not want to look at Finch; he knew the man knew his troubles and it made him ashamed; instead, he stared stupidly at the pudgy, soft fingers as they shuffled the cards.

"You look like an accident going somewhere to happen," Finch commented.

"I'm under the weather," Cross confessed. "I want to renew that eight-hundred-dollar loan I had last year—"

"Oh, yes." Finch looked up. "Your wife's been in."

White fingers took the cigar from thin lips and a brown stream of tobacco juice spewed into a spittoon. Finch replaced the cigar, chewed it, and settled it carefully again in his jaw.

"You colored boys get into a lot of trouble on the South Side." Finch gave a superior smile. "You must have a hot time out there every day, huh?"

Cross stiffened. Letting Finch call it racial behavior was a kind of compound interest he had to pay on his loan.

"Is the loan possible?" Cross asked.

"The Postmaster said it's all right," Finch said, finally stacking the cards and flinging them to one side, as though ridding himself of something unpleasant. "Half of my time's spent taking care of you colored boys. . . . What goes on on the South Side?"

Cross cleared his throat to control himself. "I don't

70

know," he mumbled. "I'm offering my house as security—"

"I'm ahead of you, Damon," Finch said. "On the strength of your wife's plea, I've had the papers all drawn up. Boy, you've got a good wife. You ought to take care of her—"

"I do," Cross mumbled.

"If you did, you wouldn't be in this mess," Finch said. He pushed the contract toward Cross. "Here, sign. . . ."

Cross signed clumsily, his nervousness letting a blob of ink smear across the page. He fumbled with a blotter to soak it up.

"Let me do that," Finch said, taking the blotter from Cross. "Looks like a chicken with dirty feet ran over this contract." He handed Cross a carbon copy of the contract, then opened a drawer and pulled out a sheaf of vouchers. "How do you want this? A check or cash?"

"Cash. I'd like the money tonight."

"Why not? It's your money."

Finch initialed a voucher for cash and flipped it at Cross.

"Okay. Get going," Finch said, yanking his thumb toward the door.

Cross stood and wanted to spit at the man. He edged forward and opened the door.

"Shut the door when you go out," Finch called, picking up his deck of cards and beginning to shuffle them again.

"Yes; of course," Cross said.

He pulled the door softly shut and sighed. Well, that was done. Then he stiffened. One of the Assistant Postmasters was bearing down upon him, his gray eyes intent on Cross's face.

"Damon, just a moment!"

"Yes, sir," Cross answered, waiting.

The Assistant Postmaster pointed a forefinger at Cross. "Damon, don't ever come to this Post Office again on an errand like this. If it hadn't been for your wife, I wouldn't touch this stink with a ten-foot pole. Look, you had one loan and paid it. Do the same with this. We're here to handle the mails, not emotional dramas. Now, this eight hundred ought to settle your little business, huh?"

"Yes, sir," he lied; it would only settle the claims of

Gladys, but it would not help him with Dot. "Let me explain, sir. . . ."

"Don't tell me about it. I don't want to know."

"I'd like the night off, sir," Cross said. "I'll take it out of my vacation days."

"And what other service can I render you?" the Assistant Postmaster asked with mockery.

"I'm ill," Cross said peevishly.

"You look it," the Assistant Postmaster said. "Okay. Take it. But I know a guy called Damon who's going to find the Post Office a hard line to walk from here on out."

Cross bit his lip, and went down to the cashier's office of the Postal Union and presented his voucher.

"Cash, eh?" the teller asked, smiling. "What're you going to do with all that money? Buy the Tribune Tower?"

Cross pretended that he had not heard. He pushed the pile of fifty-dollar bills into his wallet, sought a telephone booth and dialed Gladys.

"I got the money," he told her.

"I want it first thing in the morning," she said flatly.

"I'll bring it by at noon."

"All right."

He made for the exit, showed his badge to the guard and stepped into the street. It was snowing again; fat, white flakes drifted lazily down from a night sky. An El train rattled past overhead. He sighed, feeling relieved. He had to be careful and not let a pickpocket rob him of the money. He put his badge and the duplicate copy of the loan contract into the pocket of his overcoat and stuffed his wallet into his shirt, next to his skin. His job now was to head off Dot.

Diving into a subway, he paid his fare and, two minutes later, when a train roared up, walked into the first coach and sank into a seat, closing his eyes. The train pulled into motion; he opened his eyes and noticed another Negro, shabbily dressed, about his own color and build, sitting across the aisle from him. The movement of the coach rocked some of the tension out of him, but not enough to let him relax. He went to the front window and stood looking at the twin ribbons of steel rails sliding under the train.

A moment later, when the train was streaking through the underground, darkness suddenly gouged his eyes and a clap of thunder hit his ears. He was spinning through space, his body smashing against steel; then he was aware of being lifted and brutally catapulted through darkness. Screams of men and women rent the black air.

Afterward Cross remembered that when the lights had gone out he had involuntarily blinked his eyes, feeling that the cause of the sudden darkness was some fault in the functioning of his pupils. About him were sounds of ripping metal and then something thumped against his head, knocking him out. How long he was unconscious, he did not know. When he came to he realized that his body was in an almost upright position, jammed between what seemed like two walls of steel. The right side of his skull was gripped by pain and something wet and warm trickled down the side of his face. His left leg was being wrenched and his right leg was pinioned, crushed to numbness in what seemed like a vise. He groaned. The words: *It's a subway wreck!* shaped themselves in his consciousness.

Abruptly the thunder ceased and the only sounds he heard were screams. In the blackness that walled before his eyes, Cross was afraid to move. *How badly am I hurt? Is it over?* He became aware that he was holding his head tucked down to dodge another attack of annihilation. Lifting his eyes he saw far ahead of him a jutting spray of blue electric sparks showering down from somewhere. He had to get out of this, now, NOW . . . Gingerly, he groped with his fingers and what he touched made him project images of what his fingers felt and he screamed. He imagined he saw the profile of a human face drenched in blood. He snatched his hand away and wiped it dry upon his coat.

He breathed softly, listening: a viscous liquid was slowly falling drop by drop somewhere near him: the whimper of a woman seemed to be issuing from a half-conscious body: a quiet coughing seemed to be trying to dislodge something thick and wet from a sticky throat: an incessant grunt grew fainter and fainter until it was heard no more. . . .

He was calm now, thinking. His lighter must be in his left pants pocket. Twisting, he reached for it, felt it with the ends of his fingers. Yes! Purpose gripped him and, squeezing the tips of his fingers together, he caught hold of the lighter and slowly pulled it out. He pushed the lever and a bluish flame shed feeble light amid a welter of tangled forms. Lines zigzagged and solids floated in shadows, vanishing into meaninglessness; images dissolved into other images and his mind was full of a sense of shifting significances.

He saw that the seats of the train were above his head; the coach had turned over, twisted within the tube of the underground and he was standing on the shattered lights of the ceiling. Seats had ripped from the floor and had fallen to the ceiling where he stood.

Cross shut his eyes and bit his lips, his ears assailed by screams. He had to get out of here! He bent lower and looked; a white face with unblinking eyes was wedged at the level of his knees and beneath that face he could make out a dark pool of fluid that reflected the flickering flame of his lighter. He moved the flame over shards of glinting glass and saw again that window and the shower of blue electric sparks still sprinkling down. . . . Yes; he had to get to that window. . . . But his legs . . . He had to get them free. . . . He bent and looked closer; his right leg was gripped between the steel wall of the coach and a seat that had tumbled from the floor to the ceiling. He pushed at the seat and it would not budge. Again he shoved his weight at the seat. Why didn't it move? He stooped lower with the light and saw that the seat that jammed his leg to the wall was anchored in place by the man's head, which, in turn, was rammed by another seat. The man's face was fronting Cross.

Cross lifted the pressure of his finger from the lever and the flame went out. He thought: That man's head is keeping this seat from moving. . . . Could he get that head out of his way? He pressed the lever again and looked. He could just reach the man's head with his right hand. Yes; he had to shove it out of the way. He held the lighter in his left hand, shut his eyes, and felt the palm of his right hand touching the yielding flesh of the man's face, expecting to hear a protest. . . . He opened his eyes; no breath seemed to be coming from the nostrils or mouth. Cross shuddered. If the man was dead, then any action he took to free

74

himself was right. . . . He held his fingers to the man's parted lips and could feel no stir of air. For a few seconds he watched the man's chest and could detect no movement. The man's dead. . . . But how could he get that head out of his way? Again he pushed his right hand with all of his strength against the face and it budged only a fraction of an inch. Goddamn . . . He panted with despair, regarding the man's head as an obstacle; it was no longer flesh and blood, but a rock, a chunk of wood to be whacked at until it was gone. . . .

He searched vainly in the moving shadows for something to hold in his hand, still hearing the sounds of screams. He felt in his overcoat pocket; the gun was there. Yes . . . He pulled it out. Could he beat down that foolishly staring face belonging to that head pushing against the seat wedging his leg to the wall? He shut his eyes and lifted the gun by the barrel and brought down the butt, and, even though his eyes were closed, he could see the gun butt crashing into the defenseless face. . . . Sweat broke out on his forehead and rivulets of water oozed from his armpits.

He opened his eyes; the bloody face had sunk only a few inches; the nostrils, teeth, chin, and eyes were pulped. Cross sucked in his breath; a few more blows would dislodge it. He shut his eyes and hammered again and suddenly he heard a splashing thud and he knew that the head had given way, for his blows were now falling on air. . . . He looked; the mangled face was on the floor; most of the flesh had been ripped away. He had done it; he could move his leg.

Now, he had to free his other leg. Peering with the lighter, he saw that his left leg was hooked under a fallen seat. With his right leg free, he hoisted himself up and saw that he would get loose if he could use his left leg as a ramrod to shove at the seat. Pricked by splinters of glass, he hauled himself upward and perched on the back of an overturned seat and, with his left foot, he gave a wild kick against the seat. It did not move. Bracing himself, he settled his heel against the back of the seat, eased his overcoat —which was hindering his movements—down a little from his shoulders, shut his eyes and pushed against the seat. It fell away. Both of his legs were free. An awful stench filled his nostrils.

He looked toward the gutted window; the blue electric sparks were still falling. From somewhere came a banging of metal against metal, like an urgent warning. That window was the way out. He crept forward over the ceiling of the overturned coach, past twisted and bloody forms, crunching shattered electric bulbs under his feet, feeling his shoes slopping through sticky liquid. He moved on tiptoe, as though afraid of waking the sleeping dead. He reached the window and saw that a young woman's body had been crushed almost flat just beneath it. The girl was dead, but, if he was to get through that window, he had the choice of standing upon her crushed body or remaining where he was. He stepped upon the body, feeling his shoes sinking into the lifeless flesh and seeing blood bubbling from the woman's mouth as his weight bore down on her breast. He reached for the window, avoiding the jagged edges of glass. Outside the blue electric sparks rained down, emitting a ghostly light. He did not need his lighter now. He crawled through and lowered his feet to the ground. He had to be careful and not step upon any live wires or the third rail. . . . His feet sought for gravel.

He stood for a moment, collecting himself. His head throbbed. When he moved his right leg it pained him. His body was clammy and trembling. For a moment he felt as though he would lose consciousness, but he remained on his feet. Screams, more distant now, came to his ears. He moved forward in the bluish gloom. Yes, ahead of him were amber lights! He pushed on and could hear distant voices and they were not the voices of the wounded. He had been lucky. I'd better let a doctor look at me. . . . He now realized how fantastically fortunate he had been; had he remained in his seat, he would have been crushed to death. . . .

He picked his way catlike over wooden trestles and then stopped. His overcoat . . . ? Oh, God, he had left it somewhere back in that death-filled darkness, but he could not recall how it had gotten away from him. The gun was still in his pants' pocket. With stiff and sweaty fingers he lit a cigarette and walked on. From above ground he caught the faint wail of sirens and ahead of him he saw dim traces of light in the circular tunnel. Later he made out blurred, white uniforms and he knew that they were doctors and nurses.

He trudged past overturned coaches whose windows were gutted of glass. He could see doctors and nurses quite clearly now. He heard someone yell: "Here comes another one! He seems all right!"

They had seen him and were running to meet him. A doctor and a nurse caught hold of his arms.

"Are you all right?" the doctor asked.

"I guess so," he answered out of a daze.

"You are lucky," the nurse said.

"Get 'im to an ambulance," the doctor told the nurse. "I want to take a look back here."

The doctor hurried off into the tunnel of darkness, spotting his way with a flashlight.

"Can you walk all right?" the nurse asked him.

"Yeah."

"Does anything hurt you?"

"My leg, my right leg . . ."

"Come along, if you can manage," she said. "They'll see about it. . . . What happened?"

"I don't know."

She led him toward a group of doctors and nurses clustered on the subway station platform. He saw policemen pouring upon the underground tracks and heard someone shout: "Tell 'em the current's cut off!"

Cross felt hands lifting him onto the platform, and now another nurse had hold of his arm. About him was a babble of voices. He began to revive, feeling a little more like himself.

"I'm all right now," he told the nurse.

"But you must go to the hospital and be examined," the nurse told him. "Come. The ambulance is waiting."

She led him through a throng of policemen to the sidewalk where masses of excited people clogged the streets. The nurse tried to guide him through the crowd but they were brought to a standstill. A policeman saw them and tried to clear a path for them.

"That's one of 'em," Cross heard someone say. "But he doesn't seem hurt."

Cross could see the ambulances now; there were internes with stretchers rushing toward the subway station.

"You can get through now," the policeman said.

"Look," Cross told the nurse. "I'll go and get into an ambulance. I'm all right. Go back and help the others."

"Are you sure you're all right?" the nurse asked.

"Absolutely," Cross assured her.

She let go of him and he was alone. He started in the direction of the ambulances. The crowd ignored him. He looked down at his clothes; save for the blood on his shoes, he was all right. His overcoat had protected him somewhat. He paused. Why in hell should he go to a hospital? He was not wounded, only bruised. What he wanted more than medicine was a good, stiff drink of whisky. Were the doctors and nurses watching him? He looked around; they were not. . . . And the policeman had disappeared. The hell with it. . . . He crossed the street and peered at his dim reflection in the plate-glass window of a clothing store. His eyes were muddy and his face was caked with dirt and dried blood. He mopped at his cheek with his coat sleeve, rubbing it clean. Otherwise, he looked quite normal. Some whisky would fix him up, he told himself, and went in search of a drink.

A fine snow was falling, hanging in the air like a delicate veil. He limped down Roosevelt Road and found a second-rate bar that had sawdust on the floor and an odor of stale bread and beer. He was glad of the warmth that caressed his face; he had been too preoccupied to notice that he was half-frozen. But what happened to his overcoat? He ordered a double whisky and thought back over the underground accident. Then he remembered that he must have lost it when he had climbed on that overturned seat to free his leg. That was it; he'd had to pull his arms out of the coat and had been in such a frenzy he'd forgotten to put it on again. Well, he would buy another one. An overcoat was nothing in such a holocaust. He fingered the lump on the right side of his head; it was sore, but not serious. A man sure needs luck, he told himself.

The bar was filled with foreign-born workingmen who

78

didn't seem to notice his disheveled clothing. Over his head a loudspeaker blared. He was leaning on his elbow when he heard the radio commentator announce:

We interrupt this program to bring you a special news bulletin. One half hour ago, a southbound subway train crashed headlong into another southbound train that had come to a standstill about six hundred yards from the Roosevelt Road subway station. The cause of the accident is being investigated. Access to the wrecked trains is difficult because debris has blocked the underground tubes and rescuers are having to cut their way through thick steel beams with acetylene torches. Although it is too early to give any details, it is feared that the loss of life has been heavy. In the immediate area all subway traffic has been suspended. Doctors and nurses have been rushed to the scene of the disaster. Keep tuned to this station for further details.

Cross smiled. How quick they were! Then suddenly he started so violently that the white man drinking next to him drew back in astonishment. *That money!* He shoved his hand into his shirt. . . . *It was there!* Thank God . . . He leaned weakly against the bar. If he had lost the eight hundred dollars, the only thing left for him would have been to jump into the Chicago River.

He paid his bill and hobbled back into the street where snow was still sifting down. Tomorrow at noon he had to see Gladys. And he'd go home now and wash up and then see Dot. . . . He was hungry; yes, he'd first go to a South Side restaurant and have a decent meal. But he would not take a subway. Hell, no . . . He'd treat himself to something better this time. At a corner he limped into a taxi and called out: "Forty-seventh and South Park."

He leaned back and wondered why his life had been spared. Or had it been? To say that he had been "spared" implied that some God was watching over him, and he did not believe that. It was simply the way the dice had rolled. He stretched out his right leg, testing it; the flesh was still sore to the touch, but he could keep on his feet. Funny, that morning he had been ready to blow his brains out, but when his body had been tossed about in that darkness, he had wanted to live.

His postal badge! The loan papers! They too were in the pocket of his overcoat. He'd have to report their being lost the first thing in the morning to the postal officials. . . . The taxi swerved to a curb at Forty-seventh and South Park. He paid the driver, limped out, walked through tumbling snowflakes and entered Dug's, a small restaurant that served the kind of food he liked. He went into the men's room, washed himself and then examined his face in the mirror. Not bad . . . He looked as though he had been on a two-day drunk, that was all. He grinned, re-entered the restaurant, which was almost empty, and ordered a steak, fried potatoes, coffee, and ice cream. He took a sip of water, listening to the radio that was going near the front window.

. . . *This is John Harlan speaking. I'm broadcasting from the scene of the subway wreck at Roosevelt Road. It is snowing here and the visibility is rather bad. I have my microphone with me on the El platform and I'm able to see directly down to the subway entrance where doctors, nurses, attendants, and policemen are working frantically to bring the wounded from the underground. The scene is being illuminated by huge spotlights attached to telephone poles. Beyond the subway entrance, stretching far into the street and blocking the traffic, is a crowd of more than five thousand people standing silently in the falling snow. They have been here for almost an hour waiting for news of friends or relatives believed to have been passengers on the ill-fated subway trains that collided with a heavy loss of life more than an hour ago. . . .*

I see the internes bringing out another victim. A body is on the stretcher. It's the body of a woman, it seems; yes, I can see her long brown hair. . . . Wait a minute. I'll see if I can get the police to identify her for us.

So engrossed was Cross in listening that he did not see the waitress when she placed his food before him. They're acting like it's a baseball game, he thought with astonishment. He was glad now that he had walked so unceremoniously away from the accident. He surely would not have wanted anybody to blare out his name over the airwaves as a victim. He shrugged his shoulders. They'll give us a

80

commercial soon, he thought. The radio commentator resumed:

The name of the last accident victim is Mrs. Maybelle Broadman of 68 Green Street, Ravenswood Park. She is being taken directly to the Michael Reese Hospital. . . .

Ladies and gentlemen, I see the internes coming out with another stretcher. I can't tell yet if the victim is a man or a woman, for the stretcher is completely covered. It's a man. . . . I can tell by the blood-stained overcoat which is draped over the foot of the stretcher. . . . That is the forty-fourth victim taken so far from the wreckage of underground trains. Just a minute; I'll try to get the identity of the last victim who was brought out. . . .

In spite of himself, his interest was captured by the description of the happenings at the scene of the accident. As he waited for more news, he chewed and swallowed a mouthful of steak and lifted his cup of coffee to his lips.

Ladies and gentlemen, while we are endeavoring to establish the identity of the last man taken from the scene of the subway accident at Roosevelt Road, I'm going to ask one of the eyewitnesses, who was a passenger on the subway train, to say a few words about what he saw and felt when the disaster occurred. I have here at my side Mr. Glenn Williams, a salesman of 136 Rush Street, who escaped with but a few minor bruises. Mr. Williams, could you tell us what happened? Where were you on the train . . . ?

WELL, I WAS IN A COACH TOWARD THE MIDDLE OF THE TRAIN. EVERYTHING SEEMED TO BE GOING ALL RIGHT. I WAS READING THE EVENING PAPER. THE TRAIN WAS FULL. I WAS SEATED. I GUESS WE WERE ABOUT A MINUTE FROM THE ROOSEVELT ROAD STATION, WHERE I WAS TO GET OFF, WHEN A GREAT CRASH CAME AND ALL THE LIGHTS WENT OFF. I FELT MYSELF BEING KNOCKED OFF MY SEAT. . . .

I must interrupt you, Mr. Williams. I'm sorry. Ladies and gentlemen, the police have just informed me of the identity of the last victim taken from the subway crash at Roosevelt Road. His name is Cross Damon, a twenty-six-year-old postal clerk who lived at 244 East 57th Street on the South Side. Mr. Damon's body was crushed and mangled beyond recognition or hope of direct identification.

His identity has been established, however, by his overcoat, private papers, and his Post Office badge. . . . His body is being taken directly to the Cook County Morgue. Relatives must address all inquiries there. . . .

Now, Mr. Williams, will you kindly . . . ?

Cross was still holding the cup of coffee in his right hand, his fingers tense upon the handle. He stared, stupefied. *What?* He half stood, then sat down again. Good God! He . . . *dead?* He had a wild impulse to laugh. The damn fools! They were really crazy! Well, it was his overcoat that had led them wrong. . . . Yes, that was it. He ought to phone them right now! He looked around the restaurant; except for himself, the place was now empty of customers. That tall, black girl who had been eating in the corner had gone. . . . Dug, the proprietor, who knew him, was not there. The waitress was a new one and he did not know her and she did not know him. He saw her watching him curiously. She must think I'm loony, he thought.

"Is there anything wrong, sir?"

He did not answer. This was rich! *He was dead!* He had to tell this to the gang at The Salty Dog, right now! Old Doc Huggins would die laughing. . . .

"Is the food all right, sir?"

"Hunh? Oh, yes. Look, what do I owe you?"

"Aren't you going to eat?"

"No. I've forgotten something. I got to go at once. . . ."

"Well, sir. It's one seventy-five. You see, even if you don't eat, they had to prepare it. We can't serve that food to anybody else, sir, you know. So you'll have to pay. . . ."

"That's all right. Here," he said, tossing her two one-dollar bills.

He hurried out into the spinning snow and headed for The Salty Dog. This was the damnedest thing! It was even more freakish than his having escaped alive from the subway accident itself. When he reached the corner, he halted abruptly. He was stunned and shaken by the power of an idea that took his breath away and left him standing open-mouthed like an idiot amid the crazy flakes.

He was dead. . . . All right . . . Okay . . . Why the hell not? Why should he refute it? Why should he deny it?

82

He, of all the people on earth, had a million reasons for
being dead and staying dead! An intuitive sense of freedom
flashed through his mind. Was there a slight chance here of
his being able to start all over again? To live a new life? It
would solve every problem he had if the world and all the
people who knew him could think of him as dead. . . .
He felt dizzy as he tried to encompass the totality of the
idea that had come so suddenly and unsought into his
mind, for its implications ramified in so many directions
that he could not grasp them all at once. Was it possible
that he could somehow make this false account of his
death become real? Could he pull off a thing like that?
What did one do in a case like this? These questions made
him feel that the world about him held countless dangers;
he suddenly felt like a criminal, and he was grateful for the
nervous flakes of snow which screened his face from the
eyes of passers-by. Oh, God. . . . He had to sit down
somewhere alone and think this thing out; it was too new,
too odd, too complicated. How could he let them go on
believing he was dead? But suppose later they found out
that the body that they had dragged from the wreckage
was not his? What then? Well, could he not hide away for
a few days until they made up their minds? If they buried
that body as the body of Cross Damon, then he was dead,
really, legally, morally dead. Had any of his friends seen
him since he had come up out of the subway? No, not one.
And no one had known him at the subway station. No
doubt that doctor and those nurses had already, in their
excitement, forgotten that they had ever seen him. He was
certain that no one he knew had seen him in that dingy bar
on Roosevelt Road. And if he was really serious about this,
then he ought not to go into The Salty Dog. What wild
luck! And Dug had not been in! And that waitress was new
and could not have known him from Adam . . . !

Then, if he was to do this thing, no one who knew him
must see him now. . . . From this moment on he had to
vanish. . . . Hide . . . Now! And his mother must not
see him. . . . And Dot must not see him. . . . Gladys
must be led to believe that he was dead. . . . His
sons . . . ? Good God . . . Doing this meant leaving
them forever! Did he want to do that? He had to make up

83

his mind. . . . Well, they were not close to him as it was; so leaving them was merely making final and formal what had already happened. And how was Gladys to live? Ah, she'd get his insurance money, ten thousand dollars! His cheeks felt hot. Gladys would be taken care of. And no doubt his old mother would now swallow her pride and go and live with Gladys. And the stern logic of Dot's position would force her to have the child aborted. . . . He trembled, looking about him in the snow-scattered street, his eyes smoldering with excitement. A keen sensation of vitality invaded every cell of his body and a slow, strange smile stole across his lips. It was as though he was living out a daring dream. If, after hiding away for a few days, they discovered that that body was not his, why, he could always come forth and say that the accident had wounded him in such a way that he had temporarily lost his memory. That would be his alibi. . . . And weren't such claims being made every day? He had often read of cases of amnesia. . . . It might work. Why not? It was surely worth trying. What had he to lose? His job. It was already compromised by Dot's possible accusations against him. And only tonight he had signed an obligation to pay a debt that would take him two years to discharge. . . . And if he were dead, all of that would be at an end.

All right; what next? He could not plot or plan this by talking it over with anybody. He would have to sit down alone and figure this thing out carefully. And he had to keep shy of those sections of the city where he might meet people who knew him. Where could he go? Yes, down around Twenty-second Street, the area of the bums and whores and sporting houses. . . . And he had eight hundred dollars in cash in his shirt next to his skin! Holy Moses! It all made *sense!* This eight hundred dollars would be his stake until he could launch himself anew somewhere else. . . . It all fitted. . . . He would be a damn fool if he didn't try it. All of his life he had been hankering after his personal freedom, and now freedom was knocking at his door, begging him to come in. He shivered in the cold. Yes, he had to go to his room and get his clothes. . . . But, no . . . Someone would surely see him. He could not take that chance. Funny, it was hard to think straight about this. He had to break right now the chains of habit that bound him to the present. And that was not easy. Each act of his consciousness sought to drag him back to what he wanted to flee.

He had to act, NOW! Each second he stood here like this made it more dangerous for him to do what he wanted. Yet he remained standing as though some power over which he had no control held him rooted. His judgment told him to move on, and yet he stood. Already he felt like the hunted. Waves of realization rolled through him: he had to break with everything he had ever known and create a new life. Could he do it? If he could conceive of it, he should be able to do it. This thing suited his personality, his leanings. Yes, take a taxi to Twenty-second Street. . . . No, the driver might remember him; the South Side was a small place. The subway . . . ? No, he might meet another postal clerk. He would walk over to State Street and take a trolley northward to Twenty-second Street. He was not likely to meet anybody in that direction.

At last he moved through the shaking flakes of snow. If it did not work, he could explain it all away. But, by God, it *had* to work. It was up to him to *make* it work. He was walking fast, caught up in a sense of drama, trying to work out a new destiny.

He recalled now the other Negro passenger on the train who had sat across the aisle opposite him; the man had been about his own general build, size, and color. What had happened was simple; they had mistaken that man's body for his own! The body had been so disfigured that direct identification had been impossible, and, when they had found his overcoat with his postal badge and the contract papers in the pocket, they had leaped to the conclusion that it was the body of Cross Damon. Would anyone demand that that body be subjected to further examination to determine if it was really his? The insurance company? But why would they do that unless somebody put the idea in their heads? Would Gladys? Hell, no . . . She would be content to get the ten thousand dollars of insurance money and probably some more money from the subway company. Dot? She wouldn't know what to do. His mother? Poor Mama . . . She'll just think that God has finally paid me off, he mused.

He seethed with impatience; he was both scared and glad, yearning to find shelter before meeting anyone he knew. Anxiety now drove a sharp sense of distance between him and his environment. Already the world around him seemed to be withdrawing, and he could feel in his heart a certain pathos about it. There was no racial tone to his reactions; he was just a man, *any* man who had had an opportunity to flee and had seized upon it. He was afraid of his surroundings and he knew that his surroundings did not know that he was afraid. In a way, he was a criminal, not so much because of what he was doing, but because of what he was feeling. It was for much more than merely criminal reasons that he was fleeing to escape his identity, his old hateful consciousness. There was a kind of innocence that made him want to shape for himself the kind of life he felt he wanted, but he knew that that innocence was deeply forbidden. In a debate with himself that went on without words, he asked himself if one had the right to such an attitude. Well, he would see. . . .

He took a northbound trolley on State Street and pushed his way apprehensively into the packed crowd and stood swaying. Was there anything in his manner that would attract attention? Could others tell that he was nervous, trying to hide a secret? How could one act normally when one was *trying* to act normally? He caught hold of a strap and, his shoulders jostling others, rocked with the motion of the trolley.

He began to see that this project of deception he had taken upon himself back there in the winging snow of the street was much bigger than he had realized. It was a supreme challenge that went straight to the very heart of life. What was he to do with himself? For years he had been longing for his own way to live and act, and now that it was almost his, all he could feel was an uncomfortable sense of looseness. What puzzled him most was that he could not think of concrete things to do. He was going to a cheap hotel in order to hide for a few days, but beyond that he had no ideas, no plans. He would have to imagine this thing out, dream it out, invent it, like a writer constructing a tale, he told himself grimly as he watched the blurred street lamps flash past the trolley's frosted window.

As he neared Twenty-second Street, he edged forward through the crowd, keeping his head down to conceal his face. He swung off and shivered from the penetrating dampness that bit into his bones. He was still limping, thinking: I got to find a hotel now. . . . But . . . Who was he? His name? Age? Occupation? He slowed his feet. It was not easy to break with one's life. It was not difficult to see that one was always much, much more than what one thought one was. His past? What was his past if he wanted to become another person? His past had come to him without his asking and almost without his knowing; at some moment in the welter of his spent days he had just simply awakened to the fact that he had a past, and that was all. Now, his past would have to be a deliberately constructed thing. And how did one go about that? If he went into a hotel they would ask him his name and he would not be able to say that he was Cross Damon, postal clerk. . . . He stood still in the flood of falling snow. Question upon question bombarded him. Could he imagine a past that would fit in with his present personality? Was there more than one way in which one could account for oneself? His mind came to a standstill. If he could not figure out anything about the past, then maybe it was the future that must determine what and who he was to be. . . . The whole hastily conceived project all but crumpled. Maybe this dream of a new life was too mad? But I ought to be able to do this, he told himself. He liked the nature of this dare; there was in it something that appealed to him deeply. Others took their lives for granted; he, he would have to mold his with a conscious aim. Why not? Was he not free to do so? That all men were free was the fondest and deepest conviction of his life. And his acting upon this wild plan would be but an expression of his perfect freedom. He would do with himself what he would, what he liked.

He did not have to decide every detail tonight; just enough had to be fabricated in order to get a hotel room without rousing too much suspicion. Later, he would go

87

into it more thoroughly, casting about for who he was or what he wanted to be.

He went into an ill-lighted tavern that reeked of disinfectant and sat in a rear booth and listened to the radio pour forth jazz music that linked itself with his sense of homelessness. The strains of blue and sensual notes were akin to him not only by virtue of their having been created by black men, but because they had come out of the hearts of men who had been rejected and yet who still lived and shared the lives of their rejectors. Those notes possessed the frightened ecstasy of the unrepentant and sent his feelings tumbling in a mood of joyful abandonment. The tavern was filled with a mixture of white and black sporting people and no one turned to look at him. He ordered a beer and sat hunched over it, wondering who he would be for the next four or five days until he left for, say, New York. To begin his new life he would relive something he knew well, something that would not tax too greatly his inventive powers. He would be a Negro who had just come up fresh from the Deep South looking for work. His name? Well . . . Charles . . . Charles what? Webb . . . Yes, that was good enough for the time being. Charles Webb . . . Yes, he had just got in from Memphis; he had had a hard time with whites down there and he was damn glad of being in the North. What had he done in Memphis? He had been a porter in a drugstore. . . . He repressed a smile. *He loved this!*

When he went out he bought a stack of newspapers to keep track of developments in the subway accident. He searched for a hotel, the cheaper and more disreputable the better. If there was the slightest doubt about his being dead, he would come forth with a story to square it all; but if all sailed smoothly, he was free.

He came finally to an eight-story hotel with tattered window shades and bare light bulbs burning in the lobby. The hotels in this district were so questionable that they rarely drew a color line. Next door was a liquor store in which he bought a bottle of whisky. He entered the hotel and a short, fat white woman studied him appraisingly from behind a counter.

"I'm looking for a room," he said. "A single."

88

"For how long?"

"Maybe a week."

"You got any luggage?"

"No'm. Not with me."

"Then you have to pay in advance, you know."

"Oh, yes'm. I can do that. How much is it?"

"One-fifty a night. I'll put you on the top floor. But no noise in the room, see?"

"I don't make any noise," he told her.

"They all say that," she commented, sliding him a sheet of paper. "Here; fill that out."

He answered the questions, identifying himself as Charles Webb from Memphis. When he returned the form to her, she pointed to the bottle he had under his arm.

"Look," she said. "I don't care what you do in your room, but I don't want any trouble, see? Some people get drunk and hurt others."

"Lady, I never really hurt anybody in my life but myself," he told her before he realized what he was saying.

The woman looked at him sharply; she opened her mouth to reply, but thought better of it. He knew that that had been a foolish thing to say; it was completely out of character. He had to be careful.

"Come on," the woman said, leading him down a narrow hallway to a skinny Negro with a small, black face who stood in a tiny elevator and eyed Cross sullenly.

"Take this man up to room eighty-nine, Buck. Here's the key," the woman ordered.

"Yes'm," Buck sang.

He rode up with Buck, who weighed him with his eyes. Cross knew that a bundle of newspapers and a bottle of whisky were not the normal accouterments of a Negro migrant from Memphis. He would have to do better than this. Five minutes later he was settled in his garishly papered room. The white lip of a stained sink jutted out. The floor was bare and dirty. He lay across the lumpy bed and sighed. His limbs ached from fatigue. The hard light of the bare electric bulb swinging from the ceiling stung his eyes; he doubled a piece of newspaper and tied it about the bulb to reduce the glare. He opened the bottle and took a deep swig.

Undoubtedly Gladys had now heard that he was dead. How was she taking it? He was perversely curious to know if she was sorry. And, good God, his poor old mother! She had always predicted that he would end up badly, but he had presented her with a morally clean way of dying, a way that would induce even in his enemies a feeling of forgiving compassion. And Dot . . . ? She would find out through the newspapers or over the radio. He could almost hear Myrtle telling Dot that she had the worst luck of any girl in the whole round world. . . . He was foolishly toying with the idea of trying to disguise his voice and calling Dot on the telephone when he fell asleep . . .

Late the next morning, Cross awakened with a pale winter sun falling full into his eyes. He lay without moving, staring dully. Was this his room? Around him was a low murmur of voices and the subdued music of radios coming from other rooms. His body felt weak and he could not quickly orient himself. He swung his feet to the floor, kicking over the whisky bottle. For a moment he watched the bubbling liquid flow; then he righted the bottle, corked it, and the action helped to bring back to his mind the events of last night. He had quit, run off; *he was dead.*

He yearned for just one more glimpse of his mother, his three sons; he hungered for just one last embrace with Dot. . . . But this was crazy. Either he went through with this thing or he did not; it was all or nothing. He was being brought gradually to a comprehension of the force of habit in his and others' lives. He had to break with others and, in breaking with them, he would break with himself. He must sever all ties of memory and sentimentality, blot out, above all, the insidious tug of longing. Only the future must loom before him so magnetically that it could condition his present and give him those hours and days out of which he could build a new past. Yes, it would help him greatly if he went to New York; other faces and circumstances would be a better setting out of which to forge himself anew. But first he had to make sure that he was dead. . . .

He washed himself and mulled over his situation. When a man had been born and bred with other men, had shared and participated in their traditions, he was not required of himself to conceive the total meaning or direction of his

90

life; broad, basic definitions of his existence were already contained implicitly in the general scope of other men's hopes and fears; and, by living and acting with them—a living and acting he will have commenced long before he could have been able to give his real consent—he will have assumed the responsibility for promises and pledges made for him and in his name by others. Now, depending only upon his lonely will, he saw that to map out his life entirely upon his own assumptions was a task that terrified him just to think of it, for he knew that he first had to know what he thought life was, had to know consciously all the multitude of assumptions which other men took for granted, and he did not know them and he knew that he did not know them. The question summed itself up: What's a man? He had unknowingly set himself a project of no less magnitude than contained in that awful question.

He looked through the newspapers, finding only more extended accounts of what he had heard last night on the radio. For the latest news he would have to buy today's papers. Yes; and the Negro weekly papers would be upon the newsstands in the Black Belt neighborhoods tonight or in the morning. They would tell the tale; they would carry detailed stories of all Negroes who had been involved in the accident.

He spent the morning shopping for an overcoat and other necessities in a poor West Side working-class district where he was certain he wouldn't encounter any of his acquaintances. He was frugal, for he didn't know what the coming days would bring. How would he spend his time? Yes; he would lay in a pile of good books. . . . No. What the hell was he thinking of? Books? What he had before him was of far more interest than any book he would ever buy; it was out of realities such as this that books were made. He was full of excitement as he realized that eventually he would not only have to think and feel this out, but he would have to act and live it out.

The relationship of his consciousness to the world had become subtly altered in a way that nagged him uneasily because he could not define it. His break with the routine of his days disturbed the tone and pitch of reality. His repudiation of his ties was as though his feelings had been water and those watery feelings had been projected by his desires out upon the surface of the world, like water upon pavements and roofs after a spring rain; and his loyalty to that world, like the sun, had brightened that world and made ,it glitter with meaning; and now, since last night, since he had broken all of the promises and pledges he had ever made, the water of meaning had begun to drain off the world, had begun to dry up and leave the look of things changed; and now he was seeing an alien and unjustifiable world completely different from him. It was no longer *his* world; it was just *a* world. . . .

He bought a tiny radio and went back to his hotel room. He was so spent from yesterday's exertions that he slept again. In the late afternoon there was a soft tapping upon his door and he awakened in terror. Who was it? Had somebody tracked him down? Ought he answer? He tiptoed to the door in his stockinged feet and stooped and peered through the keyhole. It was a woman; he could see the falling folds of a polka-dot dress. The landlady? The knock came again and he saw a tiny patch of white skin as the woman's hand fell to her side. She was white. . . .

He made sure that his gun was handy, then scampered back to bed and called out sleepily: "Who is it?"

"May I speak to you a moment?"

It was a woman's voice. He hesitated, opened the door, and saw a young white girl of about eighteen standing before him.

"Gotta match?" she asked, lifting a cigarette to her mouth and keeping her eyes boldly on his face.

He caught on; she was selling herself. But was she safe? Was she stooling for the police?

"Sure," he said, taking out his lighter and holding the flame for her.

"You're new here," she said.

"Yeah," he said. "I got in last night."

"So I heard," she smiled.

"Seems like news travels pretty fast around here."

"Pretty fast for those who wanna find out things," she said.

She had black, curly hair, bluish-gray-green deep-set eyes, was about five feet two in height, and seemed to weigh around a hundred and five or six pounds. Her breasts were ample, her legs large but shapely; her lips were full but overrouged and she reeked of too much cheap perfume.

"Having fun in the city, Big Boy?" She arched her eyebrows as she spoke, then looked past him into the interior of his room.

Ought he bother with her? He wanted to, but his situation was too delicate for him to get mixed up with this fetching little tart. Yet he was suddenly hungry for her; she was woman as body of woman. . . .

"I don't know anybody around here yet," he said.

"Are you stingy with that fire water?" she asked, nodding toward his whisky bottle sitting on the night table.

"Naw," he laughed, making up his mind.

She entered slowly, glancing at him out of the corner of her eyes as she went past; he followed the movements of her body as she walked to the center of the room and sat, crossing her legs and tossing back her hair and letting her breasts take a more prominent place on her body. He closed the door and placed the bottle between them.

"What do they call you?" he asked, pouring her a drink.

"Jenny," she said. "You?"

"Charlie, just Good-Time Charlie," he said, laughing.

He saw her looking appraisingly about the room. "Traveling light, huh?"

"Just passing through," he said. "Heading west."

She sipped her drink, then rose and turned on his radio; dance music came and she stood moving rhythmically. He rose and made dance movements with her, holding her close to him, seeing in his mind the sloping curves of her body.

"Want to spend the afternoon with me?" he asked.

"Why not?"

"Look, baby, seeing this isn't the Gold Coast, what do you want?"

"I got to pay my rent," she said flatly.

"The hell with that," he told her. "How much do you want? That's all I asked you."

"I want five," she said at last.

"I'll give you three," he countered.

93

"I said five, you piker—"

"I said three, and you can take it or leave it; I don't want to argue with you."

"Okay," she said, shrugging.

"Let's drink some more."

"Suits me."

When the dance music stopped she turned off the radio, pulled down the window shade, and rolled back the covers of the bed. Wordlessly, she began to undress and he wondered what she was thinking of. Clad in nylon panties, she came to him and held out her hand. Her breasts were firm and the nipples were pink.

"I'll take it now, baby," she said.

"But why *now?*" he demanded.

"Listen, I'm selling; you're buying. Pay now or nothing doing," she said. "I know how men feel when they get through."

Cross laughed; he liked her brassy manner. Nobody taught her that; sense of that order was derived only through experience. He handed her three one-dollar bills which she put into the pocket of her dress, looking at him solemnly as she did so. She pulled off her panties and climbed into bed and lay staring vacantly.

"They could paint this damn place," she said matter-of-factly.

"What?" he asked, surprised, looking vaguely around the room.

"They could paint that ceiling sometime," she repeated.

Cross studied her, then laughed. "Yes; I guess they could," he admitted.

"You're not from Memphis," she said suddenly.

He whirled and glared at her, a sense of hot danger leaping into his throat. Did she know something or was she merely guessing? Was he that bad an actor? If he thought that she was spying on him, he would have grabbed the whisky bottle and whacked her across the head with it and knocked her cold and run. . . . Naw, she's just fishing, he told himself. But I got to be careful. . . . He was so shaken by sudden dread that he didn't want to get into bed with her.

"How do you know?" he asked.

"You don't talk like it," she said, puffing at her cigarette.

He relaxed. It was true that his accent was not completely of the Deep South. He drew upon the bottle to stifle his anxiety and when he took her in his arms he did not recall the fear that had scalded him. She responded so mechanically and wearily that only sheer physical hunger kept him with her. The edge gone from his desire, he lay looking at her and wondering how a woman so young could have achieved so ravaged a sense of life. His loneliness was rekindled and he lit a cigarette and grumbled: "You could have at least tried a little."

"You're not from Memphis," she said with finality.

"You're dodging the point," he reminded her with anger in his voice. "I said that you could at least pretend when you're in bed."

"You think it's important?" She looked cynically at him. "What do you want for three dollars?"

"You agreed to the price," he said brusquely.

"Hell, that's nothing," she said casually, squinting her eyes against the smoke of her cigarette. "I might've done it for nothing. Why didn't you ask me?"

She was fishing around to know him and he did not want it. He washed and dressed while she still lolled in the nude on his bed, her eyes thoughtful. He should not act now with these girls as he used to; things were changed with him and he had to change too. And she was taking her own goddamn time about leaving. Resentment rose in him as he realized that he had made less impression on her physical feelings than if he had spat into the roaring waters of Niagara Falls. . . .

"Haven't you got something to do?" he asked her.

"I can take a hint," she said pleasantly, rolling off the bed and getting into her panties.

"Be seeing you," she said after she had dressed.

"Not if I see you first."

"You'll be glad to see me if you're in a certain mood," she said; she touched him under the chin with her finger and left.

He lay on the bed, feeling spiteful toward even the scent of her perfume that lingered on in the room. He rose, opened the window wide, let in a blast of freezing air, and peered over the ledge of the sill, his sight plunging downward eight floors to the street where tiny men and women moved like little black beetles in the white snow. I wouldn't like to fall down there, he thought aimlessly and turned back into the room, closing the window.

He went down for lunch and got the afternoon newspapers. The final list of the dead was over one hundred, making the accident the worst in Chicago's history. The mayor had appointed a committee to launch an investigation, for the cause of the tragedy was still obscure. The *Herald-Examiner* carried two full pages of photographs of some of the dead and Cross was pricked by a sense of the bizarre when he saw his own face staring back at him. He knew at once that Gladys had given that photograph to the newspapers, for she alone possessed the batch of old snaps from which it had been taken. By God, she really believes it, he thought with wry glee.

Then anxiousness seized him. If Jenny saw that photograph, wouldn't she recognize him? He studied the photograph again; it showed him wearing football togs, sporting a mustache, and his face was much thinner and younger. . . . No; Jenny wouldn't recognize him from that. . . .

Early that evening the snow stopped falling and Chicago lay white and silent under huge drifts that made the streets almost impassable. Cross was glad, for it kept down the number of pedestrians and lessened his chances of being seen by anyone he knew. Near midnight he went to Thirty-fifth Street and bought a batch of Negro weeklies and rushed back to his room, not daring to open them on the street or in the trolley. There, on the front pages, were big photographs of himself. His funeral had been set for Monday afternoon at 3 P.M. at the Church of the Good Shepherd. He laughed out loud. It was working like a charm! He wondered vaguely, while downing a drink, just how badly mangled his body was supposed to have been. Then he saw the answer; an odd item in the Chicago *Defender* reported:

Subway officials stated that the body of Cross Damon had been so completely mangled that his remains had to be scooped up and wrapped in heavy cellophane before they could be placed in a coffin.

He giggled so long that tears came into his eyes.

A little after two o'clock that morning, when the snow-drenched streets were almost empty, he took a trolley to Gladys' neighborhood. He was afraid to loiter, for many people knew him by sight. From a distance of half a block he observed his home: lights were blazing in every window. She's got plenty to do these days, he said to himself, repressing a desire to howl with laughter. But as the image of his three sons rose before him, he sobered. He was never to see them again, except like this, from a distance. His eyes misted. They were his future self, and he had given up that future for a restricted but more intense future. . . .

He went next to Thirty-seventh and Indiana Avenue and crept into a snow-choked alleyway in back of Dot's apartment building and figured out where her window would be. Yes, it was there, on the third floor. . . . A light burned behind the shade. Was Dot really sorry? Had she wept over him? Or had her weeping been over her own state of unexpected abandonment? The light in her window went out suddenly and he wondered if she was going to bed. He hurried around to the street, watching like a cat for passers-by, and secreted himself in a dark doorway opposite the entrance of the building in which she lived. After a short time he saw Dot and Myrtle come out, moving slowly through the snow and darkness with their heads and shoulders bent as under a weight of bewildered sorrow. He noticed that Myrtle was carrying a suitcase. Yes, Dot was no doubt on her way to see a doctor about the abortion. Only that could account for their having a suitcase with them. He couldn't have arranged things so neatly if he had tried dying for real!

The next morning was Sunday and it was clear and cold, with a sharp, freezing wind sweeping in over the city from Lake Michigan. He felt driven to haunt the neighborhood of his mother. How was she taking his death? Her lonely plight saddened him more than anything else. She lived in a neighborhood where no one knew him and he waited in a bar near a window to get a glimpse of her as she left for church. His overcoat was turned up about his chin and his hat was pulled low over his eyes. He smoked, toyed with a glass of beer, keeping his eyes hard upon the entrance of her house. True enough, at a quarter to eleven she came out, dressed in black, her face hidden by a veil, and picked her way gingerly over the deep snow toward her church some two blocks away. Cross felt hot tears stinging his cheeks for the first time since his childhood. He longed to run to her, fall on his knees in the snow and clasp her to him, begging forgiveness. His poor, sad, baffled old Mama . . . But if he went to her, she would collapse in the snow and might well die of the shock.

His worry that something might go wrong with his burial was what kept Cross awake the whole of the Sunday night before his funeral. Had there been no inquiries about the Negro's body that they had mistaken for his own? Who had that man been? Would his family come forward at the last moment and ask questions? Maybe his wife would claim the body. In fact, anybody's raising a question would endanger his whole plan. But perhaps no one had known that the Negro had been on the train. As he recalled now the man had seemed rather shabbily dressed. Perhaps the man's wife, if he had had a wife, thought that he had run off? Cross chided himself for worrying. In the minds of whites, what's one Negro more or less? If the rites went off without someone's raising a question, then he would consider the whole thing settled.

Monday morning was bright and cold; the temperature dipped to ten below zero. Gusts of wind swept in from Lake Michigan, setting up swirling eddies of powdered snow in the quiet streets. Cross stood moodily at his window and stared out at the frozen world, occupied with the question of how he was to spy on his burial. The Chicago *World* had reported that his body had been laid out at the Jefferson Resting Home and that "his postal colleagues and a host of friends" had sent numerous floral wreaths; his death had been referred to as a "great loss to the South Side community." He felt that if he could get a sneaking glimpse of Gladys and the funeral procession, he would feel certain in judging how soundly his death had

98

been accepted. Spying upon the church was easy; he had, late one night, rented a top-floor room in the building opposite the church, identifying himself to the old black landlady as John Clark, a student visiting Chicago as a tourist for a week. He had already made two visits to the room, bowing respectfully to the landlady, and had observed the church at leisure.

A little after ten that morning, just after he had returned from breakfast, Jenny came to see him and her manner was so friendly that one would have thought she had known him for years. Cross was decidedly in no mood for her company, fearing that she might ask him where he was going when he was ready to leave to spy on his last rites.

"I got the blues today," he growled at her.

"Maybe I can cheer you up," she said, seating herself even though he hadn't asked her to. There was something in her manner that warned him to be on guard. She had a mouthful of chewing gum.

"Nothing to drink this morning?" she asked.

"Empty pocket, empty bottle," he lied.

"What kind of work did you do in Memphis?" she asked.

"Why in hell do you want to know that?" he demanded.

"Just curious, that's all," she answered innocently, chewing vigorously. "Something tells me you got some money."

"Yeah; I opened the safe with a bar of soap and got a million bucks," he joshed her. "Now tell me, are you working for the police?"

She paled. Her jaws stopped moving. Then she said: "Well, I never . . . !"

"Then why in hell do you keep on questioning me?"

"You *are* scared of something!" she exclaimed.

She had trapped him so neatly that he wanted to slap her. Yet he knew that it was he who had betrayed his fear and made her suspicious of him. He decided that she was honest; but honest or not, he could not use her. Her present attitude might be buttressed by good faith, but she was tough and if she found out that he had something to conceal, she might blackmail him.

"Look— Why don't you tell Jenny about your troubles? Maybe we can team up together," she said seriously.

"Forget it, Jenny. You'll save yourself time."

"You're in no mood for talking today," she said, rising. "See you when you're feeling better."

She let herself out of the room and he sat brooding. Maybe he ought to play safe and move? Was Jenny stooling for the police? But he had no criminal record and even if the police should question him, there was nothing they could pin on him. He had only a day to wait; he would remain where he was. Later, after the descent of the catastrophe, he wondered why he had not acted upon his sense of foreboding and moved. . . .

It was nearing two o'clock when Cross, filled with trepidation, took a trolley to the South Side. He found himself being irresistibly drawn to Gladys' home and, rashly, he boarded an El that passed in sight of the house and rode back and forth, snatching a quick glimpse of the front door each time the train sped past. He would ride a station past the house in one direction, get off, traverse the footbridge, and ride past the house again in the other direction to the station beyond it, get off again and return. It was not until nearly two-thirty that he saw any signs of life; the front door opened and Gladys and his mother—both dressed in deep black—came out on the sidewalk and stood in the snow. Junior, Peter, and Robert followed, being led by a distant cousin of Gladys. Excited, Cross got off the train, concealed himself behind a billboard on the El platform, and saw a man garbed formally in black go up to Gladys, his mother, and the children, and tip his hat to them. No doubt the undertaker, Cross thought. His eyes lingered on his mother and his sons and, as they left, a light seemed to go out of the winter sky. He would never see them again. . . .

His heart bubbled with hot panic when a voice sounded in his ear: "Do you know 'em?"

He spun and looked into the face of a young Negro dressed in the uniform of the El company. He had never seen the man before.

"No," he answered, relaxing.

"That's the family of a guy who was killed in the subway accident last week," the man spoke in a detached voice. "I reckon they must be going to the funeral."

"Oh," Cross said, keeping his face averted. "I read about that."

"Man, that guy wasn't nothing but meatballs and spaghetti when the subway got through with 'im," the man went on.

An El train rolled to a stop and Cross hurried into it; he had seen and heard enough. He rushed to his rented room and sat at a window overlooking the church entrance. Fifteen minutes later the hearse arrived. There's Tom . . . ! Tom was his old friend from the Post Office and he was one of the pallbearers. And there was Frank. . . . And Pinkie . . . And Booker . . . And Joe Thomas . . . He could not make out the others, for their faces were turned. He watched them lift the black coffin and march slowly into the church. The undertaker's assistants followed, carrying many wreaths of flowers inside. He saw the undertaker lead Gladys, his mother, and his three sons into the church. He opened the window a crack and caught an echo of a melancholy hymn. . . . The service was so long that he wondered what the preacher could have found to say about him. He was certain, however, of one thing: whatever was being said had no relationship at all to him, his life, or the feelings he was supposed to have had.

An hour later the church doors opened and the crowd began to file out, first Gladys, then his mother; finally his three sons came, led by the preacher and the undertaker. Again he saw them sliding the black coffin into the hearse. Soon a long procession of black cars pulled off through the snow. It was over. He had witnessed a scene about which he could never in his life talk with anybody. And he *did* hanker to talk about it. When men shared normal experiences, they could talk about them without fear, but he had to hug this secret to his heart.

The procession had gone and the church doors had shut. He had to go back to his hotel and prepare to catch a train for New York. But he did not move. He was empty, face to face with a sense of dread more intense than anything he had ever felt before. He was alone. He was not only without friends, their hopes, their fears, and loves to buoy him up, but he was a man tossed back upon himself when that self meant only a hope of hope. The church across the

101

street was still there, but somehow it had changed into a strange pile of white, lonely stone, as bleak and denuded of meaning as he was. And the snowy street, like the church, assumed a dumb, lifeless aspect. He lit a cigarette and sat on the edge of the bed and stared about the room. His movements were mechanical. The dingy walls seemed to loom over against him, asking wordlessly questions that he could not answer. Nothing made meaning; his life seemed to have turned into a static dream whose frozen images would remain unchanged throughout eternity.

He told himself that he was brooding too much; he had to get out of this room. On the snow-cushioned sidewalk, his legs led him to a taxi, but when he reached his hotel, he did not want to go in. Instead he ambled into a nearby bar, The Cat's Paw, and ordered a whisky. He drank eleven shots before he could feel the influence of the alcohol. He ordered his twelfth and the bartender told him: "If I were you, I'd get some air."

"I can pay you," Cross told him.

"That ain't the point," the bartender said. "Get rid of what you've got, then I'll sell you some more." The bartender studied him. "Worried about something, eh?"

He paid and went out. He was not drunk; there was simply no purpose in him. When he finally entered the hotel, he met Jenny in the corridor near the door of his room. Because she had no meaning, she meant everything to him now.

"Speak of the devil," she greeted him, smiling.

"Hi," he breathed.

"Look, I got a bottle," she said, showing it to him. "How about it?"

"I don't mind."

He wanted a drink. He felt her take hold of his hand and squeeze it.

"You're freezing," she said.

"Yeah."

He unlocked the door and let her go in; he followed, pulled off his coat and flopped on the bed.

"You're all in," she commented sympathetically.

"Tired," he said and closed his eyes.

"You must relax," she said.

102

He was silently grateful when he felt her cool, soft hand moving slowly across his hot forehead. Her hand left him; he heard her pouring whisky, felt the glass as she took his fingers and gently forced them about it. He pulled up and drank. She sat next to him on the bed, cradling her glass in her palms.

"Don't you want to know anything about me?" she asked him.

"Jenny, you don't understand," he said kindly.

"I'm a little better than you think I am," she said; she bent forward and fingered his ear.

"Maybe."

"You *could* do a lot worse than me, and maybe you *coul*d do a lot better. But whatever it is, it's not for keeps," she told him.

"What are you trying to say?"

"Take me with you," she said. "When you're tired of me, then dump me. I don't care. I want to get out of Chicago."

"I can't."

"Why?"

Her soft arm went around his neck and his nostrils were full of the scent of her hair; he drained his glass and a moment later he heard her ask: "What's the matter? If you talk about it, it'll be easier."

She searched for his mouth and kissed him. His world was a blur. He needed what she was trying to give him but he was afraid.

"Why do you bother about me?" he asked.

" 'Cause I like you. Ain't that enough?"

"Guess so," he mumbled. He was alone, empty. "Give me another drink."

She poured the glasses full. He drank again, stood, swayed, tugged at his tie.

"What're you doing?"

"Going to bed . . ."

"Wait, I'll help you undress," she said. "You're three sheets to the wind."

His limbs were like rubber. She aided him in pulling off his clothes, rolled back the blanket and pushed him into bed. His eyes closed; he heard her moving about, pulling down the shade, locking the door. Then he felt the sensual smoothness of her skin as she slid into bed beside him. She blended her body with his and he could feel the tender spread of her fingers on his back. His senses were dreaming. He looked at her and she was not a dangerous girl; those deep, tranquil, bluish-gray-green eyes were dark and helpful now and the heat of her body was filling him with thankfulness.

"Can't you talk to me?" she asked him.

"You wouldn't understand."

"I would. Just *try*."

He laughed, took her face between his palms and stared at her, feeling foolishly proud of the irony of his life.

"I'm dead," he said.

Her lips parted in bewilderment and she pushed his hands roughly from her face. She looked off a second and then back to him.

"You're nuts," she said.

He wanted to tell her. He knew now that she was not working for the police, but for herself. She needed a man and had fastened her hope on him. If he'd known her well, he would never have had the impulse to tell her. But a strange girl was different and he would be leaving soon. Dammit, he had to tell somebody just to make sure that his situation was not a fantasy of his own mind. He was too much alone and it was insupportable.

"I'm in a funny fix," he began. "You remember that subway accident last week? Well, I was in it."

"You were hurt in it? Is that what's making you act so funny?"

"I wasn't really hurt," he continued, knowing that he ought not to talk, but hearing the words spilling out in spite of himself. "Listen, they found a body down there all mangled and they think it's mine. . . ."

"Are you *sure* you weren't hurt?" Her eyes were round with concern.

"No. I wasn't hurt," he went on, nettled that she was not believing him. "Today, just two hours ago, they buried that body thinking that it was mine. . . ."

She pulled abruptly away from him, rose, walked across
104

the room and got her cigarettes. She lit one and sat near him.

"Are you trying to kid me? Now, come on; tell me what you've done."

Cross buried his face in the pillow to stifle his laughter. She did not believe him. He knew that his story was wild, but he had not counted upon so much outright disbelief.

"This is funny," he chuckled.

"What's so goddamn funny?" she snapped at him.

"You asked me to tell you, now you don't believe me."

"If you had done something like that, you wouldn't tell me," she said.

"Why not?"

"Because the insurance companies would want to know about it," she explained. "And you're smarter than that."

He grew sober.

"All right," he said, relieved. "I'm lying." He stood and got his bathrobe and struggled into it. "I'm not dead, then."

"Where're you going?" she asked.

"Down the hall to see a man about a coffin," he said.

He lumbered into the corridor, feeling swamped by confusion. This damn girl was making him lose control of the project he had planned. I'm really crazy to talk to her, he reproached himself. He resolved to get the hell out of the city as fast as a train could carry him. And from now on he would keep firm hold on himself. He turned a bend in the corridor, his head lowered in reflection; he drew in his breath sharply as he felt his body colliding with that of another man. Before his senses could register what was happening, he heard a familiar voice bursting in his ears and saw an old, familiar smile of incredulous astonishment spreading over a fat, black face.

"As I live and breathe! You're either Cross or his twin!"

Cross stared at the face and had the stupid desire to shake his head and make it vanish. He was looking into the eyes of a man he had known for six years! The man wore a bathrobe and had evidently just come from the bathroom. He was done for; there was no way out of this except . . . *He had to decide what to do quickly!* Tension

made him hot as fire; he had to check a crazy impulse to
wave his arm and try to sweep this man from sight and
keep his freedom. It was big, fat, black Joe Thomas who
stood in front of him, the same man he had seen acting as
a pallbearer around his coffin earlier that afternoon!

"*Speak*, man! They say you're dead, but you ain't no
ghost and I damn well *know* it! We just put your coffin in
the ground, man! What the hell is this?" Joe's eyes were
dancing in his fat, black face; he threw out his hands,
hesitated, then clapped both of them on Cross's shoulders.
"I got to *touch* you to believe it!" Joe's face was a mixture
of fear and gladness. "They all think you're dead, and here
you are in a cat house with the chippies! Good God Almighty! I feel weak. . . ." Joe blinked, his lips hanging
open. "I just came in here to knock off a piece of tail 'fore
going to work— Hell, the whole town's talking 'bout how
you died—" Joe rocked back on his heels and burst into a
gale of hysterical laughter. "This is a new way to cover up
cunt hunting! Oh, Jesus, this is hot!" Joe sobered for a
moment; he was struggling with himself to adjust his mind
to what his eyes saw. "But, *say* something! You *are* Cross,
ain't you?"

"Yes," Cross heard himself speaking. "I'm Cross."

"Well, don't be ashamed of letting me catch you in a
whorehouse, man," Joe said, blinking and trying to understand the strange expression that shrouded Cross's face.
"Come on *in* here and let me *talk* to you." Joe grabbed
Cross's hand and dragged him forward. He unlocked a
door and pulled Cross inside a room. Cross's eyes darted
about. The bed was unmade, the shades drawn, and a dim
light glowed on the ceiling. Joe's clothing was flung pell-
mell over the back of a chair. Cross's fingers ached to blot
out this black man who grinned with bewilderment.

"Sit down, man," Joe spluttered. "Tell me what this
is. . . ."

Joe shut the door and Cross heard the click of the lock;
that meant that no one could come in without warning; he
was alone with Joe. . . . Joe flopped on the bed, his eyes
full on Cross, waiting for an explanation. Cross moved on
cat's feet to the center of the room, noticing the window
which had the exact position of the window in his room,

that window through which he had peered only a few hours ago and looked at the distant, snow-drenched streets far below. . . . He then stared at the almost empty whisky bottle on the night table. Tension was so tight in him that he felt his skull would burst. Joe saw him gazing at the bottle.

"You want a drink, hunh? I scared you, didn't I?" Joe took the bottle and drained the whisky into a glass. "This bottle's dead. But we've got another one on the way." He set the bottle on the floor and handed the tumbler to Cross. "I reckon I'm about the last man on earth you ever expected to see, hunh?"

Cross emptied the glass with one swallow, and, smiling tightly, said: "That's right, Joe."

"You *are* Cross!" Joe shouted and slapped his thighs. "For a minute, I thought maybe I was making a fool out of myself. God, I'm sweating——! Cross, you're the goddamnedest man God ever made. . . ."

Cross reached for the neck of the empty whisky bottle and lifted it.

"Ain't no more whisky in that bottle, man," Joe said. "I just sent Ruth down for another fifth. She'll be back in a minute. Sit down, man! Don't be scared. . . . Lord, I can't get over this!"

"When's this Ruth coming back?" Cross asked quietly.

"In a minute," Joe said, a shadow of disquiet flickering over his face. He brightened quickly. "Say, who're you shacking up with in here? Bertha, Mamie, Della, or . . ."

"Jenny," Cross said.

"She's great!" Joe approved. "Boy, she can go when she feels like it. She's got some build. . . ."

Joe went on talking and Cross stared at him. He had to do something. But what? This clown was tearing down his dream, smashing all he had so laboriously built up. And there he sat: fat, black, half laughing and half scared, with beads of sweat popping on his forehead, his black chest showing and his bare legs sprawled out from the bed, his blue silk bathrobe flowing around him. . . .

"God, but you're sly, Cross," Joe went on. "Ain't you gonna tell me what happened? I didn't know you knew about this place. But there ain't no better place to get over the blues, is it? Kind of crummy here, but the gals are nice. Hell, man, if you ain't gonna say nothing, I'll tell 'em. They made a mistake in that damned church today. I'm gonna call up Pink. He'll die laughing. . . ." Joe rose from the bed.

Cross grasped the neck of the bottle firmly; his arm trembled; his fingers gripped the bottle so hard that he thought the glass would crush in his palm. He lifted the bottle high in the air. Joe's lips moved soundlessly, his eyes black pools of mute protest. Joe was frozen, waiting, his lips open and about to utter a question and then Cross brought down the bottle with a crashing blow on Joe's head. Just before the blow landed Cross heard Joe utter in tones of deep amazement: "Say!" The bottle caught Joe on the temple, bursting from the force of the blow, and Joe fell slowly backward without having lifted a finger; he lay still, his thick lips hanging grotesquely open. Cross moved now with the speed of a panther. He let up the shade and a tide of grayish light swept into the room; he opened the window and a blast of freezing air turned his breath to steam. He turned and faced the inert form sprawled on the bed in its bathrobe. He grabbed Joe's right arm and slid his left arm under Joe's legs and lifted him as one would a sick child. He stood a moment, looking at Joe's black, quiet face, and then he looked at the open window. He struggled to the window with the body, hoisted it up and for a moment the body was poised in space. He pushed it through and shut the window at once, all in one swift, merciless movement. He turned back to the room, picked up the glass shards of whisky bottle and opened the door. The corridor was empty. He went out and hurried to the bathroom and secreted the shards atop a tall, wooden cabinet. He examined himself minutely in the full mirror and saw no telltale signs except sweat on his face. He mopped his brow with the bottom of his bathrobe, then stood still, listening intently. He heard faint voices and the muffled music of radios. Time seemed to be flowing on normally. Through the window of the bathroom he could see that night was falling upon the frozen city. He headed for his room, feeling unsteady in his legs. He hesitated before going in, trying to control himself. Again he mopped sweat
108

from his face, then opened the door of his room. Jenny still lay on the bed.

"I thought maybe you'd flushed down the drain, you took so long," she said.

He sank into a chair, fighting down a wild, foolish impulse to tell her what he had done. She rose, smiling, and went to him; he pushed her violently away.

"What's the matter with you? You're trembling and wringing wet. . . ." She paused and narrowed her eyes. "Say, are you on the needle or something . . . ?"

"Leave me alone," he muttered.

"I wonder what you're up to," she said, turning away uneasily.

A knock came at the door. Cross stiffened and felt he could not breathe. He would not have been too surprised if the door had opened and Joe had walked into the room. But he had tossed Joe out of that window; or had he? He struggled to sort reality from fantasy. The knock came again, louder this time.

"Aren't you going to answer it?" Jenny asked him.

"You answer it," Cross said.

"Jenny!" a woman's voice called through the door.

"Yeah?" Jenny answered, going to the door and opening it.

A tall, fleshy blonde woman stood in the doorway with a bottle of whisky under her arm.

"Hello, Ruth," Jenny said. "What's the matter?"

"Sorry. Didn't mean to disturb you," the woman called Ruth said. Her eyes looked about the room, resting at last on Cross. "But Joe isn't here, is he?"

"No, honey," Jenny said, shrugging. "I haven't seen him."

Ruth's lips curled in scorn. "That black bastard's run out on me," she hissed. "If he's dumped me without paying, I'll kill him the next time I see him, so help me God! But I don't understand. . . . All his clothes are still there."

"Oh, he'll come back," Jenny smiled. "He always does."

"He tried a new trick," Ruth blazed. "He sent me down for a bottle of liquor and took a powder." Ruth forced a smile for Cross. "I'm sorry to bother you with my troubles. But, you know, the fool left his clothes behind. . . . You reckon he could be two-timing me? Maybe he's in some other room . . . ?"

"*Might* be," Jenny said, laughing at the possibility.

"I'll leave you now," Ruth said, her eyes baffled.

Jenny closed the door and turned to Cross, chuckling: "Ruth and her Joe. I do believe she's in love with him, but he doesn't give a damn about her."

"Who's Joe?" Cross asked listlessly.

"A colored postal clerk who comes here all the time," she told him as she sat on the bed again, her hands folded modestly over her pubic hair. "He's Ruth's star client; he even keeps his bathrobe and slippers in her room. God, he's a scream. Jet black, fat . . . A regular clown . . . Spends his money like water . . . Listen to this: He once told me . . ."

Cross was not listening though his eyes were on her face. He was wondering how Joe's body had fallen and where. . . . Had it landed on the street? He wanted to open the window and look out, but he knew that would have aroused questions in Jenny's mind. He had done a horrible thing; he had killed so swiftly and brutally that he hardly recognized what he had done as he recalled it to his mind. It was he who had made that assault on Joe in that room; yes, he had done that to save himself. He heard Jenny laughing.

". . . don't you think so?" she was asking.

"I don't know," he mumbled.

"Hell, you're not even *listening!*" she said angrily. "At least Joe's a good sport!"

"Well, go to him," Cross told her, relishing his irony.

If Joe's body had landed on the street in the snow, then it would soon be seen by someone and there would be an outcry. But maybe it had dropped into a deep drift? He was excited by such a prospect. If that had happened, no one would see it for a while. . . . He blinked when Jenny rose from the bed and came to him; she caught his hand and pulled him to his feet. Gently, she forced him to the bed, climbed in with him and drew the covers over them.

"Charlie, what's the matter?" she asked in a whisper. "Talk to me. . . ."

Maybe at any moment now a knock would come at the
110

door and it would be about Joe. He heard footsteps pass in the corridor outside and wondered if it was Ruth still hunting for her Joe. . . . He had had no choice; it had been either he or Joe. He had known it the moment he had looked into that fat, black, laughing face.

"Your body is trembling," Jenny whispered. "I wish I could *help* you!"

She was getting on his nerves. Why didn't she leave . . . ?

"You're always watching me, questioning me," he complained in a distant voice.

"You're too goddamn suspicious!" she cursed him.

He looked at her; there was an animal-like quality in her that made him like her, and that quality showed most clearly when she was angry.

"Okay, baby, spill your story," he consented. "You've been wanting to talk to me. Now, I'm listening. . . ."

He lifted himself on an elbow, his eyes on her face, but he was really seeking over the snowdrifts outside, looking for Joe's body.

"You sure are a great help," she complained, her anger vanishing. "I'll try— Look, Charlie, you're black and I'm white— That's what this goddamn country says, but it's the bunk, and you know it and I know it. They say it to keep us apart, don't they?"

He nodded, not quite understanding what she had said. Maybe he had made a mistake in killing Joe like that . . . ? God, he had planned to be free, and now he had killed. . . .

". . . I'd bet a million dollars that I've lived a much harder life than you have. I grew up in the slums of a small rotten town in the middle of Kansas. My father was a drunkard and a socialist of a sort. . . ."

He was conscious that the more she talked the better she talked. The gal's got some sense. . . . But wouldn't they raid the hotel when they found Joe's body . . . ?

". . . he was always yelling about the rights of Negroes and fighting for the underdog. My mother was the janitor in the town school. If it hadn't been for her, I wouldn't've even learned to read and write. My mother really supported us, brought us up and nursed Father when he had

111

the D.T.'s. She was the only decent person I've ever known in my life. . . . Surprised to hear *me* say things like that, hunh?"

He was looking at her, but was wondering what the police would say about finding Joe's body clad only in a bathrobe. . . .

". . . and I spotted you as an educated guy after you'd said only two words. I respect education. . . . It's too late for me to get one now, I reckon. But I want one; really, I do."

He nodded his head as she spoke, telling her that he was following her, but he was only reacting to the general sense of her words.

". . . everybody in our little town looked down on us. Me, my brothers and sisters, we were the drunkard's children, the scum of the earth. Then I got in trouble with a boy, got knocked up, and had to have an abortion. You wouldn't think it, Charlie, but till two years ago I didn't know where babies came from. Honest to Pete! I thought they came out of women's bowels. . . . Isn't that crazy? But I know *now*. And how! You're listening, aren't you? You're not bored?"

"Oh, no; go ahead," he said; he might be lost already. It was good that he had his gun; if the police found out about him, well, he would blow his brains out. . . .

". . . and when I got knocked up, the whole town knew it. My father drove me out of the house. I lived in a dump for a while, then got rid of the child. It was hell; I was sick with a fever of one hundred and four for three days. I thought I was a dead duck. Mama finally made Father let me come back home. But just to walk down the street to the store to buy a loaf of bread was hell. . . . When I passed people, they'd stop talking and just stare at me. . . . I ran off and came to Chicago. The first week I worked in a Greek restaurant; like a dope, I went out with the Greek. He raped me. . . ."

He wondered why she felt so deep a sense of inferiority; he was black, but he had never felt that humble in the face of life. And Joe? Maybe the sirens would start howling soon . . . ?

". . . sounds crazy, hunh? But I'm not asking for sympathy. The hell with it. I'm young. I'll fight, work. Now, why am I telling you all this? You said you were going west, didn't you? I want to go to California—"

"Movies?" he asked.

"Hell, no. I'm not pretty," she said.

Cross studied her face; she was much prettier than she thought.

"Then why California?"

"I just like the sunshine and want to be as far from Kansas and my family as I can get," she said. "Take me with you, won't you? I could be of some use, couldn't I? I don't care if you're colored. The hell with that crap—"

"Jenny," he began. "It won't work—"

"Why not? You can trust me."

"But my life— No. It won't work at all."

"I don't give a good goddamn *what* you've done," she said.

Cross smiled ruefully. She doesn't know what she's saying. . . . "Look, baby, I like you. I believe you. But forget it, honey. It's too complicated to explain."

She stood and her face grew red and her eyes blazed with anger. Would he have to do something to keep her quiet? Was she going to threaten him and make him take her with him?

"Why am I so different?" she demanded. "Do you loathe me? What's wrong with me . . . ?" Tears welled in her eyes. "Only last week Pearl Bland got a ride to New York with a guy with dough," she said bitterly. "Me? I can't even get a *Negro* to trust me!" She bent to him and asked: "*Why?* Tell me why. . . ."

"Come here, Jenny," he said.

He folded her in his arms. Good God, this child was bitter! In despair she began kissing him with passion, still weeping. He relaxed. Why not let her make him forget? He could not control the flow of events now anyway; he was probably already lost. . . . Any minute the cops would be knocking on the door. What did he have to lose? He pressed his lips to Jenny's and this time he knew that she was allowing herself to be more of a woman because she wanted his trust. When the spasm was over he lay with his hand gently touching her face, mutely thanking her for the

113

benediction that she had shed upon his distraught senses.

"Darling, what's your real name?" she asked him quietly.

The respite was over; he felt danger again. He had to shake this girl off him quickly. But, what about Joe? He had pushed Joe out of that window and time had flowed on as though nothing had happened. No one here knew his name or that he had known Joe. So, when they found Joe's body, there would be no thought of him in connection with the death. They might even think that Ruth had done it. He lay still, plotting. He would not hurt Jenny; killing her would be a sure way of putting the police on his trail. He would fool her and ditch her. She thought that he was heading west. All right; agree to take her, dump her at the last moment, and strike out for New York alone. Cunning was better than violence; he must not allow himself to be confronted again with the unexpected, as he had been with Joe. . . .

"You really want to come with me?"

Her arms tightened about his neck in gratitude.

"Where're we going?" she asked.

"We'll take a bus to Denver, then later we'll go to the Far West," he said.

"But we have to have dough. How much have you got?"

"Leave that to me," he said. "I'll get you to the West Coast if you want to go."

"When do we leave?"

"Tonight." He rolled swiftly from the bed and began washing up. "I'll go down for the tickets now."

"I'll believe it when I see those tickets," she said, rising and commencing to dress also.

"You better start packing," he told her. "How much luggage have you got?"

"Just a suitcase." She studied him, then rubbed her fingers together. "I need some nylons and things. . . ."

He gave her ten dollars.

"Aw, come on," she exploded. "Be a sport."

"I'll give you more tomorrow," he said. "Now, go." He pushed her out of the door, looked both ways in the corridor, then shut the door and locked it. He hurried to the window and opened it. A clear night sky sent a sheen over

114

the snow-blown world. He stared down, searching for Joe's body. Ah . . . There it was, on that roof! He could see it lying straight out, a black mark on the white snow. The soft snow had no doubt cushioned its fall and the impact of the body on the roof had not been heard. He had time to get away before anyone discovered it. He closed the window and stood in the center of the room. Why had that damn fool come on him at that time? But he could not think of Joe now; he had to plan how to ditch Jenny. . . .

He rode down in the elevator with Buck, who was grumbling: "Jesus! Why can't that bitch leave me alone?" He spoke to no one in particular. "She keeps yapping at me about Joe, Joe. . . . What the hell do I care about Joe? It ain't my job to keep track of her damn men! These whores make me sick. Let a bobby pin get lost, and they come running to me."

"Don't let 'em break you down," Cross told him.

"You damn right I won't," Buck seethed with anger. "I don't do my day's work at night, like they do, flat on their backs. Man, a woman'd make a man jump out of a window; *she would!*"

Cross walked from the lobby on legs he did not feel. He knew that Buck knew nothing about how Joe had died, but his talking of jumping from a window had almost paralyzed him. His body was seized with a chill and he felt so weak that he went into an alleyway and sank down upon an empty wooden soda-water case under the spreading glare of a street lamp. He started when a door opened and an aproned man came out with a garbage can and dumped its contents near him; the man glanced curiously at Cross, then went back inside, slamming the door and bolting it securely. Cross rested his wrists on his knees and his eyes traveled without purpose over the steaming pile of refuse, the top of which was crowned with a mound of wet, black coffee grounds that gleamed in the light of the street lamp; some of the grounds spilled over a flattened grapefruit hull; there was part of a fried sausage with grease congealed white in the porous grains of meat; there was the crumpled cellophane wrapping from a pack of cigarettes glittering with tiny beads of moisture; there was an electric bulb still holding its delicate filigreed web of wires even though its glass globe had been shattered; there was a bone from a piece of roast beef still holding traces of red and gray meat; there was a lemon ring molded to a light green color; there was a clump of cigarette butts whose ends were blackened and whose tips were stained red from the rouge of a woman's lips; there was a limp wad of lettuce whose leaves glistened with a fine film of oil; there was a clean piece of wood jutting out with a shining nail bent at the end of it; there were several eggshells showing bits of yellow yolk; there was the stump of a cigar bearing the marks of a man's teeth; and there was a clump of fluffy dust freshly gathered from some floor. . . .

His blood felt chilled. He had to shake off this dead weight and move on. He pulled to his feet and took a cab to La Salle Street railroad station and went directly to the reservation window.

"Have you any sleeping accommodations for New York?"

"For tonight?" the clerk asked.

"For the earliest possible train," Cross said.

"Just a minute," the clerk said.

Cross waited nervously while the clerk telephoned.

"We have one, a compartment," the clerk informed him.

"Okay. Fix it up. When does the train leave?"

"At six on track eight, sir."

He paid, received the tickets, then rushed by cab to the Greyhound Bus Terminal and bought two tickets to Denver. Back in the hotel, Jenny was waiting for him at the door of his room. She smiled warmly, but there was nervousness in her manner. When they were inside, he handed her her ticket for the bus.

"Where's your ticket?" she asked suspiciously.

"Here," he said, showing it to her. He had thought that she would ask that; it was why he had bought two tickets. The extra money he had paid for his ticket was his insurance that she would believe in him long enough for him to take the six o'clock train to New York.

"You know where the Greyhound Bus Terminal is?" he asked.

"Sure."

"The bus leaves at eight. I've got to see some people; I'll

116

be gone about an hour." He looked at his watch. "It's five now. I'll be back at six. We'll eat and then we're off."

She seemed satisfied with his story and he left her. He got into a cab and rode over to the La Salle Street railroad station. A porter guided him to his coach. He showed his reservation and ticket to the conductor, got on, and, when he was in his compartment, he locked the door.

He cursed softly: That damn fool Joe . . . ! And Jenny did not know how lucky she was. From now on he had to cope with this impulse of his to confide. If circumstances had been just a little different, he would have had to kill Jenny too, or give up the game. He had thought he was free. But was he? He was free from everything but himself. Loneliness had driven him to confess to Jenny, and fear could have made him kill her as he had killed Joe. He kept his fists tightly clenched as he waited impatiently for the train to pull out. At last he heard the distant calling:

"All aboooooard!"

He stood at the window as the train began to move. A light snow was falling softly. Two hours from now Jenny would be searching frantically for him at the bus station. And she would never know that he had done her the greatest favor of her life.

But what was he to do with this conflict of his? This urge to confide and the fear of the danger of confiding? The outside world had fallen away from him now and he was alone at the center of the world of the laws of his own feelings. And what was this world he was?

The dreary stretches of Chicago passed before his window; it was a dim, dead, dumb, sleeping city wrapped in a dream, a dream born of his frozen impulses. Could he awaken this world from its sleep? He recalled that pile of steaming garbage, the refuse the world had rejected; and he had rejected himself and was bowed, like that heap of garbage, under the weight of endurance and time.

As the train wheels clicked through the winter night, he knew where his sense of dread came from; it was from within himself, within the vast and mysterious world that was his and his alone, and yet not really known to him, a world that was his own and yet unknown. And it was into this strange but familiar world that he was now plunging. . . .

BOOK 2: Dream

The train had been plunging through the wintry night for
some hours before his memory of the happenings of the
last days in Chicago had dimmed in his consciousness
enough for him to feel somewhat relaxed. Whenever he
recalled the past there returned to him not only the mere
constellations of events through which he had lived, but
also a psychological grasp of the role that his desires,
hates, hopes, or loves had played in them. What helped
him most was that he possessed the lucky capacity of reducing and referring his memories to an intense and personal
basis, and could, therefore, once he was emotionally free
of the concrete context from which they had sprung, live
with them without a too-crushing sense of guilt.

His memory of his relationship with Dot was not only a
recollection of a man's sensual affair with a pretty girl
whom he had forsaken in the trouble he had brought on
her; but, above all, Dot had been to him a representation
of a personal hunger which he had projected out of his
heart on her, and the two of them—Dot and what she
subjectively meant to him—had been something he had not
been able to cope with with satisfaction to himself and
honor to her. There had been no element of sadism in his
love for Dot, and he would have gladly, if such had been
possible, taken upon himself in a spirit of atonement the
hurt she had sustained. But who can reverse time? What
was done was done and the only part of the past that he
could alter was that portion lingering on in his heart. The
118

mirage of desire that he had sought so pathetically was still his to mull over in regretful recollection.

In breaking his life in two he had left his baffled mother to fend for herself as best she could, but that baleful gift of the sense of dread which she had, out of her life's hysteria, conferred upon him in his childhood, was still his beyond his right to surrender. More definitely than ever her fateful gift was shaping and toning his hours even now on this fleeing train, was subtly sculpturing the contours of his destiny, staining all the future that he was to embrace even to that lonely grave which he would some day have to fill alone.

Being quit of Gladys was infinitely more than shedding a vindictive wife; it meant insight into those quicksands of appalling loneliness that had sucked him into her waiting arms in the first place. He did not remember her in a way that made him yearn to return to her; his memory assumed the form of an intense appropriation of that intimate part of himself which had seduced him into embracing her, and toward that part of his being he had now a change of heart —he wanted never again to seek fulfillment of desire in that direction.

He was, however, far from being resigned; an urge to launch again into life was still strong in him. His sorrow for Dot, his mother, and Gladys originated in his knowing that they had hoped for something from him which he did not possess; his pity for them was his knowledge of himself, a regret for ever having allowed them to build their dreams upon the mercurial instabilities of his emotions.

His memory of Joe's death was simpler. His killing of Joe had been dictated by his fear of exposure, and he knew that what had happened with Joe could happen again under conditions he couldn't control. Given a situation of danger and the dreaded tension that went with it, his impulse to save himself would sweep him toward what horizons? He knew that his being able to reflect coolly upon this did not mean that he was free of it, that to see was not to control, that self-understanding was far short of self-mastery. He was afraid of himself.

Had they discovered Joe's body yet? Or would that snowdrift on the roof hide it for a few days longer? He would keep track by reading the Chicago newspapers. . . . But he had no real fear of ever being accused of killing Joe, for his relation to Joe had been twice removed and no apparent motive for his having killed him could be easily deduced. For days the Chicago police would no doubt sniff about aimlessly in the hotel corridors, accusing first this whore and that, and, in the end, they would probably mark it down either as suicide or death at the hands of parties unknown. . . . Or maybe they'd conclude that his death had been accidental . . . ?

The next morning, as the train neared New York, he made his way apprehensively into the dining car for breakfast. He was afraid that his preoccupation with his burden of nonidentity and his fear of sudden surprises would distract him to the point of robbing reality of its naturalness and innocence. The serried white faces floating above the tables about him were signs whose meanings he had to decipher in terms of wondering if they suspected him. Or could he find with them some basis for a relationship to still his loneliness?

Seating himself circumspectly at a vacant table, he looked about for the waiter. Coming from the front of the dining car, grinning broadly, holding aloft in his right palm a tray of steaming food, was a short, nervous, brown-skinned man who winked smilingly at Cross and kept on looking at him as he passed. The waiter had given him an innocent, racially fraternal greeting common among Negroes. Cross knew that most whites never dreamed that their behavior toward Negroes had bred in them, especially when they were in the presence of whites, a defensive solidarity that had, except for latent white hostility, no valid reason for being. He idly observed the waiter's movements as the brown hand deftly placed succulent dishes under the impassive faces of whites. Having emptied his tray, the waiter turned, paused at Cross's table, dusted his napkin at imaginary bread crumbs on the white tablecloth, and whispered: "How you, guy?"

"Fine," Cross answered. "And you?"

"Just dragging my black ass, serving these white sons of bitches," the waiter said in a sniggling whisper. "Be with

120

you in a sec. I'm the only waiter in this car. My pal took sick and got off in Cleveland. So I got my hands full of white shit." The waiter clapped his hands over his mouth and widened his eyes at Cross in a sign-language laugh.

"Take your time," Cross told him. "I'm in no hurry."

"Wish these white monkeys felt like you do," the waiter whispered in appreciation. He handed Cross a folded newspaper. "Want the paper?"

"Thanks," Cross mumbled.

He gave Cross another wink and moved swiftly on between the crowded tables. Cross opened the paper and glanced at the headlines. Was there any news of Joe? It was not until he had reached the bottom of page four that he saw a small caption:

POSTAL CLERK'S BODY FOUND

He lowered the paper quickly, reading:

The almost nude body of a Negro postal clerk, Joe Thomas, 39, of 3433 St. Lawrence Avenue, was found dead early this morning on the near South Side by an emergency line repairman. The body was lying clad only in a bathrobe in a deep snowdrift atop the roof of a four-story dwelling.

The victim had apparently been drunk and it has not been determined if Thomas leaped, was pushed, or died from exposure.

That was all. Could they trace Joe's death to him? But how could they discover that he, Cross Damon, had been in the hotel? He felt safe. He looked through the moisture-streaked window at the sunny fields of snow glittering and turning slowly outside. The train rumbled on, clicking wheels of steel. Ice-encrusted telegraph wires shot past, rising and dipping like strings plucked by invisible fingers. It was a normal world whose events flowed intelligibly and each object had a sharp, precise meaning. He looked in the direction of the waiter and was surprised to see the waiter looking at him, winking, smiling. . . .

Out of a void, anxiety rose and captured his senses; he could feel the reality of the dining car falling away as his

121

consciousness projected menacing meanings on the look of the world. Was he being followed on this train? Wasn't that waiter being especially friendly to allay any fears he might have that he was being watched? Hadn't that waiter cursed the white folks with the idea of inducing in him a false notion of security?

He had no objective evidence that anything extraordinary was happening in the dining car, but this rational perception didn't down his fear. Why was that tall white man staring at him? And why had he looked off when their eyes met? In vain his mind protested this delusive mood that was stealing his sanity away. . . .

Passing to get another tray of food, the waiter again paused at Cross's table, grinning, whispering: "These white bastards think they're smart, hunh? But one of these days we'll show 'em, won't we, boy?"

The waiter knew and was teasing him! He had spotted him for the police and was so sure of himself that he could joke about it! Cross blinked and fought to control the sensations of his body; he had the illusion of something crawling over the surface of his skin. When the waiter finally came to take his order, he was so confused that he kept his eyes on the menu and mumbled what he wanted to eat. He was conscious of the irrational nature of what was transpiring, but he could not master it. His sensibilities clamored to believe in this delusion; his emotions needed the certainty of this transparent fantasy; yet, in the end, his mind was tough enough to cling to its anchorage in the hard ambiguities of normal reality. When his bacon and eggs came, he had no desire to eat. But would not that make him conspicuous? He picked up his knife and fork and forced himself, praying for this spell to pass.

He was loading his fork with a bit of bacon and a part of egg yolk when a stretch of black cloth appeared before him. He lifted his eyes and saw a Catholic priest, tall, heavy, florid of face, and with a white, turned-about collar.

"Good morning," the priest said, smiling.

"Good morning," Cross answered.

The priest sat down, then nodded toward the white landscape. "We've had a lot of snow."

"Yes."

122

"Did you sleep well?" the priest asked.

"Yes," Cross lied.

"I didn't," the priest said. "I can never sleep on trains. By the way, do you live in Harlem?"

"Yes."

Why was he being so closely questioned? The priest stared thoughtfully out of the window and Cross wondered what he was thinking. . . . He gripped his knife and fork hard. Goddamn . . . He had to keep his head above this dangerous water and not go under. As the waiter passed, the priest caught hold of his arm and asked: "May I keep this seat for my friend? He'll be here in a moment."

"Certainly, sir," the waiter said and, when he was out of the range of the vision of the priest, he made a grimace with his lips to Cross.

Cross's anxieties now condensed themselves into an attitude of sullenness toward the priest. He disliked most strongly all men of religion because he felt that they could take for granted an interpretation of the world that his sense of life made impossible. The priest was secure and walked the earth with a divine mandate, while Cross's mere breathing was an act of audacity, a confounding wonder at the daily mystery of himself. He felt that the attitude of the priest was predicated upon a scheme of good and evil ordained by a God whom he was constrained out of love and fear to obey; and Cross therefore regarded him as a kind of dressed-up savage intimidated by totems and taboos that differed in kind but not in degree from those of the most primitive of peoples. Cross had to discover what was good or evil through his own actions, which were more exacting than the edicts of any God because it was he alone who had to bear the brunt of their consequences with a sense of absoluteness made intolerable by knowing that this life of his was all he had and would ever have. For him there was no grace or mercy if he failed.

The waiter paused with a loaded tray at his table and said: "I'll be serving your coffee next."

"Good," Cross mumbled.

He saw the waiter bend with a dead-pan face to serve a white woman who sat across the aisle from him.

"I'm sorry I had to make you wait, Ma'm," the waiter mumbled.

Cross watched the waiter place a tumbler of orange juice before the woman, then a platter of ham and poached eggs. The waiter was about to lift a silver pot of steaming coffee to fill her cup when the woman turned abruptly with her whole body, opening her mouth to speak. Cross saw the woman's plump, naked elbow describe a tiny, swift arc and collide with the coffeepot as it left the tray. There was a ringing clatter of metal and a brown spout of boiling coffee, emitting a cloud of vapor, splashed over the woman's bare arm and onto her bosom. The waiter's movements froze and the woman leaped to her feet and screamed, her face distorted with fury and pain.

"You nigger, you're burning me!" she yelled.

The waiter stood paralyzed, his mouth open. The woman's frantic eyes swept the dining car, then rested upon the table. In one flowing movement, she seized the handle of a silver water pitcher and raised it above her head, her eyes bulging and her darkly rouged lips curled in pain.

Cross was on his feet before he knew it and had traversed the aisle and was standing between the woman and the waiter, fronting the woman, blocking her action with his uplifted right hand, which still clutched his napkin. The woman lowered her hand.

"You're not hitting me, nigger," the woman said quietly.

"You're not hitting anybody either," Cross said.

The priest rushed to the side of the woman, put his arm about her, then looked from Cross to the waiter. The dining car was full of the rumble of the train speeding over steel rails. In the middle of the car a tall, hard-faced man stood up and glared.

"What's the matter down there?" the man called.

"I'm sorry, lady," the waiter crooned in humility.

The woman pawed at her arm, which gleamed a brick red where the coffee had scalded it. Steam still rose from her dress. She began to weep.

"I got something for that burn, Ma'm." The waiter found his tongue and ran toward the rear of the car. The tall, hard-faced man rushed to the side of the priest and now

124

two men were holding the woman and looking at Cross. Cross's hand fell to his side. He was surprised to find that he was smiling; he had acted before he had known it. Another white woman came forward and took hold of the injured woman.

"Darling, I've got something in my purse for burns," the woman said and led her from sight, toward the women's lavatory. The waiter came running with a tube of salve and stood staring helplessly at the backs of the two retreating women.

"It wasn't my fault," he said, looking at the silent, thoughtful faces in the car. "She turned round—like this." He imitated the woman's movement. "And she knocked the pot out of my hand."

The train whistled a long, mournful blast and Cross could feel the centrifugal pull of its speed as it struck a stretch of curving track. He went to his seat and sat before his half-empty plate and stared out the window. Low voices were murmuring in the car.

"It's a shame— Was she burnt badly?"

"But I *saw* her; she knocked the pot out of his hand. . . ."

"What happened? Did somebody hit the woman?"

"Oh, no; it was an accident. It wasn't the waiter's fault."

Cross became aware that the priest had also sat and was staring at him; when their eyes met, the priest looked off toward the snow-filled fields. Cross realized that he had sprung without thinking to his feet to block the woman's tossing the pitcher into the waiter's face and he knew that the priest had leaped up to defend the woman. Both of them had acted before they had been fully conscious of what they had wanted to do. And now shame made them avoid each other's eyes.

"It's a strange world, isn't it?" Cross asked the priest softly.

The priest ruefully smiled his answer and nibbled thoughtfully at a slice of buttered toast.

The injured woman came briskly down the aisle with lips pursed and eyes glazed. The other woman followed.

"I'm going to report you," she told the waiter.

The waiter paused, stared, his lips hanging open in dismay. He shook his head and when he spoke his voice was so high-pitched that it was ludicrous.

"It wasn't my fault, Ma'm." It was a plea issuing from a soul that hated its shame and humility.

"You were careless and I'm going to sue," the woman said.

She tossed her blonde hair and flounced out of the car. The waiter's face was a mask of distress and Cross chided himself upon ever having thought that he could have been spying on him.

"Oh, there you are!" a sonorous voice came from a hunchbacked man who slid into the seat beside the priest.

"What kept you?" the priest asked.

"I went in the wrong direction looking for the diner," the man said, laughing and letting his eyes settle upon Cross's face.

Suddenly the priest beamed at Cross and spoke: "By the way, I'm Father Seldon and my friend here is District Attorney Ely Houston of New York City."

"How do you do?" Cross asked, full of fear, nodding to the hunchback. A district attorney? *The* Ely Houston of whom he had heard? The celebrated crime-buster? At once his tensions began to deform the look of the world. Though the two white faces regarded him with friendliness, he projected on them an air of the sinister. Maybe the Chicago police had wired ahead and Houston had gotten on the train to apprehend him? How had they come to seat themselves *exactly* at his table? And he recalled that the priest had *expressly* asked the waiter to save the chair next to him for Houston. . . . Was Houston armed? He imagined he could see a slight bulge under the man's right armpit and he mentally pictured a gun nestling there. . . .

"You live in New York?" Houston asked.

"Yes."

Could this be a trap? He did not volunteer to tell his name and they did not ask him to do so. Would they think it odd that he had not identified himself?

"Mr. Houston and I are very much interested in your people," the priest said to Cross.

Cross knew exactly what the priest meant, but he allowed his eyebrows to lift in surprise. He did not want to be drawn into any discussion with them, yet he did not want to make them feel that he was afraid.

"*My* people? What do you mean?"

Father Seldon chewed industriously upon his mouthful of bacon and eggs and kept his eyes on his plate, answering: "I mean the colored people—"

"Oh," Cross said, giving a play-acting laugh. "But they were born that color. Nobody *colored* them."

Houston and the priest were startled for a moment, then both of them laughed. Houston continued to examine Cross in a friendly manner; finally he nodded his head affirmatively.

"That's good. I must remember it," Houston said.

"Well, Ely," Father Seldon said, turning and smiling at Houston, "if you should ever run for the Senate, you'd know how not to make a mistake before an audience in Harlem."

"I sure would," Houston admitted.

Cross was through eating and he wanted to go back to his compartment. But he must not act too fast and arouse unnecessary suspicions. He lingered on, studying Houston closely. The man had a huge head of remarkably black, unruly hair; a long, strong, too white face; clear, wide-apart brown eyes; and a well-shaped mouth that held always a hint of a smile at its corners. His shoulders were Herculean with long arms that terminated in huge hands with delicately strong fingers. The hump on the back was prominent but not as noticeable as Cross would have thought it would be, so naturally did it blend in with the man's general build. Cross had not particularly noticed this deformity when Houston had first sat down, but now he remembered that Houston had moved forward to the table with a motion that slightly resembled that of a creeping animal, holding his trunk still as he walked. He reminded Cross of a patiently waiting, giant white spider whose temper was never ruffled but whose mental processes ground both fast and exceedingly fine. He had the impression of a man possessing stealthy reserves of physical and emotional strength, and he felt intuitively that this was exactly the kind of man whom he had to fear, not only because he was a defender of the law, but because Houston

127

had an ability to delve into life. He was afraid of this man and yet his fear made him want to know him.

"Where's your parish, Father?" Cross asked.

"In Harlem," Father Seldon said, obviously glad to speak of it. "We also operate a school for delinquent boys in upstate New York. Maybe you've heard of it? The Sanctuary, it's called. We have about sixty Negro boys up there now."

"I see," Cross said.

Houston dawdled his fork in his plate and spoke in a tone that made Cross know that he was expressing thoughts of deep interest to himself, thoughts touched and lighted by passion, almost.

"I'm profoundly interested in the psychological condition of the Negro in this country," Houston said. "Only a few people see and understand the complexity of this problem. And don't think that my interest is solely political. It's not; it was there long before I ever thought of entering politics." He smiled cryptically and let his eyes wander over the icy landscape flowing past the train's window. "My personal situation in life has given me a vantage point from which I've gained some insight into the problems of other excluded people."

Cross's impulses were at war. Was Houston raising the question of the Negro to mislead him before he was told that he was under arrest? Why didn't he come right out with what he wanted? He had a foolish desire to reach forward and grab Houston's shoulder and say to him: All right; I know you're after me. . . . Let's get it over with. . . . His stomach muscles tightened as he checked himself. He knew that Houston, in identifying himself with Negroes, had been referring to his deformity. Houston was declaring himself to be an outsider like Cross and Cross was interested, but he kept his face impassive to conceal it.

"The way Negroes were transported to this country and sold into slavery, then stripped of their tribal culture and held in bondage; and then allowed, so teasingly and over so long a period of time, to be sucked into our way of life is something which resembles the rise of all men from whatever it was we all came from," Houston said, the smile on his lips playful and knowing.

128

"I follow you," Cross said.

"Yes; I see you do." Houston smiled with satisfaction. "We are not now keeping the Negro on such a short chain and they are slowly entering into our culture. But that is not the end of this problem. It is the beginning. . . ."

"What do you mean, Ely?" Father Seldon asked.

"I mean this," Houston hastened to explain. "Negroes, as they enter our culture, are going to inherit the problems we have, but with a difference. They are outsiders and they are going to *know* that they have these problems. They are going to be self-conscious; they are going to be gifted with a double vision, for, being Negroes, they are going to be both *inside* and *outside* of our culture at the same time. Every emotional and cultural convulsion that ever shook the heart and soul of Western man will shake them. Negroes will develop unique and specially defined psychological types. They will become psychological men, like the Jews. . . . They will not only be Americans or Negroes; they will be centers of *knowing*, so to speak. . . . The political, social, and psychological consequences of this will be enormous. . . ."

"You are much too complicated, Ely," Father Seldon said. "The problem's bad enough without trying to make it into *everything*. All the colored people need is the right to jobs and living space."

"True," Houston said. "But their getting those elementary things is so long and drawn out that they must, while they wait, adjust themselves to living in a kind of No Man's Land. . . . Now, imagine a man inclined to think, to probe, to ask questions. Why, he'd be in a wonderful position to do so, would he not, if he were black and lived in America? A dreadful objectivity would be forced upon him."

"Oh, Ely, you're always climbing some rocky goat-track of speculation," Father Seldon protested. "Take the simple facts of life just as they are found—"

"That's what I'm doing," Houston said. "And when you look at them closely, those simple facts turn out to be not so simple."

"I think Mr. Houston's close to the truth," Cross said, pretending a smile, relishing an irony that came from referring both to his own feeling that maybe Houston was trying to track him down and to the aptness of the man's remarks. "The problem really starts once the Negro gets his so-called rights. Is he going to be able to settle down and live the normal, day-to-day life of the average white American? Or will he still have his sense of outsidedness?"

"Right," Houston agreed by stabbing the air with his fork. "You've got it. Say, where did you go to school? Not that you learn things like that in school. . . ."

"Fisk," Cross lied. He rose; this was getting too close. "I'm sorry, gentlemen." Cross smiled at them. "But I must leave. It's wonderful to talk like this."

"Well, sit down and talk," Houston said.

"No; really, I must go. I've a lot to do," Cross lied vaguely. "Good morning." He made his way nervously out of the dining car. Goddamn. . . . He was frightened of that hunchback, that outsider who understood *too* much. Houston was a man crammed with guilty knowledge. What weird luck to encounter a kindred type to whom he wanted to talk and who wanted to talk to him. And this would be his life until he found himself an identity behind which he could hide.

The Pullman porter had made up his bed and he was alone; he sat and stared moodily out the window. He who had a secret to hide loved talking! When one tried to conceal oneself, didn't one make oneself conspicuous? And that seductive fear that always surged up in him, how was he to handle it? And why did he always yearn to embrace those delusive fantasies? What unearthly greed made him want to feed upon what he knew to be unreal? He could run away from Dot, Gladys, his mother, but he could not run away from this; it was he and he was it. A tapping came at the door and he rose in dread, his lips parting. Was it Houston? The tapping sounded again and he opened the door.

"Hey, guy." It was the waiter, holding a scared smile on his lips.

"Hello," Cross said, relieved.

"Can I speak to you a minute?"

"Sure; come on in."

The waiter came hesitantly into the compartment.

130

"Man, that bitch is raising hell," the waiter began. "She's gonna sue the company for damages, and she's saying it's all my fault. If she wins, it's my job." The waiter's eyes danced in his head.

"What're you going to do?" Cross asked.

"I got to get some witnesses," the waiter said. "You know, that priest won't witness for me. Can you feature that? Man, what can we do with these white folks?" He spoke in a low, nervous tone of voice charged with bitterness. "I'm gonna take it up with the union; they'll fight for me. But I got to have evidence, see?"

"Sure," Cross said.

"My name's Bob Hunter," the waiter said.

Cross knew that Hunter was waiting for him to give his name.

"Mine's Addison Jordan," Cross said, feeling that he was speaking out of a dream.

"Would you be a witness if that bitch makes trouble?"

"Sure," Cross said, beginning to hate the man.

"Give me your address and the union'll get in touch with you," Hunter said, taking a frayed address book from his pocket.

"It's 128 West 137th Street," Cross lied, never again wanting to look into Hunter's eyes. He could not explain his unavailability to this man, yet it was wrong to allow him to think that he had his help.

"Thanks," Hunter said, jotting down the address. "You don't live so far from me. Here; take my address." He wrote it on a slip of paper. "If you're ever up there, drop in and we can kill a bottle, hunh?"

"Sure," Cross agreed.

Hunter made him feel his impotence so keenly that he wanted to spit in his face. Hunter's manner of pronouncing certain words bothered Cross and Cross asked him: "Where were you born, Hunter?"

"Texas, man," Hunter said, eying Cross closely. "Why?"

"I don't know. Just curious, that's all."

"Say, you need any help with your bags?" Hunter asked.

"Oh, no," Cross said. "I've only one suitcase."

"Just want to help you, man," Hunter smiled. "We colored folks got to stick together, don't we?"

"Oh, yes," Cross agreed with pretended heartiness.

"Good-by, now," Hunter said, leaving and closing the door.

Christ Almighty! Hunter was believing that he had his help, that he would be a friend. He had made Hunter a promise that he could not keep, just as he had made his mother, his sons, Dot, Gladys, and Jenny promises that he could not keep. . . . His nonidentity was making Hunter believe in the unreal. Cross sighed. He had to break out of this dream, or he would surely go mad. He had to be born again, come anew into the world. To live amidst others without an identity was intolerable. In a strict sense he was not really in the world; he was haunting it, pleading for entrance into life. . . . He sat and rested his head in his hands. He must eventually find Bob Hunter and try to square this deception. But why did he care about Bob Hunter? No; it was not Hunter himself that bothered him; it was Hunter's delusive belief in him that he found offensive. He started as another knock came. Hunter again? If so, he'd explain to the man that he could not help him. He rose and opened the door.

"I'm not disturbing you, am I?" Houston asked him, smiling.

"Oh, no," Cross lied. His body seemed suddenly made of soft, melting wax. "Come in."

"Are you sure? I just wanted to talk a little," Houston said.

Houston's manner seemed sincere. Maybe he was wrong? As he talked to Houston, he would be waiting for the trap to be sprung. Houston sat and held out his pack of cigarettes. Cross took one and Houston held out his lighter. Cross strove for nonchalance, meeting Houston's gaze with a smile. Houston studied Cross for some minutes. Why in hell doesn't he speak . . . ?

"It's not often that one meets someone who can grasp ideas," Houston began. "If I'm bothering you now, it's a little of your own fault; you ought not to have agreed with me in the dining car." Houston laughed. "You know, to get to the point, I've never had a chance to talk to Negroes as I'd like to. There's something about the Negro in America that almost hypnotizes me, really. . . . By the way,

132

quite frankly, talking about this problem doesn't bother you, does it?"

"Not at all," Cross said, in spite of his anxiety.

"People are so tender-skinned these days," Houston went on. "Everybody's trying to be other than what they really are: something official, approved of, safe—"

"They are afraid," Cross said, suppressing his own fear.

"You strike me as being a man of pretty cool judgment and having some insight into life," Houston said.

Cross wanted to laugh out loud. If the man only knew how lost and guilty and scared he was! How steeped in anxiety!

"I don't know," Cross said.

"Whenever I've tried to talk to most educated Negroes, I've felt a barrier," Houston continued. "I can understand why they feel constrained. They feel that I'm enjoying their humiliation. And many whites do enjoy talking to Negroes about this problem; it makes them feel superior and secure."

"That's all too true," Cross agreed.

"But this hump on my back ought to give me some license," Houston argued. "I know what it means to be an object outside of the normal lives of men. I know how it feels to be stared at, to have some silly woman want to touch your hump for luck. . . . When I was a child, I hated myself, cursed my ill fortune; but now I'd not want to give up what my peculiar situation has taught me about life. This damned hump has given me more psychological knowledge than all the books I read at the university.

"My deformity made me free; it put me outside and made me feel as an outsider. It wasn't pleasant; hell, no. At first I felt inferior. But now I have to struggle with myself to keep from feeling superior to the people I meet. . . . Do you understand what I mean?"

"I do," Cross said quietly.

"Some men are so placed in life by accident of race or birth or chance that what they see is terrifying," Houston said, carried away by his theme. "Life converts the lives of such men into something almost dreamlike. And I've often wondered why I couldn't detect this feeling of the outsider in the Negroes I've met. In America the Negro is outside.

Our laws and practices see to it that he stays outside.
. . . Or, am I mistaken in looking for this in Negroes,
Mr. —?"

"Addison Jordan's the name," Cross lied, murmuring
softly. Was Houston spying on him? If he acted afraid,
Houston would wonder why. The best policy would be to
talk frankly, and when he spoke he was talking of himself,
a self pushed away from him and described in abstract
terms. "Yes, Mr. Houston, the Negro feels exactly what
you are asking about. But he hides it. He's scared to reveal
what he feels. He fears reprisals from his white neighbors."
Cross was feeling how much he was hiding from Houston.

"But they ought to be able to talk to *me* without fear,"
Houston said with a note of pleading in his voice. "After
all, in a psychological sense, I'm a brother to them."

"They're even afraid of you," Cross said, smiling,
wondering if Houston too was being ironical.

Cross could feel that Houston sensed the quality of the
demoniacal in him, and he could feel the same in Houston.
But this man, of all men, must not get too close to him. He
represented the law and the law condemned what he was
and what he had done. Cross felt the hot breath of danger
as Houston continued.

"My position's difficult," he said. "I feel outside the lives
of men. Yet my job demands that I enforce the law against
the outsider who breaks that law."

"How do you manage it?" Cross asked with a con-
stricted throat.

Houston laughed and did not answer.

"Do you have sympathy for those who break the laws of
civilization?" Cross felt compelled to ask.

"In a way, yes," Houston confessed. "But it all depends
upon *how* the laws are broken. My greatest sympathy is
for those who feel that they have a *right* to break the law.
But do you know that there are not many criminals who
feel that? Most of them almost beg you to punish them.
They would be lost without the law. The law's vengeance is
what gives meaning to their lives." Houston paused and
stared at the floor. "You asked something about civilization.
. . . Civilization," Houston repeated the word, letting it
roll slowly on his tongue. He looked at Cross, smiled, then

asked teasingly: "You call this *civilization?* I don't. This is a jungle. We pretend that we have law and order. But we don't, really. We have imposed a visible order, but hidden under that veneer of order the jungle still seethes."

"But why do you call it a jungle?" Cross asked. "Isn't it normal life and we've tried to hide it with order because it's too terrible, maybe?"

"Maybe," Houston admitted.

"Isn't life exactly what it ought to be, in a certain sense? Isn't it only the naïve who find all of this baffling? If you've a notion of what man's heart is, wouldn't you say that maybe the whole effort of man on earth to build a civilization is *simply* man's frantic attempt to hide himself from himself? That there is a part of man that man wants to reject? That man wants to keep from knowing what he is? That he wants to protect himself from seeing that he is something awful? And that this 'awful' part of himself might not be as awful as he thinks, but he finds it too strange and he does not know what to do with it? We talk about what to do with the atom bomb. . . . But man's heart, his spirit, is the deadliest thing in creation. Aren't all cultures and civilizations just screens which men have used to divide themselves, to put between that part of themselves which they are afraid of and that part of themselves which they want to try to preserve? Aren't all of man's efforts at order an attempt to still man's fear of himself?"

"And what is man that he has to hide from himself?" Houston asked, smiling; there was a look of frightened delight in his eyes.

Involuntarily Cross drew in his breath and looked past Houston to the bleak landscape of snow sweeping past the train's window. The conversation was making him feel a sense of intense isolation, and, even though Houston was there in the compartment with him, for a moment he was unaware of it. He was man who had killed and fled, man who had broken all of his ties and was free. . . .

"Maybe man is nothing in particular," Cross said gropingly. "Maybe that's the terror of it. Man may be just anything at all. And maybe man deep down suspects this, really knows this, kind of dreams that it is true; but at the same time he does not want really to know it. May not

135

human life on this earth be a kind of frozen fear of man at what he could possibly be? And every move he makes, couldn't these moves be just to hide this awful fact? To twist it into something which he feels would make him rest and breathe a little easier? What man is is perhaps too much to be borne by man. . . ."

Houston rose quickly; there was intense excitement in his face and Cross grew afraid. Maybe he had talked too much?

"Maybe my theory is too wild," Cross said with hasty self-deprecation.

"No. I've had the same notion and I can't get rid of it." Houston looked directly at Cross and smiled. "I *knew* that this existed! By God, I knew that some day I'd hear this from your side of the fence. The Negro *has* to know this. How could he escape knowing it? He looks right at it every day of his life, every hour. . . ." Houston paused, smiled cynically. "All my life I've been haunted by the notion that this life we live is a pretense, and all the more deadly because it is a pretense. And woe to the man who dares to try to reveal that pretense! *He* is the *criminal*. . . ." He pulled deeply at his cigarette and laughed softly. " 'Man's nothing in particular,' " he repeated Cross's words. "I think you're pretty close to something there. Say, we seem to be getting into the city. . . . Look, here's my card. Call me up sometime and we can chat a little, eh? I'd love it."

"Sure," Cross said, rising and taking the card. "I'd be glad to."

Houston left, smiling, seemingly satisfied. Alone, Cross sat again and stared unseeingly at the dreary apartment-building landscape of the Bronx as it heaved into view. Of one thing he was certain: he could never see Houston again. It was Houston's job to bring him to justice. The man's mind seemed to find its recreation by delving directly into problems of consciousness like those that were possessing him. He felt like a bird veering and fluttering toward the wide, unblinking eyes of the crouching cat. . . . He had to master himself; he had to steer clear of being always drawn toward that which he dreaded. And, intuitively, he knew that Houston was caught in the same psychological trap. That was why Houston was a district

136

attorney sworn to uphold a system of law in which he did not really believe. Houston was an impulsive criminal who protected himself against himself by hunting down other criminals! How cleverly the man had worked out his life, had balanced his emotional drives! He could experience vicariously all destructive furies of the murderer, the thief, the sadist, without being held to accountability!

The train slowed and was passing 125th Street and Cross looked down at the wintry drabness of Harlem, at its rows of tenements, at black men and women huddled in overcoats, trudging through snowy streets. Well, here I am. . . . I've made no promises. . . . I'm nobody. . . . I'm responsible for nothing. . . . He sighed as the train slid into the underground, making for Grand Central Station.

Half an hour later, Cross, lugging his heavy suitcase, followed the crowd up the ramp toward the waiting rooms. As he edged forward his anxieties began to mount. Care seemed to bring him these compulsive moods which, when they first made their presence felt, when they first declared their emotional authority, were nothing definite. They simply rose seemingly out of nowhere and in defiance of his rational capacity and began seeking their own object; failing to find it, they created it out of what was at hand, anything. . . . Cross knew that this was himself acting, and that self was alien to him.

He passed the train's huge engine and longed to become as uncaring and passively brutish as that monster of steel. But, no; his was to feel all of those anxieties in his shivering flesh. Goddamn! To swap the burden of this sorry consciousness for something else! To be a God who could master feeling! If not that, then a towering rock that could feel nothing at all! His life was becoming a tense prayer interspersed with curses. He wondered if the priest felt life as keenly as he did. Or hadn't the priest become a priest precisely in order *not* to feel it?

Through the bars of the gate he saw crowds milling in the station; porters rushed to and fro; hand trucks piled with luggage rolled toward the exits; he heard shouts of friends greeting friends. If his apprehensions were true, if Houston were playing a game, he could expect the police to accost him. When he was out of the gate, he saw Hous-

137

ton and Father Seldon smiling and waving at him and he smiled and waved back. He was still safe.

Twice before he had been in New York, with Gladys on summer vacations, and he knew his way about. He headed for the Grand Central subway station and took the shuttle to Times Square where he changed for a Harlem train. He stood at the front window of the first coach with his back to the other passengers, his emotions reading a secret language in the red and amber and green lights that swept past in the noisy night of the underground. At 110th Street he began to wonder where he would get off. Such were now the tiny decisions that clogged his consciousness. He was *too* free! For no reason at all he rode past 110th Street and at 125th Street he decided to get off simply because it was one of the best-known thoroughfares in Harlem. Standing uncertainly on the platform, he debated: Maybe 125th Street is *too* crowded; it's just possible I might meet somebody I know. . . . He waited for a local and rode to 135th Street and got off and climbed the stairs to the upper world.

Loitering, holding his suitcase, his cheeks stinging from the icy wind, he pondered what direction to take to find a room. When he finally ambled forward, he avoided looking into the faces of the passers-by, feeling instinctively that he did not have the right to do so. He was without a name, a past, a future; no promises or pledges bound him to those about him. He had to become human before he could mingle again with people. Yet he needed those people and could become human only with them. Dimly he realized that his dilemma, though personal, bore the mark of the general. The lives of children, too, were subjected to this same necessity; they, too, could become human only by growing up with human beings. . . .

He came to Seventh Avenue and walked up to 136th Street, turned left, looking for FOR RENT signs. At last he saw a brick house set well back from the sidewalk with shutters closed and it appealed to him. It was as though his doubt about his right to exist blended with the closed shutters and the distance the house was from the street. He mounted stone steps and rang the bell; the opening door

138

disclosed a woman with a brown face—a burning cigarette slanting across her chin made her seem sluttish at first—wearing a dark blue dressing gown. He saw the tip of a soiled brassiere struggling to keep her bulging breasts to the dimensions of modesty. She was about twenty-eight or thirty, had hard surfacy eyes that might have indicated that she was limited in her thinking. Woman as body of woman shot through his senses, but he pushed the impulse from him; he was in too much danger now to play around. . . .

"What can I do for you?" she asked bluntly.

"You have a room for rent, I think," Cross said, a little taken aback by her abrupt manner. Yet he liked her. She was the kind of woman who would most likely take him for granted and not pry into his past; her attitude seemed to place her in the sane, ordinary events of Harlem life.

"Come on in if you want to see it," she said.

He stepped inside, set his suitcase in a corner, and followed her down a hallway and up a flight of steps to a second floor. She trailed an odor of tobacco smoke. She opened the door of a large room and threw him a defiant glance.

"There it is," she said flatly.

He sized her up as a naïve woman who had created about herself a hard-boiledness of manner to protect a too believing nature that had been tramped on and abused by sundry men. In appearance, she was intensely feminine, seemingly ready to surrender in a yearning for a happiness which she was certain she would be cheated out of in the end.

"How much is the rent?" he asked her.

"Ten dollars a week," she said.

"I'll take it."

"You don't have to decide right now," she told him; she seemed to be uncertain of herself.

"I want a room and here is one: large, airy, clean. I'll take it." He smiled at her, took out his wallet and gave her a ten-dollar bill.

"When do you want to move in?" she asked.

"I'm here," he said. "My bag's downstairs. It's simple."

139

Having identified himself as Addison Jordan, Cross, half an hour later, was lying on his bed, trying to plot out his life.

The weather continued bitterly cold. An icy wind swooped from a bleak sky, ripped against windowpanes, and clawed at passers-by in the streets. Cross, overcome by a listlessness which he could not shake off, spent his days either lounging in his room or in the consoling shadows of movie houses. He was Mrs. Hattie Turner's only paying guest and he heard rather than saw her, slightly in her cups at times, stumbling around downstairs in her dining room or kitchen. He learned from a gossipy drugstore clerk that she was a widow who owned her own home, that she drank a little too much, and that she had recently begun to receive the attentions of two men. Most of the time he could hear her playing blues or jazz records whose wild rhythms wailed up to him through the thin flooring.

The raucous blue-jazz became his only emotional home now and he listened with an appreciation he had never had before. He came to feel that this music was the rhythmic flauntings of guilty feelings, the syncopated outpourings of frightened joy existing in guises forbidden and despised by others. He sensed how Negroes had been made to live in but not of the land of their birth, how the injunctions of an alien Christianity and the strictures of white laws had evoked in them the very longings and desires–that that religion and law had been designed to stifle. He realized that this blue-jazz was a rebel art blooming seditiously under the condemnations of a Protestant ethic just as his own consciousness had sprung conditioned to defiance from his relationship to his mother, who had shrilly evoked in him exactly what she had so desperately tried to smother. Blue-jazz was the scornful gesture of men turned ecstatic in their state of rejection; it was the musical language of the satisfiedly amoral, the boastings of the contentedly lawless, the recreations of the innocently criminal. . . . Cross smiled with depressed joy as he paced about his room, his ears full of the woeful happiness of the blues and the orgiastic culpability of jazz.

He had enough money to keep him for a while. Each night he vowed that on the following morning he would do something practical about his problem of identity, but the morning found him ready with excuses for inaction. He avoided trying to justify his fear of activity, but in his heart he knew that to exert himself was to invite down upon him those spells of dread; so he remained inert, hoping that by blending his bleak mood with the empty hours he would elude his compulsions.

Of a morning or of an evening he would encounter Mrs. Turner in the downstairs hallway and they would exchange greetings. Whenever she asked him if he were comfortable, he would tell her that everything was all right in a tone of voice that sought to hold her off from him, for he sensed slumbering in her strained manner a nervousness whose content he did not want to know. Now and then he noticed two well-dressed Negroes coming to visit her, but they roused neither his interest nor jealousy.

When she did finally break in on his jealous solitude, it was with a naïve brusqueness that swept him before it and he was again acting with swift heartlessness to save himself. His anxiety rose when he noticed her staring at him. Inflamed, his dread distorted innocent events. Wasn't she suspicious about his background? Why did those two men come to see her? Why were they always *together?* Didn't policemen act that way? Why wasn't Mrs. Turner more relaxed with him of late? He even wondered if she searched his suitcase when he was out. . . .

On the morning of the day of his flight, Mrs. Turner failed to return his greeting in the hallway. Late that evening, she knocked at his door. He made sure that his gun was handy, then rose and confronted her. She stared at him blankly, embarrassed.

"God, I'm rattled tonight," she complained. "I came up here to say something, and now, for the life of me, I can't remember what it was." She tapped the knuckles of her hand against her forehead. "It'll come back to me in a minute. If it doesn't, then it couldn't've been so *very* important, could it? I'm silly." She forced a smile and left.

Cross was frantic. Had she come up to make sure that he was in his room? He ached to grab her and shake the truth out of her. He was certain that she had not forgotten the object of her errand; a mere failure of nerve had swamped her before she could speak. Quickly he packed his suitcase. Maybe she was trying to tempt him . . . ? Or maybe the cops were waiting downstairs? Or perhaps she wanted to talk to him about some problem of her own? But how could he tell? He sat on the side of the bed and sweated.

A moment later he heard water running in the bathroom. He leaped from the bed, grabbed his suitcase and softly groped his way out, tiptoeing. In the hallway he heard the sound of water still coming from the bathroom and he could see a light shining from beneath the sill. He crept down the stairs to the front door and paused; he opened it and saw a bluish haze hanging in the dim streets. It was late, far past midnight; the world was wrapped in silence. He ran over the snow to the sidewalk, walked to Seventh Avenue, and ducked into a subway, relieved that he was free, free to wrestle again with the tyranny of himself. His fear drove home to him the unreal nature of his life; he was defenseless. He had to work out of this dream somehow. . . .

Cross's opportunistic rejection of his former life had been spurred by his shame at what a paltry man he had made of himself. What little external pressure had compelled him to this stance was also a part of that self which he had rejected, for he alone had been responsible for what he had done to Gladys and Dot. His consciousness of the color of his skin had played no role in it. Militating against racial consciousness in him were the general circumstances of his upbringing which had shielded him from the more barbaric forms of white racism; also the insistent claims of his own inner life had made him too concerned with himself to cast his lot wholeheartedly with Negroes in terms of racial struggle. Practically he was with them, but emotionally he was not of them. He felt keenly their sufferings and would have battled desperately for any Negro trapped in a racial conflict, but his character had been so shaped that his decisive life struggle was a personal fight for the realization of himself.

What really obsessed him was his nonidentity, which

negated his ability to relate himself to others. He realized that what was happening to him now had been buried implicitly all along in his past life, had slumbered there in the form of a habit of acute reflection, in the guise of a certain coldness in judging even those closest to him, all because none of them really interested him.

He had long yearned to be free of all responsibilities of a certain sort, but not because he hadn't a capacity for responsibility. What had irked him about his past responsibilities had been their dullness, their tenuity, their tendency simply to bore him. What he needed, demanded, was the hardest, the most awful responsibility, something that would test him and make him feel his worth. And his South Side Chicago environment had held forth no hope of his ever being able to find any such responsibility.

Where could he find such experiences, such spheres of existence? In the main he accepted the kind of world that the Bible claimed existed; but for the sufferings, terrors, accidental births, and meaningless deaths of that world, he rejected the Biblical prescriptions of repentance, prayer, faith, and grace. He was persuaded that what started on this earth had to be rounded off and somehow finished here.

He had reckoned that getting rid of the claims of others would automatically open up to him what he wanted, but it had merely let him live in the empty possibility of action whose spell, by a purging reality of its aliveness, had bound him more securely in foolish drifting. The world became distant, opaque; he was not related to it and could find no way of becoming so.

It was this static dream world that had elicited those acts of compulsion, those futile attempts to coerce reality to his emotional demands. There was in him a need to stabilize his surroundings. The world of most men is given to them by their culture, and, in choosing to make his own world, Cross had chosen to do something more dangerous than he had thought.

One walks along a street and strays unknowingly from one's path; one then looks up suddenly for familiar landmarks, and, seeing none, one feels lost. Panic drapes the

143

look of the world in strangeness, and the more one stares blankly at that world, the stranger it looks, the more hideously frightening it seems. There is then born in one a wild, hot wish to project out upon that alien world the world that one is seeking. This wish is a hunger for power, to be in command of oneself.

Cross's heart was full of a longing to search for himself and create a future as he walked up the exit stairway of the 116th Street subway station the night he had fled from Hattie and started looking again for a room in which to hide. When he reached the sidewalk the weather had turned to sleet and it was bitter cold. Lugging his suitcase through the slush underfoot, he leaned against the stinging wind and squinted his eyes, seeking a FOR RENT sign. He was tired; it was after two o'clock in the morning. Now and then he felt the pavement beneath his feet trembling from the rush of underground trains. Ahead he saw faint blobs of traffic lights wink from red to green and back again. Here and there a few neon signs glowed, half lost in murkiness. He went into a little bar that was almost empty and ordered a whisky.

As he sipped his drink, his eyes fell upon a series of crude signs on the dingy walls. He smiled as he read: IF YOU SPIT ON THE FLOOR AT HOME, YOU MAY DO SO HERE. Under the wording was a drawing of a coarse-faced man in a nicely furnished room reclining in an easy chair; his legs were stretched out and his feet rested upon a sofa. He was expectorating upon the floor, much to the horror of his long-suffering wife, who was on her hands and knees with a scrub rag trying to keep the floor clean.

Another sign read: DO NOT ASK FOR MR. CREDIT. HE DIED A LONG TIME AGO AND WE BURIED HIM. Under this drawing was the picture of a neglected grave in a hideously dilapidated cemetery. Engraved on the headstone was: MR. BROKE, BORN APRIL 1, 1949—DIED APRIL 2, 1949.

Cross wondered who thought up such legends. The image of the grave made him think how *he* was supposed to be dead. How fantastic it seemed. How did his grave look? And where was it? He did not even know the name of the cemetery. . . . He sighed and closed his eyes. Wonder
144

what Gladys engraved on my tombstone . . . ? He visualized big words hewn into marble:

CROSS DAMON
1924-1950
In Loving Memory

Would Gladys say more than that? Hell, would she even say *that* much . . . ? Perhaps she might; people had a way of forgiving you when you were dead. And why not? You could not hurt them then and maybe their forgiving you was an expression of their joy at your being dead . . . ?

He downed his last drop of whisky, then held his breath, caught in the grip of a paralyzing idea. Good God! Why in the name of all that was reasonable hadn't he thought of it before? It was *too* easy, that's why. He had often read about such things in newspapers; it had been reliably reported that underground Communists had established new identities by such methods. Why not? It more than answered his problem. Sure; all he had to do was to go to a cemetery and find the name of a man born on his birthday or any birthday that would make his present age and appearance seem normal! Why, if he were clever about it, he could even have a birth certificate! He had been pounding his brain for days for a new identity, and all he had to do was go to a graveyard and copy down a name. And there might be a hell of a wide choice; he could even afford to be critical about whose name he took. First thing in the morning he would go.

"Hey, another whisky here," he called to the bartender. When he was being served, he asked: "Say, you know where a guy can find a room for rent in this neighborhood?"

The bartender pursed his lips, put down the whisky bottle and stood thoughtfully.

"I know a Mrs. Crawford who lives up the street," the bartender told him. "She's been asking me to send her somebody. She's kind of old, but she's got a nice place. I lived there once myself, 'fore I got married."

Cross took down the number; he gulped his drink, thanked the bartender and was about to go when the door

145

flew open and two Negro policemen entered. Dread froze him to his stool. One cop sat to one side of him and the other went to the end of the room and looked about the bar carefully, his eyes at last resting upon Cross's face. Cross scarcely breathed. Was this *it?* He kept his head down, hiding his features. Goddamn, why did he always have to have that suitcase with him? He looked up and saw one of the cops coldly examining the reflection of his face in the mirror opposite him. Yes, they were looking him over; there was no doubt about it. He slipped his hand slowly into his overcoat pocket and grasped the gun. Then he started violently.

"It's okay, Jerry. Set it up in the back," one of the cops boomed out.

"Right," the bartender said.

Both cops disappeared wordlessly into the rear and Cross felt his muscles relaxing. The bartender took a bottle of whisky back to the cops. When he returned, Cross said in a whisper: "I thought they were raiding the joint."

"*Them?* Hell, naw. They want a drink. They're on duty this time of night and they're just making sure no spotters are about, that's all. Say, you gonna take that room?"

"Yeah, sure," Cross said. "Thanks a million."

Ten minutes later he was climbing dirty, smelly stairs to the door of Mrs. Crawford. He rang the bell, waited, then he heard an old woman's voice ask: "Who is it?"

Cross told her that Jerry, the bartender, had sent him for a room. She opened the door and peered at him. She was about sixty years old and had on a dressing gown. She'll be safe, Cross thought.

"Oh, you want a room? Kind of late you know. . . . Well, come in."

"I just got into the city," Cross lied.

"I see," she said, trudging slowly down the darkened hallway.

Mrs. Crawford was a brown-skinned, talkative, motherly, and slightly crippled old woman who was rather nervous at his sudden appearance.

"When did Jerry tell you 'bout this room?"

"A few minutes ago, Mrs. Crawford. I just left the bar," Cross assured her.

146

He accepted the room, paid his rent, and an hour later he was in a warm bed and feeling more hopeful than he had felt in a long time. Soon he would have an identity. But what kind of man would he pretend to be? What kind of beliefs would he pretend to have? Would he pretend studiousness or gaiety? He would choose the kind of disposition that would make people like him and accept him. Wasn't that the way life was lived in this world? Didn't people select deliberately the types of personality that would get them the kind of attention that they thought would help them? He laughed silently on his bed, enjoying the insight into life that his outlandish position was giving him. He felt that at last he was beginning to grapple with his problem, was getting near its meaning.

The next morning near ten o'clock Cross was roused from sleep by the solicitously soft voice of Mrs. Crawford calling to him through the partly opened door.

"Good morning. Wouldn't you like a hot cup of coffee?" she asked, smiling shyly.

"I'd love some, Mrs. Crawford. Would you mind if I came out in my bathrobe?" he asked her.

"Come right along. Make yourself at home here, son," she said. "I've no dining room; you'll have to take it in the kitchen."

"That's all right with me," he told her.

He liked her and felt secure; she was homey. Unlike Hattie Turner, her concerns were simple. He slipped into his bathrobe and lumbered into a spotless, tiny kitchen.

"Hope I didn't wake you up too early," Mrs. Crawford mumbled.

"Not at all. I should have been up hours ago," Cross said, sipping black coffee and wondering about how to find a graveyard.

"That weather outdoors beats everything!" Mrs. Crawford exclaimed.

Through the fogged windowpane Cross could see a world of churning bits of snow and could hear the wind whimpering like a thing in agony as it tore past the corner of the building.

"Looks like we're in for it," Cross commented.

"A body needs something hot in the stomach first thing

147

in the morning, especially on days like this." Mrs. Crawford proceeded to give her views on life.

She was skinny, brittle, fragile in her bone structure; her
eyes were sunken, cloudy, weak.

"There's nothing better than a good cup of hot coffee,"
he agreed, feeling that this woman was lucky to have such
elementary preoccupations.

"Planning to stay in Harlem long?"

"I don't know yet," he answered honestly.

"Where're you from, if you don't mind my asking?"

"Not at all; I'm from Maine," he lied, naming the first
state that popped into his mind.

"Maine? Well, what do you know about that! Are many
colored people up there?"

"Plenty," he continued lying, beginning to relish it.

"I didn't know that." Mrs. Crawford sighed over a world
much too big and complex for her. "Well, you're young
and you keep on the go," she philosophized. "Me, I'm old
and I'm not long for this life. I just pray and keep my
house straight and wait for the Good Lord to call me
home." Her voice was charged with courageous resig-
nation.

"Oh, no! You'll be around for a long time yet." Cross
spoke with make-believe sincerity. She looked as if she
would die in two weeks. Malnutrition, maybe, he said to
himself.

"The only thing I worry about is keeping up my insurance payments," the old woman went on, as though talking
to herself. "I'll have just enough money to lay me away
decently. I don't want a pack of strangers toting this old
body of mine off to some potter's field. If I thought something like that would happen to me, why, I wouldn't be
able to sleep at night. Before my poor husband died he
bought us a little plot out in the Woodvale Cemetery.
That's where my blessed husband's sleeping now. I'll be
joining him soon, please God."

Cross's interest heightened.

"Is Woodvale a nice cemetery?" he asked casually.

"It's *beautiful*," the old woman cried enthusiastically.
"I'm so happy I'll be sleeping there till God calls me to rise
from the dead." She paused and looked quizzically at
148

Cross. "But son, you're young. How come you interested in cemeteries?"

"I was thinking about taking out some insurance," Cross explained. "I'm alone too and I've got to look out for myself. I may as well buy a plot somewhere. . . ."

"You're wise," Mrs. Crawford approved. "Ain't too many young folks these days serious enough to worry about important things like that. . . ." Her dim eyes shone. "Just a minute—I want to show you something." She rose and hobbled hurriedly out of the kitchen.

Poor woman, Cross thought. Mrs. Crawford returned with a huge bundle wrapped in thick brown paper. She placed it upon the kitchen floor and commenced to unwrap it. Cross saw a pile of filmy summer clothing, each piece of which was delicately folded in white tissue paper.

"This is what I'm going to wear," Mrs. Crawford said, looking at him appealingly. "Don't you think it's nice?"

"Yes; it's nice," Cross said, puzzled. "But where're you going to wear it?"

"When I pass to the other shore to meet Jesus, this is what they're going to dress me in," Mrs. Crawford told him sweetly.

Cross quickly bent forward and fingered the aged material. There was a pearl-handled fan made of large, colored feathers; there was a faded silk, cream-colored parasol; there was a long, tea-colored ruffled voile dress which had huge pleats and a décolleté neckline; and there was a pair of fragile, high-heeled slippers. Cross noticed that she had even included a pair of nicely starched drawers and a pair of nylon stockings from which the price tags had not been removed. Christ Almighty! The woman was acting as though she was preparing to go to a cocktail party. He opened his mouth to tell her that her burial wardrobe was for summer and not this raging blizzard outdoors, but thought better of it. Yes, each time he thought that he was mad, he met someone else with a head full of sane, socially acceptable madness.

"Where is Woodvale?" he asked gently, sighing.

"Out near White Plains—"

"Is it a colored cemetery?" he asked.

"*Strictly* colored," Mrs. Crawford assured him. "And

149

only the best colored folks are buried there. You'd be surprised at how well they keep those graves. Why, in the summertime, it's like a garden. I was lucky to get my plot when I did, for the prices have gone up something awful."

"You're right," Cross said, thinking that he would go out to White Plains at once. "Thanks for the coffee, Mrs. Crawford."

" 'Twasn't nothing, young man," she told him.

Half an hour later Cross was hurrying toward the subway through the blizzard. He was grateful for the lack of visibility, for that would obscure him when he was pillaging the tombstones of the graveyard for names and dates.

Arriving at White Plains, he inquired his way to the Woodvale Cemetery. He had to take a long bus ride and then tramp almost a mile through deep snowdrifts. At last the cemetery came into view, veiled by snowflakes dancing crazily in the winter wind. Myriads of white marble crosses and tombstones stretched away in a white shroud. The huge, iron gate was locked; no one was about. He climbed over the fence and stood in the white silence, a feeling of unreality filling him. He went to the nearest grave and peered at the inscription on the headstone: MARY HAWKINS. The hell with her . . . He searched farther and read: MAYBELLA SMITH. Shucks . . . Even people with the name of Smith have to die. . . . He looked at yet another which said: BESSIE ROUNDTREE. Hell were only women buried here? He walked a good way into the cemetery, looking over his shoulder to make certain that he was not being observed. He approached another batch of graves, bent and wiped snowflakes from a slab of marble with his hand and read: JAMES HOLIDAY—1934—1948. Hunh. . . . Cross was thoughtful. Only fourteen years old, just a kid . . . He looked farther, reading: NEIL BROWN—1870 —1950. That old bugger had a long span. . . .

It was harder to find a good birth date and a name than he thought. Snow was heaping up on the crown of his hat and his feet ached with cold. He stood breathing gusts of vapor into the snowflakes that flitted about his face and clogged his eyelids. Dammit, he couldn't give up now. But an hour later he had not found what he wanted; he had seen graves containing young girls, old men, babies, middle-aged women, the twin graves of husband and wife, of brother and sister, all kinds of graves, white and eternally silent in the shuddering snow. But all these dead seemed to have been born either too early or too late for him to use their abandoned names. . . . Hell, there *must* be some young men here my age, he told himself bitterly, his teeth chattering, his body shivering in an icy gale. Finally, when he discovered that he was examining the same graves twice, he saw a plain, obscure grave he had somehow overlooked, whose cheap, wooden board at the head of the mound read: LIONEL LANE—1924, June 29th— 1950, March 3rd. . . Ah, this was something like it. The guy had been buried only two days ago. . . . He scraped the clinging snowflakes from the headboard and read the rest of the inscription:

Sleeping secure in the Faith of the Second Coming
of Our Lord and Savior, Jesus Christ, Amen.

Awkwardly, Cross copied down the name and the date; he hesitated at the expression of sentiment regarding Jesus' second coming; but, what the hell, take it all down; it couldn't do any harm. Had this guy been widely known? Would it be wise for him to go to the Bureau of Vital Statistics and ask for a birth certificate in the name of Lionel Lane? What proofs of identity would the clerks ask him for? He would have to invent a good pretext. . . . Well, he would try it. What could he lose? After all, the identity he was seeking didn't have to be foolproof; he wanted a mask of normality just airtight enough to enable him to start living again without too much fear. He would create his own past if he could find a respite of but a few weeks.

But if he wanted to assume Lionel Lane's name, shouldn't he try to learn something about him? Where he had worked? How he had lived? Did he have a family? His ardor ebbed somewhat when he realized that he hadn't the remotest idea of how to find out about the name. But there must be a caretaker somewhere around who could tell him if Lane had belonged to a church, or the name of the funeral home from which he had been buried. . . . He looked about in the sea of frightened snowflakes, full again of that old sense of dread. But there's nothing to be scared of. Find the caretaker and tell him that Lionel Lane had been an old pal of his, that he had just come from the army and had learned that poor Lionel was dead, and that he was searching for Lionel's folks. . . .

Cross struggled through the snowdrifts back to the huge, iron gate and peered about for signs of life, a house. . . . Nothing but silence and scudding swirls of whiteness. He was about to leave when he noticed on the gate a square, wooden plaque whose face was obscured by a thick layer of snow crystals. He cleaned the flakes away with his coat sleeve and read: Address all inquiries to Mr. Sloane, 6 Pine Road, White Plains. . . .

More frozen than alive, he dragged himself out of the cemetery and tramped back to the street. When the bus rolled silently toward him he stumbled on board and had difficulty getting his money out of his pocket, his fingers were so frozen.

At the office of the Woodvale Cemetery in White Plains, Cross found a colored girl of about eighteen years chewing gum behind a typewriter. In reply to his plea about the relatives of his "long-lost pal," Lionel Lane, the girl said: "You'd better come back this afternoon at four when Mr. Sloane's in, because I'm not allowed to give out information like that to anybody—"

"What harm could that do?" Cross asked. "My friend's dead now. Come on, have a heart." Cross aped nostalgic distress. "I want to see his mother—"

"Why don't you try his pastor at his church?" the girl suggested.

"I don't know his church or his pastor—"

"And you say you were an old, dear friend of his, huh?" the girl asked him in a light, taunting voice.

"But I never asked him about his religion—"

"He lived in Harlem," the girl said. "But that's all I can tell you. I'm sorry, but you'll have to see Mr. Sloane. . . ." The girl resumed her gum chewing and turned back to her typewriter.

He decided not to press her further; he thanked her and left. He didn't want that girl to recall that a young man had been demanding details about Lionel Lane. . . . Dammit, he had failed in his first try. But perhaps he could phone the office later in the afternoon and pretend that he was. . . . Who could he pretend to be? He stood musing in the street amid the circling columns of snow, then he looked again at the scrap of paper on which he had written the data from the wooden headboard of Lionel Lane's grave, rereading the words: "Sleeping in the Faith of the Second Coming of Our Lord and Savior, Jesus Christ, Amen." Where and when had he heard words like those before? They reminded him of something. *Yes!* Of course. That inscription expressed the cardinal article of faith of the Seventh Day Adventist Church! He had, in his childhood in the Deep South, met and known Adventists. True, it was a guess, but not at all a bad one. His task, now, was to find the Seventh Day Adventist Church from which Lane had been buried. The girl had said that Lane had lived in Harlem, and it would be safe to assume that the church was there. . . .

During the subway ride to Harlem, he pondered over the difficulties involved in his quest. As the excitement wore off he realized that he was attempting a long-shot gamble. For instance, he did not know if Lionel Lane had been born in the state of New York or not. Suppose it turned out that Lionel Lane had been born in, say, Ohio? What could he do then?

At 110th Street he got out of the subway, went into a drugstore and consulted a telephone directory. There were three addresses of Seventh Day Adventist organizations in Harlem. One was on West 135th Street and another was on West 123rd Street; and there was still another organization called the Seventh Day Adventist Conference on West 150th Street. . . . Yes, he'd call the Conference. He dialed and heard a suave, masculine voice answering: "Hello."

"This is the Eastern Insurance Company," Cross lied smoothly. "I wonder if you'd be kind enough to give us some information, please?"

"Yes. What is it?"

"We are searching for the address of a man's family; the man, we believe, was buried from one of your Harlem

153

churches about two or three days ago. The name is Lane, Lionel Lane. Could you tell us where his parents are living? Or do you know the last address of the deceased?"

"Just a moment, please."

Cross waited, looking uneasily over his shoulder at people shopping at the counter of the drugstore.

"We have no direct information here, sir. But I understand that there was a funeral three days ago at our Ephesus Church at 101 West 123rd Street. Why don't you get in touch with Elder Wiggins there?"

"Thank you," Cross said.

He dialed Elder Wiggins and, still impersonating an insurance official, asked for the whereabouts of the Lane family.

"Oh, yes," the gentle, tired voice of a man answered. "We held services for the departed at our church last Thursday. But I cannot help you very much, sir. My secretary's not here for the moment. But I know that the Lane family lives in Newark, New Jersey. The departed lived here in Harlem, I'm fairly certain. You see, the departed was not himself a member of our church. His mother, Mrs. Mary Lane, is one of our oldest members and, though she lives in Newark, she wanted her son buried from our church. If you'd care to phone later today. . . ."

"It won't be necessary," Cross said. "Our Newark office will be able to locate the family. I thank you very much."

So Lionel Lane had parents in New Jersey. Well, he'd go there right now. Twenty minutes later Cross was in Pennsylvania Station, hunched over a Newark telephone directory, feverishly thumbing the thin, crisp leaves, searching under L's. Good Lord, there was a long list of Lanes: there was an Albert Lane, a Bernard Lane, a Daniel Lane, a Harry Lane . . . and then there came Mary Lane . . . . This undoubtedly was Lionel Lane's mother. He jotted down the address and an hour later he was in Newark, inquiring for the street on which the Lanes lived. He was so excited that he had to calm himself when he learned that the street was located in the heart of the local Black Belt: on Broome Street in the Hill District. *This* was it!

When he reached the bleak slum neighborhood, he slowed and mapped out his plan of attack. Presuming that

154

he was on the track of the right family, to go to the Lane house directly and ask questions carried a risk. If, when using the name of Lionel Lane, something happened to him and that name got in the newspapers, someone might recall that a stranger had been around asking vague questions. It would be better if he posed as a social worker or a salesman of some sort and in that way pick up bits of information from neighbors or shopkeepers. What kind of a family were the Lanes? Working class or professional? If they turned out to be a family of prominent citizens, then it would be almost impossible to go to the Bureau of Vital Statistics in a city like this and impersonate Lionel Lane and demand a birth certificate without getting into serious trouble. He first had to get hold of some basic facts.

The Lane house proved to be a ramshackle, wooden affair, sitting unpainted on a run-down, dirty, treeless street. If Lionel Lane came out of this hellhole, then not many people of any consequence could have known him. But was this the house of the family of Lanes whose son was buried in Woodvale?

At that moment he saw an elderly Negro postman bent under the weight of a mailbag coming toward him over the snowy street.

"Say," Cross stopped him, "have you got a minute? Maybe you can help me?"·

The postman paused, spat a stream of tobacco juice into a snowdrift, eyed Cross cynically, and mumbled: "That depends on what kind of help you want. I'm on my rounds."

"I'm from the Central Credit Bureau of New York City," Cross lied. "I'm trying to track down a young chap by the name of Lionel Lane."

"Lionel Lane?" the postman echoed, smiling ironically. "He owed money somewhere?"

"Confidentially, yes."

"Well, the people who let him have money didn't have good sense," the postman observed, spitting another spout of tobacco juice. "And you got a fat chance of collecting, 'cause that baby's where you can't get at 'im. He's six feet deep with snow in his face. He kicked off four or five days ago. Had consumption—"

"Did he live with his family?"

"When he didn't have any dough, he did; and that was almost all the time. He holed up somewhere in Harlem, with a dame. Didn't want his family to know where he was when he was with that dame. Had to forward all his mail there. . . ."

"What kind of a family has he got? Do you know 'em?"

"Ain't but one person in that outfit that you could call human, and that's the mother. . . . She's solid, religious. But the rest of 'em—I've seen 'em, but I don't know 'em and don't want to know 'em. Boy, if you're thinking of giving the Lanes any more credit, then just don't."

"What kind of work did Lionel Lane do?"

"Work?" the postman mocked Cross, chuckling. "He used to work in a laundry, but for the past two years he used all his energy pulling at the neck of a bottle—"

"Thanks, buddy," Cross said.

He felt he had a chance. He went into a bar, The Fat Man, and over a whisky schemed out his next move. How soon was a death reported to the clerks in the Bureau of Vital Statistics? Lionel Lane had died in Harlem and it was safe to assume that the Newark officials did not yet know that he was dead. When he approached the clerks about a birth certificate, there must not be in their minds any doubt whatsoever that he was Lionel Lane. One blunder and the whole structure he was so carefully building would tumble. How was he to handle it? He thought hard, calling up everything he knew about white and black race relations to help him. If he could ever act the role of a subservient Negro convincingly, this was the time to do it. He would have to present to the officials a Negro so scared and ignorant that no white American would ever dream that he was up to anything deceptive. But why would any black wastrel be wanting a birth certificate? Cross knew that the authorities were chronically watchful these days about handing out birth certificates, for spies were using such documents to establish their claim to having been born in the United States. In the end Cross decided that a simple, an almost silly reason was the best reason that an ignorant Negro could have for demanding a birth certificate; it would have to be a reason that whites, long

156

schooled in dealing with Negroes as frightened inferiors, would accept without question.

He went to the City Hall and presented himself at the window marked DUPLICATE BIRTH CERTIFICATES. Looking apprehensively about, he took his place in line. When his turn came to face the young white clerk, he said in a plaintive, querulous tone: "He told me to come up here and get the paper."

The clerk blinked and looked annoyed. *"What?"*

"The paper, Mister. My boss told me to come and get it."

"What kind of paper are you talking about, boy?"

"The one that say I was born," Cross told him as though he, in his ignorance, had to teach this white man what to do.

The clerk smiled, then laughed: "Maybe you weren't born, boy. Are you *sure* you were?"

Cross batted his eyes stupidly. He saw that he was making this poorly paid clerk happy; his pretense of dumbness made the clerk feel superior, white.

"Well, they *say* I was born. If I wasn't born, I can't keep my job. That's why my boss told me to come here and get the paper." Cross let a tiny edge of indignation creep into his voice.

The clerk regarded him with benevolent amusement and turned and yelled behind him: "Say, Jack! Come here and get a load of this, will you?"

Another clerk, somewhat older, came forward and asked: "What's up?"

"This coon clown says he was born somewhere," the young clerk said.

"I *don't* believe it," the older clerk said.

"Oh, yes, sir. I *was* born," Cross said, his lips hanging open, his eyes wide with desperation.

"Can you prove it?" the first clerk said.

"Now, look here, Mister. I ain't done nothing to nobody, 'specially to no white folks," Cross wailed in deep distress.

"The worst thing you ever did was to be born," the older clerk said.

157

"But I ain't done nothing wrong, Mister," Cross protested.

"You're always wrong," the young clerk said. "Say, Jack, what in hell do we do with 'im?"

The older clerk pulled down his mouth and muttered: "Hell, go ahead and give 'im a certificate if he *was* born around here. These clowns don't mean any harm."

"If I can't say I was born, I'll lose my job," Cross complained.

"Where do you work?" the young clerk asked.

"Machine Tools Company, in Brooklyn."

"What's the address?"

"I don't know the number, not exactly, Mister. But you take the Fulton Street bus and ride—"

"Can that," the older clerk said. "You were born in Newark, you are sure of that?"

"Yes, sir."

"Wait, Jack. He ought to know something about his job," the young clerk said. "Say, boy, what's your boss's name?"

Cross stared in blank amazement, then he shook his head as though trying to avoid the worst trap of a black man's life.

"Mister, I don't ask white folks their personal business," he told them.

The clerks shouted their laughter.

"Where were you born in Newark?" the young clerk asked.

Cross blinked again, then looked up brightly, as though his memory had returned, and said: "In the Third Ward." He pointed elaborately in the direction.

"Whereabouts in the Third Ward?"

"Over the hill— Why, Mister, everybody knows where that is."

The two clerks howled with laughter. The young clerk asked: "What street were you born on 'over the hill,' as you call it? And on what date were you born? And what's your name? You got a name, I suppose?"

"Yes, sir. They gave me a name," he said, falling silent.

"Well, what in hell is it?"

"But you know," Cross said, amazement showing on his face. "They say you got all the names here."

The two clerks bent double with mirth. And as he stood there manipulating their responses, Cross knew exactly what kind of man he would pretend to be to kill suspicion if he ever got into trouble. In his role of an ignorant, frightened Negro, each white man—except those few who were free from the race bias of their group—would leap to supply him with a background and an identity; each white man would project out on him his own conception of the Negro and he could safely hide behind it.

"All right, boy," the young clerk agreed. "We'll give you your certificate if we can find your record. But we've got to have your name and the year of your birth. We're pretty smart here, I admit. But we're not so smart that we can guess your name."

"They call me Lionel Lane," Cross admitted at last.

"In what year were you born?"

"My mama told me it was in 1924; the twenty-ninth of June."

"Give us a dollar and we'll mail you a duplicate certificate," the young clerk said.

"But my boss told me to bring it in the morning, or I ain't got no job," Cross complained.

"Okay. Sit down over there on that bench. We'll see what we can do. We'll look it up," the older clerk said resignedly.

Two hours later Cross had the duplicate birth certificate of Lionel Lane and had left in the minds of the clerks a picture of a Negro whom the nation loved and of whom the clerks would speak in the future with contemptuous affection. Maybe some day I could rule this nation with means like this, Cross mused as he rode back to New York. All you have to do is give the people what they want. . . . He knew that deep in their hearts those two white clerks knew that no human being on earth was as dense as he had made himself out to be, but they wanted, needed to believe it of Negroes and it helped them to feel racially superior. They were pretending, just as he had been pretending. But maybe men sometimes pretended for much bigger and graver stakes?

Cross was now as solidly identified as he felt he could be for the time being, and the first desire that sprang into his mind was to try to redress, to some extent, the unintentional wrong he had done to that waiter, Bob Hunter, whom he had met in the dining car more than two weeks ago. He fished in his pocket for the address, made his way to Harlem, and found the grim tenement where Hunter lived. Climbing six flights of rickety stairs, he squinted in shadows from doorway to doorway until he came to a white card whose printed legend read: MR. & MRS. ROBERT HUNTER.

He pushed the bell and a moment later he was staring into Bob Hunter's brown and nervous face. The man was in his shirt sleeves and held a pamphlet with a yellow and red back in his left hand.

"Remember me?" Cross asked.

"Man, where in hell have you been?" Bob exclaimed, his face breaking in a broad grin. "I've been looking for you everywhere! Come in."

Cross walked into a large, clean, rather bare apartment and Bob led him into the living room.

"You *are* Mr. Jordan, ain't you?" Bob asked to make sure.

"How are you, Bob?" Cross asked, ignoring the question.

"Sit down, man," Bob said. "I ain't complaining, though I got a lot I *could* complain about." Bob's eyes were fixed intently upon Cross's face and the lips held a nervous smile.

Cross felt that he could not deceive the man any longer.

"Bob, I suppose you wondered about me, hunh?" Cross asked.

"Well, I sure needed you, man. . . . I went to that address you gave me, but it was a funeral parlor and nobody knew you there. Is your name really Jordan?" Bob asked in an appealing yet venturesome tone of voice.

Cross placed his right hand reassuringly upon Bob's shoulder. "Take it easy, Bob. I'll explain everything. Say,

160

how did you make out in that little trouble you had on the train?"

"Hunh? What trouble?" Bob asked.

Cross knew that Bob was pretending that he had not understood. He's trying to save face. . . .

"Did that woman on the train make any trouble for you?" Cross asked.

Bob shrugged his shoulders and laughed, but there was no mirth in his voice. "*Trouble?* Hell, man, I got *fired!* I lost my goddamn job, that's all." Bob's eyes were evasive but he could not hide that he felt that Cross had betrayed him unpardonably. "I ain't blaming you none, man. After all, you did jump up and stop that bitch from hitting me with that water pitcher, didn't you? And if you gave me a bum steer 'bout your name and address— Well, you know your own business."

"But didn't the union help you?" Cross asked.

"Man, I'm too goddamn militant for my union," Bob explained. "I had a hell of a fight with 'em. My union's got a left wing and a right wing. I'm with the left. When the company brought me up on charges, the rightists piled in on me, and I was out. Man, only *you,* an eyewitness, could have saved me. How come you fooled me like that? You could've said you didn't want to help me— Maybe I could've found some other witnesses. But I didn't look for any till it was too late. I was counting on you. . . ."

Bob related how the white woman had sued the railroad, how the railroad had charged him with carelessness, how the leftists in the union had tried to defend him, and how, in the end, because he could not get a single witness to establish independent corroboration of his version of the accident, he had lost.

"But what about that priest?" Cross asked.

"I went to see 'im," Bob said. "Told me he didn't want to get mixed up in it. Said his job was saving souls and stuff like that. Then he went off to Rome to see the Pope—"

"I'm sorry, Bob."

"Hell, man, it's nothing," Bob said defiantly. "Me and Sarah's making out."

"Are you working now? I can let you have a loan—"

"Man," Bob's face spread in a wide, glad grin, "I'm working for the biggest outfit in the world!"

"What's that?"

"The Party, man."

"What party?"

"Hell, man! There ain't but *one* Party and that's the Communist Party," Bob explained proudly.

"What are you doing for them?"

"Organizing! What the hell do you think?"

"Do you like it?"

"I'm crazy about it," Bob confessed with a smile. "I'm going to be a professional revolutionary, working twenty-four hours a day beating these rich white bastards. It makes me feel *good!*"

Bob went into the kitchen and brought out two bottles of cold beer and, opening them, set them on the table.

"Listen, Bob," Cross began, "I don't trust many people in this world—"

"I know *that!*" Bob agreed. "You lied to me on that train so smooth that I would have died trusting your word. Man, you can *lie!*" Bob's howl of laughter was so infectious that Cross was forced to join in.

"Bob, I'm going to trust you as far as I dare—"

"Man, I'm black like you and you can trust me till death. Race means a lot to me. I love and trust my own," Bob swore his fidelity.

"My name's not Addison Jordan," Cross said.

"Hell, I found *that* out," Bob said, exploding with laughter. "But what is it? You don't have to tell me unless you want to."

"Lionel Lane," Cross said.

Bob looked at Cross with skeptical eyes and grinned, a light of admiration showing in his face. "You telling me the truth now?"

"Well," Cross hedged, feeling that it was impossible really to fool the man now, "I'm Lionel Lane for the moment." Cross could not help laughing at himself. "But it's the name I'm giving to everybody from now on."

"You did something to the white folks and they're looking for you, hunh?"

Cross looked away, chagrined. His life had become a

vast system of pretense; one act of bad faith necessitated another, and in order to prove the sincerity of a new lie he had to fall back upon lying still further. Bob was asking him if he had committed some act of racial heroism against whites, and the only people he had wronged thus far had been black.

"Something like that, Bob," he said vaguely with an embarrassed mumble.

"Brother!" Bob exclaimed, seizing hold of Cross's hand and pumping it vigorously in fraternal friendship. "I'm with you till the curtain comes down."

Cross's teeth felt on edge, but he managed to say: "I feel I made you lose your job. I want to help you—"

"Just be my friend, man; that's all the help I want." Bob's voice rang with hope, his words pouring out in a gush of forgiving generosity. "Now, *I'll* tell you something, see? I ain't no American. I'm British, see? But I'm black, like you. . . . I came to this goddamn country from Trinidad ten years ago. . . . Had to run off; was an organizer and they were after me. . . . So I got to be careful too."

"Your secret's safe with me," Cross told him; he now understood why Bob's accent had seemed strange to him on the train.

"Now, tell me what you did," Bob asked.

"You'll just have to trust me. I can't tell you. . . ."

"You ain't no *spy?*"

"If I was, do you think I'd tell you?"

They laughed. Bob was overcome with wonder. Cross's secret loomed in his mind more important and intriguing than any concrete crime.

"You were Mr. Jordan on the train, and now you're Mr. Lane," Bob mused, laughing. "That's all right with me." His eyes narrowed and he stared silently for a moment in deep thought. "Man, the Party could *use* you—"

"Really? Why do you say that?"

"You can be so *many* things at once—"

"Maybe I'm *too* many things," Cross said quickly.

"Lionel," Bob said, his mind working fast, "I'm sorry my wife, Sarah, ain't here to meet you. You'll like her, man. She's down to earth and takes nothing off nobody; she's militant. . . . Say, we're having some folks over to a

163

late dinner tonight. Why don't you come over about nine-thirty and eat with us?"

Cross knew that Bob was trying to recruit him. He had no desire to join the Communist Party, but he knew that he would feel somewhat at home with Communists, for they, like he, were outsiders. Maybe communism would be the best temporary camouflage behind which he could hide from the law. And his secret past would make Communists think that he was anxious for their help. To be with them was not at all a bad way of ending his isolation and loneliness. . . .

"Who's going to be there?"

Bob's face beamed with a look akin to worship.

"Man, you talk just *like* the Party folks! I *declare* you do!" Bob laughed uproariously, delighted and amused.

"Why do you say that?"

"You're so *suspicious*— You don't want to take a step without knowing *where* you're going. . . ." Bob sobered. "They're Party folks who's coming."

"Who are they?"

"Man, you're sure careful," Bob commended him. "There's gonna be Gil and Eva Blount, friends of mine. Gil's a member of the Central Committee of the Communist Party. A damn nice guy. Man, he's sharp, cold as ice. You'll like him; he's a lot like you— And there's gonna be my goddamn organizer, Jack Hilton. Then there's me and Sarah, that's all. And you, if you'll come."

"It's a deal," Cross said, his eyes deep and thoughtful.

Cross said good-by, descended into the streets, entered a bar and sat brooding over Bob's believing mind. He found himself amused and a little intrigued at the prospect of meeting some Communists tonight. In all his attempts to find some disguise for his outlaw existence, he had never seriously considered communism. But why not? Did not the Communists, like him, have a secret to hide? And what was the Communist secret? Cross felt that at the heart of all political movements the concept of the basic inequality of man was enthroned and practiced, and the skill of politicians consisted in how cleverly they hid this elementary truth and gained votes by pretending the contrary. If, by pretending, he could find a hiding place, why, he would

164

pretend that he believed in the Communist pretensions. Why not? They are deceivers and so am I. That ought to be fair enough, he thought as he took a long gulp of beer.

But the Communists were shrewd; they'd hardly be taken in by his birth certificate; he would have to buttress his pretensions of being Lionel Lane by some other document. What? Of course. Lionel Lane's draft card. . . . The postman had said that Lane had died of consumption, so it was highly likely that Lane had been classified in the draft as unfit for military duty. . . .

He paid for his beer and went out into the falling snow. There was a black cop standing at the corner and he accosted him, telling him that he had been six months in Arizona for his health, that he had lost his draft card, and that he had forgotten the address of his draft board. . . . He gave the cop Lionel Lane's address and in turn the cop directed him to the draft board which was located in the basement of a church.

Cross was feeling better by the minute. When he found the church, which was on West 134th Street, he saw a throng of young men loitering about the entrance. No; he wouldn't go in now; he'd wait until nearly closing time. He mingled with the boys and learned that the draft board did not close until nine o'clock that night. It was now a little after seven. He spent the hour and a half in a nearby movie and at ten minutes to nine approached the church, entered the basement and saw that a young Negro clerk was in charge; there were three or four other young men hanging about. When the clerk came to him, Cross recited his prepared lie:

"Look, I'm listed as unfit for military duty with this board. I've been in Arizona for the past six months for my health and I'm sailing for France in the morning; I'm on my way to Switzerland. . . . But I've lost my card. I've got to get a duplicate, or I won't be allowed aboard the ship—"

"What's your name?"

"The name's Lionel Lane."

The clerk left. Cross was nervous. If Lane's death had already been reported, why, he'd simply bolt for it. . . . The clerk returned with a folder.

"We've got your record here," the clerk began. "But how do I know you're Lionel Lane?"

"Here's my birth certificate," Cross said, presenting the duplicate he had gotten in Newark.

"Look," the clerk said, examining the certificate, "I'll fix up a duplicate card for you and I'll have the chairman sign it, but the secretary of the board is the man who gives the final okay and he's not here. You'll have to come back in the morning—"

"But I'm sailing in the morning. I've got my ticket. I'm packed to go—"

"Gosh," the clerk said. "This stumps me—"

"But I got to have that card," Cross insisted.

"But I don't have the authority to give it to you—"

"You're looking at my birth certificate," Cross pointed out.

"Look, anybody can have a birth certificate," the clerk said. "We do things here by routine. The chairman'll sign your card tonight. But the secretary's not in; he won't be in till tomorrow morning—"

"Okay," Cross assented to the fairness of the clerk's statement. "But, look, if I was trying to dodge the draft, do you think I'd come here and ask for a duplicate?"

"I guess not," the clerk grinned. "Say, what time do you sail?"

"I've got to be at the boat at ten—"

"Okay. I'll get the card ready, have the chairman sign it. You be here at nine sharp in the morning and the secretary'll give it to you."

"Is that all you can do?"

"That's all, buddy."

"Okay. Thanks."

The clerk turned to another young man and Cross walked into the corridor. When the office closed tonight, his draft card would be signed and on the desk of the chairman of the board. How could he get that card? If he waited till morning, the secretary might raise questions and cause trouble. He walked along the corridor, thinking frantically. He looked around; the lights in the inner offices had been turned off. He glanced over his shoulder and saw that the clerk was busy, bent over the files. Cross walked

166

quickly to his left, not knowing where he was going. Could he hide in the office? No, that was too dangerous. . . . How in God's name could he get back here tonight, after everyone had gone? He had it, yes; he'd open a latch on one of the windows near the ground. . . . He advanced slowly and softly into the dark, his hand outstretched to prevent his colliding with unseen objects. He flicked on his lighter and shielded the flame with his hand. Yeah; there was a window. . . . But could he reach it easily from the outside? He doused the light, pushed the latch on the window and lifted it slowly. Peering out, he could see that the window gave onto a fetid areaway. This was no good. . . .

Footsteps in the corridor made him freeze; through the open doorway he saw that a light had been clicked on in the office next to him. He waited. Maybe he could hide in a clothes closet? The light went out and he heard footsteps retreating. The clerk had gone into that office for something and had returned to the front. . . .

He crept into another office and at once saw the dim reflection of a street lamp. This was it. . . . He unlatched the window and slid it up noiselessly. Fumbling in the dark, he took out his address book and tore off a page and inserted it beneath the sill, then stood debating. Maybe he ought to leave by this window? Naw; it was too risky. He closed the window; the piece of paper would help him to identify the window from the outside.

Re-entering the corridor, he walked out boldly. Outside, he ambled along in the drifting snow, scanning the street in both directions. There were not many passers-by, but he saw lights shining through the stained-glass windows of the church on the first floor. If a service was about to begin, all the better; it would mean that no one would be prying around in the basement. He walked on till he spied the bit of paper jutting from the window sill. Lights still blazed in the draft office. Sheltering himself in a doorway, he waited.

Ten minutes later the lights in the draft office winked out, one by one; finally, the clerk, flanked by two other men, emerged. Was it safe to enter now? Yes; he'd try it. He stood beneath the fluttering piece of paper and lingered

167

till the street was empty; then, in one quick movement, he hoisted the window, climbed into the office and dropped to the floor amid a shower of heaped-up snow from the sill. He closed the window, pushed the lever of his lighter and peered about. The office was deserted. He went into the corridor and looked into all the rooms. . . . Now, where was the desk of that draft board chairman? He approached a big, shiny desk that had a swivel chair and saw a neat pile of manila folders.. He grabbed them, thumbed quickly through them. Yeah; goddammit, *here it was!* He detached his draft card; it was signed. He then read the items describing the physical appearance of Lionel Lane and grew thoughtful. Lionel Lane had weighed 158 pounds and he weighed only 148. . . . Well, he could always say that he had lost ten pounds, couldn't he? That's what tuberculosis did to you, didn't it . . . ? But this other item was more difficult; Lionel Lane was listed as being five feet six inches in height and he was five feet eight. It was a little thing, but it might cause him trouble. . . . Oh, yes; he could fix that. . . . He looked about for a typewriter; he would type an 8 over that 6! He uncovered a machine; holding his lighter in his left hand, he inserted the card, jiggled it until the figure 8 coincided with the 6 and hit the key. There . . . He put the card into his billfold, doubled the folder, stuffed it into his inside coat pocket. Now, get out of here. . . .

He stood, thinking. Soon the death of Lionel Lane would be reported to the board and the personnel would be wondering what had happened to the folder of Lionel Lane. There would be some sort of inquiry. . . . A solution clicked in his mind. Yes, *all* the files should be destroyed. If *his* file alone was missing, questions would be raised; but if *all* the files were missing, then he had a chance. . . . And he noticed that each manila folder was wrapped in cellophane and cellophane burned like hell. . . . He opened a window so that a draft would feed the fire, then bent forward and ignited a folder; he watched the cellophane smoke, curl, leap into flame. He backed away, seeing the flames grow, spread from folder to folder; soon the top of the desk was one blazing, red sheet with thick, acrid smoke. He opened the door and hurried out, then

168

stiffened in his tracks. Good God! His lips parted in stupe-
faction. He heard the surging of a lusty hymn coming from
above! He had forgotten that he was in a church! But there
was no help for that now. . . .

He left the door of the office open so that a current of
air would sweep into the room; then he went down the
dark corridor to a stairway and mounted to the street level.
The singing came loud and sonorous:

> Let the lower lights be burning!
> Send a gleam across the wave!
> Some poor fainting, struggling seaman
> You may rescue, you may save.

He hurried into the street and looked back at the
church, then up to the tall steeple which was faintly visible
in the feathery flakes. He walked on slowly to the end of
the block, wondering when the smoke or the flames would
show. He saw a fire-alarm box and paused. A man passed.
Then a child. He waited until the street was empty, opened
the box, pulled the lever, then walked briskly to a corner
drugstore, entered, perched himself atop a stool where he
could watch the front of the church. He ordered a cup of
coffee, sipped it, waiting.

Suddenly he saw a man hurry from the church; then a
small knot of men came out; soon a throng of people was
pouring from the church door. A moment later he heard
the sound of distant sirens.

"Looks like there's a fire somewhere," the clerk behind
the counter said.

"I see some people running out of the church down the
street," Cross said casually.

The clerk went to the window. "By God, you're right!
Fire's coming out of the basement window of the church!"

He joined the clerk at the window. Yes, the draft office
was blazing. . . .

"How much is this cup of coffee?" he asked.

"Huh?" the clerk grunted.

"How much is this coffee?"

"Ten cents."

Cross left a dime on the counter and walked calmly

169

from the drugstore. He had a dinner engagement to meet some Communists.

A quarter of an hour later Cross climbed six flights and pushed the bell of Bob's flat. Bob himself opened the door and grabbed his arm.

"Man, give me your coat and hat—Sarah's here and raring to meet you," Bob said, guiding Cross straight to the kitchen where Sarah, a brown-skinned woman with a strong, hard face, was cooking dinner. "Sarah, honey! C'mere! I want you to meet Mr. Lane!"

Sarah was bent over a table busily flattening dough with a rolling pin; she glanced up at Cross, then quickly back to her biscuit board.

"Just a sec," she answered placidly.

She was solidly built without being fat, and her soft, pliable muscles seemed as strong as any man's. She had black hair, a well-shaped mouth and a firm chin. Her movements were deft as she cut the thin spread of dough into biscuits and placed them swiftly into tin pans and shoved them into an oven. She wiped her hands on a dish towel, turned and smiled. Then her face grew solemn as she came toward Cross and stared with eyes full of surprise. Cross's muscles grew rigid. Had Sarah seen him before? Maybe he had known her in Chicago? Because she was staring at him, he stared at her. Sarah advanced to within a few inches of Cross and broke into a wide grin.

"What's the matter, Sarah? Can't you say hello?" Bob exclaimed.

Sarah cupped her right palm under Cross's chin, cradling it gently. Then she began to laugh, still holding Cross's face. She said:

"Look at that face—*Lead Kindly Light* . . . And he's meeting some Communists tonight, hunh? Honest to Pete, man, you got the *sweetest* face I ever saw!"

She turned from Cross, laughing even louder. Bob joined in, but more sheepishly than Sarah. Their laughter filled the corridor. Maybe they were getting even with him for his having deceived Bob . . . ?

"Don't be mad, man! You got to get used to Sarah—

170

She just blabs out what pops into her mind, that's all," Bob explained through his laughter.

Cross had had the illusion of feeling at home with these outsiders, but now he felt himself being pushed more than ever into that position where he looked at others as though they weren't human. He could have waved his hand and blotted them from existence with no more regret than if he were swatting a couple of insects. Could he ever make others realize how dangerous it was for them to make him feel like this? He lowered his eyes and stared at them, a tight smile hovering on his lips. He trembled to do something, but he held himself back. He knew that he had the kind of face that would always look much younger than his age, but never in his life had another person grabbed hold of that face with their bare hands and made blatant fun of it. What kind of life had Sarah lived that made it possible for her to laugh at him so openly? Pity for her came into his mind, but he banished it, realizing that it was hard to pity someone who most likely did not want it. She and Bob were still laughing.

"Okay," Cross said finally. "Maybe I look funny to you."

"Naw— You ain't funny!" Sarah spluttered. "You're just out of this world— And you want to be a Bolshevik! Why, child, they'll eat you for dessert!"

Cross sank into a chair and stared at a print of the Moscow subway that hung on the wall. He had conquered his impulse to anger now; he did not respect them enough to be angry. In his eyes their value as human beings had gone; if they existed, all right; if they did not exist, that was all right too. . . .

"Okay. Don't you think I deserve a drink for all that?" he asked them in tones of mild reproof.

"All right, honey," Sarah said at last. "I'm gonna show you my heart's in the right place. I'm gonna give you a *whole* glass of whisky— You had whisky before, ain't you?"

"You'd be surprised," Cross told her.

"Know one thing," Sarah said, pouring whisky into a tumbler. "I'm laughing, but I wonder about you—"

171

"Why?" Cross asked.

"I see now how Bob made a mistake to trust you on that train," Sarah said soberly. "But I wouldn't've trusted you. No, sir! That nice suit you got on, that nylon shirt, that woolen handmade tie—all that don't mean nothing to me. I'd trust that face of yours as far as I could throw an *elephant,* and you know that ain't far! What you reckon the Communists gonna make out of you?"

"I don't know," Cross answered.

He understood now. Sarah and Bob felt that Communists ought to look like Communists; that is, ragged, desperate, with a slightly crazy air. Of course, there were exceptions: white men with cold, sharp minds who sat in dim offices and who ran things, the intellectuals. But Sarah and Bob never expected to see a black intellectual and did not know one when they saw one.

"When did you join the colored race?" Sarah asked, sniggling.

"I never joined," Cross said.

Sarah went off into the kitchen, shaking with laughter. Bob stood near him and kept his right hand on Cross's shoulder. Cross took a long swig from the tumbler; he needed it.

"Don't be mad, man," Bob said. "If we laugh at you, it's 'cause we like you, see?"

"I'm not angry," Cross said in a faraway voice that made Bob sober quickly.

The doorbell rang and Cross was glad. If white guests were arriving, Sarah and Bob would stop baiting him. Bob went to the door.

"Gil and Eva! Come in! I got somebody here I want you to meet," Bob greeted his guests.

A stolid white man and a tall, blonde white girl came in. Cross rose to meet them.

"I'm Gilbert Blount," the man said, extending his hand, holding a fixed smile on his face. The man's eyes were hard, watchful, gray, and bulbous.

"How are you, Mr. Blount?" Cross asked.

"I'm Gil to my friends," Blount said.

"I'm Lionel," Cross lied.

172

"And I'm Eva," the girl said and extended an incredibly soft white hand.

"There's something in here to wet your throats!" Bob called to them to come into the living room.

It was clear that Bob intended to leave them to talk together and Cross sensed that the meeting had been arranged. What had Bob told Gil about him? Had he led Gil to believe that he had done some great stroke of racial retaliation against whites? That would be like Bob. All right, he'd let these Communists look him over and he'd look them over.

But he didn't like Gil; there was about the man, even before he had found more valid reasons for his aversion, a rigidity of bodily pose that irked him. Gil was thin without being wiry, tall without being big, aged without being old, and intellectual without partaking of the processes of thought. He spoke in a manner that seemed to indicate that he had difficulty getting the words out of his mouth. Life to Gil was a stubborn, humorless effort that revealed itself in the stiffness of lips that barely moved as he spoke and a kind of mouthing of his huge teeth when he laughed, which was not often. And back of this was a cold hunger in the man that Cross could not name, a waiting, calculating consciousness whose ends seemed remote.

Gil caught Cross's elbow in a firm grip and said: "Bob told me you were coming here tonight, and I'm glad you came. Whatever your background is, you can feel at home with us."

Cross smiled a smile that he hoped would be interpreted as gratitude. How quickly they work together, Cross thought with wonder. Gil had swallowed the lies he had palmed off on Bob and his reference to his background delighted him. What would Gil think if he really knew? Two strange backgrounds are meeting tonight, Cross told himself. I'm just as complicated as they are. . . .

"I'd like to talk to you," Gil continued, guiding him into the living room. "Let's sit over here."

Yes, they've discussed me and they're losing no time. They feel that my being wanted by the police will make me rest my weary head on their red pillow. . . . A slow tide of confidence and curiosity was seeping into Cross's consciousness.

"Sure. Whatever you like," Cross said, allowing himself to be led to a sofa in the corner of the room. Gil was going to try to recruit him, all right. But this baby doesn't know what he's got hold of tonight, Cross mused ironically.

Gil sat opposite Cross and Eva pulled over a chair and sat beside her husband. Bob came in and poured drinks, handed each of them a glass and left.

"What are you doing now?" Gil asked him bluntly.

Cross smiled and spread out his hands. "Frankly, nothing."

"How do you live?"

"From hand to mouth."

"Where do you live?"

"On 116th Street in a rented room."

"Are you married?"

"Well, I was once—"

"That's all right. We're not prudes or moralists. That's your business. I just wanted to know if you are free—"

"I'm quite free," Cross said readily. He doesn't know how free I really am, Cross mused. If he knew he'd jump out of his skin. . . .

He was not a little shocked at Gil's colossal self-conceit. He acts like a God who is about to create a man. . . . He has no conception of the privacy of other people's lives. . . . He saw Gil's eyes regarding him steadily, coolly, as though Gil was already seeing to what use his life could be put.

"You don't mind my questioning you like this, do you?" Gil asked with a cold smile.

"No. Why should I?" Cross lied with friendly unctuousness.

"We Communists do not admit any subjectivity in human life," Gil said with a slow, even smile, as though proud that he could utter such a horrible statement so lightly.

"I see," Cross said, striving to keep his voice neutral.

He was seething with resentment at Gil's effrontery. Who in hell does he think he is? He had to brace himself to keep from taking issue not only with Gil's statement but

174

with the whole attitude toward life implied in it. Cross felt himself slowly coming awake, feeling the real world about him. Here was a challenge the measure of which might meet his needs. . . . Keep still, he told himself.

"Do you know anything about the revolutionary movement?"

"I know it sketchily in general outline, from 1917 onward—"

"Where did you pick it up?"

"From books, of course. What do you think?" Cross had difficulty keeping irritation out of his voice.

"Accounts written by counter-revolutionary historians, no doubt," Gil pronounced placidly. He brought out his pipe and began to fill it leisurely with an aromatic tobacco.

Cross had come by his account of the Russian Revolution from the pens of Russian Bolsheviks themselves, but he did not bother to correct Gil. He sensed that accuracy was not the point here. Gil was trying to impress him, not with learning, but with an attitude of scorn so deep that argument was futile against it. Instead, he took advantage of Gil's silence to observe Eva, who sat with her shapely nyloned knees close together and regarded him with wide, enigmatic eyes. When his gaze met hers, she smiled and looked off. She seemed tense, yet rigidly contained. She was a fragile girl of about twenty-four; her attitude was so distracted that one could feel that she would never speak frankly what was really on her mind. Despite this, she seemed kind, impulsive. Her eyes were a clear hazel; her nose small and straight; and her mouth, which was only slightly rouged, was almost severe in its sharpness. The over-all aspect of her face, despite the shadow of a smile that flitted over it now and then, was one of tortured, organized concentration. Cross wondered how on earth she had come to be married to a coarse, inhuman character like Blount. Cross now shifted his gaze to Gil and was chagrined to find that Gil had been observing his observation of Eva. Gil smiled tolerantly and Cross found himself boiling with rage. He thinks I've never met a white girl before. . . .

Something decisive was transpiring in him regarding Gil. He knew that Gil did not take his inner life into account and he felt compelled to do the same with Gil. This damn thing's catching, he told himself. You have to descend to their level if you are to deal with them. There's no other way out. . . . But he really liked this; there was an absoluteness about it that appealed to him, excited him. To grapple with Gil would involve a total mobilization of all the resources of his personality, and the conflict would be religious in its intensity.

"What do you think of the position of the Communist Party on the Negro question?" Gil asked him.

"I know nothing concrete about the Communist position on the Negro," Cross replied. "I know that you fight for Negro rights—"

"I'm surprised," Gil said rudely, ignoring what Cross had been about to say. "How can a man of your intelligence afford not to know the most important contribution on the Negro question that has yet been made?"

"Look, Gil," Cross said in spite of himself; he had not met this provocative kind of argument before and he felt a desire to plead extenuating circumstances. "I haven't come across this question in a way that would make me want to go into it that deeply. I'm twenty-six years old and I haven't paid much attention to politics."

"The whole of human life is politics, from the cradle to the grave," Gil said, sweeping Cross's explanation into a heap of dust. "For those who don't know this, so much the worse for them. In England and Germany the ruling classes start training their future rulers when they are mere boys. The Party does the same. That's why Communists have something to say about what happens on this earth. Men are not born masters; they are made into masters. We Communists understand that. And, my friend, it's time that you understood it too. History will not respect you nor forgive you for not knowing it. How can you sit there and be indifferent to the forces that shape and control your destiny? It's your job to find out how this world is run, Lionel. What do you know about dialectical materialism?"

Cross knew the theory, but he answered: "Nothing."

"Too bad for you," Gil said; there was no pity in his voice; he spoke as though a man as ignorant as Cross did not deserve to live.

176

Cross looked at Eva, whose eyes flittered at once from his face. He clenched his teeth to keep down his anger. His feelings were bridling so that he found himself picking nervously at his lips with his fingernails. Goddamn this cool, brash man who, though in a different way, was treating him as Bob and Sarah had. How easily he could kill Gil, with no regret; Gil was making him feel that he was his enemy, not his personal enemy, but his enemy in general and in principle. And at the moment he could think of no words that he could ever muster that would convey to Gil the depth of his rejection of him. Cross recalled that he had once wished to be a rock that could feel nothing; well, he had met a man who had apparently tried to turn himself into one. . . .

Bob came to the open door, poked his head in, grinned, and asked: "Everything's all right?"

"We're doing all right," Gil told Bob.

You conceited sonofabitch, Cross told Gil in his mind.

Gil leaned back and stared at the ceiling, puffing gently at his pipe. Yes, they are definitely trying to recruit me, Cross mused. But I need them, just as much as they need me . . . Then, why not? He could always leave them when he wanted to, couldn't he? And in the meanwhile he would have a chance to establish a new base, a new set of friends. . . . As Cross waited for Gil to speak, he did not let his facial expression betray his acute consciousness of Gil's consciousness; through it all he sat listening with a soft, ambiguous smile. But could he, even for the sake of his own selfish ends, stomach this preposterous Gil?

"You must never be a victim," Eva said, stressing the word "victim."

Cross loved her for saying it so sweetly, but hated her assumption of superiority. Yet, in the end it was the soft light in Eva's eyes that made Cross say at last: "Well, Gil, we're not all lucky enough to be able to keep abreast of events as well as you do."

"I'm not keeping abreast of events," Gil corrected him with imperturbable aloofness. "You learn revolutionary logic by working in the revolutionary movement. Yes, Lionel, you need to stop throwing your life away in individual protests against your exploiters. Pool your strength

177

with your natural allies; get in the revolutionary movement and soak up the lessons of history."

"I'd never try to act before knowing what I was about," Cross told him.

"Look, guy." Gil took his pipe from his mouth and leaned and pointed the stem at him. "I like you, see? I've seen you for about ten minutes and I'm willing to take a chance on you. If I made you a gift, would you accept it?"

Cross smiled and looked at him. These Communists mean business. . . .

"My mother used to tell me: 'When somebody gives you something, take it; when somebody takes something away from you, cry,' " Cross said.

Gil managed a wry smile, as though he did not approve of the folk saying because it hadn't been sanctioned by Karl Marx; but Eva clapped her hands and laughed delightedly.

"I want to send you to the Workers' School," Gil said, "at my own expense. But there's only one catch to my offer. . . ."

"What's that?"

"If I stake you to study, then you'll have to come and live with us."

"Why?" Cross asked, puzzled.

Did this man want him in the same house with a girl as beautiful as Eva? He was crazy. . . .

"For many reasons," Gil explained. "First, I'd like to keep track of your progress. Second, I want you to help me in a fight against racism which I'm going to wage in the building in which I live. Third, I want to demonstrate to a certain man, my landlord, who needs to learn a lot, that a Negro is not afraid to live in his building. My landlord's a Fascist, an open Fascist! I want you to move into my apartment. We've a spare room."

Cross looked at Eva.

"We'd be happy to have you," she said; but she did not smile.

Cross sighed. He had not expected this. Well, why not? This man thinks he is cold; well, I'm just as cold as he is. . . .

178

"I like to gamble sometimes," Cross said, rising. "I'm doing nothing with myself. I'll take you up on this and see where it leads. About the Fascist, lead me to him. I've been accused of many things in my life, but no one has yet said that I was afraid."

Gil rose; he beamed for the first time since he had been in the room and he clapped his hand on Cross's shoulder.

"You're a man in a million! That's the spirit I like to see."

"The freedom of your people ought to be the most precious thing on earth to you," Eva said solemnly.

Hiding his irony with an acquiescent smile, Cross stood to one side and watched them. As if at a signal, Bob and Sarah came into the room; there was no attempt to conceal the fact that all of them had discussed Cross previously and had decided to make the offer that Gil had tendered him. Bob was jubilant, slapping Cross on the back and telling him:

"You ain't got no worries now, boy. The Party'll take care of you. . . . From now on, the Party's going to be your mother and your father."

Sarah whispered to him, grinning and struggling to repress her laughter: "You're something new, something special. You can go far with that face of yours. Nobody'll think you're up to anything."

Why do they have to crow so openly over me? Cross asked himself. Though he had agreed to give Gil's offer a try, he could not avoid feeling cheapened at the way they boasted of how they had been wise enough to know a "good man" when they saw one. I'll show 'em how good I am, Cross told himself.

Sarah turned and looked at the clock on the mantel; then she and Bob looked at each other.

"Where's Jack?" Bob asked.

"My dinner's being ruined," Sarah complained.

"I say let's eat," Bob said defiantly. "He knew what time we were eating."

"Ditto," said Sarah. "I don't like slaving over a hot stove cooking a good meal and letting it get cold. That Jack Hilton's always doing that. Who does he think he is?"

179

"He's held up at a meeting," Gil said.

"Come on, folks," Sarah called, beckoning. "Go into the dining room and sit down."

Cross detected in Bob a feeling of hostility toward the absent Jack Hilton and he wondered about it. He joined the others at the dinner table, but even the deliciousness of Sarah's cooking could not banish his sense of their regarding him as a strange fish that they had hauled up out of the sea. Gil downed his food wordlessly, his attention far away. Eva gossiped with Sarah, and Bob ate lustily, now and again looking proudly at Cross. They were eating dessert when the doorbell rang.

"That's Jack," Sarah said with disgust.

"I'll let 'im in," Bob said, rising and going to the door.

Cross heard Bob greet the new guest: "Hey, Jack! You're late. We're eating dessert."

There was a low rumble of voices in the hallway and then Cross saw a slender white man of about thirty enter the dining room with his overcoat still on. Flakes of melting snow clung to his hat, and a faint haze of vapor, precipitated by the warm air of the apartment, rose from his clothing. His eyes were dark brown, limpid, deep-set, and stared almost unblinkingly. The face was emaciated, the lips thin and hanging slightly open. He had a shock of blond hair and his skin was sallow. Under his arm he carried a roll of papers which were slightly damp from the weather outside, and he held both of his hands, which had no gloves, clasped tightly in front of him, as though his strained nerves had to have something to hold on to for support. Cross had the impression that a slight emotional push would set him off.

No one save Bob had spoken to him and so far he had said nothing to anyone. All waited for him to speak. He glanced at Sarah and said dryly: "I'm sorry I couldn't come in time to eat. But I was detained at the Control Commission."

Sarah forced a smile and mumbled: "That's all right, Jack."

"The Party comes first," Bob agreed.

"Sit down and have a drink, won't you?" Sarah asked him.

180

"I don't want a drink," he said. "I can stay but a minute. In fact, I've come on an important errand, to speak to Bob."

"We can go into the bedroom," Bob suggested.

"No. I can say it right here," Jack Hilton said in hard, cold, precise tones.

He paused and Cross noticed that Hilton's shoes had cracks in them. The man's feet must be frozen. . . .

"Bob Hunter," Jack Hilton began in a tone that sounded as though he was declaiming a prepared speech, "the Party has decided that you must not proceed any further in your attempt to organize any cells in the Dining Car Waiters' Union. The Party does not wish to see that task undertaken at this time. You must forthwith desist from all and any activities in that direction. For further instructions, you will report to your Fraction Cell. Is that clearly understood?"

The man's voice had gradually risen to a high pitch of oratory before he had finished; Cross felt that the importance of the message did not justify such a method of delivery, but he sensed behind the manner an attempt to impose a respect for higher authority.

"But, man," Bob protested, "what are you saying to me? I'm working at it night and day."

"Then stop it!" The words shot from Hilton's mouth.

"But, Jack," Bob yelled, "I already sent out the letters for a meeting—"

"Then send out letters and cancel the meeting!" Hilton said.

"But— Man, you don't know what you're doing! I declared myself to 'em in public as a Party member—"

Hilton took a step closer to Bob, and, taking the papers he had held under his arm, he doubled them in his right fist and slapped them against his leg to underscore each word he spoke.

"Hunter, when will you ever learn to respect a decision of the Party? You don't discuss decisions of the Party. You *obey* them!"

"But what am I gonna do?" Bob wailed. "I want to organize my union like the Party told me."

"The Party has altered its decision!" Hilton stated flatly.

"Jack," Sarah spoke in a low, calm tone of voice, "listen, this is not as easy as you think. Bob has exposed himself as a member of the Party in order to recruit for the Party. Now, if he drops this work, what is he to do? He can't work for the union and he can't work for the company. . . . And now you're telling him he mustn't go on working for the Party—"

"This has *nothing* to do with *you*," Hilton told Sarah. "This decision is between Hunter and the Party—"

Sarah leaped from the table and confronted Hilton. "It *has* something to do with me!" she blazed. "Bob's my husband, and what concerns *him* concerns *me!*"

"Not in the Party it doesn't," Hilton said.

"Then Bob's *not* going to obey any such damned decision!" Sarah shouted. "You wanted Bob to organize the waiters on the dining cars. Now, he's doing that. Then you say stop. Now, why, why?"

"The Party is not obliged to justify its decisions to you or anybody," Hilton said.

"I'm gonna keep on organizing," Bob said uncertainly to Hilton.

"Then you will be disciplined," Hilton said.

"What discipline? What can you do to me?" Bob asked, his eyes wide with wonder and anxiety.

"You can be expelled," Hilton told him. "And the Party will blacklist you throughout the labor movement. The Party will kill you. You can't fight the Party. Understand that?"

There was silence. Cross looked about the dining room. Gil leaned forward, listening, sucking contentedly at his pipe, his elbows resting on the table. There was a quiet twinkle in his eyes as he looked from Bob to Hilton and back again, following their dialogue. Eva was pale, stiff, and seemed not to be breathing; her eyes were full of a look that seemed to be protest. Sarah's eyes were blazing and her chest rose and fell rapidly; Cross could see the throbbing of a tiny vein in her neck. Bob stood bent forward a little, his lips hanging open, his eyes wide and glassy. His stance was a combination of subservience and aggression; it seemed that he was about to bow to Hilton's demands and yet at the same time he could have been

182

ready to leap forward and grab Hilton's throat. Cross wondered if it occurred to Bob that he was trying to drag him into an inhuman machine like this. . . . Maybe Bob's mind did not possess enough elasticity to realize it. . . .

"But what can I do?" Bob finally asked in a wail.

Gil rose and walked around the table to Bob and pointed the stem of his pipe into Bob's face. He spoke with jerky authority: "You're going to be a Bolshevik and obey the Party."

"But my fellow workers'll think I'm crazy if I change my mind like that," Bob pointed out.

"That does not matter," Gil said. "You are an instrument of the Party. You exist to execute the Party's will. That's all there is to it."

"But I *feel*—" Bob began.

"Goddamn your damned feelings!" Gil spat. "Who cares about what you feel? Insofar as the Party is concerned, you've got no damned feelings!" Gil paused a moment; there was a look of wild exasperation in his bulbous eyes. "Bob, there's a hell of a lot you don't understand. What do you think men like Molotov do when they get a decision? They carry it out! Do you think the Party exists to provide an outlet for your personal feelings? Hell, no! What do you think the Party would be if this happened? We're not Socialists. . . . We're *Communists!* And being a Communist is not easy. It means negating yourself, blotting out your personal life and listening only to the voice of the Party. The Party wants you to *obey!* The Party hopes that you can understand *why* you must obey; but even if you don't understand, you *must* obey. If you don't, then the Party will toss you aside, like a broken hammer, and seek another instrument that will obey. Don't think that you are indispensable because you're black and the Party needs you. Hell, no! The Party can find others to do what it wants! Is this asking too much? No. Why? Because the Party needs this obedience to carry out its aims. And what are those aims? The liberation of the working class and the defense of the Soviet Union. The Party, therefore, does not and cannot ask too much of any comrade. It's logical, isn't it? The Party is conducting this fight on your behalf and you must fit into it. Is that clear?"

Bob nodded his head affirmatively and then Gil turned and stared at Cross. And Cross felt that a better demonstration of what he was in for could not have happened even if it had been arranged.

"Lane," Gil said. "You are looking at a Party problem. Do you understand it?"

"I understand it," Cross said.

"I must go," Hilton said; he turned and without another word walked out of the room. No one had moved to open the front door for him; Cross heard it slam shut. He looked at Gil and was astonished to see Gil watching him and smiling.

"Do you understand what I mean, Lane, when I say you can't learn this out of books?"

"Yes. But listen. I see here two points of view. I see—"

His eyes caught sight of a gesture of Gil's hand, a motion that meant for him to remain silent; Cross knew that Gil did not want him to discuss Bob's Party problem in front of Bob.

"It's late!" Gil exclaimed. "We must be going, Eva."

"Oh, dear, yes," Eva said. She turned to Sarah. "Thank you for the wonderful dinner."

"It's nothing," Sarah said; she could not lift up her eyes.

Gil asked Cross, when he was close enough to him to talk in a whisper: "Can I give you a lift to 116th Street?"

"Sure," Cross said. He longed to talk to Bob, but felt that it would be better to do so without Gil.

Bob pretended to be brave; he grinned, wagged his head, and crooned: "Boy, the Party's tough, hunh? It's a great Party—"

"That's the spirit," Gil said, going for his overcoat.

"I don't like it," Sarah said, taking a pile of dirty dishes into the kitchen.

"She'll be all right," Bob apologized for her.

"I *won't* be all right!" Sarah shouted at him, her face twisted with anger.

"Darling, let's go," Eva said.

Cross shook hands with Bob and went to the kitchen door to say good-by to Sarah. The door was closed and when he pushed it open he saw Sarah sitting with her head bowed. Her shoulders were shaking; she was weeping. She

184

had not heard him open the door, and Cross closed it softly and joined the others. He followed Gil and Eva silently down the stairs to the street. Not a word was spoken until they had all gotten into the car and were rolling over the lumpy drifts of snow. Cross was next to Eva and his nostrils were full of the delicate perfume that she wore. He stared straight ahead of him, feeling that his life had at last touched something that stirred him to his depths. He was not angry or outraged, just deeply thoughtful, full of wonder. He had witnessed a scene of naked force in which obedience had been exacted through fear and the intensity of the emotions involved shook him.

"Well, what are your impressions, Lionel?" Gil asked, smiling and looking ahead of him.

"It's interesting," Cross said; he did not want to talk now.

"Is that *all?*" Gil asked, chuckling.

"It's impressive," Cross conceded.

"I didn't expect you to see that tonight," Gil said soberly. "I'm just wondering if you understand it correctly. If you got the right interpretation."

"I got the right one," Cross said tersely.

"You have a big future ahead of you," Eva said in a neutral, faraway tone that made Cross wonder what she meant.

"You'll be all right," Gil said.

"Here's 116th Street; you can drop me here," Cross said, relieved.

The car slowed and Gil and Eva looked solemnly at Cross.

"Well, Lionel, have you changed your mind?" Gil asked.

"Absolutely not!"

"Then we can expect you?"

"When do you want me?"

"Tonight. Tomorrow. This week . . . Whenever you want to come," Gil said. "Here's the address."

"I'll be there about ten in the morning," Cross said. "I've one suitcase, that's all."

"Right," Gil said.

"Good night, Lionel," Eva said.

Gil waved his hand and the car moved off through the

dim, snowy streets. Cross stood a moment, watching its red taillight disappear. He mounted to his room, undressed, and lay on his bed. There was a smile on his face as he stared up into the darkness. They think I'm a little child, he told himself. I don't mind the way they act in organizing. I don't mind the wild way they give out their decisions. I don't even mind their self-righteousness. But that naked force . . . Why? At the mere recollection of Hilton's biting tones, he sucked in his breath. They didn't *have* to treat Bob that way. Bob'll follow any strong person. You can take his hand and lead 'im. . . .

He sat on the side of the bed; sleep was far from him. "Once you get that kind of attitude in an organization that goes on from year to year, how can you ever get it out . . . ?" he asked out loud.

Cross felt that he was at last awaking. The dream in which he had lived since he had fled Chicago was leaving him. The reality about him was beginning to vibrate: he was slowly becoming himself again, but it was a different self.

Finally, toward dawn, he turned over on his side and slept like a rock for the first time in many weeks.

BOOK 3: Descent

> For that which I do I allow not: for what
> I would, that I do not; but what I hate,
> that do I.
>
> — ST. PAUL

Cross was aware of every echo of meaning surrounding his
decision to live with the Blounts. He had accepted their
invitation in bad faith which was now almost a congenital
condition with him; but he realized that his adversaries
were also acting in bad faith, a bad faith of which they
were cynically proud. Bad faith wasn't unknown to Cross;
not only had he long been guilty of it in his personal
relations, but he was convinced that bad faith of some
degree was an indigenous part of living. The daily stifling
of one's sense of terror in the face of life, the far-flung
conspiracy of pretending that life was tending toward a
goal of redemption, the reasonless assumption that one's
dreams and desires were realizable—all of these hourly,
human feelings were bad faith. But when Cross saw bad
faith being practiced as a way of life, when he saw men
mobilizing the natural hopes and anxieties of other men for
their own selfish ends, he became all but hypnotized by the
spectacle.

He had no illusions regarding the complexity of the situation into which he was voluntarily entering. His past-life
had prepared him for such compounded duplicities. His
temperament made him love to understand those who
thought that they were misleading him and it was fun to
use his position of being misled to, in his turn, mislead
them into thinking he was misunderstanding them. He

187

knew, of course, that such complicated games carried a risk of *his* misunderstanding those whom he was supposed to understand, but he was willing to shoulder the handicap. Perhaps we might both misunderstand each other, he mused.

Need for money was not pulling him into this. Nor did he have the itch to right wrongs done to others, though those wrongs did at times agitate him. And, above all, he possessed no notion of personal or social wrongs having been done to him; if any such wrongs had existed, he felt fully capable of righting them by his own lonely strength and effort.

It was an emotional compulsion, religious in its intensity, to feel and weigh the worth of himself that was pushing him into the arms of the one thing on earth that could transform his sense of dread, shape it, objectify it, and make it real and rational for him. Logic was guiding his sense of direction, but his emotional needs were dictating the kind of directions he chose.

His affinities with the turbulent instincts of Gil and Hilton were undeniable; he was, in a manner, their brother, just as Ely Houston was his. The difference lay in his violence being at bottom sharper and more secretive. He was too full of personal pride to regard himself as an exploited victim; he didn't demand that he be given his share of a mythical heritage. His was a passion to recast, reforge himself, and he was certain that Gil and Hilton had once in their lives felt what he was now feeling, that his reaching out for another pitch of consciousness had haunted them just as now it plagued him. But they had resolved their tangled emotions in the rigid disciplines of Communist politics, thereby rejecting from their hearts the pathos of living, purging their consciousness of that perilous subjective tension that spells the humanity of man. And now they were warring to slay in others that same agony of life that had driven them to the wall.

What malevolent psychological advantages were theirs in the waging of their war! Who better could track down criminals than reformed criminals! Gil and Hilton were spiritual bloodhounds on the trail of men whose spirits had not yet been broken as theirs had been. Since they had been defeated, they had decreed that defeat be the lot of all. . . .

It was not the objective reality of the revolutionary movement that was pulling so magnetically at Cross; it was something that movement had and did not know it had that was seducing his attention. It was its believing that it *knew* life; its *conviction* that it had mastered the act of living; its *will* that it could define the ends of existence that fascinated him against his volition. Nowhere else save in these realms had he encountered that brand of organized audacity directed toward secular goals. He loathed their knowledge, their manners, their ends; but he was almost persuaded that they had in a wrong manner moved in a right direction for revealing the content of human life on earth. He knew that their bristling economic theories were simply vastly clever fishing nets which they dragged skillfully through muddy social waters to snare the attention of shivering and hungry men; but many men, the best of them, would not yield their allegiances on purely economic grounds and he knew that the Party knew this.

While packing his suitcase, he was struck by an idea. Suppose Gil was right in assuming that the Party was justified in coercing obedience from others purely on the basis of its strength? What was there, then, to keep an individual from adopting the same policy? Apparently nothing save cunning and ruthlessness. . . .

"Gil'd want to kill me if he knew how I felt," he chuckled, lumbering down the stairway with his suitcase.

A yellow sun was flooding the buildings with a pale light that had no warmth. He headed for the subway and had gone but ten yards when the image of Bob's face rose before his eyes. Yes! How was Bob making out? Had he kept the Party's decision? Instead of going to Gil's place, he rode uptown and made his way to Bob's apartment. Bob answered the door.

"Speak of the devil!" Bob greeted him. "Come in, man. We were just talking 'bout you. You got your suitcase— Going to Gil's, huh?"

"Yeah." Cross looked searchingly at Bob, whose face was a mask of cheerfulness. "You seem all right after what happened last night."

"Yeah, man," Bob boasted. "That ain't nothing—"

"The hell it ain't!" Sarah's voice boomed from the living room.

Bob became crestfallen at the sound of Sarah's voice. "Man, Sarah's mad. Go on in."

Bob followed him and the moment Cross stepped into the living room he saw Sarah's angry face.

"Hey, Pretty," Sarah greeted him in cold tones.

"I thought you were going to laugh at me today," Cross said.

"I ain't laughing at no sonofabitch today," Sarah replied.

"She don't understand that the Party has to have discipline," Bob explained. "Women think we men can do as we like—"

"You joined the Party to organize, didn't you?" Sarah demanded.

"Yeah; sure, Sarah. But listen— Lemme explain—"

"You ain't explaining nothing!" Sarah overrode him. "A white man held out a stick to you and said, 'Jump!' And, by God, you jumped, just like any nigger—"

"Listen, woman! This is the *Party!* This—"

"But it's a *white* man's Party, ain't it?" Sarah demanded.

Bob turned to Cross and shook his head helplessly.

"Why don't they want you to go on with your work?" Cross asked Bob.

"He don't know," Sarah answered for Bob. "They walk in here and tell 'im what to do, and he hates it, but he *obeys!* They don't even tell 'im why, but he *obeys!*" She glared at Bob. "Even in the South when the white folks lynched you, they told you *why!* You didn't agree with 'em, but, by God, they told you *why!*"

"Sarah," Bob began, "the Party's an army—"

"Goddamn your Party!" Sarah blazed, leaping to her feet. "What in hell did I marry, a Marxist or a mouse? Listen, nigger, you're going to *organize,* you hear?"

"Baby," Bob whined. "Look, Lionel's new to the Party—"

"Let 'im hear it all!" Sarah yelled. "Let 'im know what he's getting into." Bitter tears filled her eyes; she turned to Cross. "All my life I've seen niggers knuckling down to white people. I saw my mama knuckling down when I was a child in the South. And nothing hurt me so much as when I saw a white man kick her one day. . . . Know what I mean? *Kick* her! I said kick her with his *goddamn* foot. I was 'bout six; Mama was serving in the white man's house; I was watching from the kitchen door. Mama tripped and fell with the tray and boiling soup splashed all over her. But the white man wasn't worried 'bout that. Hell, naw! He was mad 'cause his dinner was spoiled, so he *kicked* her. It'll stay in my mind till my dying day. . . . And everywhere I've looked since I've seen nothing but white folks kicking niggers who are kneeling down. . . . Know why I don't go to church, Lionel? 'Cause I have to *kneel* in front of that white priest, and I'll be goddamned if I'll do it. Now, we're in the revolution and the *same* goddamn white man comes along. But he's in the Party now."

"Baby, it's different," Bob wailed.

"Don't tell me it's different; it's the *same* damn thing!" Sarah sat heavily in a chair and her head dropped; she seemed ashamed of her outburst. "Maybe the Party wanted you to expose yourself that way," she began again in a reflective tone. "You're no good to the union, you're no good to the company, and, if you don't obey the Party, you're no good to them. They got you trapped—"

"Sarah," Bob spoke solemnly. "A good Bolshevik obeys. Lenin obeyed, didn't he? Molotov obeys—"

"Then, honey," Sarah sneered at him, "I want you to be one of them who tells the *others* to obey, see? Read your Marx and organize. *That* scares you, don't it? They done put the fear of God in your soul!" She rose again, trembling with anger. "Listen, I'm working and helping to support you to *organize!* I'm feeding you to *organize!* Now, you either *organize* or *go!*" She whirled to Cross. "The Party scared the pee out of him this morning. He went to the Control Commission to find out why they didn't want him to go on with his work. When he got back here, he was sick—"

"I *wasn't* sick," Bob protested, ashamed that Cross should know.

"You looked *green*," Sarah said. "And when a man as dark as you looks *green*, he's *sick!*"

Bob grabbed his head with his hands, sank into a seat;

his body began to tremble. He was suffering, a wet rag flopping between Sarah and the Party. Cross was unable to look at him; he stared out the window.

"What are you going to do, Bob?" Cross asked patiently.

"Hell, man. I don't know," Bob sighed.

"What do you *want* to do?" Cross asked.

Bob's eyes searched Cross's face as though seeking an answer there; he licked his lips and mumbled despairingly:

"I want to organize Negroes——"

"Well, why don't you?"

"You reckon I could do it? Reckon I ought to?" he asked sheepishly.

"You ought to do what you want to do," Cross told him.

Sarah watched Bob with the cold eyes that only a woman can have for her husband. Cross knew that Bob would never win. Bob was too scared to act alone; he had to have a master. The Party had sunk its hold deep in Bob's heart and if Bob left the Party he would have to find another. . . .

"I'm gonna stick to my own people," he said heavily, his eyes glistening. He had run from one master to another: his race. "That's what I'm gonna do."

"Then, *do* it, Bob," Cross said. "I'll help you."

"You want to help organize Negroes?" Bob asked eagerly, jumping to his feet.

"No. I want to help *you*." Cross told him in clipped tones.

Bob was puzzled; he brushed the meaning in Cross's words aside. He paced nervously with eyes full of anxiety. "One thing's got me worried," he mumbled. "The Party knows I'm illegally in this country——"

"So what?" Sarah asked.

"Suppose they turn me in to the Immigration folks to get rid of me——?"

"The *Communists?*" Cross asked.

"Sure, man," Bob said. "When the Party fights, they fight with everything."

"They wouldn't dare," Sarah said.

Cross felt that Bob's worries were farfetched. After all, was Bob that important to the Party? He rose to leave and Bob grabbed his hand in gratitude. Sarah followed him to the door. As Cross descended the stairs he wondered why some men wanted to be free and some did not, why some needed freedom and others did not even feel its loss when they did not have it.

After witnessing Bob's turmoil, he had doubts about going to Gil's. Wasn't Gil another Hilton? And why did the Party demand abject obedience? He recalled Bob's having told him that the Party was "now your mother and your father," which meant that if he obeyed, the Party would take care of him, but if he disobeyed, the Party would destroy him. And he didn't have the right to know *why* he was obeying. . . . Why blind obedience? Yet, upon reflection, he found some cynical merit in the Party's demand for it. If no reasons are assigned for a given command, then you cannot criticize, for you do not understand what you are doing. And if obedience without reasons is demanded for little things, it would hold, as a matter of ingrained habit, for bigger and more dangerous things. . . . But why had the Party chosen that procedure? Had they found that men would *not* obey otherwise? That could hardly be true, for each day millions of southern Negroes obeyed southern whites; millions of South African natives obeyed the white powers above them; millions of Germans had obeyed Hitler; and in most cases these millions had been given some fantastic excuse to justify the command of obedience. The Nazis tried to win the loyalty of their subjects by conferring upon them ornate titles, noneconomic rewards of various sorts, and by devising schemes of sport and joy. But the only motive that Hilton had held out to Bob was fear. Did the Communists *prefer* fear? He sighed and glanced out of the subway window just in time to discover that the train was slowing for his stop. Well, the answers to his questions were in Gil's apartment. . . .

The Blounts lived in a sparsely furnished, seven-room apartment on the second floor of a red brick building on Charles Street. Eva was not in and Gil received Cross with determined stolidity. The questions that had thronged Cross's mind were now informing his sensibilities. If there was something here to understand, then he, Cross, would get it.

"How are you?" Gil asked offhandedly.

"Fine."

"Follow me," Gil said, heading down a narrow hallway.

Gil showed him a small room overlooking a depressing stretch of straggling wooden fences separating back yards.

"Will this suit your needs?" Gil asked.

"Certainly."

"Leave your suitcase and let's have some beer," Gil said and left.

Cross placed his suitcase in a corner and walked slowly down the hallway, passing first what was obviously Gil's bedroom, then Eva's bedroom, and next the dining room, the living room, and finally coming to the kitchen, in which Gil stood pouring beer into two tall glasses.

"You get the layout of the place?" Gil asked without looking around.

"Yes; I see it." *He knows I've looked the joint over.* . . .

"The bathroom is next door," Gil said. He pointed to a rear door in the kitchen. "That's Eva's studio. She paints, you know."

"Oh; I didn't know," Cross said.

"She's a good painter," Gil told him. "Now, follow me."

Gil took the glasses into the living room and set one glass for Cross and another for himself on the end tables by two easy chairs. Cross noticed the slow precision with which Gil moved.

"You're observant," Gil observed.

"Just a habit," Cross said.

When they were seated, Gil studied Cross silently for some seconds, took a swallow of beer, lit his pipe and puffed the bowl to a glowing red. He held the burnt-out match delicately in his fingers, then laid it aside carefully in an ashtray. *Why does he act like that?* Cross asked himself. *Or, maybe he was observing the man too closely. He acts like he wants to mesmerize me; if he does, he certainly picked the wrong subject.* . . .

"Did anyone see you come up?" Gil asked.

"Not a soul. Why?"

Gil did not answer; he acted as though he had not heard.

"I'd like for you to sit around for a week, go to

meetings, listen a bit before you start your studies in the Workers' School," Gil said.

"Just as you say," Cross agreed.

Gil rose and went to his bookcase and took down a volume, parted the leaves to a certain page, and stood reading for some minutes, puffing slowly on his pipe. He finally sat and spoke while looking out of the window.

"We are going to launch a campaign against realtors who discriminate against Negroes here in Greenwich Village," Gil explained. "There is no law against Negroes living anywhere in this city they want to, but landlords have banded together and made codes against Negroes. One of the leading supporters of this code is the man who lives downstairs; he is my landlord."

Gil's attitude began to assume a pattern of meaning. Cross recalled that Gil had asked him if he had been observed by anyone on his entering the building, and when he had told Gil that no one had seen him and had asked Gil to explain why he had asked such a question, Gil had remained silent. It was clear that Gil was jealously reserving to himself the right to tell Cross the facts in his own way, to paint the entire picture, put in the shadings, the interpretations, the sense of direction. And the words Cross heard would constitute a law which he had to memorize carefully. . . . But *why?* Cross asked himself. Let him come out and say what he wants.

"This'll be a tough fight," Gil went on. "We'll be attacking the most deeply entrenched money interests in this city. The man downstairs is called Langley Herndon; he's an ex-real-estate broker; he's now retired. He's a dyed-in-the-wool Negro hater. He has told me that if he had his way, he'd kill every Negro he could lay his hands on. . . .

"Now, here's our strategy. He's going to know soon enough that you're living in my apartment, and the moment he knows, trouble will start. Just enter and leave the building normally. Maintain a polite attitude toward everyone you meet. We mustn't let any side issues develop here; we mustn't give anybody a chance to say that you were rude or insulting to them; understand? Be reserved. If this Herndon should speak to you, and he will, just act as if

195

you were not aware of trespassing his racial boundaries. Let him take the offensive in every instance, that is, up to the point of violence. Now, Lionel, I have a lease. . . ." He paused and pulled a batch of papers out of his inside coat pocket. "It's drawn between you and me. The lease I hold with Herndon gives me the right to sublet in whole or in part. Now, the lease I want you to sign was drawn up by a Party lawyer. This whole plan has been most carefully mapped out. Your staying here is perfectly legal; not only human and decent, but *legal*.

"Now, armed with this lease, Herndon has no real recourse to law to throw you or me out. But, of course, he has his goons, his tough boys who may try to waylay you. The cops will be on his side; make no mistake about that.

"Now, let me tell you the kind of man this Herndon is. I said last night that he was a Fascist. He is. I'm not understating it. Herndon began his life as a Texas oil man and he made piles of money. He has the old-fashioned American racist notions, all of them, right up to the hilt, including the so-called biological inferiority of the Negro. He even claims that he has found a philosophical basis and justification for his racial hatred. Understand? He hates not only Negroes, Jews, Chinese, but *all* non-Anglo-Saxons. . . . And he is smart enough to give you a mile of specious arguments, gotten out of crackpot books, for his anti-Semitism, anti-Negroism, and the rest. All of his arguments boil down to this: God made him and his kind to rule over the lower breeds. And God was so kind and thoughtful as to arrange that he be paid handsomely for it. Of course, he has conceived this God of his in the image of a highly successful oil or real-estate man, just a little more powerful and wonderful than he is. Herndon is quite anxious to collaborate with God by shouldering a rifle, if necessary, and helping God to defend what God has so generously given him. Herndon feels that God was absolutely right in giving him what he's got, but he does not completely trust God's judgment when it comes to his keeping it.

"As soon as he knows that you're in the building, the entire neighborhood will know it. That ought to happen within the next few hours. From that moment on, you'll have to watch out. Now, I'm getting you a gun and a permit to carry one. . . ."

"I've got a gun," Cross told him. "But no permit."

Gil frowned and studied the floor. "How long have you carried a gun?"

"A few weeks. Especially when I travel—"

"You carry it on you?"

"Yes."

"May I see it?"

Cross tendered Gil his gun and Gil broke it, copied down the serial number and returned it.

"A Party contact will help get you a permit," Gil continued, but the tone of his voice had changed.

He's worried about the gun, Cross thought. Otherwise, I've acted in a way to make him trust me, to make him feel that he is the boss; but my having a gun makes him feel that I might have a will of my own. . . .

"If and when Herndon moves against us," Gil resumed, "we'll break the case in the *Daily Worker*; we'll break it in England, in France, in China, and the Soviet Union—"

"You don't think a court would uphold your lease?" Cross asked.

Gil seemed annoyed. He gazed down at the figures in the carpet for a moment.

"Lionel, courts are instrumentalities of bourgeois law," he said slowly. "We are going to try this case in the public mind. Above all, this case must serve the Party's organizational interests."

Cross was worried. What would the publicity mean for him? Should he tell Gil that he couldn't risk that? No, he would wait; he could always disappear if things went in the wrong direction. . . .

"Are you in agreement with this plan?" Gil asked.

"Of course," Cross lied.

"Then tell me what you would think of anyone who tried to defeat this fight for Negroes to live where they want to?" Gil asked slowly.

"Why," Cross stammered, "he'd be a sonofabitch, to say the least."

Gil did not react to this definition. He stared straight at Cross and then leaned back in his chair. His pipe had gone out and he relit it. Suddenly Gil's eyes seemed to become unseeing.

"He would be a counter-revolutionary," Gil pronounced at last. "And he would deserve to be destroyed by the Party."

Gil's words made Cross at last understand what had been bothering him all along. It came in the tone of Gil's words, in the chilled promise of cold vengeance that edged his voice. *Power!* This was power he saw in action. That was why Gil had evaded answering his questions; Gil had made him assume a position of disadvantage, of waiting to be told what to do. The meaning unfolded like the petals of a black flower in the depths of a swamp. That was why fear was used; that was why no rewards of a tangible nature were given. It worked like this: Gil could lord it over Cross; and, in turn, as his payment for his suffering Gil's domination, Cross could lord it over somebody else. It was odd that he had not sensed it before; it had been *too* simple, *too* elementary. His mind worked feverishly, analyzing the concept. Here was something more recondite than mere political strategy; it was a *life* strategy using political methods as its tools. . . . Its essence was a voluptuousness, a deep-going sensuality that took cognizance of fundamental human needs and the answers to those needs. It related man to man in a fearfully organic way. To hold absolute power over others, to define what they should love or fear, to decide if they were to live or die and thereby to ravage the whole of their beings—that was a sensuality that made sexual passion look pale by comparison. It was a noneconomic conception of existence. The rewards for those followers who deserved them did not cost one penny; the only price attached to rewards was the abject suffering of some individual victim who was dominated by the recipient of the reward of power. . . . No, they were not dumb, these Gils and Hiltons. . . . They knew a thing or two about mankind. They had reached far back into history and had dredged up from its black waters the most ancient of all realities: man's desire to be a god. . . . How far wrong most people were in their appraisal of dictators! The popular opinion was that these men were hankering for their pick of beautiful
198

virgins, good food, fragrant cigars, aged whisky, land, gold.
. . . But what these men wanted was something much
harder to get and the mere getting of it was in itself a way
of keeping it. It was power, not just the exercise of bureau-
cratic control, but personal power to be wielded directly
upon the lives and bodies of others. He recalled now how
Hilton and Gil had looked at Bob when Bob had pleaded
against the Party's decision. They had enjoyed it, loved it!

"Do you understand?" he heard Gil asking him.

Cross sighed, looked up and met Gil's eyes with a level
stare. "Yes, I understand," he said.

He understood now why Gil had moved so slowly, why
his manner was so studied. He had been giving Cross a
chance to observe! And he remembered that Gil had been
watching him to see that he was watching! The heart of
communism could not be taught; it had to be learned by
living, by participation in its rituals.

He heard a key turning in the lock of the door.

"That's Eva," Gil said.

A moment later Eva, wind-blown and cherry-cheeked,
with an armful of packages, rushed into the room. Her
face held a bright, fixed expression of cheerfulness.

"Welcome," she sang out in her nervous, high-strung
way.

Cross stood and smiled at her and wondered if her
strained manner was covering her distaste at his presence
in the apartment. . . . There was something in her attitude that bothered him.

"Thank you," he told her. "I'm here and we're planning—"

"And you'll get action," Eva promised him self-consciously. "If Gil planned it, it's really planned. Huh, darling?" She bent and kissed Gil lightly on the forehead. "I
must get lunch ready now." She turned to Cross. "Just
make yourself at home."

"Oh, Eva," Gil called. "I'm not eating lunch in. In fact,
I must leave now. Why don't you eat with Lionel? I've got
to make a speech at the Dyers' Union. I'll be in for
dinner."

"Very well, Gil," Eva said; her face showed no expression.

Gil turned to Cross. "Keep your eyes open, boy." He laughed for the first time. "The fight is on!"

Eva walked slowly into the hallway and a moment later Cross heard her rattling pots and pans in the kitchen. Gil got into his overcoat and left. Cross went to his room and stretched out on his bed, thinking, mulling. His was the hungry type of mind that needed only a scrap of an idea to feed upon to start his analytical processes rolling. This thing of power . . . Why had he overlooked it till now? Well, he had not been in those areas of life where power had held forth or reigned openly. Excitement grew in him; he felt that he was beginning to look at the emotional skeleton of man. He understood now the hard Communist insistence on strict obedience in things that had no direct relation to politics proper or to their keeping tight grasp of the reins of power. Once a thorough system of sensual power as a way of life had gotten hold of a man's heart so that it ordered and defined all of his relations, it was bound to codify and arrange all of his life's activities into one organic unity. This systematizing of the sensual impulses of man to be a god must needs be jealous of all rival systems of sensuality, even those found in poetry and music. Cross, lying on his bed and staring at the ceiling, marveled at the astuteness of both Communist and Fascist politicians who had banned the demonic contagions of jazz. And now, too, he could understand why the Communists, instead of shooting the capitalists and bankers, as they had so ardently sworn that they would do when they came to power, made instead with blood in their eyes straight for the schoolteachers, priests, writers, artists, poets, musicians, and the deposed bourgeois governmental rulers as the men who held for them the deadliest of threats to their keeping and extending their power. . . .

He saw now that those who, in trying to rationalize their fears of communism, had said that the practice of communism was contrary to human nature were naïve or blind to awful facts which they hadn't the courage to admit; for, as Cross could see, there was not perhaps on earth a system of governing men which was more solidly built upon the sadly embarrassing cupidities of the human heart and its hunger to embrace the unembraceable. And this system of sensualization of the concept of power wasn't restricted to the Communist or Fascist worlds; the Communists had merely rationalized it, brought it nakedly into the open. Cross began to see that this systematization of the sensuality of power prevailed, though in a different form, in the so-called capitalistic bourgeois world; it was everywhere, in religion as well as in government, and in all art that was worthy of the name. And bourgeois rulers, along with the men of the church, had forged through time and tradition methods of concealing these systems of sensual power under thick layers of legal, institutionalized, ritualized, ideological, and religious trappings. But at the very heart of this system were the knowing and conscious men who wielded power, saying little or nothing of the real nature of the black art they practiced, the nameless religion by which they lived.

He knew instinctively that such subjects could not readily be explored in discussions with others, for its very victims—if, in strict sense it could be said that they were victims—would deny its reality perhaps more vociferously than those who controlled this system of power. Cross's insight into men like Gil or Hilton enabled him to isolate his own past actions and gain some measure of insight into them; it had been the blind coercions of a hungry sensuality that had made him try to hug delusions to his heart when he had suspected malevolence in the innocent and had tried to credit the unknowing with motives that they could not possibly have had. He rolled over and sat up in bed, his mouth open. He was seeing a vision, but at long last it was not an unreal one. This vision made reality more meaningful, made what his eyes saw take on coherence and depth. For the first time since that snowy evening in Chicago when he had decided to flee, when the waters of desire had drained off the world and had left it dry of interest, meaning began to trickle back again. . . . He was, in his mind and feelings, isolating this central impulse of informing action by which he and other men lived. There was a hunger for power reaching out of the senses of man and trying to say something in symbols of action.

201

What message, if any, was written in those hieroglyphics of energy? These actions were far more basic than the economic relations between rival social classes, he was convinced. Maybe . . .

A light knock came upon his door.

"Lionel!" It was Eva calling.

"Yes?"

"Lunch is waiting—"

"Coming."

He washed up and went into the dining room and sat at the table facing Eva, who now, though friendly, still seemed to avoid his eyes.

"I don't know what you like to eat," she said, smiling.

"Anything'll do me, Eva," he told her, seeing her now in the light of his ponderous reflections of a moment ago.

"I suppose you and Gil went over a lot today. You'll see that Gil has a grip on life," she said in a strained matter-of-fact tone devoid of any boasting.

"He has indeed," Cross agreed, merely to keep the talk going.

As she served him he studied her and was amazed to find that she looked even younger without rouge on her lips and cheeks. How did this child—for there was an undeniable childishness about her—fit into his dark broodings and interpretations of Gil's politics? He longed to ask her how she had come to marry Gil, for every move she made and every word she uttered belied her being his wife.

"Are you a native New Yorker; that is, born here, I mean?" he asked.

"Yes; I'm one of those rare ones. I was born about three blocks from here," she said, laughing, keeping her eyes down.

"Did you grow up in the Communist Party?"

"Oh, God no. I was an orphan. . . . I encountered the Party when I met Gil." She still did not look at him.

"Oh, I see."

"Do you like music?" she asked.

He had hoped that she would discuss politics; but either she didn't want to or she evaded the subject because it didn't interest her.

"It's the one thing I know least about, I'm ashamed to

202

admit," he confessed. "I've heard some classical music and liked it; but my level is jazz and folk songs, I'm afraid."

"Really?" She was surprised and thoughtful for a moment. "The reason I asked is that we have stacks of symphonic records in the living room and you're free to play them if you like."

As the lunch progressed, she spoke in a quietly melodious voice of her love of music, painting, and poetry, and the beauty of France, which she had seen last summer. Without seeming to, she avoided all mention of herself and made no political observations at all. The simplicity of her manner made him doubt the validity of the theory he had hatched out a few minutes ago. Yet she lives in the Communist world and she must know, he thought.

"Say, what was behind that little scene at Bob's last night?" he asked boldly.

"What scene?" She looked startled.

"Hilton's laying down the law to Bob—"

"Oh, *that* . . ." She frowned and murmured. "I'm afraid that Gil will have to explain that."

Either she did not know or she did not want to tell. He didn't want to create the impression that he was fishing for information so he quickly assumed an attitude of naïveté.

"There's so much to learn," he said wistfully. "I must be patient."

"I was *once* as bewildered as you are," she said meaningfully.

It was definite that she was evading him; he sensed reserves of emotion in her and he cast about for a way to make her open up.

"Look, don't think I'm nosy, but are you active in the Party?"

"Not exactly," she said. "I paint." She was frowning.

"Oh, really? Social subjects?"

A flicker of dismay darted across her face. She's afraid to talk, he thought. She bit her lips and her long eyelashes shadowed her cheeks. She took up a slice of bread, broke it nervously, then put it aside as a sudden impulse came to life in her.

"No. I'm a nonobjective painter," she said modestly.

203

Cross stared. The wife of a Communist leader painting nonobjectively?

"You don't like nonobjective painting, do you?" she asked, putting a soft challenge in her voice.

"But I do; what I've seen of it," he answered honestly.

"Not many people do," she said. "I'd not have thought that a colored person would. Your people are so realistic and drenched in life, the world. . . . Colored people are so robustly healthy."

"*Some* of us," he said.

"And you're not? How did that happen?"

"It's a long story," he said. "Some people are pushed deeper into their environment and some are pushed completely out of it."

"Do you feel *that* much aloneness?" she asked in surprise.

"Yes; and you?"

"Yes," she said simply and was silent.

"I'd like to see your work."

"All right. But . . . ."

"But what?"

"I'd rather you didn't tell Gil we talked about this," she said, flushing.

"I see," he said. What's she afraid of?

After lunch she took him into a cluttered, dusty room behind the kitchen; it reeked of oil and turpentine. She stood timidly behind him as he looked at walls covered with canvases; more were stacked in corners. The odd power of her work was immediately apparent; Cross saw a bewildering array of seemingly disassociated forms—squares, cubes, spheres, triangles, rhombs, trapezoids, planes, spirals, crystals, meteors—struggling in space lit somberly by achromatic tints. He advanced to the canvas on which she was evidently working and which rested upon a huge easel. Out of a darkly brooding background surged broken forms swimming lyrically in mysterious light stemming from an unseen source. The magical fragility of this light, touching off surprising harmonies of tones, falling in space and bringing to sight half-sensed patterns of form, was like Eva herself, like her sense of herself. In her work she

204

seemed to be straining to say something that possessed and gripped her life.

"Have you exhibited?"

"Yes; last year. Just before I married—"

"You have enough for another exhibit now."

"I shan't exhibit again soon," she said.

"How was your work received?"

"Very well," she muttered.

"And why aren't you going to exhibit again soon?"

"Oh, Lionel, I must go," she said hurriedly, ignoring his question. "Stay and look at them as long as you like. . . . Here are the keys to the apartment; one's for the downstairs and the other's for the front door up here. I'm off to do some shopping and then I'll do a concert." She flashed him a quick smile. "Come and go as you like. But watch for Herndon downstairs. . . ."

She left him and a few moments later he heard the front door open and close. She had not wanted to talk to him, but what she had seemed too shy to say in words shouted and pleaded for her in images. For two hours he looked at every canvas in the room, placing them in the light, examining them from far and near. He had the illusion, while studying them, of standing somehow at the center of Eva's ego and being captured by the private, subjective world that was hers, a world that was frightening in the stark quality of its aloneness; and he knew that it was out of a sense of aloneness that these haunted images, nameless and timeless, had come with the force of compulsions. At least she's lucky to be able to say her terrors and agonies in form and color, he said a little enviously to himself.

With a cigarette glowing in his lips, he went back into the apartment and wandered aimlessly from room to room, probing and idly searching. He smiled, feeling the presence of Eva and Gil as he spied among their belongings. Why did they have separate bedrooms? Twin beds were all right, but two bedrooms? He recalled the little, pecking kiss that Eva had given Gil when she had come in from her shopping and he was certain that there was something wrong between them.

He ended up in Eva's bedroom, prowling in drawers and

desks. At the bottom of a pile of dusty sheets of music lying on the floor of a clothes closet he came across a stack of bound notebooks; he opened one. They were Eva's diaries. . . . He glanced guiltily over his shoulder. When would she be back? To be caught reading her diary would be awful. . . . He stepped into the hallway and saw that there was a safety night-chain on the door. He put the chain in place. If Gil or Eva returned suddenly, he would say he had put it on in case Herndon came up. . . . He went back into Eva's bedroom and picked up a volume of the diary that dated back six months of that year. He began reading the small, clear, schoolgirlish handwriting:

June 10th

—I'm at last in Paris, city of my dreams! What a wedding gift from Gil! Poor dear, he's too busy with Party work to show me the beauty of this wonderful Paris; his assignments keep him going from morning till night. But I do manage to see it for myself. The art exhibits, the artists' studios, the sense of leisure, the love of beauty—will I ever be myself again after all this?

Notre Dame! Rising nobly in the warm summer night like a floodlit dream— The tourist bus is crawling away, taking from me this vision of beauty, remote, fragile, infused with the mood of eternity. At the next stop I got off the bus and walked back to Notre Dame; I could not keep to the schedule of a tourist bus! I sat on a bench and gazed at Notre Dame till almost dawn. How quiet the city is. A lonely, shabby man is pushing a handcart through the city streets. Lines, space, harmony softened by dark mists . . . Dusk of dawn kissing the pavements with tenderness . . . I doubt if Gil would understand feelings like these, yet they mean so much to me, to my heart. Mine is the glory of those angels against the background of that pearly, infinite sky.

June 15th

I'm so numbed with shock that I can hardly think. Is this my honeymoon? Is it possible that Gil has betrayed me so cruelly, so cynically? For days now I've pretended to be ill to avoid having it out with him, but in the end I must do it. It all began

206

that afternoon when I went to see a Left Bank art exhibit. I stayed behind and got to talking to some of the younger artists, both American and French, all of whom were complete strangers to me. One young man, an American expatriate, obviously a Trotskyite, began a violent tirade against the Party, charging that membership in the Party was death to artists. I told him that I was a painter and did not think so. He then told me not to be naïve like that Eva Blount who had had such a stunningly successful exhibit in New York last spring. He didn't know who I was, and I asked him what was so naïve about Eva Blount. He said that it was common knowledge in radical circles that Gil Blount had been ordered to marry her, to get her into the Party for prestige purposes. He went on talking of other instances where such had happened. I was silent; I felt cold, dead. To stand in a crowd of people and hear them talk of you like that!!! I asked him how he knew this, and what right he had to spread such foul gossip about people he did not know. He then went on to tell things which only someone close to the revolutionary movement could know. He said that Gil's secretary, Rose Lampkin, was his mistress and had been for years, and that at the same time she was spying on Gil. I could not contradict him.

To hear one's private life spoken about so brutally, in public! God, it *can't* be true! Yet his words explain so much. Is that why Gil is away from home so much? Is that why he never comes to me except when he's drunk? Oh, God, I feel I've no ground under my feet any more—I must confront Gil with this. . . .

And that Rose Lampkin woman, Gil's secretary . . . Is she his mistress? Is that why he insisted that she accompany us to Paris? The more I think, the sicker I get. I try to tell myself that this cannot be true, yet in my heart I know it and feel it.

June 17th

Gil has all but said that it's true. Which means that when I confronted him, he would not say anything. He raves at me, telling me that I'm trying to undermine his Party position, that I'm slandering him. I asked him to send Rose back to New York, and he said that it was the Party's decision that Rose remain with him. And Rose, when she came to the hotel this morning, had a cold smirk on her face. She knows that I know. According to Gil, I must accept this betrayal and be loyal to the Party; to be loyal to my feelings means betraying the Party. I don't know what to do—I feel that everybody's laughing at me, that everybody knows—*I could kill Gil.*

June 18th

I must be calm—I've only my work left; that's all. I tell myself all day long that I must give my life to my work. If I make a sudden, hysterical move I'll lose my grip on myself. Gil has predicted as much. Can there be betrayals as intimately cynical as this? I'm a fool to wonder, for it is true; it stares me in the face. But I don't want to believe it. That's what makes it possible; no one *wants* to believe it. What coldness people are capable of! I walk the streets all day to keep thoughts of suicide from filling my head—

June 19th

My whole life seems tainted, unclean. . . . I've asked Gil to take me back to New York; he says he will as soon as his duties with the French Party are over. I begged him to give me the fare, and he says no. I'm alone again, just as I was in the orphans' home. I didn't lose heart then and I mustn't now. I won't; I can't give up; I must work, work, work, paint. . . . But can I paint again?

Gil warned me that I must not talk of this. He demanded to know who told me about the Party deciding that he was to marry me. He accuses me of having anti-Party friends.

I'm afraid. If I stay with Gil, I'll loathe myself; if I run off, the Party will attack me publicly, branding me a renegade. All of my friends are Party people and they would no longer speak to me. Night and day Gil demands that I be loyal to the Party. But I owe myself some loyalty too. How can I face myself in the years to come, knowing that I have been bought, and in such a shameful way? Gil says that my personal feelings do not count. Doesn't he know he's killing me?

June 20th

I've been hurt; there's no doubt about it. I stand before my easel and cannot paint. I'm numb; my love of work is gone. When Gil comes into the hotel room, I begin to tremble with shame and rage. And he tells me that I *must* not, *cannot* talk

208

to anybody. If I protest, the Party will destroy me. . . . Last night he relented a tiny bit and said that I could be free only if I let the Party choose a husband for me. It seems that I'm guilty not because of what I've done, but because of what I know.

June 21st

I've begun to notice things that I've never noticed before. Is this because of what Gil and the Party have done to me? I feel like a victim and everywhere I look I think I can see other victims in the making. . . . I've just come from an American movie where I saw mothers with their young children. It was a horrible gangster film with a tense, melodramatic atmosphere. How can mothers take their children into such places? I should hate to have my children getting used to sights of violence, death, brutality. When for years a child has seen men hitting other men, killing or getting killed, he gets used to it. In time it does not impress him any more, and death, betrayal, deception become just unimpressive facts of life, just "one of those things." . . .

June 23rd

Gil came in at 2 A.M., drunk. He's ashamed to face me when he's sober. I understand it: drunk, he's still a free Communist; sober, he's still a slave of his boyhood upbringing in the Bronx and is ashamed of what he's done. To every argument I raise, he has one answer: "You don't understand!" I've got a knife with which I cut canvases and I sleep with it under my pillow. Gil will *never* touch me again, drunk or sober.

My eyes are red from weeping and sleeplessness. I never dreamed that I'd be brought to this. Before, the world was a sad place, but now it's both sad *and* dangerous. The worst part of all this is that I've no preparation for it; there was no warning. There's nothing I've ever read or heard that could have prepared me for this. . . . After father died when I was six, I lived in that orphans' home; but even there life seemed rational. Hunger, cold, study; making sacrifices to attend art school—all of that was rational. When I began to win scholarships, all the deprivations were redeemed. But this deliberate deception—? Where does it fit in?

Gil is sullen, silent; a cold wall— He has his friends; I'm

alone— I've no friends unless I consent to accept what has been done to me! I must be a partner to this crime in order to be forgiven! I see it now; there can be no crimes like this unless there is the consent of the victim! My fear to talk, my silence makes this possible! But dare I speak? Who would believe me? Who'd care? How can I go on like this?

June 24th

I'm afraid my loneliness and melancholy are making me morbid. Injustice has always been merely a word to me, now it's a reality. Gil and the Party have opened my eyes and I see. . . . In the Paris Métro today I saw something that made me sad. In front of me, on one seat, sat a young mother, middle class, her face well made-up and glowing with motherly pride; she was holding a little girl about two years old on her knees. And that sweet little baby girl, all dressed up in delicate, lacy things took a liking to a pale little boy of about nine or thereabouts. He was filthy, badly dressed; he seemed too mature for his age; he sat next to a huge, vulgar, toothless, harsh-voiced woman—no doubt his mother. Both the little children were at once keen on each other, but the big woman kept telling her son to stop looking and smiling at the baby. The little girl's hands tried to take hold of those of the boy and the boy was enjoying it. The young mother did not like it, but she was too well bred to want to hurt the little boy's feelings. Maybe the big woman was afraid of what the smartly dressed young woman would say? Anyway, the two women got terribly nervous and finally the young mother pried the tiny, playful, rosy little fingers out of the boy's dirty hands. The baby cried and I wanted to cry too —I wonder if Gil realizes how awful people can feel when something happens to them that they cannot understand? I've sworn that Gil will never touch me again. I'll die first!

July 10th

We're back in New York. My friends are asking me about my honeymoon and I'm forced to smile. God, how can I keep up this deception any longer? I'm noticing other victims now. I've become aware of colored people. God, how they take it! Compared to their deception, mine is nothing. Yet they manage to go on living, even smiling. How do they do it? They must be strong, healthy, unspoiled by the lies of the white man's world.

July 12th

My world has failed me and everything in it. . . . What Gil and his Party have done to me is ruining my life, making me possess fantastic notions. My loathing of Gil has gone so far that I cannot any longer abide the color pink. I no longer want to paint in reds and blues and greens. They now remind me of Gil's deception. That's why I'm beginning to adore colored people; I could live my life with sunburnt people; I wish I was a warm, rich, brown color—

July 18th

I've begged Gil for a little money to start out for myself and he says no; the Party says no; it's no everywhere. . . .

We're in a new apartment and the landlord is truly a Fascist! This morning I met him on the stoop and said good morning to him. For some reason I asked him if there were any black people in the neighborhood. He must have thought that I objected to them, for he said: "Oh, no; nothing like that around here, lady. But there's a Chinese laundry down the street—" "But Chinese aren't black," I said. "Oh, lady, you don't know. They're *almost* black. These colored people are all the same. God's marked 'em all red, yellow, brown, and black so we could know 'em." Good God, what a world we live in!

Cross smiled and flipped the pages of the diary and began reading the last entry:

March 3rd

Bob Hunter, one of the Party organizers, came rushing in to see Gil. When I told him that Gil was out his face fell and he pouted like a child. I like him because he is so open about his desire to fight and free his people from oppression. Bob told me to tell Gil that we must be sure to come to his apartment for dinner tonight—Bob bubbles over with the news of his finding a new, wonderful recruit for the Party. He is a young Negro living under an assumed name, a fugitive from Southern racists. He is, according to Bob, who swore me to secrecy, a bright young Negro intellectual who had some dire trouble with whites and committed some crime and is in hiding to save his life. Bob met the young man on a train and he is certain that he has killed a white man and that there is a price on his head. It sounds so exciting, terrible, pitiful. . . . And they're bringing him into the *Party!* Another victim? I wish I could talk to him and tell him something. Colored people are so trusting and naïve. He's going to be misled by Gil, just as I have been. . . .

Cross closed the diary; he did not want to read any more. He knew enough to make a numbing sense of recognition go through him. Impulsively he wanted to run to her and talk to her, to tell her that she was not alone. But that was foolish. Secrecy was how the world was run. Millions felt alike, but were afraid to admit it. Here was a lost woman who had enough sensitivity and intelligence to understand what he had to say. She was a victim like him; the difference was that he was a willing victim and she was an involuntary one. . . . She protested and he said yes. And a world yawned between his yes and her no. . . .

But, Christ, how could she go on living that life? Her tense, artificial manner was now clear. She did not want to talk about politics; she was afraid of what she would say. . . . She wanted to help him; and he wanted to help her. . . .

And Gil was trusting him because of Bob's foolish stories! Yes; that was rich. Bob had led the Party to feel that it had found a real victim of race hate! Well . . .

He felt sluggish; he replaced the diary and decided to take a walk. He went out of the front door, listening to hear a harsh voice challenging him. But nothing happened. He ambled to Washington Square and stood looking at the pigeons fluttering around the trees, alighting in the snowy grass. He went past the bookshops on Fourth Avenue, browsing here and there. It was cold; he would go home.

He was entering the building when the door of the apartment of Langley Herndon opened. Cross saw a white face watching him from behind thick spectacles. He shut the door to the street, taking his time, then turned and started up the stairs.

"Hey, *you!* Wait a minute!"

It was the voice of a man who was used to issuing orders. Cross paused, turned his head, and registered a look of make-believe surprise.

212

"What do you want here?" the man asked, coming up to him.

"What do you mean?" Cross countered. "I'm going up to my room."

"Your *room?* Are you *living* here?" Herndon demanded.

"Of course. And who are you? Why are you asking me all this?"

"I just happen to own this goddamn building, that's all," Herndon said with rough irony. "I say who can and can't live here!"

"But I'm not going into *your* apartment," he pretended to misunderstand. "I live upstairs—"

"I don't give a good goddamn *where* you live!" Herndon snapped. "You can't stay in this building—"

"Now, wait a minute! I've signed a lease with Mr. Blount—"

"You can't talk to me that way!"

Herndon advanced and Cross doubled his fist.

"Watch out! You're old and I don't want to hurt you!" He saw Herndon pause and blink his eyes. "If you want to talk to me, all right. But don't touch me, see?"

Herndon was short, gray, flabby, with a wide mouth. His eyes were inflamed and teary at the corners. His hair was black and slicked flat to the crown of a large, partly bald skull. He was violently agitated and seemed not to know what move to make. His face grew brick red.

"How long have you been in this building?" Herndon asked finally.

"For almost a week," Cross lied.

Herndon looked him over, his eyes traveling from Cross's necktie to his shoes.

"Say, come in here," Herndon said suddenly. "I want to talk to you."

Cross thought, he's going to try to scare me in another way now. . . . He stepped into a nicely furnished room which had a large desk. A wood fire burned in the grate and shadows danced along the walls. Herndon studied Cross for some seconds.

"Listen," he began in a tone of voice that indicated that he was stooping to give advice to someone who he doubted had sense enough to profit by it. "You are being misled.

213

For thirty years I've had a strict policy about renting, and nobody's going to make me change it. This lease you're talking about—it's nothing. Forget it. The quicker, the better for you. I'm going to see Blount tonight and give 'im hell. Get me straight. I don't give a good goddamn about what happens to you, see? I could crush you, if I wanted to. Now, go upstairs and pack your stuff and get the hell out of there! You're black and you don't belong here and you goddamn well know it."

"Thanks," Cross said in a low, clear voice. "I'm staying here as long as Mr. Blount says I can. It's your move."

"So, you're a Communist, hey?"

"No, I'm not."

"Oh, yes, you are, and you think you're being smart," Herndon's voice was rising. "I can take care of your kind. You Reds think you—"

"I told you that I'm not a Communist; I'm *anti*-Communist!" Cross said sternly.

"I don't give a good goddamn *what* kind of a Communist you are!" Herndon shouted.

"I didn't think you did," Cross said quietly. "That's why I insisted on telling you. I'm black and that's what's riling you. But I will not move from here."

Herndon, his lips quivering, yanked open a drawer of the desk.

"Be careful, man," Cross warned him, ramming his hand into his coat pocket. "I'm armed. If you pull out a gun, I'll shoot you!" Cross was bent forward, his entire body tense, his eyes not blinking.

Herndon slammed the drawer shut and came to the side of his desk.

"Get out of here, you black sonofabitch!" he shouted, his body trembling with rage. "Get out of this house! Get out of this building! Get out of my sight! If I see you again, I'll kill you, you hear?"

Cross did not move; he stood towering over Herndon, whose mouth held flecks of foam at the corners.

"I'm going, but I never turn my back on a man who's yelling at me," he said slowly.

Herndon's lips moved soundlessly. Cross kept his eyes on Herndon and walked backward to the door, still clutching his gun. With his left hand he groped for the knob, turned it, and pulled the door open.

"Mr. Herndon, whenever you're in my presence, be careful," Cross said. "You've threatened me and I won't forget it."

He went through the door and shut it. Things would happen fast now. He smiled as he went upstairs. The encounter with Herndon had given him a lift, had almost made the last shred of dreaminess leave him. This thing'll be decided tonight one way or the other, he told himself as he entered the apartment.

Eva returned an hour later. He had to be careful in her presence; he must not let her feel that he had spied on her intimate life.

"Oh, Lionel!" she called.

He went into the hallway and saw Eva still wearing her coat; her cheeks were red and excitement was in her eyes.

"Yes?"

"Herndon says he wants to see Gil as soon as he comes in," Eva said breathlessly. "What happened? Did you have a run-in with 'im?"

"We had it," Cross said.

"Did it get rough?"

"He wanted to pull a gun, but I told him I had one, too."

"Oh, Lord—" She leaned weakly against the wall. "Poor Lionel . . ."

Her eyes were full of pity, and Cross knew that she felt that he too was a victim of the Party, that the Party was using him for bait. I'm tougher than you think, he said to himself.

"It's nothing," he said. "I like his kind."

"Oh, dear! Where's Gil?" She was trembling.

"Now, Eva, don't worry," Cross tried to soothe her. "Nothing's going to happen for the moment, anyway. His next move will be to try to scare Gil, and I don't think Gil scares easily."

"Don't you want a drink or something?" she asked, looking at him as though she expected to see him collapse.

"I never refuse a drink," he said.

She brought out a bottle of cognac.

"I brought this from France last summer, thinking I might need it sometime," she said. "And now's the time."

Cross looked at her and smiled. Bless her; she's feeling good because she feels that she's of some use to me. . . .

"Look," he said, pushing the glass she had filled to her. "I think you need this more than I do."

She drank from the glass and poured one for him.

"What do you think will happen, Lionel?" she asked in a whisper. "That Herndon's capable of anything— Oh, God, Lionel, do you think it's *worth* it?"

Cross could see that she was on the verge of telling him to ditch the Party, to get out, to save himself. At that moment he heard Gil's key turning in the lock of the door and a pall of anxiety came over Eva's face. Cross could see Gil hanging up his coat in the hallway. As Gil entered, Eva turned as though to speak to Cross, but checked herself.

"Hello, everybody," Gil said placidly.

"Tired, Gil?" Eva asked; she was trying to act natural.

"Not especially," he said, shrugging. He drew his wallet from his coat pocket and extracted a paper from it, saying: "Here's the permit for your gun, Lionel. The Party had a lawyer pull some strings. . . . But be careful, guy."

"Thanks," Cross said. "I might really need the permit. I met Herndon today."

"Really? And how was it?"

"Rugged."

Eva rushed forward and caught hold of the lapels of Gil's coat. "You mustn't let Lionel get into this," she said hysterically. "Herndon said he wanted to see you the moment you came in. . . . And he's already threatened Lionel with a gun—"

"Let Lionel tell me what happened," Gil said, gently pushing Eva to one side, struggling to master his annoyance.

"Well," Cross began, "I was returning from—"

"Just a moment," Gil said. He took out his pipe and began to fill it with tobacco; then he paused and looked intently at Eva. Eva stared; she seemed on the verge of speaking, but controlled herself.

"I must see about dinner," she mumbled, flushing red. She left the room and Gil lit his pipe, sucked at it.

"I'm listening," he said.

Cross related what had happened, leaving out nothing. Gil made no comment; he rose and stood at a window looking out, smoking silently. Then he turned, sat at his desk and began writing. Eva came on tiptoe to the door, peered in apprehensively, then left. Cross lit a cigarette and waited. I'll make him guess at what I'm feeling just as I have to guess at what he's feeling, he told himself.

The doorbell pealed. Gil paused in his writing, lifted his hand from the page, then began writing again. Eva came to the door, her eyes round with fear.

"Gil," she called timidly.

"Yes," Gil answered, but not turning or looking at her.

"Maybe it's Herndon— Shall I answer?" she asked in a whisper.

"You're always to answer the door," he said calmly.

As though seeking support, Eva looked at Cross.

"If it's Herndon, do be careful," she said.

"Eva!" Gil barked at her.

"I'll answer it," Cross said.

"No, Lionel. Eva will answer the door," Gil said in slow, heavy accents of authority.

Cross wanted to rise and take the man by the throat. Why does he act like that? Then he tried to dismiss it from his mind. After all, I'm no angel, it's really none of my business. . . . He was now sorry that he had read Eva's diary; his knowing her as he did made it impossible for him to regard her with detachment. Eva lingered a moment longer at the door, then vanished.

"Oh!" Eva's frightened voice came from the hallway a moment later.

"I'm sorry, Eva— Did I scare you? Is Gil home? I got to see 'im quick— It's awfully important—"

"Come in, Bob— But what's the matter? You look sick— Did you have some trouble downstairs?"

"Trouble? Yes. But not downstairs . . . What do you mean? Is Gil here?"

"He's in the living room," Eva said.

Gil had stopped writing, his pen poised over the sheet of paper. His eyes hardened as Bob, his face twitching, his eyes bloodshot and staring, appeared in the doorway.

"Hey, Lane," Bob called to Cross; there was no heartiness in his voice.

Gil whirled in his seat and demanded: "What do you want here, Bob?"

Bob acted as if he had not heard; he sank weakly into a chair. He looked at Gil and forced a sick grin that faded quickly and his face went lifeless, his eyes staring at the floor in a kind of stupor. A large drop of mucus formed at the tip of his flat, brown nose, hovered there for a second, then dropped to his upper lip. He licked at it, unaware that he did so.

"Gil," he begged, "you've got to help me."

Eva stood in the doorway. Cross sat watching. Gil was looking at Bob with half-turned body. Bob turned to Cross.

"Lane, you got to talk to 'im for me—"

"Bob!" Gil shouted, his tone full of warning. "Lane has nothing to do with this, and you damn well know it! What are you trying to do? Disturb his faith in the Party? You've said enough already to be brought up on serious charges!"

"I just want to talk to 'im—"

"You're trying to influence Lane!" Gil shouted again, leaping to his feet. "You're organizing against the Party right *here* in my presence!"

"No, no, Gil—"

"You're trying to turn Lane against the Party right under my eyes."

"Oh, God, no!"

"You are guilty right now of ideological factionalism!"

"What's that?" Bob asked incredulously.

"You are trying to get Lane to support your ideas," Gil accused.

Bob sighed; he had come to plead innocent to one crime and now he found himself accused of still another crime. Cross felt certain that Gil did not want him to witness this.

"I'll go to my room," he offered.

"No; stay right here," Gil ordered.

And Cross suddenly realized that Gil wanted him to see what was happening. Gil's chastisement of Bob could either be a warning or an object lesson. How efficient this is, Cross marveled. Not a single word or gesture is wasted. By observing this, Cross, too, could learn how to break and ravage the spirits of others, or he could see what would happen to him if he disobeyed. Eva remained in the doorway, her eyes fixed upon Bob's face. Gil was looking at her with eyes full of warning, but she wasn't aware of his gaze. Then, the moment she saw it, she blushed and hurriedly left the room.

"Now, what's the matter with you, Bob?" Gil asked at last.

Bob had not taken off his hat or his coat. Dirty snow melted on his shoes and tiny rings of water were forming on the carpet. Bob spoke in a broken whimper: "The Party voted to expel me, Gil—"

"I know that," Gil said calmly.

"But Gil, I don't wanna leave the Party— You got to help me— My life's in the Party— The Party's all I got in the world— I made a mistake—"

"Tell that to the Party," Gil said, turning and sitting again at his desk.

"Oh, please, Gil— You don't understand— I don't even want to say it, man— You *know* my problem—I'm British — Only the *Party* knows it!" Bob rose and went to the back of Gil and whispered despairingly: "Listen, an hour ago the Immigration men came to my flat, see? Lucky, I didn't go to the door—Sarah went. She told 'em in a loud voice that I was out— I heard 'em talking to Sarah and I slipped down the back stairs—I came here, to *you*, Gil— You're my friend— Gil, for God's sake, don't let 'em do this; don't let the Party do this to me—"

"How do you know it was the Party?" Gil asked.

"But *only* the Party knew!"

"But how do you *know* the Party did it?" Gil demanded.

"Listen, I once heard Hilton threaten another West Indian Negro like me— He said he could drop an unsigned note to the Immigration folks if he didn't behave—"

"But have you any *proof* that the Party told the Government?" Gil demanded.

Bob shook his head; his eyes were blank and empty. Cross saw the point; if Bob had no proof, what harm could Bob's accusation do?

"Naw; I ain't got no proof. . . ."

Gil rose and stood over Bob.

"Are you accusing the Party of playing the role of stool pigeon?" he thundered.

Bob winced as though he had been slapped.

"No!"

"Then what in hell *are* you saying?"

"Gil, listen to me. Ten years ago I had to run off from Trinidad to keep the British from putting me in jail for Party activity— If I go back, they'll snatch me off the boat and take me straight to jail for *ten* years— Ten years in jail in the tropics is death—I mean *death*, man—don't you understand?"

"I understand," Gil said, nodding his head. "But that doesn't explain why you fought the Party."

"I didn't know I was *fighting* the Party. . . . I don't want to fight the Party. . . ."

"You took a position *against* the Party. . . . That's counter-revolution. And for counter-revolutionists the Party has no mercy," Gil told him.

"Gil, you got to tell 'em to give me another chance. . . . The Party can *hide* me. . . . Let me go to Mexico, anywhere—"

"Who are you to defy the Party?"

"I ain't nobody, *nothing*. . . ." Bob slid from his chair and lay prone on the floor. "This is *too* much, Gil— Please, please, don't let 'em do this to me. I was wrong. I confess. And I'll do anything you say, Gil! You're on the Central Committee and they'll listen to you. I been to headquarters and they won't even talk to me—"

Cross was stunned. He wanted to rise and place his foot on Bob's neck and cut off the flow of whining words. Gil watched Bob with calm, placid eyes and Cross wondered how many men and women Gil had seen in that prostrate position of penitent surrender that he could stare at Bob with so aloof and yet engrossed a passion.

"Did you meet anybody when you came up here?" Gil asked suddenly.

Bob blinked his eyes bewilderedly. "Meet anybody? No; I didn't see anybody. . . . Gil, *please!*"

"All right, Bob. You can go now."

Bob sat up; his hand went to his mouth in dismay.

"Where?"

"I don't care *where* you go—"

"But they'll get me, Gil! Look, I'll give my *life* to the Party!"

"The Party doesn't want your life." Gil smiled.

Cross closed his eyes. He hated Bob for his weakness. No wonder Gil wouldn't give in! The more merciless Gil was the more Bob would yield. Eva came to the door, her eyes avoiding Bob. Cross could see her legs trembling.

"Gil, dinner's ready."

"Go ahead and eat, Lionel. I'll join you later," Gil said.

Cross rose and went out of the room, his eyes avoiding Bob, who sobbed on the floor. He had no appetite, but he sat at the table and Eva served him. As he chewed his food, he heard Gil's voice rising in accusation, then Bob's voice falling in meek pleas. Then came a pause during which Bob coughed loudly. Finally there was a sound of footsteps in the hallway. Gil was saying something to Bob at the door, then the door closed. Cross looked at Eva; her eyes were full of fear, and her hand shook slightly as she ate. Gil came briskly to the table, sat, keeping his eyes in front of him. He volunteered no information and acted as though he knew no one would dare ask for any.

"God, I'm hungry," Gil said pleasantly and reached for the platter of roast beef.

After he had served himself generously, Gil turned to Cross and asked: "Say, did you see who won the chess tournament in Moscow? I was too busy to buy a paper."

"No, I don't know who won," Cross said, slightly non-plused.

"Do you play chess?" Gil asked.

"No."

"You ought to learn. It's wonderful for relaxation," Gil advised him.

As dinner proceeded in silence, Cross was aware that a feeling of tranquillity had descended upon him. In his mind Gil had receded far off until he had become a tiny, little luminous figure upon which all of his attention was focused. It was as if he were squinting his eye along the barrel of a rifle toward some distant and elusive target and at long last the center of the target had come within the hairline of the sight.

After he had drained his cup of coffee, Gil chuckled softly and asked: "What time is it?" He looked at his wrist watch. "Hummm . . . Ten past nine— I'd better get down and see Herr Herndon."

"Do you want me to come with you?" Cross asked.

"Why?" Gil asked, lifting his brows in surprise.

Cross said nothing. Eva sat stiffly, staring with protesting eyes into her empty coffee cup. Then she lifted her eyes to Gil and Cross saw the light of protest die. God, she's scared, Cross thought. If she's that afraid of him, how she must hate him!

Gil stood and went into the hallway, then out the door. Eva rose suddenly, as though she had to drown her anxieties in activity, and began clearing the dishes from the table.

"I'll help you," Cross said, taking a stack of plates and starting for the kitchen.

"No, Lionel—"

"Why not?" he said.

"You don't have to, you know," she said.

"I want to," he said. He wanted to be near her.

Then they both were still. They heard loud voices coming from downstairs. Cross could distinguish Gil's voice, then Herndon's. They were at it strongly. The dishes slid from Eva's hands to the table with a clatter; then she clutched the back of the chair till her knuckles showed white.

"Do you think I ought to go down?" he asked Eva.

She shook her head.

"No. If he said no, then don't. He'd be awfully angry, and when he's angry he doesn't speak for weeks—" She caught herself; she had said more than she had intended. "Lionel, really, don't bother with the dishes. Do what you like. . . ." Irritation was in her voice.

He knew that he was making her more nervous; she didn't want him to see her state of mind.

"Okay."

He went to his room and the voices were clearer; he put his ear to the floor and heard shouts full of hot anger, but no words were distinguishable. He lay on his bed, then jerked upright; he heard a sharp snapping like wood break-

222

ing, then a dull thump, and all was silent. The door of his room flew open and Eva stood there, clasping her hands in front of her, staring at him with eyes filled with terror. "What was that?"

Cross went to her; she clutched his hands tightly.

"Don't you think I ought to go down?" he asked.

"Yes," she agreed impulsively. Then her body flinched and she shut her eyes in desperation. "No; no; he'd be angry. He'd think that you thought he couldn't handle it—" Tears leaped into her eyes and she turned from him. "If he gets hurt, he'll wonder why we didn't do something. He'll think I did it on purpose—"

"On *purpose?*" he asked.

Yes; she was fighting against a wish for something to happen to Gil; she was longing for someone to put him out of her life. . . .

A hoarse scream came from downstairs.

"I'm going down," Cross said suddenly.

"Yes, Lionel," Eva breathed; she was pale, trembling.

He went quickly into the hallway. He realized as he went down the steps that he was acting more as a kind of proxy for Eva's feelings than his own. *I* really don't care, he thought. When he reached the landing of the first floor, he paused, listening to the sound of grunts, scuffling feet, and the thud of blows. He crept on tiptoe to the door. . . . Was it locked? He turned the knob; the door swung in and Cross looked at the two men grappling with each other. Gil lashed out with his right fist, bashing Herndon on the ear and sending him reeling backward. Herndon collided with a table and when he turned Cross could see that he had the fire poker in his right hand. Cross looked quickly at Gil and saw that his face was covered with bloody streaks where the fire poker had ripped into his flesh.

Both men were oblivious of Cross, who stood in the doorway with a bitter smile on his face. Cross could barely contain himself as he watched the battle. Which man did he hate more? Many times during the past hours he had wished both of them dead and now he was watching them batter each other's brains out. . . .

He spun round at the sound of footsteps behind him on

the stairs. Eva was descending with wild eyes, her hair flying behind her. He grabbed her shoulders and held her, wanting to keep her out of the room. Eva twisted loose and ran to the doorway. Cross followed and stood behind her. Eva grabbed hold of both jambs of the door and screamed as she saw Gil sinking to the floor under the blows of Herndon's fire poker.

Herndon turned and stared at Eva, still clutching the poker in his right hand. He had the look of a man struggling to awaken from a dream. Then Cross saw the muscles of Herndon's face twitch as he advanced menacingly toward them.

"Get out, or I'll kill you both!" Herndon growled.

Eva screamed again, backed violently into Cross, then turned and ran up the stairs. Before Cross could move, Herndon was upon him and he ducked in time to save his head from a blow from the poker, which caught him on his right shoulder, leaving a searing line of fire in his flesh. He leaped aside and watched Herndon stumble toward the rear of the hall. Cross felt for his gun, then decided to run —not through fear of Herndon but because he hoped Herndon would re-enter the room and battle again with Gil. . . . He took the stairs four at a time, then, halfway up, he heard another scuffling lunge behind him; he glanced back. Gil had rushed out of the room and had grabbed Herndon; the two men now wrestled for possession of the fire poker, rolling, clawing, going from Cross's sight as they fell through the doorway back into the room. Cross caressed his bruised shoulder and looked upward; the door of Gil's apartment was open and he heard Eva's frantic voice.

"Don't you understand? I want the police! For God's sake—" Cross entered the hallway. Eva thrust the telephone into his hands.

"Lionel, here; call the police. . . . I can't make the operator understand anything."

"Okay," he breathed.

"Are you hurt?"

"Not much . . ."

He picked up the telephone, jiggled the hook, then

paused, turning his head as another burst of sound came from downstairs. Eva sprang through the doorway, heading downstairs.

"Eva!" He left the phone and ran after her, catching her on the landing and dragging her back into the apartment.

"No, no," he told her. "You can't go down there. . . . *You* call the police—"

"I don't know what to do," she cried.

"I'll go down and help Gil," he said.

Eva stared at him helplessly. He thrust the telephone into her hands and ran from the room, stumbling down the stairs. In the lower hallway, he stood, hearing the sound of the fight. He debated: yes; he *had* to help Gil. . . . What would Gil say if he didn't? His failure to help would be something he could never explain. . . .

Again he stood in the doorway of Herndon's apartment. Herndon was rushing at Gil, the poker raised to strike. Gil backed off, his hands lifted to protect his face and head. Herndon crashed the poker into Gil's hands, which seemed to wilt under the blow. The poker flew from Herndon's fingers and clattered to the floor. Gil snatched it up quickly and charged into Herndon, his face livid with fury; he whacked Herndon's head and face and Cross heard the tinkling of glass shards as Herndon's spectacles broke and showered from his eyes.

Cross watched, disdainful, detached. He saw a broken table leg lying near the fireplace; one of them had no doubt crashed into the table and the heavy oaken leg had snapped in two near the top. Teeth bared, Gil lifted the poker again to smash Herndon; but, as his arm was about to descend, the tip of the poker caught in the glass chandelier swinging from the ceiling. There was a musical storm of falling crystal and the ceiling light went out, leaving the room lit only by the leaping shadows of the fire. The force that Gil had put behind that swooping blow now carried him headlong to the floor, the poker bounding free.

Catlike, Herndon was on it and before Gil could rise Herndon was covering him with deadly blows.

Suddenly Cross knew what he wanted to do. He was acting before he knew it. He reached down and seized hold

225

of the heavy oaken leg of the table and lifted it high in the air, feeling the solid weight of the wood in his hand, and then he sent it flying squarely into the bloody forehead of Herndon. The impact of the blow sent a tremor along the muscles of his arm. Herndon fell like an ox and lay still. He had crushed the man's skull. Tense, he stood looking down at Herndon, waiting to see if he would move again. He was concentrated, aware of nothing but Herndon's still, bloody form. Then he was startled; he whirled to see Gil struggling heavily to his feet, blood streaming from his face and neck, clotting his eyes. Cross stared for a moment. He was not through. The imperious feeling that had impelled him to action was not fulfilled. His eyes were unblinkingly on Gil's face. Yes, this other insect had to be crushed, blotted out of existence. . . .

His fingers gradually tightened about the oaken table leg; his arm lifted slowly into the air. Gil was dabbing clumsily with his handkerchief at the blood on his neck and cheeks. Cross let go with the table leg, smashing it into the left side of Gil's head. Gil trembled for a split second, then fell headlong toward the fireplace, where flames danced and cast wild red shadows over the walls. Cross's hand sank slowly to his side, the table leg resting lightly on the floor, its edges stained with blood. There was silence save for the slow ticking of an ornate clock on the desk.

He filled his lungs and sighed deeply. For perhaps a minute he did not move; his senses gradually assumed a tone of anxiety and he stared more intently at the two bloody forms stretched grotesquely on the smeared rug. Then he sucked in his breath and whirled toward the door. Oh, God, it was still open! Had anyone seen him? He rushed to it and closed it; then turned back to the room and the two inert forms. Were they dead? He touched Herndon's shoulder; the man was still; the wide, thin lips hung open; blood oozed from one corner of the mouth. Cross hesitated a second, then lifted the table leg and chopped again into the skull. The body rolled over from the force of the blow.

Cross now turned to Gil, whose head lay near the fire. He caught hold of one of Gil's legs and yanked the body from the fireplace into the center of the room where he could get a better chance to deliver another blow at the head. Again he lifted the table leg and whacked at Gil and he knew that Gil would never move again.

The universe seemed to be rushing at him with all its totality. He was anchored once again in life, in the flow of things; the world glowed with an intensity so sharp it made his body ache. He had had no plan when he had dealt those blows of death, but now he feared for himself, felt the need for a plan of defense. He knew exactly what he had done; he had done it deliberately, even though he had not planned it. His mind hadn't been blank when he had done it, and he resolved that he would never claim it had been.

He took one last quick look about the room. One of the drawers of Herndon's desk was open and Cross could see the butt of Herndon's gun half pulled out. He could almost reconstruct what had happened between the two men. Gil had no doubt grabbed Herndon just as Herndon had been about to seize the gun. And after that they had fought so desperately that neither of them had had a chance to get the gun, or they had forgotten it. . . .

The plan sprang full and ripe in his imagination, his body, his senses; he took out his handkerchief and quickly wiped the table leg which he held in his hand, making sure that no trace of his fingerprints would remain. He went to Herndon, holding the table leg with the handkerchief so that his hand would not touch it, and forced the fingers of Herndon's right hand about it several times so that the man's prints would be found. . . . He was breathing heavily. The winking shadows of the fire flicked warningly through the room. Still holding the leg with the handkerchief, he went to Gil and closed Gil's loose fingers about it. He took the fire poker, wiped it clean and inserted it in the fingers of Herndon's right hand. . . . No; he changed his mind; he'd let the fire poker rest a few inches from Herndon's hand. That was more natural. . . . He looked swiftly around to make sure that he was leaving no marks of his having been in the room. He had to hurry. . . . The door? Fingerprints on the knob . . . ? No; he would not bother about them. After all, if he made things *too* clean, the police would get suspicious. . . . And he had been down here talking to Herndon earlier this afternoon. . . . Sure . . . His prints had a right to be on the door. Go up to Eva. . . . What would he tell her? There would be questions from the police, from Party leaders, from Eva, from everybody. . . . The newspapers . . . ? What would they say? Well, he was just a Negro roomer who had gone down at the suggestion of Mrs. Blount to see what was happening and had seen them fighting. . . .

He opened the door; the downstairs hallway was empty. He caught hold of the door handle and was about to shut it when an idea came to him. Suppose someone came to see Herndon and found both Herndon and Gil dead? Ah, yes; it was better to push the tiny lever on the lock and let the door lock itself. The door would be locked when the police and the Party leaders arrived. That was the trick. They would have to knock down the door. *And he, on his second trip down, had not been able to see what was happening; he had only heard sounds.* . . . He adjusted the lock and pulled the door to, hearing it catch. He tried the handle; it was locked. Now, what motive on earth could he have had in killing the two of them? Let them figure that out. . . .

He started up the stairs, then paused and looked down at himself. Was there any blood on him? He looked at his hands, his coat, his shoes. He could see nothing. Oh, yes; his handkerchief; it was bloody from where he had wiped the fingerprints from the fire poker and the table leg. . . . He would have to burn it. Yes; he'd put it into the kitchen incinerator the first chance he got. And, to be absolutely sure, he would ditch the clothes he was wearing. The police had scientific ways of examining particles and arriving at damaging conclusions. He stood in front of Gil's apartment door and composed himself. Yes; he had to act hurriedly and frantically now. He grabbed hold of the door knob and rattled it brutally. It was locked.

"Eva!" he yelled.

"Is that you, Lionel? Is Gil with you?"

"It's me; Lionel! Open the door quick!"

He heard the night-chain rattling; she had locked herself

228

in. She opened the door and backed fearfully away from him.

"Did you call the police?" he asked her.

"No. I called Jack Hilton; he's calling the police— What happened?"

He searched her face; her eyes were bleak and frightened. Would she be glad that Gil was dead? Didn't she want him dead so that she could be free?

"The door down there is locked and I can't hear a thing," he told her. "Gil's still in there. . . ."

"Oh, God," she whimpered.

He longed to know what was going on in her mind. Was she hoping that Gil was dead? And was she feeling guilty because she was hoping it? If so, then she'd act violently now; she'd try to ease her burden of guilt.

"The door's locked?" she repeated in a quiet voice.

"Yes."

"I'm terrified. . . . Lionel, call Jack Hilton again and tell him— He thinks maybe Gil's all right now—"

Her voice died in her throat and she had spun around and was out of the door before Cross could grab her. He debated: he had a wound on his shoulder to prove that he had tried to help Gil and maybe it would be a good thing for Eva to see that the door was locked. Then Eva, panting and whimpering, came rushing in again.

"He's there!" she gasped. "He's coming up here. . . ."

"Who?"

"Herndon—I saw 'im on the stairs— He has his gun—"

Was she crazy? Herndon was dead. Eva ran past him into her bedroom. Cross approached the door and looked out; he heard footsteps mounting the stairs to the floor above him. Ah, Eva had thought she had seen Herndon, but she had mistaken another man for Herndon. . . . He shut the door and put on the night-chain. Yes; that was something that could be used in his favor. Eva had thought that she had seen Herndon coming up the stairs! *That meant that her testimony would indicate that Herndon was still living after he had come up to the apartment for the second time. . . . That could mean that Gil and Herndon killed each other!* By God, *that* was the plan! He would stick to that story. . . .

"Eva!" he called to her. "Give me Hilton's phone number!"

When she did not answer, he went to her. She was lying on the floor of her bedroom; she had fainted. He lifted her to her bed, got a wet towel from the bathroom and patted her face with it. Her eyelids fluttered.

"Give me Hilton's phone number," he insisted.

"My purse," she murmured.

He got her purse and she gave him an address book and whispered: "Find the number there, under H. . . ."

Cross found the number, then walked slowly toward the telephone. His mind clearly grasped the entire situation and every muscle of his body was relaxed. Now, I'd like to see them figure that out, he told himself with a grim smile. I killed two little gods. . . . He paused, frowning. But they would have killed me too if they had found me like that. . . . Yet he could not get it straight. Just a moment ago it had all seemed so simple. But now it was knotted and complicated. There was in him no regret for what he had done; no, none at all. But how *could* he have done it? He too had acted like a little god. He had stood amidst those red and flickering shadows, tense and consumed with cold rage, and had judged them and had found them guilty of insulting his sense of life and had carried out a sentence of death upon them. As Hilton and Gil had acted toward Bob, so had he acted toward Gil and Herndon; he had assumed the role of policeman, judge, supreme court, and executioner—all in one swift and terrible moment. But, if he resented their being little gods, how could he do the same? His self-assurance ebbed, his pride waned under the impact of his own reflections. Oh, Christ, their disease had reached out and claimed him too. He had been subverted by the contagion of the lawless; he had been defeated by that which he had sought to destroy. He sank listlessly into the chair by the side of the telephone. Yet, no matter what happened, he had to call Hilton; he had to phone that little god . . . ! He was limp. What was the matter with him? He was, yes, he was trapped in the coils of his own actions. He had acted, had shattered the dream that surrounded him, and now the world, including himself in it, had turned

230

mockingly into a concrete, waking nightmare from which he could see no way of escaping. He had become what he had tried to destroy, had taken on the guise of the monster he had slain. Held to a point of attention more by the logic of events than by his own reasoning, charged with a sense of meaninglessness, he bent toward the telephone and dialed. . . .

BOOK 4: Despair

> *The wine of life is drawn; and the mere lees*
> *Is left this vault to brag of.*
>
> — SHAKESPEARE'S *Macbeth*

In talking to Hilton over the telephone, Cross was careful to assume the role of a subordinate, a humble outsider, a man speaking for a temporarily incapacitated woman.

"But Eva phoned and told me that you'd gone down to help Gil," Hilton said in a baffled tone of voice.

"But the door was *locked* this time—"

"Did you try to get in?"

"Yeah. I banged and knocked and hollered—"

"And Herndon didn't answer?"

"No."

"And did you hear anything?"

"Fighting, like I told you—"

"Did you try to get help from anywhere?"

"Eva called you—"

"And the first time you went down, he hit you?"

"Yes, with the fire poker—"

"Where's Eva now?"

"She fainted. She's lying down."

"You hear any noise now?"

"Nothing; nothing at all."

"And Herndon ran Eva back into the apartment, hunh?"

"Yes; I was trying to phone you and she ran out—"

"He had a gun?"

"She said so. I didn't see him. I bolted the door when she came running back in."

"Did Gil seem badly hurt?"

232

"Gosh, I don't know. I only got a glimpse of 'im." Cross was purposefully vague. "Look, you ought to come over and I could explain it all. I just moved in this morning, see? This Herndon jumped me at sight, told me to get the hell out, wanted to pull a gun on me, said he'd kill me—"

"Where was Gil when you first looked through the door?"

"He was lying on the floor."

"Herndon knocked him down?"

"Seems like it. Herndon had the fire poker in his hand—"

"Did you *see* him strike Gil?"

"Yes."

"Was Gil conscious?"

"I don't know—"

"And you're sure that Eva saw him on the stairs a few minutes ago?"

"Sure; she said so."

"Okay. Now, listen, don't let anybody into the apartment until I come, unless it's the police or somebody from the Party, see?"

"All right."

"That's all. I'll be right over." The line clicked.

Not once had any emotion entered Hilton's voice as he questioned Cross over the telephone, but Cross noticed throughout Hilton's inquiries a theme that puzzled him. Then he had it. Hilton was already trying to establish the fact that Herndon was the *aggressor*. Cross, knowing that Gil was dead, decided that his own defense could be best served by his feeding the Party's hunger for a martyred hero, dead or alive. He marveled at how instinctively Hilton was reacting in terms of the Party's organizational needs. If, in describing what he had seen when he had looked into the doorway, he said that Gil had seemed to be getting the worst of it, that Herndon had been standing over Gil with the fire poker, then the Party would claim, when it found that Gil was dead, that Herndon, the Fascist beast, had killed him, and had later died of wounds which Gil, in self-defense, had inflicted on him during the course of the struggle. And then there was that fantastic luck of Eva's thinking that she had seen Herndon after Herndon

233

had been killed and after the door had been locked! Cross knew that he had to be careful in relating what he had seen, had always to keep sternly in mind that he must do no interpreting at all, that the Party and the police had to weigh what had happened and place their own assessment on it. His aim would be to establish in the minds of the police and Party leaders that Herndon had been alive when he had last looked into the room, that Gil had been hurt, unconscious, maybe dying, and after that the door had been locked. . . .

And wouldn't Eva be his unconscious ally? He was convinced that her actions had been determined by an awful sense of guilt toward Gil. The fantasy of seeing Herndon with a gun on the stairs sprang from her guilt—Herndon ought to kill *her* now that he had done her secret bidding by killing Gil. . . . And Eva no doubt felt that Cross was, like her, a victim of the Party's complicated duplicities. . . . Yes, he had a chance to stand clear of suspicion as long as he could manipulate or count upon the guilt feelings of others.

Cross took a deep breath and tried to keep the facts straight in his mind. This thing had come upon him so suddenly that its full reality hadn't sunk home to him. Had he killed them or was it a teasing fantasy? They both must be dead, or his whole plan was crazy. Or, if Gil lived, he was in deadly trouble, both with the police and the Party. He longed to creep downstairs and make sure that they were both dead. But they *must* be dead. God knows he had crushed them hard enough. Gil would have to be a superman to live after the slashes from Herndon and the heavy whacks from the table leg. Of Herndon he could be certain; that Fascist was dead. . . .

"Lionel . . ." Eva's voice was calling.

"Yes?"

He went to her; she was leaning on her elbow in bed and she looked at him with eyes full of fear and guilt.

"Did Gil seem badly hurt?"

"I don't know," he answered her softly.

"What did Hilton say?"

"He said for us to stay here; he's on his way over now. He's phoning the police and the Party."

234

"But we should try to *do* something for Gil—"

"The door's *locked*; Eva—"

"Oh, God," she cried, "I wish Hilton'd come. Do you hear anything down there now?"

"No," Cross said. "I was listening in the front hall, but I couldn't hear anything."

She broke down again and began weeping. "I can't stand this life—this deception—this everlasting violence— Isn't there any way to be human any more?"

Before he could stop her, she had sprung from the bed and was running on swift feet down the hall to the door.

"Gil—Gil!" she was screaming.

"Eva!" he yelled and started after her.

"He'll blame me if we don't help him," she sobbed hysterically. "And the Party'll want to know *why* we didn't help him. . . ." She sobered quickly and stared at him, realizing that she was trying to explain something that he could not possibly understand.

Yes; she, like him, was wondering if Gil was really dead. A wounded Gil, a living Gil, would be a calamity for both of them. He longed to put her at peace, to tell her that she was free. But he could not. He caught her on the landing, about to descend the stairs. He grabbed her shoulders.

"The door's *locked!*" he insisted. Yes, he would stress that she must be loyal to the Party, something which she feared more than she feared Gil. "The Party will make a test case of this, see? We *can't* interfere. . . ." A better idea leaped into his mind; she felt that he was a victim of the Party and he would try to exploit her delusion. That's it. . . . "Look, Eva," he argued solemnly, "this is complicated. The reason that Hilton doesn't want me to go down there is that I'm *colored*, see? You know the police. . . . They'd try to frame me. . . ."

She wilted, turned, and buried her face on his shoulder. Hers was a world ruled by fear. He led her back into the apartment and bolted the door; sweat stood on his forehead. He guided her steps to the bed and gently helped her upon it. They were silent; they heard footsteps in the hallway. Eva strained, lifting herself almost to a sitting position. Could that be the police or Hilton? Cross heard the footsteps mount the stairway. No; it was somebody who lived upstairs.

"The Cushmans," Eva whispered. "They're anti-Party."

Cross stared at her in amazement. To her the world was either Party or anti-Party, and all in between did not count. He sat on a chair at the side of the bed. Eva was shaking. He longed to take hold of her and soothe her, but dared not.

"You think they'll blame us if Gil's badly hurt?" she asked in a whisper.

"We did what we could," he told her. "This was not our idea, Eva. They should have sent someone to help Gil. . . . And he wouldn't let me go down with him. . . ."

Cross rose and Eva reached impulsively and grabbed his hand and clung to it.

"Don't go," she begged.

"I was going to try to listen at the door—"

"Don't leave me here," she pleaded in a whisper of panic.

He sat again on the edge of the bed and felt nervous tremors going through her body. If only he could tell her that she was free! But, no . . . If he told her that he had killed, the horror she felt for the Party would be transferred to him. . . .

He was aware of her slim, willowy figure on the bed, the legs that tapered with such a long, slow curve, the suggestively dramatic roundness of her hips, the small but firm breasts, the long and delicate neck, and the hazel pools of her eyes now dark and anxious with dread; and desire for desire rose in him for her for the first time. Oh, God, he must not think of that now. . . . He felt the soft pressure from her thin, almost transparent fingers on his hand and she became woman as body of woman for his senses. The depths of him stirred as he realized that she was now alone in the world and did not know it; in a peculiar sense she was at his mercy. What he did or did not do, what he said or did not say would affect her more profoundly now than anything that would ever happen to her. Already she was his in a deeper sense than the sexual, in a sense that included the sexual. At this moment she was again an orphan; she had only him to depend upon and he could

236

now, as Gil had done with Bob, ravage her entire being without any resistance from her. From the poignant pages of her diary and from the fact that Gil was dead and she did not know it, he possessed a comprehension of her existence that she had not the capacity to imagine. Would she suspect him? *Could* she suspect him? She believed that colored people were caught up in life, healthy, untouched and unspoiled by the cynical world of political deceptions. . . . Had she not referred to "us" when she spoke of her fear of the Party?

For the first time since he had killed, he felt guilty. It was not a guilt for his having murdered; it was because he now saw that he held over the life of Eva a godlike power and knowledge that even Gil or the Party had not held. He had killed Gil and Herndon because they had wanted to play god to others, and their brutal strivings had struck him as being so utterly obscene that he had torn their lives from them in a moment of supreme conviction that he and he alone was right and that they were eternally wrong. And now Gil lay still and dead downstairs amid the trembling red shadows and he sat here holding Eva's hand, desiring her body. And the wall of deception which he had begun to erect to conceal the nature of her husband's death would throw her, perhaps, into his arms. . . .

If the actions of Gil and Herndon were monstrously inhuman, then wasn't what he was doing also devoid of humanity? If there was a valid difference, just where did it lie? Was the guilt of Gil and Herndon the less because they had millions of supporters, because time and tradition, law and religion, had mounted a shield of justification before them? And his guilt, was it the more because he was alone and had no counsel but his own? If Gil or Herndon had done what he had done, would it have worried them? Wasn't his worrying proof that he was wrong? Didn't he need about him the sanctioning buttress of the faces of his brothers in crime to make him feel at home with his deed?

His sense of despair deepened and he yearned for the first time to be free of this circling brooding that filled his skull, this elusive shadow of himself that tortured him. To go on killing would only sink him deeper into the quicksands of guilt which he wanted so much to avoid. But what

237

way was there out of this? The desperately naïve idea of confessing everything to Eva came to him. Might not she, being another victim, understand and help him? *No!* That was crazy. . . . She believed him an *innocent* victim, not a *guilty* one! No; he could talk to no one now; he had to tread this guilty treadmill alone. . . .

He recovered himself as the fingers of Eva's hand tightened about his own.

"Are you frightened, Lionel?"

"No."

"What can we tell them?"

"The truth. We'll tell them what happened. . . ."

He knew that, childlike, she was already thinking that maybe a lie would be a better kind of truth to tell than to try to conceal the guilt that had so long smoldered in her heart. Why was he mulling and hesitating? Ride this thing out and take this lovely girl and live with her . . .

"What are you thinking, Lionel?"

"Nothing," he breathed.

"They'll say we acted wrongly, won't they?"

"How could they?" he asked. "We couldn't do any more than we did—"

"Oh, why did the Party push *you* into this?" she wailed.

"We're in it together," he told her.

The doorbell rang.

Cross let in Jack Hilton and another man. They stared at one another for a moment in silence. Eva came running from the bedroom.

"He's still down there, Jack— Can't you do something?" she implored. "Maybe he's hurt. . . ."

Hilton's face turned pale and he spun to Cross.

"But the police? Aren't they here *yet?*"

"No," Cross told him.

"And Gil's *still* down there?"

"Yes."

"And that door's still locked?"

"I guess so," Cross stammered.

"My God—" Hilton said, whirling and going through the door. He halted, turned, and beckoned to his companion. "Come *on*, Menti!"

They thundered down the stairs. Eva followed Menti; and Cross, lingering, followed Eva, watching Hilton's movements, wondering what his tactics would be. They paused momentarily in the downstairs hallway. Hilton advanced to the door of Herndon's apartment.

"Is this the door?"

"Yes," Cross told him.

Hilton grabbed the knob and rattled it.

"Gil! Are you there?" Hilton called loudly.

"Gil! Gil!" Eva yelled, hammering on the panels of the door with her fists.

"You'd better break it down," Cross said. "I've called and called—"

Hilton hesitated, then ran to the rear door and tried the handle. He walked back toward them with worried eyes.

"Put your shoulder to it, Menti," Hilton said.

"Okay," Menti agreed eagerly.

Menti, tall, black-haired, with a nervous, too-white face, backed off to the bottom of the stairs, quickly hunched his shoulders and sent himself toward the door; the second his body hit the panels, the door burst in, banging loudly against the wall inside. Menti blocked Cross's vision and he could see nothing; he remembered the room lit by flames and dancing shadows, but the wood fire had died down. Eva pushed past him, then stopped, her face gazing at the floor of Herndon's study.

"Gil! Oh, God, Gil!" she screamed.

Cross could now see the dim outlines of Gil and Herndon lying outstretched on the rug. They were as he had left them, the table leg and the fire poker lying near their right hands, their faces darkened with splotches of blood.

"Good Christ," Menti breathed.

"Gil! Gil!" Eva was still screaming, advancing slowly into the room.

Hilton stood without moving, his thin lips hanging open. Eva was now bent over Gil, her hands reaching out as though to touch him; then she closed her eyes and leaned weakly against a wall, sobbing. Cross watched closely, waiting for questions. Hilton was the first to master himself; he rushed forward, knelt at Gil's side and felt for his pulse. His eyes lifted to Eva's face; then he looked at Cross; he

239

stood slowly, turning and looking at Menti. Only later did he glance at Herndon, then kneel and feel for his pulse.

"Help him," Eva begged, staring at Gil as though she expected him to rise and accuse her.

"We better call the police again," Menti said.

"Better call a doctor," Cross ventured.

"No; wait," Hilton said, his eyes straying from face to face. "Look, don't touch anything here. . . . Let's get upstairs!"

"Get a doctor," Eva begged. "He's bleeding. . . . Somebody *do* something. . . ." She knelt to touch Gil, but Hilton grabbed her arm.

"Gil's dead, Eva," Hilton told her. "Don't touch anything."

Cross held her by her shoulders, conscious that Hilton's eyes were upon him. He knew that the time of his drastic test was beginning, a test he did not want, for, if he won it, what had he won? Eva? He hadn't killed to get her. Hilton was still staring at him; then Hilton turned and walked slowly to the hall door. Menti ran to Hilton and grabbed his arm.

"Hadn't I better call the Party again?" he asked.

"We haven't time," Hilton said. "The police'll be here any minute now."

Menti was nonplused; "I think we should call the Party," he said.

"Take it easy, Menti," Hilton said with a slow, ironic smile. "This is more complicated than you think. I'm in charge here. I spoke to Blimin over the phone and he told me to take complete responsibility. *This* is political."

"I see," Menti said, dropping his eyes.

Hilton was now staring at Cross. And Cross, as he watched Hilton, knew that this was the man he had to cope with, and a slow hatred for Hilton began to surge up in him. He still kept his arm about Eva, who was trembling against him. Why was Hilton staring at him so? Was he already suspecting him? Hilton was a member of the upper circles of the Party and he was no fool. Cross held himself alert, every atom of him striving to be aware of what was taking place.

"We've no time to lose," Hilton told them roughly.

240

"Everybody get upstairs at once. Stay in the apartment until I come."

"No, no," Eva sobbed. "Help Gil—"

"Go upstairs, Eva," Hilton said. "It's too late."

Cross led Eva into the hallway and struggled up the steps with her; Menti helped him, but kept looking over his shoulder to see what Hilton was doing. Inside the apartment, Eva clutched Menti and begged: "Can't something be done, Menti? It's not too late, *is* it?"

"Take it easy, Eva," Menti said. "Hilton's doing everything. . . ."

Cross eased Eva upon the sofa of the living room and Menti sat next to her, holding her shoulders. Hilton entered a moment later and Cross could see sweat on his forehead.

"He should've broken that door down," Menti told Hilton, nodding to Cross.

"No; he did right," Hilton said. "He's colored. . . . This thing is complicated. . . ."

Hilton left the room and Cross could hear him putting the night-chain on the front door. Hilton returned and knelt at Eva's side.

"Eva," he began in a hurried but composed voice, "can you understand me? Are you fit to be questioned? We don't have much time—"

"But maybe he's not dead, Jack," Eva whimpered. "Try . . . try to *do* something. . . ."

"They're *both* dead, Eva," Hilton said sternly. "We've no time for that. . . . You must get hold of yourself. You're in the Party. You must rise above personal feeling. This is important to the memory of Gil and I must discuss it with you. You hear me?"

"Yes," Eva breathed, trying to still the shaking of her body.

"Gil's been killed by a Fascist," Hilton explained. "He was carrying out Party orders when he was killed; he fell in line of duty. . . . That must be understood. This is a *Party* matter. The bourgeois press'll try to twist those facts downstairs, and we must see that they don't. I'm sure that Gil, if he were with us now, would agree emphatically to that."

"Yes," Eva said, nodding her head slowly; she glanced at Cross and buried her face in her hands.

Cross grasped the approach; it was as he had hoped it would be. But they had not questioned him yet; that was to come.

"Now, Eva," Hilton was saying, "tell me quickly what happened. . . ."

"Ask Lionel. . . . I only saw Herndon beating Gil," she said.

"You were not in the room at all?" Hilton asked Eva.

"No. . . ."

Hilton rose and faced Cross.

"Were you in the room?"

"No," Cross said. "I was looking in through the door. He came at me, hit me with the poker— Right here—"

"Start from the beginning and tell me quickly," Hilton urged.

Cross sketched the story briefly, telling the facts just as they had happened, but omitting that he had been in the room.

"God, I'm sorry about Gil," he ended up.

"This is war," Hilton said. "We must expect casualties. Gil was brave." He studied Cross. "I saw you at Bob's last night, didn't I?"

"Yes."

"What's your name?"

"Lionel Lane."

"You've got to help us with this thing," Hilton said. "You were Gil's friend. . . ."

"I'll do what I can."

"Listen to me carefully, all of you," Hilton began. "The important thing here is who died *first*. Get it?"

"What do you mean?" Menti asked.

"If it's proved that Herndon died first, then they'll want to brand Gil as a murderer," Hilton explained swiftly.

"But Eva saw Herndon alive with a gun. . . . He was after her," Cross told him.

"Yes; I know that," Hilton said. "But when you looked into the door and saw Herndon beating Gil . . . Gil was not able to defend himself, was he? Herndon was killing him. . . . Do you understand? It's important."

242

Menti approached Cross and caught his arm.

"Look, guy, Gil was killed by that Fascist," Menti said. "Do you understand that?"

"Gil died fighting for your people, for *you*," Hilton reminded him.

"I know that," Cross said, simulating bafflement; he didn't want to seem to grasp it too quickly. He squinted his eyes and looked at the floor; he felt like laughing out loud. They were now begging *him* to believe something that he was praying that *they* would believe!

Cross looked at Eva. Though she had stopped sobbing, Cross could see that she didn't quite follow what was being said. Cross felt that now was the time to co-operate with the Party, to demonstrate class consciousness, to cast his solidarity with the revolution. He nodded his head, looking slowly from Hilton to Menti.

"When I looked through the doorway, I saw Herndon with his foot on Gil's chest— He was hitting Gil— With the poker— I don't know how many times he hit him— Then Eva came down and Herndon saw us. He ran us back upstairs with the fire poker. . . ."

"Yes," Eva sighed.

"And Gil couldn't move when you looked into that door?" Hilton demanded.

"No, he was out, unconscious, it seems to me. . . ."

Hilton turned to Eva.

"And you saw Herndon *after* Lionel was up here? He was coming to get into the apartment? You ran back in and shut the door, didn't you, Eva? He had his gun?"

"Yes," she said.

"That is *proof*," Hilton said.

Cross wondered if Eva really believed it. Her sense of guilt was making her paint a picture that was helping him.

"Lionel, you just tell the cops what you saw; stick to your story," Hilton said. "Cops are your enemies. Look at what they've done to your people. . . . Don't forget the lynchings. . . . No matter *what* they do to you, say nothing but the truth; you hear? Gil gave his life for you. Herndon miscalculated; he thought he could scare Gil. When Herndon killed Gil, he was really killing *you;* you understand?"

"I understand," Cross answered.

"You better call those cops again," Menti said.

Hilton left and a moment later Cross heard him dialing the telephone. Menti stood looking at Cross and Eva, and Cross could guess what was going through the man's mind. Menti was hoping that Eva would be able to keep him in line, keep him loyal to the Party; and no doubt that same idea was in the back of Hilton's mind.

"Poor girl," Menti said to Cross, nodding toward Eva. "We owe it to her to protect the name of Gil."

"You can depend on me," Cross assured him; the corners of his mouth twitched, for he was wondering just what they would depend upon him for: to lie for the Party or to try to win Eva? And, back of it all, he was protecting his own wild despair at having surrendered to his pride to the point of having killed. . . .

Hilton returned to the room absent-mindedly puffing at a cigarette. His bony, ascetic face was tensely concentrated. Cross marveled at the self-possession of this man who, twenty-four hours ago, had mercilessly reduced Bob's enthusiasm for organizing to a heap of whimpering flesh, and Cross was certain that no regretful memories lingered on in Hilton's mind as he coldly grappled with this new crisis. Men like Hilton did not spend their days scheming how to get hold of dollars; they worked at organizing and exploiting the raw stuff of human emotions. In being close to the common impulses of men, in their cynical acceptance of the cupidities of the human heart, in their frank recognition of outlandish passions, they were akin to priests. Now that he had killed Gil and had elected to remain near Eva, this man was his adversary, an adversary who played a game whose stakes held nothing less than life and death. . . . Cross fought feebly against an intellectual pride that was rising in him and making him want to cope with Hilton, to show him that he and his kind did not possess a monopoly of knowledge about the emotional nature of man. And again Cross was dismayed at himself for contracting the ailment he hated. To fight Hilton meant fighting Hilton on Hilton's own ground, just as he had had to kill Gil and Herndon on their own ground, and that in itself wás a defeat, a travesty of the impulse that had first

244

moved him. . . . Was all action doomed to this kind of degradation? How did one get around that? Or maybe you couldn't get around it? Perhaps he was staring right now at the focal point of history: if you fought men who tried to conquer you in terms of total power you too had to use total power and in the end you became what you tried to defeat. . . .

Hilton was restless, shifting from foot to foot, as if he feared that if he stood still he would commit some violent act. Here was a human instrument that had placed the total capacities of its life completely at the disposal of the Party. . . . Cross could feel that Hilton, at this very moment, was pondering some question concerning him, for Hilton's wary eyes were fixed upon his face. Finally Hilton said to Cross: "Come into the kitchen a moment."

"Sure."

Menti was talking to Eva now in low, consoling tones and Cross followed Hilton. When they were inside the kitchen, Hilton shut the door. He smiled and asked: "How's she taking it?"

"As you see," Cross answered, on guard.

"You think we ought to get somebody to be with her?"

"Gosh, I don't know." He thought the question odd, for Hilton had shown no concern about Eva's state until now. "She doesn't seem to show much of what's going on in her."

"*That's* what I'm scared of," Hilton said in a tone of amused wonder. "She might even be glad that Gil is dead when she's over the shock. Gil was a first-class sonofabitch if ever there was one. He was an absolutely cold fish whom I tried always to avoid, if I could. . . ." He caught hold of Cross's arm and squeezed it. "You're not so bourgeois that speaking the truth about the dead bothers you?"

"Hell, no," Cross said; he was genuinely surprised. What was the man getting at?

"Gil was snobbish to the point of inciting murder, really," Hilton went on, smiling wryly. "Frankly, I've no sympathy for him. I'm a Communist, and a dead man, so far as I'm concerned, is just so much cold meat." He chuckled uneasily. "He never liked me. I'm just an ex-schoolteacher, but Gil's father was a 1905er. . . . His real

245

name was Bernstein. He grew up in the Bronx with the air of revolution in his home and it always made him feel that he was of the Red elite. He hit at me several times politically, but I dodged him. He was widely hated in the Party."

"I didn't know that," Cross said. *Why's he telling me this?*

"And Eva's a cold one too," he went on in a tone of voice that told Cross that he was now getting to his point. "There was no love lost between Gil and Eva. . . . Don't kid yourself. In the Party, we know things."

Hilton looked at Cross curiously. *He's worried about Eva and he's wondering how much I know. . . .* He decided not to tell Hilton that he knew Eva's marriage had been arranged by the Party, and that Eva had been in revolt, had been seething with hatred and despair.

"She knows a lot about the Party, but Gil was her only real link to us," Hilton pursued his theme. His lips moved without emitting words.

"Have you heard her say anything against the Party?" he asked finally.

Cross decided at once that he would defend Eva: their interests were identical.

"Never." He reflected that he was a newcomer and his word would not mean much. "She's never spoken an anti-Party word. In fact, I've asked her about political issues, but she'd never talk. Of course, you know that I'm not yet a member of the Party. . . ."

"She likes colored people," Hilton said. He hastened to add: "I'm not saying that in a nasty way. She does. Tell me, do you think she trusts you?"

Cross understood at last. Hilton was asking him to watch over Eva! And he was longing to do just that, but not for Hilton's or the Party's sake. And, no doubt, in the living room Menti was hinting to Eva to keep an eye on Cross. . . .

"I don't know," Cross said cautiously.

"From what I see of her reactions, I think she does," Hilton said with a sly smile.

Cross was angry, but he hid his feelings. He sensed that at some time in the past Hilton must have made advances to Eva and had been repulsed; and now, in the interests of the Party, he was giving her up. What a man! Cross thought.

"Why aren't you a member of the Party?"

"Well, I just met Gil and Eva last night."

"That's long enough. You are a Negro and you've an instinct for this sort of thing. I don't mean a racial instinct; it's a socially conditioned instinct for dissimulation which white Americans have bred in you, and you've had to practice it in order to survive. Look, every day in this land some white man is cussing out some defenseless Negro. But that white bastard is too stupid to realize that his actions are being duplicated a million times in a million other spots by other whites who feel hatred for Negroes just like he does. He's too blind to see that this daily wave of a million tiny assaults builds up a vast reservoir of resentment in Negroes. At night at home Negroes discuss this bitterly. But the next morning, smiling, they show up on their jobs, swearing that they love white people. Why? You know the answer. They have to live, eat, have a roof over their heads. So they collaborate with people who they feel are their sworn enemies. . . . White America has built up something in you that can help the Party now. Defend yourself against these cops who are coming, and, if you do, you are defending the Party and your own interests at the same time. If you are honest in your heart, you can't deny the Party. What about it, Lionel?"

How astute the man was! The average white American could never drag such simple truths past his lips, and here was a man confessing it with fluent passion. Did the average white American suspect that men like Hilton existed, men who could easily rise above the racial hatred of the mob and cynically make use of the defensive attitudes instilled in Negroes as weapons in their own bitter struggle for power? This Hilton knew his country as only a man who had lived in it but was not of it could know it. He was a man who, like Houston, like Gil, was an outsider and was free. But I'm an outsider too, Cross thought musingly. I'll let him use me for what *I* want to be used for. . . .

"I have no objections," Cross said softly.

What greater protection could he dream of than this?

The Party he loathed was going to help defend him. . . .

"Now, when the police questioning is over, I want to talk to you," Hilton said, giving Cross a card with his address upon it. "I don't live far from here—"

"Okay," Cross agreed, taking the card from him.

They shook hands.

"Just look after Eva," Hilton said. "If anything develops, get in touch with me. In fact, I think you'd better stay close to her."

Cross did not trust himself to answer. He simply nodded. Hilton looked nervously at his wrist watch.

"The police are slow in coming," he commented.

They returned to the living room. Eva was stretched out on the sofa. Cross went to her, bent down and asked: "Can I get you something, Eva?"

She shook her head, forcing a wan smile to her lips. Menti looked at Hilton and winked. Hilton knelt at her knees and caught hold of her hand.

"Eva, Gil's gone, but the Party's still here," he said in solemn tones. "I've no doubt but that you're going to be able to do what you're called upon to do. Here's the situation: Herndon called Gil down to make him put Lionel out of the apartment. You heard noises and you and Lionel went down to see what was the matter. Herndon was beating Gil. He drove both of you upstairs, beating Lionel with the poker. You heard more noises. Eva, you tried to phone the police, but couldn't get through. So you phoned me and I phoned the cops; understand? Then you and Lionel heard more noises and screams. You sent Lionel down to help Gil. . . . But the door was locked. Lionel came back up to phone the cops and, Eva, you started down again. But Herndon ran you back up with his gun. You saw him on the stairs with his gun. You both then locked yourselves in. You phoned me again. I came with Menti. We broke down the door—" Hilton gripped Eva's arm tightly. "Now, listen, we *didn't* tell you what we found down there, Eva. . . . You hear? You *understand* that?"

"What do you mean?" Eva asked, baffled.

"I mean this," Hilton explained. "You and Lionel *did not* go down with us— You and Lionel remained up here; understand? You don't know that Gil's dead. When you
248

hear that he's dead, you must scream. Your husband's been murdered. Herndon's guilty of *murder*. That's all. Herndon's the murderer. The rest of the burden's on us. . . ."

Eva nodded her head, tears streaming again down her cheeks.

"You are a *Communist*, Eva," Hilton emphasized. "We Communists do what we have to do. It's our life."

Then the room was deathly still; in the distance came the faintly rising wail of a siren.

"Are you all right, Eva?" Menti asked.

"I'm all right," Eva said, steeling herself.

The police are coming, Cross told himself. If Eva could face them, then, God knows, he ought to be able to. Buttressed by these two men whose profession was based on a defiance of the law, he would have more than an equal chance. For a moment a nostalgic regret seized hold of him. Why wasn't he *with* them? As allies against racist white Americans, they had no peers. But he knew that that was not all. He recalled Bob's squirming on the floor, begging for mercy that the Party would not grant. No; no, he wouldn't swallow that happening to him. . . . The sirens were near now. Then he couldn't hear them and he knew that the police were downstairs in the snow-choked streets in front of the house.

Cross knew that another world, Herndon's world, was coming; the police agents of that world were as much against him as the dead man Herndon had been. And Hilton and Menti were his allies and wanted to defend him, whatever their motives. He was black and, in the baleful eyes of the men who were coming, he had no right to be here in a white apartment building in a white neighborhood. He leaned against the wall, waiting, thinking. Why was it like this? As a Negro, he was not even free to choose his own allies.

What a cheap price Hilton was paying for his loyalty! And for men like Hilton, detached from impulses of racial hatred, what a trifling effort to expend to capture the allegiance of millions of people! Wasn't a world that left itself open to such easy attacks a stupid world, a doomed world, a rotten world not worth fighting for or saving? Since Herndon's world considered him only half human, why

249

didn't he, out of spite and in defense of his own human dignity, turn on that world and, with the help of such base and dubious allies as Hilton and Menti, destroy it? But what would happen to him after that world was destroyed . . . ? He would be at the mercy of the Hiltons and Mentis. . . . What a black choice!

He heard the slow, heavy tramp of feet on the stairs, and the sound of wrenching at the doorknobs; then the bell pealed impatiently. Cross moved to the center of the room, but Hilton waved him back.

"Stay put. I'll get this. I'll do the talking until they ask you something."

Menti sat holding his arms about Eva and looking at Cross. Cross winked at Menti and Menti smiled. He had to give these men some assurance. He heard Hilton open the door.

"What's the trouble here?" The voice was rough and aggressive.

"There's been an awful fight downstairs," Cross heard Hilton explaining. "I think you'd better go down and see—"

"Whose apartment is this and who are you?"

"I'm a friend of one of the men downstairs, Mr. Gilbert Blount," Hilton's voice came clear and steady. "But, say, I think you ought to take a look quick—"

"I asked you your name."

"Hilton, Jack Hilton."

"And where do you live?"

"At the Edward Hotel near Washington Square."

"And what were these men fighting about?"

"Well, it seems that the landlord, Mr. Herndon, objected to a certain tenant—"

"We'll see about that," a flat, brutal voice said.

There was silence. Cross could hear voices but could not make out what was being said.

"What are you doing here now?"

"Mrs. Blount, the wife of one of the men downstairs, asked me to come over," Hilton explained. "Look, don't you think you ought to take a look and see what's happened to the men down there—?"

"Where's Mrs. Blount now?"

"In the living room," Hilton answered. "But maybe a doctor could help those men—"

"Look, Mister, we know our job, so don't try to tell us what to do, see?"

"Well, I just thought—"

"We want to see Mrs. Blount," the hard voice insisted.

"Sure. Come in. That way— She's in the living room."

Cross heard feet coming down the hallway. Eva sat up, supported by Menti's arm. Two policemen, tall and seemingly Irish, came into the room and at once stopped dead in their tracks at the sight of the dark face of Cross. The older of the two policemen stared at Cross, Eva, Menti, then at Hilton, and finally his large, bold, gray eyes rested on Cross again.

"What's the matter with you people? Are you color-blind?" he demanded with a faint sneer on his lips.

"Who are you?" Menti asked.

"Lieutenant Farrel. This is Officer Clark, my aide." He turned toward Eva. "Are you Mrs. Blount?"

"I am," Eva whispered.

"What seems to be the trouble, lady?" Farrel asked.

"My husband— He's downstairs— I'm afraid he's hurt — He had an argument with the landlord, Mr. Herndon—"

"Who are these people?" Lieutenant Farrel asked, glancing at Menti and then Cross.

"My name's Herbert Menti, a friend of Mrs. Blount. And this is Lionel Lane, who lives here."

"*You* live here?" Farrel asked Cross, lifting his eyebrows.

"Yes," Cross answered.

"Why?"

"Why not?" Cross countered.

Farrel stared, then rocked back on his heels and looked over the people. "Are you *married* to anybody here?" Farrel demanded.

"No. I room here. I'm a student," Cross said.

"Uh huh," Farrel said.

"Is there anything illegal about Mr. Lane's being here?" Hilton asked pointedly.

"No," Farrel said, pulling down the corners of his mouth. "It's legal, just *legal*."

There was silence in the room as the pounding of feet on the stairs was heard. An officer stumbled through the door, panting, his face red and his eyes round with shock.

"Farrel, downstairs—" he gasped. "Quick, man—God! Looks like they bashed each other to death! It's a regular slaughterhouse, for real. . . . You have to *see* it to believe it—"

"*Two?*" Farrel asked, his mouth dropping open.

"Yep. *Two*."

Cross's eyes went quickly to Eva's face. Could she cope with this? He saw her hesitate a second, then rise, her eyes blazing with disbelief.

"No, *no* . . . ! *What* are you saying? Gil, Gil, *Gil!*" she screamed.

"Lady!" Farrel called to her.

"Oh, my poor Gil!" Eva cried, running toward the door.

Farrel grabbed her. Eva struggled, trying to break loose.

"Let me go; let me go. . . . Gil— Gil—"

She pulled from Farrel's arms and sank to the floor, sobbing convulsively.

"They've killed my poor husband— Oh, God, help poor Gil—"

"Is that his wife?" the new policeman asked.

"Yes," Menti answered.

"You'd better get her to lie down," Clark said.

"Eva, come with me," Menti said, lifting Eva from the floor. "Darling, take it easy— We don't know for sure yet—"

"I want to go to Gil," she cried.

"No, no; you must stay here," Menti insisted. "Lie here on the sofa—"

Cross was transfixed. She had done it. She had conquered her genuine grief and had replaced it with a pretended one, and somehow he felt that the pretended one was more real than the other. It rang with a sincerity that stemmed from a conscious act of creation.

". . . one used a table leg and the other a fire poker, it seems," the cop was explaining to Farrel.

Farrel's eyes widened in wonder.

252

"Is it too late to do anything for 'em?" Hilton asked, making sure to include Herndon in his question.

"Clark, stand guard here," Farrel said, ignoring Hilton. He beckoned the other policeman. "Come on. We'll have to get the Medical Examiner if what you say is true. . . ."

Grim-lipped, Clark towered over Eva, Menti, Hilton and Cross. Sounds of voices and commotion could be heard downstairs now.

"He didn't seem to like you, Lane," Hilton said.

"Look," the policeman on guard held up his hand in a warning, "I must tell you that I can repeat anything I hear you say, see? So be careful."

"I don't give a damn what you do," Hilton shot at the cop. "I've nothing to hide here. None of us has. Now, I say that that damned Lieutenant Farrel made some nasty cracks here about Mr. Lane. He called us color-blind. He wanted to know if Lane was married to anybody here. . . . Now, you can damn well repeat *that* to Headquarters, if you want to. If you don't, I will. Mr. Lane has more than a legal right to be here."

The cop reddened with embarrassment.

"I reckon you got something there, buddy," he said in tones of conciliation.

Cross assumed a relaxed, detached air, but he managed to keep a furtive eye on Eva. He knew that two main lines of development were possible: the average cop would either consider him fair game and concentrate upon him as a Negro, or he would seize on the Communist political angle for purposes of public exploitation. I'm going to sit tight and see which way the cat jumps, Cross mused, proud that he was conscious of their consciousness. It was, of course, possible, but not probable, that they might combine the two issues and whip up a lynch atmosphere. Barring some fantastic facts coming to light, he did not see how they could think of him in relation to the deaths of Gil and Herndon. And, even if they did, there were the machinating temperaments of both Hilton and Menti working to advance the interests of the Party by placing the blame for Gil's death on Herndon, and thereby protecting him.

He noticed that Eva was now as calm as marble. Balling a handkerchief in her right fist, she sat looking bleakly in front of her. His eyes caught hers and he saw in them a glint of recognition. Yes, she's with me. She thinks I'm a victim too. . . .

Lieutenant Farrel came back into the room, puffing from climbing the stairs; his heavy brows were knitted in perplexity. Following him was another policeman with a notebook and pencil in hand. He demanded the names, ages, occupations, and identification of all present. Cross accounted for himself as a student and showed his birth certificate and draft card. Hilton was a free-lance writer and Menti spoke of himself as an unemployed printer. The room was quiet; no one volunteered any further information. The burden of getting at what happened fell upon Farrel, and he was a more chastened man now that he had seen the charnel house in Herndon's living room.

"Well, who'll lead off and tell what happened?"

There was silence. Menti looked at Hilton and Hilton looked at Cross. Cross cleared his throat and spoke in low, polite tones: "I'm afraid that you'll have to rely upon me for the details as to how this started."

"And what did you have to do with it?"

"Nothing, directly. But I saw Mr. Herndon striking Mr. Blount with a fire poker. . . ."

Under questioning by Farrel, Cross related what he and Hilton and Menti had agreed upon. He kept his account terse, making no interpretations at all, leaving the cops to make their own inferences. Farrel frowned, looking from face to face. Briefly, Hilton related how he had received two phone calls, one from Eva and another from Lionel. He told of phoning the police, of picking up his friend Menti and rushing over. He related how they had found Lionel and Eva huddled in fear in the apartment, how they had gone down and bashed in the door and found the men lying there, bloody, still. . . .

"We didn't tell Mrs. Blount anything. . . . We waited for you . . . ," Hilton wound up.

"Madam, do you know of any reason why anyone would want to kill your husband?" Farrel asked Eva.

Eva rose magnificently to the question; she threw her hands to her mouth and screamed: "He killed my husband! He killed poor Gil!"

254

"You mean that *Herndon* killed him?" Hilton demanded, looking at Farrel. "Didn't he?"

"We don't know," Farrel said.

"But there are eyewitnesses who saw Herndon beating Blount . . . ," said Menti.

"That's for the Medical Examiner to say," Farrel hedged.

"But where *were* you guys?" Hilton demanded. "I phoned you thirty minutes ago. I got here in ten minutes—"

"We're pretty busy these days," Farrel said. "We got here as soon as we could— This may be a job for the D.A."

Cross was attentive. *Ely Houston?* God. . . . Would Houston recall his false name? He was certain that Houston would remember the talk they had had in his compartment on the train. Houston was capable of finding out the truth about him, could even *guess* the truth. . . . Houston, a hunchback, an outsider, a man whose physical deformity had forced him to live in but not of the normal rounds of ritualized life, knew the demonic feelings of men who played god because he himself was of the demonic clan, having hidden his kinship with the rebellious by publicly upholding the laws and promises that men live by. . . . And Cross knew that Houston would find his crimes not only engrossing but challenging. Houston understood those rare judgment-feelings that made men kill for no motives defined or known in the realms of law. Cross had no real fear of Farrel, or Clark, or the other flatfoots who wandered blunderingly in and out of the apartment, but for Houston he had something akin to terror. . . . The cops were baffled, half-scared men who hid their bewilderment by loud-mouthed blustering; but Houston was so placed psychologically in life that he would feel intuitively at home with his crimes, for he was akin to Gil, to Herndon, to Hilton, and to Cross in temperament and outlook; he had the kind of consciousness that could grasp the mercurial emotions of men whom society had never tamed or disciplined, men whose will had never been broken, men who were wild but sensitive, savage but civilized, intellectual but somehow intrinsically poetic in their inmost hearts.

Farrel left the room and made a lengthy telephone call in the hallway; at last he came in with his verdict.

"All of you must consider yourselves under house arrest," he began. "I'm posting an officer at the door of the apartment for tonight. There are a lot of questions that must be answered. In the morning all of you must face the District Attorney and give him your stories and account for yourselves. The Medical Examiner is downstairs working now—"

"But what is the meaning of this?" Hilton demanded.

"We must determine how those men died downstairs," Farrel said.

"But it's all very simple," Menti said.

"Mr. Lane told you what happened," Hilton said.

"I'm only obeying orders," Farrel said.

"You mean we have to stay here all night—?" Menti asked.

"Absolutely," Farrel snapped.

"But my wife; she'll be upset," Menti objected.

"You got a phone at home?"

"Yes."

"Then call her," Farrel directed.

"And I'll have to stay too?" Hilton demanded.

"I'm afraid so, sir," Farrel said.

"But why?"

"Listen, I'm acting under the orders of the District Attorney. He is acting according to the reports he's getting from the Medical Examiner downstairs. If you want to, I can take you to see an Assistant D.A. Maybe you can arrange something with him. . . ."

"The hell with it," Hilton said.

Eva was weeping now afresh.

"I want to see Gil," she sobbed. "Please, please—"

"I'm sorry, lady," Clark said. "They've taken his body to the morgue."

". . . and it looks like they killed each other," Farrel was saying in a low voice to another officer.

"It's the most freakish thing I ever saw," the other officer said.

256

Finally Cross, Eva, Hilton, and Menti were alone; the police had gone, stationing a young cop on guard in the hallway in front of the apartment door. For a while there was silence among the four of them. Eva was weeping noiselessly but earnestly now, and Cross observed that her grief at this moment had none of that spontaneousness that had characterized the grief she had pretended for the cops. She was free now; her secret wish had come true. . . . Was that why she was weeping?

Cross was frantically trying to weigh all the possibilities involved. Could the Party let Eva, with her guilty knowledge, go free? And the Party's attitude toward him? For the moment the Party was his ally, but Communists were not naïve enough to accept him merely on a basis of declaration of solidarity. They wanted something more. . . . And what could that be . . . ? For its own defense, the Party was trying to dump Eva into his arms, knowing that black and white love could find shelter nowhere so readily as under its red aegis. . . . Well, for the time being he'd accept the situation as it was, but not for the Party's reasons. . . .

Cross watched Hilton. Eva was resting on the sofa with her face buried in the crook of her elbow, her chest heaving. Menti patted her shoulder. Hilton paced the floor, puffing at the inevitable cigarette that protruded from his lips.

"It didn't go too badly." Hilton spoke as though wanting to share his thoughts. "But, of course, the real showdown will come in the morning with the D.A." He looked at Cross. "You did well. Maintain the same attitude tomorrow. We're behind you."

"I'll try," Cross mumbled; he wondered if he ought to tell Hilton that he had already met the District Attorney. He decided not to; there was no purpose in adding to Hilton's suspicions. I'll try to take care of it when it comes, he told himself. But Hilton worried him. The man was *too* calm, *too* collected, his face always a tense, blank mask. How *much* of his reactions was he concealing?

"I'm sleepy," Hilton said, stretching his arms above his head and giving a yawn that was *too* genuine.

"Why don't you and Menti sleep in Gil's room," Eva suggested in a whisper.

"Okay, I'm turning in," Hilton said. But even now he did not demonstrate any feeling of sympathy for Eva. "Good night," he said, and headed for the hallway.

"Is there anything I can do for you, Eva?" Cross asked.

"No. You should rest, Lionel," she said, looking pityingly at him. "We brought you into a mess, didn't we? I'm sorry. . . ."

"Good night," Menti called to her.

An hour later Cross was in bed, turning sleeplessly from side to side, trying mentally to cope with the threat of Ely Houston. What would he think of these deaths? Would he not think it somewhat odd that both Gil and Herndon had been men of extreme ideas? Oh, God . . . Cross sat upright in bed with a wild jerk of his body. Jesus . . . *That bloody handkerchief . . . !* He had to get rid of it before the District Attorney showed up in the morning; it had been in the pocket of his pants until now. . . . He got out of bed, pulled on his bathrobe, took the wadded handkerchief and put it into the pocket of the robe and softly opened the door to the hallway. The apartment was quiet and dark. If anybody demanded where he was going, he could always say that he was on his way to the bathroom. . . . He stole silently down the dark hallway to the door of the kitchen. He paused, listening for sounds, then turned the knob, pushed the door inward, and went inside. Faint blue light fell through a window, casting a ghostly radiance over the gas stove, the sink, and the refrigerator. Yes, there was the incinerator. . . . He could see and would not have to turn on the light. He crossed the floor and lifted the lid and tossed the guilty handkerchief quickly down. He smelled a whiff of smoke; it would burn soon. His tension ebbed a bit. He turned to go to his room and suddenly the kitchen light blazed on. He caught his breath; Hilton was sitting in a chair near the wall, the habitual cigarette hanging unlit from his lips.

"I didn't know you were there," Cross breathed, struggling to stifle his panic.

"What's the matter?" Hilton asked. "You can't sleep either?"

Cross thought rapidly. Had Hilton seen him throw the handkerchief away? He didn't think so. Then his job now was to act natural and not rouse Hilton's suspicions.

"I thought I'd get a glass of milk," Cross mumbled. "Ha-ha—I threw my cigarette down the incinerator—I smoke too much." Ought he have said that? Good God, this sonofabitch Hilton . . .

Moving self-consciously, he took a tumbler from a cupboard and went to the refrigerator and poured some milk.

"Aren't you going to sleep?" Cross asked, taking a sip from the glass.

"I never sleep much," Hilton grumbled. "Just sitting, thinking . . ."

"That's a goddamn shame about Gil, isn't it?" Cross felt compelled to say.

"Yeah," Hilton drawled.

"I should've broken down that damned door," Cross accused himself.

"You did what he told you to, didn't you? You've nothing to worry about."

"Yes. But to die like that—"

"A Communist is a soldier, Lane. He's prepared to die."

"I'm so new at all of this—"

"You're not so new. You know what you're doing."

"But I don't understand—"

"You understand enough," Hilton cut him short.

What was Hilton thinking? The very manner in which he spoke bothered Cross. But what the hell! He was going to sleep. . . . Hilton knew nothing yet.

"I'm tired; good night," Cross said.

"Good night, Lane," Hilton said, staring at the far wall.

Had Hilton seen anything? He went down the hallway, then paused, listening. There were no sounds. No, Hilton had seen nothing; if he had, he surely would have said something about it. Hilton was no bashful boy. . . . Now that he felt out of danger, Cross's heart began to pound with excitement. If Hilton had caught him with that bloody handkerchief, he would have been in Hilton's power for the rest of his life. He would either have had to kill Hilton on the spot, or make a break for it through one of the windows of the apartment. To be in the power of a cold little god like Hilton was about the most awful thing that could happen to a man. He would have trampled on me night and day, Cross thought, shivering with relief. He entered his room and, fumbling in the dark, he pulled off his robe and got into bed.

"Lionel—"

It was Eva's voice coming from nearby; it was low and plaintive. Terror flooded him. Maybe they *all* knew what he had done!

"Eva?"

"Yes."

What was she doing here in his room in the dark? Did she know that he had just burned the handkerchief? He reached out to turn on the light and his hand knocked over a book.

"No," Eva whispered.

He felt her fingers seize hold of his hand.

"Don't turn on the light."

"What's the matter, Eva?"

He felt both of her hands now gripping his own, as though she was trying to hang on to him for life's sake.

"I didn't know you were out of your room," she began, her voice catching in her throat. "I knocked and when you didn't answer, I came in. . . ."

Cross felt hot tears dropping onto his fingers.

"Lionel, forgive me— But I'm so *scared*—and I'm so much *alone*— You'll never know how alone I am— I'm bothering you, I know— But I can't stay in my room alone," she sobbed. "Oh, God, I'm no good—I'm too scared—" For a second she was silent. Then she spoke again in a changed tone of voice: "You're colored and you're strong. I'll never know how you managed to face those awful people and never flinch or quail. . . . You're prepared for them and I'm not. . . . Have pity on me and let me stay here near you. . . ."

Her breathing filled the darkness. Her soul was reaching toward him for protection, solace. Cross smiled, feeling that he was listening to her words as perhaps God listens to prayers. . . . A wave of hot pride flooded him. She was laying her life at his feet. With a gesture of his hand

260

he could own her, shield her from the Party, from fear, from her own sense of guilt. . . .

"You'll be cold," he said softly.

"No, no . . . I'll be all right."

"Here; take my robe. . . ."

"All right," she consented.

He heard her moving amid a rustling of garments in the dark, and then he felt her hands again, her fingers entwining themselves in his own.

"You don't mind, Lionel? Please don't send me away. . . ."

"No, Eva."

"I just can't stand fear, and I'm full of fear when I'm alone in times like these. . . . And I've been scared so long. . . ."

"Just rest easy. You'll be all right. Don't worry. . . ."

"I thought you'd understand. . . . Don't tell the others I came in here," she begged. "I'm ashamed of being so scared."

"No one will ever know," he told her.

"I don't mind so much if I cry before *you,* but I could never cry before *them,*" she whispered. "And I *need* to cry. . . ."

Her weeping now was real, different from the pretended weeping for the police and different from the weeping she had done in front of Hilton and Menti. In the universe of white skins, she was too frozen with fear to cry; but with people of color who she felt were victims too and so more understanding, she could weep without check. He wanted to hold her and take her into the bed, but he felt it would violate her budding trust.

"Lionel," she called in a whisper.

"Yes?"

She controlled her sobbing and was silent for some moments.

"We could have saved Gil," she whispered, and choked.

"But, Eva, how could we know that that would happen?" he asked gently, trying to purge her of her sense of guilt.

"But the Party might think that we *let* him be killed," she breathed.

She was not confessing to him, but she was near it.

"But, *why?*" he asked in make-believe astonishment.

She wept afresh, resting her head on his shoulder.

"You don't understand," she said despairingly. "People are worse than you think. . . . They treat you bad because you're colored, but me—people like me, they take our *lives* away. . . ."

He was silent. He had given his life away. How could he ever tell her that he understood what had blasted her self-confidence?

"You'll be all right," he said soothingly.

"You shouldn't be in this. You've suffered enough—"

"I'm used to it, Eva."

"Why's there so much cruelty? I want to die; life's *too* much, *too* much. . . . Is it wrong to feel like that, Lionel?"

"We all feel it. But we have to fight it," he told her.

"Did you ever want to kill yourself?"

"Yes."

"Oh, Lionel!"

Her fingers gripped his like bands of steel. Then he felt her fingers disengage themselves from his and a moment later they were touching his lips, his eyes, his hair, tenderly, softly.

"Those cops were horrible to you tonight, weren't they?"

"It was nothing."

"I'm so sorry, Lionel," she sighed. "You have it hard enough, and then we drag you into this. . . ."

He understood. She was pitying him for being black and having to take the scoffs and insults of the white world; and, in doing so, she was pitying him for the wrong reasons. But he couldn't tell her that. Oh, God . . . if only he could find a way of begging her pity for having killed Gil, for having let his soul take on the shape of monstrousness, for having forsaken his humanity. That was the pitying he needed. . . . He knew that Eva, too, had been forced to live as an outsider; she, too, in a different sort of way, was on his side. Maybe, in the future, he could tell her, could unburden himself and feel free once before he died?

262

He felt her moving and then she was sliding into bed with him.

"Just hold me a little, Lionel," she whispered, shivering and clinging to him.

He held her, feeling her hot tears on his face.

"I'm so cold, so scared, so lost."

At last she grew quiet and later he could tell that she had gone to sleep. It was then that he knew he loved her, wanted to try to banish the dread that haunted her, wanted to tell her what he knew of terror and hopelessness. He held in his arms one woman who was willing to understand, whom life had so tempered that he could talk to her, but between them stood a wall not of race but of mutual guilt, blood, and false identity. . . .

Pale dawn crept into the room. Cross looked down at Eva's wan face; she slept as one exhausted. He shook her gently, calling softly to her: "Eva . . ."

Her eyes fluttered open; when she saw him, she buried her face in his bosom.

"Darling, go to your room," he told her. "It's better that way with Hilton and Menti in the apartment."

"Yes; you're right, Lionel."

She kissed him lightly on his lips and whispered: "Thank you, darling."

And she was gone. The more he thought of her the more he began to care about what would happen to him. Could he fight his way through and have this girl? It seemed impossible, yet that was what he wanted. I mustn't think about it, he told himself. He closed his eyes, but he could still smell the faint odor of her hair, feel the delicate pressure of her fingers upon his face, her lips on his. . . . He gritted his teeth and mumbled aloud: "Oh, goddamn . . ."

Hilton roused him at eight-thirty by rapping on the door.

"Lane, come and get some coffee," Hilton called.

Cross tumbled from bed. Oh, yes . . . he must wear a different suit. . . . And at the first opportunity he would get rid of the clothes he had worn when he had struck down Gil and Herndon. . . .

When he went into the kitchen, he found that Hilton had set up breakfast. Eva and Menti were already at the table. Cross sat and began sipping his coffee. What about that bloody handkerchief? Hilton was busy making toast and everything seemed normal. He saw Hilton go to the incinerator and dump some waste paper into it. Yes, he was safe for the time being. . . .

Menti ate broodingly. Hilton moved quickly about the kitchen like a man who must either do something or become exasperated. Cross let his eyes rest on Eva; she was pale and tired, looking off into space; finally she did glance at him and her eyes told him that she was with him; he felt better.

The doorbell rang and Hilton started nervously.

"This is it, I think," Hilton said.

Hilton left and a moment later, before Cross could prepare himself, the hunched form of Ely Houston filled the doorway. Cross stared unblinkingly. Houston entered the kitchen and paused; his eyes traveled swiftly around the room and at last rested on Cross.

"Well," Houston exclaimed, "what in the world are you doing here?"

Cross stood, smiled, and reached out his hand to Houston, who shook it warmly.

"How are you, Mr. Houston?" Cross said evenly. "I live here."

"At last I've tracked you down," Houston said.

Hilton, Menti, and Eva were thunderstruck. Hilton was staring at Cross with an open mouth and Cross could tell that he was thinking that maybe he was a police spy.

"How is it that you know the District Attorney?" Hilton asked bluntly.

"Mr. Houston and I have met before," Cross explained lightly.

Houston advanced into the kitchen, followed by Farrel and a tall, lean, gray-haired man on whose chest Cross could see a police badge. Farrel too stared at Cross and said:

"Why didn't you tell me you were a big shot?"

"I'm not," Cross said.

Everyone was standing now except Eva; tension and distrust hung in the air. The tall, lean man stood in one corner and surveyed the faces of Cross, Menti, and Hilton.

264

"I've asked about you," Houston began, addressing himself to Cross, "but I couldn't get a line on you. . . . I didn't forget that talk we had. Know one thing? I made notes on your ideas." Houston seemed to have forgotten that he had come to investigate the deaths of two men; he was excited and seemed in a holiday mood. "Now, what was it you said . . . ?" Houston paused, ran his hand into his pocket and pulled out a notebook. "I've got it right here, you see." As he thumbed the leaves, the tall man stared in bewilderment at Houston, saying nothing. "Ha— here it is: 'Man is nothing in particular. . . .' You see? I don't forget."

"I see you don't," Cross said.

Hilton was so nervous that he could not control the shaking of his hands. Menti stared, but there was a sardonic smile on his thin lips. Only Eva was listening to Houston.

"Well, what is this all about?" Houston asked Cross, rubbing his hands together. "We can talk about special problems later— Oh, yes— What was the name you gave me?"

"The name is Lane, Lionel Lane," Cross said.

"Lionel Lane," Houston repeated, paused; then went on. "Mr. Lane, this is the Medical Examiner, Dr. Stockton. . . ."

Cross nodded to Dr. Stockton and the doctor nodded to him.

"Farrel," Houston demanded. "What have we got here?"

As Farrel outlined to Houston what he had found downstairs, Houston moved with vacant eyes about the kitchen, his lips pursed, his hat in his hand, his hump seeming to follow him. He walked softly, flat-footedly, as if he feared that he would disturb some delicate process of thought by jarring his brain. He began to frown as Farrel described details of the scene of blood and death.

"And these two men, what were their backgrounds?" Houston asked at last.

"That's a damned strange thing, Mr. D.A.," Farrel said. "Gilbert Blount was a member of the Central Committee of the Communist Party of the United States—"

"You're kidding," Houston protested with wide eyes.

265

"No, sir," Farrel insisted. "It's a fact—"

"And who's the other one?"

"Langley Herndon—"

Houston snapped his fingers, as though trying to recall something.

"Langley Herndon . . . ! Ah! I remember him— He used to write for the *Crusader* sometimes," Houston said. "A violent baby—bloodthirsty— Welcomed Hitler and publicly lauded his extermination of the Jews. Said that America should use the Negro as a scapegoat around which to unify the nation—" He looked at Cross and smiled. "Herndon was perfectly cynical. He argued that anything could be done for any reason. . . . He had the Negro singled out as a target, a menace, a danger. . . . The Negro was America's ace in the hole if the nation ever experienced any real internal stress. You could say that the nigger was the cause of it and get the rest of the nation to forget its problems and unite to get rid of the niggers. . . . Ingenious, huh?" Houston chuckled and turned to Dr. Stockton. "Well, Doc, how does it look to you? What's your verdict?"

Dr. Stockton cleared his throat, advanced to the kitchen table and rested his brief case upon it. He took out a sheaf of papers and leafed through them. He lifted his eyes at last to Houston.

"Mr. District Attorney, this is either very simple or very complicated. . . ."

"Make it simple," Houston said.

"I'll let you decide that," Dr. Stockton said.

"Oh, wait a minute," Houston interrupted him. He turned and faced Eva, Hilton, Menti, and Cross. "Who are these people? Is anybody here related to either Blount or Herndon?"

"This is Mrs. Blount," Cross told Houston.

"Oh, madam, I beg your pardon," Houston apologized. "If I'd known it was you, I'd not have spoken as I have. I'm awfully sorry. . . ."

"It's nothing," Eva mumbled.

"These things are unpleasant, but we have to get these facts straight— Oh, yes; and the other two gentlemen?"

Farrel introduced Hilton and Menti as friends of Eva.

266

"All right, Dr. Stockton, you may proceed—"

"Well, Mr. District Attorney, I've all the reports right here. What we can make of these reports is quite another matter. Our pathological chemist, Dr. Reddick, has submitted a mass of details. I'll begin first with Blount. . . ." He began reading from the report: " 'Multiple incised wounds of scalp; congestion and edema of brain . . .' "

"Dr. Stockton," Houston interrupted him. "Forgive me — Suppose we save all that for the formal hearing, eh? Right now I just want to know if I'm to look for a murderer or not. Give me this wrapped up in a nutshell. . . ."

"Right," Dr. Stockton replied, putting his papers aside. "To all intents and purposes, Mr. District Attorney, these two blokes battered each other to death. All concrete evidence points toward that. . . . Let's take that aspect of it first. And, mind you, I'm leaving out all question of motive for the time being. The definite ascertaining of a different motive could alter the entire picture of our findings. Now, due to the great disorder of the room downstairs, we've not yet been able to reconstruct exactly what happened. Yet, the concrete evidence we possess points to the fact of an argument that led to a fist fight. There's evidence that Herndon attempted strangulation upon Blount. Blount must have freed himself, for the next stage of the fight was with the fire poker. Who grabbed the fire poker first, we do not know. Now, here's the strange thing. *Both* men bear evidence of having been hit with the poker, which means that during the course of the fight the poker must have gone from one to the other; they took turns lamming each other with it. . . . Follow me?"

"Right," Houston said.

"Now comes a third stage of the fight. The table leg is used as the weapon. Just how they got hold of it, we don't know. It seems utterly unlikely that either of the two men had time enough to stop the fight and break the leg off the table. We surmise that one of them crashed against the table in falling and broke the table, the leg coming off, breaking in two. . . . The first man who saw that table leg dived for it and took it as his weapon.

"At the present moment, with what we've got to go on, we surmise that Blount got hold of the leg first—"

"How do you figure that?"

"It's a guess," Dr. Stockton said. "The most single powerful blow dealt with that table leg was against the forehead of Herndon. . . . That blow could have caused death, not at once, but certainly Herndon would have died of it eventually. Most certainly he was stunned by it and we further surmise that he kept on his feet and continued the fight. . . . Now, here's another strange fact. *Both* men bear marks of that table leg on their heads. That can only be accounted for, too, on the basis that the table leg, like the fire poker, changed hands during the course of the fight, which is highly likely. . . . *But*, and this puzzles me, was Herndon *able*, physically *able* to deliver such death-dealing blows upon Blount's head *after* he had received that crushing blow on his own forehead? Yet the facts point to such. It's possible. . . . Men have been known to possess remarkable strength just before dying; men have been known to aim and fire a gun with sharp accuracy and then die straightaway. . . . *If* Herndon was able to deal a death-dealing blow to Blount, after having received such a blow himself, then the case is simple."

"Is there any way of telling, Dr. Stockton, how much *time* intervened between these blows?" Houston asked.

"That's impossible," Dr. Stockton said. "Our impression is that those blows were all delivered at approximately the same time. At the most, a half hour could have intervened, but we think the whole fracas took place in about fifteen minutes."

"In other words, you don't think that one man could have been knocked out, then have come to, and resumed the fight?" Houston asked.

"That's highly speculative," the doctor said. "It *would* explain how Herndon was able to deal such hard blows after he had been mortally wounded. There are some 'ifs' here. . . . But these 'ifs' only make the whole picture more complicated." Dr. Stockton paused and pulled forth a batch of photographs from his brief case. "This is how they looked when the officers arrived. . . ." He handed the photographs to Houston.

Houston looked at the photographs and his eyes bulged

268

with suppressed horror. Cross could see a slanting glimpse of the pictures and at once there leaped into his mind the image of that red room with its flickering flames and the two still, bloody forms stretched out on the carpet, drenched in their own blood. . . .

"Lovely," Houston commented softly, returning the photographs to Dr. Stockton. He turned to look at Eva. "Would the lady mind excusing herself?" Houston asked.

"Not at all," Eva said; she rose and left the kitchen.

Cross's eyes followed her with anxiety as her wan, tight face went from view.

"There's no use in her hearing this sordid mess," Houston mumbled. He rubbed his hands together, glanced about the room, and then spoke in a loud, sonorous voice: "Perfect setup. Two extremes meet. A plus and a minus— And they cancel each other out. . . . And who could hate each other more than two men like that? It's the Russian-German war all over again, eh? Could be . . . Sounds like it. It fits, doesn't it? Motives? Dr. Stockton, you spoke of leaving out motives. Why? You have all the motives on earth here. These two men were totally opposed to each other in all aspects of life. You might call such motives *natural life* motives. . . . Oh, I know that there is no such thing in law as that. But there will be one day. . . . I'm sure of it. We might call such motives jealousy. But it's total jealousy. The kind of jealousy the Bible speaks of when it refers to God's being a jealous God." Houston looked around the room and smiled.

Cross was trembling; he felt that maybe Houston knew that he was guilty and was mocking him. Was Houston teasing him by speaking his *own* ideas out loud, testing them on the people present? Whose ideas belonged to whom? What crazy luck he had in having this hunchback, the one man he had ever met who understood him, to track him down? Did Houston know how maddeningly close he stood to the truth?

"There's another possibility," Dr. Stockton's voice sounded patiently.

"There are millions of possibilities," Houston said, waving his hand. He looked at Cross. "Of course, there's this problem of Herndon hating to have Negroes in his building, but I take it that that was simply a tiny aspect of his total jealousy toward Blount—"

Hilton and Menti were silent, tight-lipped, staring first at Houston and then at Cross. Cross waited, wondering what other versions of the crime the Medical Examiner had in mind.

"So they killed each other," Houston went on. He turned on Farrel. "According to you, Herndon killed Blount, huh? Yes, he was seen standing over Blount with the fire poker. . . . He was strong enough to chase Mrs. Blount up the steps with a gun. . . . That fits. He later dies of wounds that Blount had inflicted on him. A double murder, or double manslaughter, whatever you want to call it." Houston faced Dr. Stockton. "Is that more or less your opinion?"

A trace of hesitancy showed in Dr. Stockton's eyes; then he shrugged and said: "More or less."

"More or less?" Houston was astonished. "What's your reservation?"

"Somebody could have come upon them while they were fighting and killed them both," Dr. Stockton said somewhat sheepishly; he was obviously embarrassed at the far-fetched nature of his theory.

Cross felt suspended over a bottomless void. He had thought that Houston would have arrived at that solution first; but, no, it was Dr. Stockton who had put his finger on the truth.

"Good Lord!" Houston exclaimed. "Why can't you fellows take facts just as you find them? Why do you want to make life more complicated than it is, and it's damn well complicated, if you ask me. Now, Dr. Stockton, what motive on earth could anybody have in coming upon those two men fighting and then killing both of them?"

"I don't know." Dr. Stockton shrugged his shoulders.

"I don't know either," Houston said. "The damned thing's simple. Two hotheads met and had a fight over their total views of life. They fought. One died and then the other died. And for my money, there's something of poetic justice in the whole damn thing."

270

"Is that the official interpretation, Mr. District Attorney?" Dr. Stockton asked.

"Oh, Dr. Stockton, I'm not trying to encroach upon your duties," Houston said, smiling blandly. "If not this interpretation, then what have you to offer?"

"I don't know," Dr. Stockton said. He turned to Cross and stared at him for several seconds. "You're the young man who saw them fighting?"

"Yes, sir," Cross answered.

"What time did Blount go down to see Herndon?" Dr. Stockton asked.

"It was about ten past nine," Cross answered.

"How do you know that?" the doctor asked.

"Just before leaving the dinner table, Mr. Blount looked at his watch and told the time to us, and said he had to leave."

Houston came forward and stood in front of Cross. Cross felt that his feet were resting on air, that he could sink right down through the floor.

"How long was Blount gone from the apartment before you went down there?" Houston asked.

Cross frowned, thinking. He felt that it was not really a matter of time; either they found a motive, *his* motive, and accused him or they did not. So he could tell the truth.

"That's really hard to say. . . . It's better to tell you what happened. Mrs. Blount was worried. I was too. I offered to go down with Blount, to help him, defend him if anything happened. . . . But he wouldn't hear of it. He was a proud man. . . . And Mrs. Blount warned me not to interfere. She said he'd be angry, wildly angry if I did. . . . I was helping Mrs. Blount clear away the things from the table. Then we began hearing loud voices. We knew that they were quarreling. I offered to go down and Mrs. Blount said no, that he'd be angry. I went to my room and was lying on my bed. . . . It was then that I heard that loud noise, like something breaking, a big piece of wood. . . . That was the table, maybe. . . ."

"No doubt," Dr. Stockton said. "Go on. . . ."

"Mrs. Blount came running to me. She was terribly upset. It seems—"

"How long were you in the room before Mrs. Blount came running to you?" Dr. Stockton asked.

"I don't know," Cross said truthfully. "Maybe five minutes; maybe longer. . . ."

"And Mrs. Blount asked you to go down?"

"Well, not exactly . . . she didn't seem to know what to do. . . . So I offered to go down. But she said no. Then we heard a scream—"

"Could you tell who it was that screamed?"

"No," Cross said. "This time I said I'd go down, and she agreed. . . . But she was still afraid. You see, really, she was more afraid of Blount himself than of anything happening to him. The moment I got downstairs in the hallway, I knew a fight was going on. . . . I ran to the door, opened it, and saw Herndon beating Blount with the fire poker. . . . Blount was on the floor and Herndon had his foot on his chest and was lamming away. I didn't hear Mrs. Blount come down, but all at once I felt her hand touching my back. She started screaming and Herndon saw us. . . . He came at us with the fire poker . . . I blocked him just long enough for Mrs. Blount to run upstairs, and he swiped me across the shoulder with the poker. . . ." Cross paused, pulled off his coat, opened his shirt and showed his shoulder.

"Why didn't you call the police?" Houston wanted to know.

"When I got upstairs, Mrs. Blount was calling the police. . . . She didn't seem able to get connections. . . . She asked me to call, then she ran out of the room to go downstairs again. . . . I was scared she'd get hurt, so I ran after her, caught her on the landing and brought her back to the apartment. We kept hearing the fighting; there were shouts, screams. . . . Mrs. Blount asked me to phone the police—"

"And didn't you phone?" Houston asked.

"No; I wanted to try to help Mr. Blount. . . . I told her to phone and I ran downstairs. But I found the door locked this time. I rattled the knob—I called, yelled—I could hear 'em fighting—"

"Whose name did you call?" Dr. Stockton asked.

272

"Mr. Blount's name. I didn't know what to do. I went back upstairs and——"

"How long were you downstairs the second time?"

"I don't know. Maybe five minutes, maybe longer. . . . When I went back to tell Mrs. Blount, she told me that she'd phoned Mr. Hilton and that Mr. Hilton was phoning the police. You see, she thought surely Mr. Blount was coming up with me. And when I told her that he was still down there, she went really wild. . . . I was trying to call the police when she ran out of the door again. This time she came flying back. She said Herndon had his gun and was on his way up. . . ."

"Did you see him?" Houston asked.

"No. I barred the door. Mrs. Blount fainted and I put water on her face. . . ."

Dr. Stockton turned to Farrel, frowning.

"Where was Herndon's gun, Lieutenant?" Dr. Stockton asked.

"In the drawer of his desk," Farrel explained. "The drawer was half pulled out. Seems like somebody had just tossed it in there. Might have been the last thing Herndon did before he died."

"Perhaps," Dr. Stockton said slowly.

Cross was as still as stone. He could feel that they were not satisfied with this interpretation, but they could find no other that would explain the facts. Houston seemed inclined to accept the picture that Cross had painted. Good. Let the doctor and his scientists discover something else, if they could. Things were not going so badly. But he had to be careful of this man Houston; after all, he might be stalling just to see how he would react. The doctor had hit upon the right solution, but he had no background of ideas to make it stick, no understanding or grasp of the range of motives that could explain it all. And Houston had that, but he seemed not to care to bother with it. Was Houston playing a game?

Dr. Stockton began putting his papers and photographs back into his brief case.

"Well, I'll have to leave the motives to you, Mr. District Attorney," he said. "My findings are as follows: double

273

murder or double manslaughter. . . . The two men died so close together that I wouldn't like to say who died first, so—"

"Mr. District Attorney," Hilton spoke up for the first time. "There's more to this than you gentlemen are admitting. A man has been murdered. That man was Gilbert Blount. The murderer was Langley Herndon. Now, allow me to identify myself a little more before I continue. I'm a member of the editorial board of the *Daily Worker*. I was a colleague of Gilbert Blount. I want to protest against the light-handed manner in which this case is being handled. The issues here are basically social, and you gentlemen are playing around with probabilities and psychological facts. I'm insisting that some measure of responsibility be shown here. This case has a background of politics, sir. I said *politics*, and I mean it. And you do not want to look into that phase of it, yet the only real motives can be found there. We have *proof* that Herndon killed Blount. Mr. Lane here is an eyewitness. He saw Herndon striking Blount with a poker about the head. Herndon later struck Mr. Lane with the same fire poker. I'm speaking of the moral side of this case. . . . You saw that frightened little woman who just left this room. Herndon chased that poor woman with a gun, terrorized her! Now, I maintain that it's unfair to leave the impression in the public mind that her husband was a murderer—"

Dr. Stockton had his brief case in his hand.

"Mr. District Attorney, I must be off. . . . The rest is up to you. There is no possibility of my giving you an opinion as to who died first. From a clinical point of view, we've nothing to go on. Good morning, gentlemen."

Dr. Stockton walked briskly out of the room. Hilton's thin face turned livid; he whirled to Houston and began to shout: "Mr. District Attorney, it's only fair to warn you that the *Daily Worker* will fight you about any interpretation of this case that points to Blount as a murderer. He was defending his life against a Fascist attack! He was defending his home, his wife, his friend against a man who has publicly advocated the extermination of all racial minorities. Herndon *sent* for Blount to come and see him. Mrs. Blount will testify to that. And Herndon was wildly

274

angry when he did it. He later pulled a gun on Mrs. Blount herself. . . . There was only one issue in this thing: Could Mr. Lane, a Negro, remain in this apartment? You know that's true, and so do I. We all know it. Only yesterday morning Herndon threatened the life of Mr. Lane here. . . ."

"Look, Mr.— What's your name?"

"Hilton. John Hilton."

"I see your point, Mr. Hilton," Houston said. "In this particular investigation our aim is to determine *who* died first. And that is something for the Medical Examiner to find out. I asked him who died first, and he says he doesn't know."

"But there's another angle to this." Hilton was persistent. "Look, Mr. District Attorney, this Herndon has threatened Mr. Blount many times. He threatened Mr. Lane here. He had the *intent*. Now, there is a *real* difference."

"But no proof," Houston said.

"Yes, there is proof," Hilton overrode Houston. "This man's writings are fascistic. He had advocated the extermination of non-Anglo-Saxon minorities—"

"Oh, Christ, man!" Houston exploded. "That's farfetched. If you're going to bring that up, why not cite all the Communist arguments and threats against the bourgeoisie? That would make Blount the guilty one, wouldn't it?"

"No," Hilton said.

"Why not? If you're going to be fair, you'll have to admit it," Houston insisted. "Now, look, here is how things stand. We don't know which man died first. We are not going to call this case an instance of double murder. What right has anybody to make Blount a murderer in the eyes of his wife? And, by the same token, what right has anybody to make Herndon a murderer in the eyes of his relatives even if they are not here to protect his name? All right, in the light of what the Medical Examiner has said, I'm going to call this double manslaughter. . . ."

"And we'll call it just plain murder!" Hilton's voice rose. "You're taking the side of property in this investigation—"

Cross listened with amazement. Yes, sane men did misread reality. Just as he had once had fantasies, so now he was looking at men who were passionately arguing about

275

their own fantasies, trying to decide which fantasy was to be taken for reality. No one in the room knew the truth of what had happened but he, and yet they were ready to fight, if need be, for what they thought was the truth.

"Farrel, ask Mrs. Blount to come here a moment, will you?" Houston asked, ignoring the angry Hilton.

"Yes, sir."

Farrel left the room and a moment later Eva appeared in the doorway.

"Mrs. Blount, I'm sorry this has to happen in your home," Houston began. "I must question each person here separately. I'd like the use of your living room, if I may."

"Of course," Eva answered in a lifeless manner.

"Now, Farrel, in about ten minutes, send me these people one by one," Houston instructed. "Begin with Mrs. Blount— You are well enough to answer questions, aren't you?"

"Yes," Eva whispered.

Houston went out of the kitchen.

Hilton went over to Cross and forced a smile. "You're some fellow, Lane."

"What do you mean?"

"How did you get to know *him?*"

"So you think I'm in the pay of the police?" Cross asked, laughing. "I met him once on a train. That's all." A look of doubt was still in Hilton's eyes. "If you don't believe it, then I can't help it. You can check my statements, if you like. After all, how did I know that I'd ever meet him again?"

His words seemed to have some effect.

"Just the same, I'd like to know more about that," Hilton said.

"Sure," Cross said. "Whenever you like. I've no secrets."

The hell with him, Cross thought. Only one thing worried him about Hilton. Would the man try to poison his relations with Eva? Anger rose slowly in him. He would fight for Eva. He tried to catch her eye, but she was sunk in deep thought, staring blankly before her. He longed to be at her side when she was with Houston, but he knew that that was impossible. What would his relationship to

276

her be now that Gil was dead? Did it mean that he would have to move from the apartment? After the police had gone, he would talk to her about it. He would tell her, openly and frankly, that he did not ever want to leave her.

Farrel came to the door.

"Mrs. Blount," he called.

Eva rose and followed Farrel into the hallway. Hilton at once closed the kitchen door and turned to Cross.

"What are your plans, Lane?"

"I have no plans," Cross told him.

"Do you intend to stay here?"

"I don't know."

"If you don't, who does?"

"I'm going to speak to Eva about it," Cross said.

"When?"

"Look, I can't very well bother her *now*," Cross protested.

Hilton paced the floor. This man is after me, but why . . . ? He thought of Bob squirming on the floor, weeping; he thought of Bob dodging the Immigration authorities, and again he was drifting into that state of danger where he was judging others with supreme and final contempt. What right had Hilton to say who could live and who could not live? Damn him . . . Hilton must have sensed his mood, for he came close to Cross and clapped him on the shoulder.

"You're okay, Lane," he said. "We just have to be careful, that's all. But I must see you sometime, *soon*. As soon as this is over."

"Sure," Cross said.

At some time in the future, he had a score to settle with this little god and it filled him with anger to think of it; then he was angry with himself for getting angry. Farrel came to the door and beckoned to Hilton, who strode out with defiance in his eyes and manner. A moment later Cross could hear Hilton's strident voice rising in vehement argument with Houston. Why didn't the damn fool let well enough alone? If he kept hammering at Houston, Houston would, in the end, start wondering about the case, start trying to find what new theories he could make fit it. He strained to hear what was being said in the living room, but could not make out any words. He looked at Menti and Menti smiled.

"He's tough, that Hilton," Menti said, nodding approvingly.

"Yes," Cross agreed.

"Eva likes you," Menti said.

"She's a wonderful person," Cross said.

Cross thought that Menti was a weak man who followed Hilton's lead. Could he placate Hilton a little through Menti? He would try.

"Hilton seems suspicious of me," Cross said. "Is it because I know Houston?"

"Well," Menti drawled, pulling at his ear and smiling with embarrassment, "knowing cops isn't exactly in our line, you know."

"But I've no relations with this man," Cross defended himself. "I met him simply and honestly in the dining car of a train some weeks ago." He recalled that Bob had witnessed their meeting and he added: "Look, I remember now. . . . Bob saw it happen—"

"Bob? Bob Hunter?"

"Yes. You know Bob?"

"Let me give you a tip," Menti said. "From now on, it's not wise to give the name of Bob Hunter as a reference in the Party."

"Why?"

"He's a counter-revolutionary," Menti said simply.

Cross blinked. He had blundered. He felt that he had become entangled in moving shadows.

"You're new to all this," Menti told him kindly. "I believe you're solid. But Hilton trusts nothing and nobody but the Party."

Cross decided to beg and wheedle a bit; he wanted to remain near Eva, and the Party had the power to take her from him.

"Look, I've been in connection with the Party for only twenty-four hours," he argued. "I've worked for Hilton, so far. . . . I'd like to set his mind straight. What does he think I'm after?"

"What *are* you after?" Menti demanded.

That shot caught Cross squarely unawares. "You distrust me too?"

"We distrust everybody," Menti said.

"Why do you distrust me?"

"We don't know you."

"All right," Cross said, feeling trapped. "Tell me what I should do in order to be trusted by the Party—"

"You have to belong to the Party," Menti said.

"I'm going to join—"

"I don't mean that."

"What *do* you mean, then?"

Menti chuckled cynically, scratched his chin, and looked quizzically at Cross.

"You have to *belong* to the Party," Menti said.

Then Cross understood. The Party would have to have some hold on him before it could trust him; the Party would have to own him morally. And Menti had spoken of it as casually as if he had been reciting the number of inches in a foot. . . .

"Do you *belong* to the Party?" Cross asked softly.

"Yes. I've no life except that of the Party. I have no wish, no dream, no will except that of the Party," Menti confessed.

They both started at the vicious slamming of a door down the hallway. Hilton came into the kitchen, his face distorted with anger.

"That goddamn sonofabitch," he railed.

Farrel came into the kitchen, beckoned to Menti and said: "You're next."

Hilton took hold of Menti's arm and said: "Tell him to go to hell for me!"

"Take it easy," Farrel warned.

Alone with Cross, Hilton changed his attitude quickly.

"When you go in there, stick to your story, see?"

"You can depend on me," Cross assured him.

"We'll see."

"Look," Cross could no longer hold himself in, "you make me feel that I'm guilty of something. You don't trust me. Okay. Distrust breeds distrust. Now that I feel that you don't trust me, I wonder if I ought to trust you—"

"You want to change your story to the D.A.?" Hilton asked.

"Hell, no! Why should I? My talking to the D.A. has nothing to do with it. But, hell, man, don't make me feel I'm dirt under your feet. I don't like it."

Hilton grinned and relented.

"Lane, there's only one thing I want to ask of you—"

"What's that?"

"Take care of Eva."

"I'll do my best."

"I *know* you will," Hilton said, and went abruptly out of the kitchen and out of the apartment.

What had he meant? Cross's hands twitched. I'd like to ram that bastard's head against a wall, he muttered to himself.

A few moments later Farrel tapped him on the shoulder. "You're the last."

When Cross entered the living room, Houston was sitting smoking a cigarette.

"There you are," he greeted Cross. "Sit down."

As Cross sat Houston rose and began to pace the floor, chuckling, now and then tossing a glance at Cross. Had Houston changed his mind? Was he about to spring a trap?

"Tell me, Lane, what do you make out of all this?"

"I hardly know, really, Mr. Houston."

"I wonder how many men in this land refuse to acknowledge the laws of our society?" Houston mused out loud.

"That would be hard to find out, wouldn't it?" Cross asked.

"Yes. And that's just why I'm asking," Houston continued. "Farrel, like the Medical Examiner, keeps mumbling about how somebody could have come upon those two men while they were fighting and killed both of them. That's possible, but highly improbable. What kind of motive could such a killer have? That's what's puzzling me."

Cross was silent. Houston had returned to this dangerous ground. Why? He had to watch himself now. If he disputed such a theory, Houston might think that he was afraid of it. But if he acted casual, nonchalant about it, that would make Houston think he was disinterested.

"I thought you had accepted the idea that they killed each other," Cross said, simulating surprise.

"Maybe yes, maybe no," Houston mused. "I'm just playing with this idea. Now, such a killer could not be either a Communist or a Fascist, could he?"

"Why not?" Cross asked.

"Why would a Communist want to kill another Communist in the presence of a Fascist? And the other way around."

Cross thought he saw a way of confusing the issue and he put in quickly: "Suppose a Communist came upon two men fighting. . . . Suppose Blount was killing Herndon and his brother Communist helped Blount finish him off and then killed Blount too?"

"Why?" Houston asked.

"I don't know," Cross said. "I'm just exploring possibilities. Or suppose a friend of Herndon showed up under the opposite circumstances? Suppose he helped to finish off Blount and then killed Herndon——?"

"Why?" Houston demanded again.

"I don't know."

"I don't know either," Houston said. "But while we're on this theory of a third man, suppose either Blount or Herndon killed the other and a third man came upon the victor and killed him. Why? No, your theory is wrong. If there's anything in a third man showing up, after you left, and joining in this fight—and I doubt this—he'd have to be somebody psychologically akin to either Blount or Herndon and yet somehow outside of them. I can't see either a Communist or a Fascist acting in that way.

"Only a brother absolutist would have any motives for killing them on purely ideological grounds," Houston went on. "Let's suppose a normal person came upon those two men fighting. . . . What would he do? He would do what you did—you called the police, or you had Hilton call the police. Now, we've checked the time. It *is* possible that, after you left the door, somebody did go into the room. But, in order to kill the two of them on ideological grounds, this killer would have to have the support of a *third* set of ideas. . . . We've checked Herndon's apart-

281

ment; nothing has been stolen. He had plenty of enemies, but they were nowhere near that apartment last night. Now, who is that *third* man with the *third* set of ideas?"

"And what is that third set of ideas?" Cross asked.

"That no ideas are necessary to justify his acts," Houston stated without hesitation. "Our mythical killer is as lawless as the other two; they're all three alike because of the identity of the impulses in their hearts."

Cross felt a spasm go through his body. Yes, Houston was on the right track. But such a track did not lead to proof. He gave a gentle laugh to cover his terror.

"Mr. Houston, that's a rather fantastic assumption," he said. "How can you *prove* that the same impulse actuates all three men?"

Houston looked at Cross and then slowly tapped his broad chest with his right thumb.

"I have proof right *here*, Lane," he said quietly.

"What do you mean?" Cross asked, trying to keep anxiety out of his voice.

Houston did not answer at once; he resumed his pacing, his eyes deep with reflection.

"The proof is easy to see, but it is a rather daring kind of proof. Of course, this kind of proof cannot be introduced into court. It has a psychological basis," Houston explained. "It's an 'as if' proof. . . . It's an intuition; it must first come from your own heart, see? How do I know that all three men feel alike? I know because *I* feel that way. . . ." Houston sized Cross up. "And I think you feel that way too; that is, if I recall correctly your attitude on the train. The only difference is this: you and I have not acted upon this impulse of ours. The moment we act 'as if' it's true, then it's true; get it? But we've both *got* it. We both understand it; that's the proof.

"A lawless man has to rein himself in. A man of lawless impulses living in a society which seeks to restrain instincts for the common good must be in a kind of subjective prison. How such a man must live and sweat behind the bars of himself! God, the millions of prisons in this world! Men simply copied the realities of their hearts when they built prisons. They simply extended into objective reality what was already a subjective reality. Only jailers really believe

282

in jails. Only men full of criminal feelings can create a criminal code. Only an enemy of Christianity, like Saint Paul, could establish Christianity. Men who fear drink want laws passed against drinking. Men who cannot manage their sexual appetites launch crusades against vice. . . . Lane, we're outsiders and we can understand these new twentieth-century outlaws, for in our hearts we are outlaws too.

"Here are the psychological origins of tyranny. Don't kid yourself. Napoleon, Mussolini, Stalin, and Hitler knew what they were doing when they cast their beady eyes upon their subjects. . . . When a man stood accused, objective evidence didn't matter. The dictator had but to glance into his own heart, and he knew at once that the prisoner at the bar was guilty! For, he reasoned, had he stood in the prisoner's place, he would have been guilty. . . . How in hell did he become dictator without becoming guilty? Without breaking all the laws in sight . . . ?

"Now, let's get back to our *third* man who's realized all of this without acting upon it. . . . Two tyrants are fighting in a room and our *third* man shows up. He feels toward those two men as those two men feel toward the masses of people. . . . He's playing the same game, but on a much smaller scale. Who knows, maybe he's been hurt by both sides? He kills 'em, and with no more compunction than if he were killing flies. . . . That man who kills like that is a bleak and tragic man. He is the twentieth century writ small. . . . Do you get what I'm driving at, Lane?"

Was Houston teasing him? Or was he only talking? Cross laughed again to still his nervous dread. He told himself that he should keep quiet, that he was a damn fool to talk, yet he felt an overpowering desire to help Houston develop his theory.

"The man you are describing," Cross said slowly, listening with numbed dread to the sound of his own voice, "is one for whom all ethical laws are suspended. He acts like a god."

"That's it exactly," Houston said. "But how can you tell when a man feels like that? You walk along the street and all faces look more or less alike. There's no clue to what

283

each man feels or thinks. This man would be hard to detect, because he'd act like other men, maybe a little more subdued. But, above all, this man must feel that he *knows* what's right. Then, all at once, he sees something that violates that sense of right and he strikes out to set it as it ought to be. Then he resumes his cool and correct manner of living. But that, of course, is purely external. What must go on in a man like that? He must be something like an inferno." Houston paused and stared again off into space, and when he spoke there was a note of wonder in his voice: "I wonder if such men have any value? Might not they be the *real* lawgivers. . . . Maybe . . . Who knows?"

Houston stood in front of Cross and laughed. Cross joined him in laughter, feeling as though something were creeping over his skin.

"Some idea, huh?" Houston asked.

"Yes," Cross said.

Cross waited to be challenged, to be accused. Houston turned and went to the door.

"Farrel," he called.

Cross held his breath. Had he called Farrel to arrest him?

"We'll wash this thing up," Houston said over his shoulder to Cross.

Farrel came to the door.

"Make it manslaughter," he told Farrel. "Double manslaughter. Any other theory is too fantastic."

"Just as you say, Mr. D.A.," Farrel said.

"Now," Houston began, "let's talk about us. Can I see you sometime?"

"Any time you like."

"What are you doing now?"

"I'm planning to attend some classes at the university. . . ."

Cross was conscious as he talked that he was speaking as out of a dream. A moment ago he had been positive that he was about to be arrested, and now he sat here free. The room seemed to sway slowly around him.

"Will you have dinner with me some evening?"

"Of course."

"What about Sunday evening at Frank's in Harlem?"

"Sure. What time?"

"Eight. Right?"

"Right."

"And forget this mess about Blount and Herndon," Houston said, winking. "Good riddance, I think."

They shook hands and Houston strode to the door, then turned and said casually: "You'll have to testify, maybe, at a hearing of the Medical Examiner, you know."

"All right," Cross murmured.

Houston left. Cross sat alone and closed his eyes; he wanted to keep them closed and not look any more on the sight of the world. He recalled Houston's saying that most lawbreakers longed to be punished and he wondered if such a longing was smoldering in him. . . . Why didn't this thing rest easily on his heart? Or was he only deluding himself in thinking that he was free? He was suddenly tired. Was it worth while going on? Eva . . . Yes. There was a hope that one day he could talk to her. She would understand. She too was a victim. But—suppose she knew what he had done? How would she feel about him then? He leaned his forehead on the palm of his hand and the only answer he could find was no answer. . . .

Half an hour later he pulled to his feet and went in search of Eva. The door of her room was open and he saw her lying fully dressed across her bed. He should leave; his staying was no good for her. . . . He pictured himself getting his suitcase, hat, and coat and going in search of a hiding place. . . .

"Lionel?"

"Yes."

"Come in," she said.

He went to the bed and bent to her.

"Are you all right?" he asked.

"I'm numb. Are they gone?"

"Yes."

"What did they decide?"

"It's double manslaughter."

"Poor Gil . . ."

"Listen, Eva—"

"Yes."

"You know that Gil asked me to come and stay here. He wanted to send me to the Workers' School. Now, Gil's gone. I don't know what to do."

She lifted her head and her hazel eyes looked at him.

"Do you want to leave, Lionel?"

"No. I never want to leave you, Eva."

Her eyes fell. She finally looked at him, reached out her hand to touch him, and said in a low, clear voice: "If you leave, I shall kill myself—"

"God, no," he said. "I'm here. I want to be here near you— Listen, tell me; have you any money?"

"Money?" she repeated with a bitter laugh. "I've nothing. I've not worked at my painting in six months. All Gil and I had was his salary from the Party. I've not sold a picture in over a year. . . . I don't know what the Party thinks of me."

Her voice died and her eyes assumed a scared, haunted look. Cross knew that she was wondering if they would let her wander free with her guilty knowledge.

"Look, I have a few hundred dollars," he said.

"Oh, no, Lionel," she protested. "That's impossible! I can't touch that."

"Why?"

"It isn't right. I must work—"

"Eventually, yes. But right now, I don't want you to worry. Look, after this is over, let's go away somewhere together. The Gatineau Mountains in Canada. It'll be safe there, quiet, far from all this—"

Her eyes shone, then tears clouded them.

"I'm sorry about Gil, but, Lionel, I'm glad you're out of that trap," she spoke softly.

"Trap?" he asked; he could not let her know that he knew.

"There's so much I have to tell you—" She gazed off. "Gil told you he wanted to fight for you. It's true; he wanted to. But he was fighting for something else too. His idea of the world—"

"But aren't the two things one thing?" he asked to get her notion of it. "He's fighting for Russia; Russia needs men like me; so when he fights for me he's hitting at the

286

rotten basis that holds up the world that's against Russia. Isn't that it?"

Eva sighed and shook her head.

"You were only a means," she said. "Lionel, the Party sets facts in motion. . . . God, what language! But there's no other way to say it. *Facts in motion.* . . . You are a fact to them, not a person. You're oppressed, so, to gain your help, they claim they'll fight for you, but only when your fight helps them." She looked fearfully about the dim room, as though afraid that someone was listening. "You must break away from this. . . ."

He agreed with her, but where could he go? She thought him a helpless victim; but, rather, he was what she hated. He had been using the Party in the same manner that the Party had been using him.

"I'm free now," she breathed. "But for how long? What will they say to me now that Gil's gone? Will they let me go? Will I be able to work again? Can I find new friends?" A twisted smile was on her lips. "Don't mind me, Lionel. I'll tell you what's worrying me later."

"Tell me now, Eva," he urged her. "It's better for you." She hesitated; she was struggling with herself.

"Lionel, I've been deceived in a way that you'll never know," she said, trying to keep her lips from trembling. "You're colored and maybe you can understand. . . . Perhaps you've lived all of your life with something that I've met only recently. . . . When you were a child, you studied the same books I studied in school, yet you knew that what you read in those books did not apply to you; you knew you were colored and that the white world made an exception. . . . You could prepare yourself against disillusionment. With me, I believed in the Party, all they told me. . . . Then I found that it was make-believe. . . . I can't even now tell you what they did to me. . . . They've ruined me, my life, my work. . . . I'm filled with shame and I want to hide. . . . Where can I hide, Lionel?"

"Eva, I'd feel happier than I ever dreamed if I could make you believe in life again. . . . You *can!* You must. . . . I trust you, and if my trust helps you, then you'll trust me in the end. I know it. You've never really been trusted; you've been told what to do, what to think and what to feel, and when it failed you, betrayed you, you hated yourself and the world. I trust you—"

"Oh, God, Lionel, I do so much want to try," she cried, reaching out her arms and pressing him to her.

He held her tightly, full of a sense of despair. What was he doing? Did he, as lost as he was, have the right to talk to her like this? How could he make promises to her? How could he believe in her when he did not believe in himself? Could he tell her how he had abandoned his mother, Dot, Gladys, his three sons, how he had killed Joe Thomas, Gil, Herndon . . . ? Could he tell her that his life was steeped in deception, that he was the essence of the world that she hated and feared? Yet he felt that the cure of his nameless malady lay in winning her trust and love. . . .

But could this delicate Eva bear the mere hearing of his story? She would turn from him in loathing. He felt her tiny, cool hands on his face; he looked into her giving, pleading eyes.

"I want your people to be my people," she said, surrendering her life to him. "I want to feel all the hurt and shame of being black. Let me bear some of it, then I'll feel that I'm worth something. I wish I was black. I do, I *do*—Let me share the fear, the humiliation—"

She was wanting to love him for his being black, and he wanted her love to help him to redeem himself in his own eyes for his crimes! Could he allow her to love him for his color when being a Negro was the least important thing in his life? He closed his eyes and rested his head on her shoulder. Yet he wanted that sensitive heart of hers to be his monitor, to check him from sinking into brutality, from succumbing to cruelty, and she wanted to love him because she thought he was an innocent victim!

"What's the matter, darling?" she asked.

"Nothing," he whispered. "Just tired."

"Poor Lionel . . ."

He was not Lionel Lane. He was nothing, nobody. . . . He had tossed his humanity to the winds, and now he wanted it back. He would shatter this poor girl's heart if he took what she was offering. He pulled away from her and walked aimlessly about the room, his eyes unseeing.

288

He needed her if he was to go on living, but would his taking of her kill her?

"Don't worry, Lionel," she smiled at him. "In the future when white men strike at you, they'll see me there at your side."

He buried his face in his hands, closed his eyes and groaned: "God . . ."

She rose and ran to him.

"What's the matter? Don't you want me to be with you?"

"Yes," he whispered despairingly.

"Then why are you so upset?"

He held her face tenderly and forced a smile to his lips.

"I'll be all right," he said.

"I only want to help you," she said. "For the first time in my life I am beginning to feel I can help somebody—"

Gently Cross crushed her to his chest to keep her from seeing the bleak look on his face.

"Bless you, Eva," he whispered.

"We'll be together," she pledged.

"Together," he repeated wonderingly; but his eyes were gazing toward a distant shore which he was certain he would never reach.

The doorbell rang. Eva broke from him, smiled, kissed him and ran to the door. It was Sarah, grim, gaunt of face, her eyes dark and full of anger.

"Is Hilton here?" she asked without ceremony.

"No; he's gone," Eva told her.

Cross went to Sarah.

"What's the matter? Where's Bob?" Cross asked her.

"I want to see Hilton," Sarah said, ignoring his question. "I'm going to kill him—"

"Oh, darling," Eva cried. "What's wrong?"

Sarah doubled her fists and lifted them toward the ceiling in a rage of bitter hate.

"The Party told on Bob— The Immigration men caught him this morning when he came to the apartment for his clothes— Bob's dead— He can't live out those years in that prison in Trinidad— And I'm going to pay off whoever did it— Bob said that Hilton threatened to do it, and

289

only Hilton and the Party knew about Bob's being illegally in the country. . . ."

She sank into a chair and sobbed.

"But how could that be possible?" Eva demanded, turning to Cross.

Cross was witnessing the birth of a new Eva. He knew that when she had been with Gil, she would never have been able openly to question or challenge a Party decision. And now she was demanding answers.

"It's all my fault," Sarah wept. "I pushed him to disobey the decision. . . . He did what I asked and now they got 'im. . . . He was screaming when they took him away." She clenched her teeth. "How they fooled 'im. Last night he phoned me and said that Gil had told him that everything would be fixed. He was to go to Mexico—"

"Sarah." Cross took hold of her shoulder. "I have something to tell you. Gil is dead. He was killed last night."

Sarah stared. "What did you say?"

"Gil's dead. He was killed last night—he was in an argument with his landlord downstairs. . . ."

Sarah rose and stood as though she herself had been condemned. Then impulsively she put her arms about Eva.

"God have mercy," she cried.

Cross watched the two women, both of whom had lost their husbands. One man had died suddenly; the other would die slowly over the years behind the bars of a prison on a hot island.

"I could kill whoever did that to Bob," Eva said.

Cross's lips parted. That was what he had been wanting to do to Hilton, *kill* him; but he had fought down the notion. Now Eva was planting it again in his mind. No, no; he would not kill again. Then what did one do when confronted with the Hiltons of this world? Let them trample freely over whom they liked? Never . . . But then what? To kill Hilton was a way of redeeming what Hilton had done to Bob. But it was also a way of making Hilton's acts right somehow. To kill him was a way, really, of exonerating him, of justifying him. Yet, what other course was there? To make an appeal to the heart of a man like Hilton was out of the question, for he was beyond sentiment. This was a problem only men akin to Hilton and Gil could

290

really see and understand, for they alone knew how far cut off from life one was when one assumed the godlike role. Was there no turning back? Once the tie had snapped, was it forever? Cross knew that the only difference between him and Hilton was that his demonism was not buttressed by ideas, a goal. So why should he care? But he did. And he hated Hilton as one can only hate something which is a part of one's own heart.

"Lionel, can't we do something?" Eva asked, oblivious of the gravity of her question. "Let's start *now!* Let's redeem ourselves and help Bob some way."

"But what can we do? Bob's gone now—" Cross explained gently.

"It's too late to help Bob," Sarah said. "They've got 'im."

"This has got to stop," Eva cried. "Isn't there some way, Lionel? There must be. . . . Men like that should be *killed!*"

She embraced Sarah again and the two women wept for the men they had lost.

"Sarah, tell me, what Party plans did Bob hurt when he continued to organize?" Cross asked her.

"They were planning to launch a campaign for peace, and if Bob's union had been known as Red—and it was bound to be if Bob had kept on—everybody would have balked at signing any peace appeals. That's all. . . . Bob got in their way and they kicked him to death." Sarah's eyes narrowed. "The police give you the third degree but the Party gave Bob the fourth degree. . . ."

"This must not *be*," Eva said in tones of horror.

Cross wandered restlessly back into the living room. He searched in his pockets and found Hilton's card, then stood staring, holding his wallet in his hand. Yes; if he went to see Hilton, it would be better to leave his money behind. God only knows what might happen. . . . He secreted his wad of greenbacks in his suitcase and again stood brooding. Suddenly he moved with purpose; he strode into the hallway and put on his overcoat.

"I'm going down for a bit," he told Eva. He studied Sarah for a moment. "Sarah, why don't you stay with Eva awhile?"

"Sure. I hate being by myself in that empty flat now. . . ."

When Cross went down into the snowy street, his gun was nestling close to his hip as he walked. He reached the corner, paused, staring thoughtfully. He should go back and remain with Eva. He was safe there, safe from himself. To mull over Hilton's crimes would unhinge his impulses and make him want to act in that wild, crazy fashion again. But he kept on walking until he saw the dark red brick bulk of the Edward Hotel where Hilton lived. Was he in? And what would he say to Hilton when he found him? He did not know. Yet he had an irrational compulsion to see Hilton. . . . He entered the hotel lobby and walked to the desk.

"Is Mr. John Hilton in?" he asked the clerk on duty.

"Mr. Hilton, Mr. Hilton—" The clerk turned and studied the board on which hung the keys to the rooms. "Room 342 . . . I'm sorry, sir. But he's out."

"Do you know when he'll be back?"

"I'm sorry. I don't know. He left no message."

"Thank you."

Cross went out into the streets again, walking at random. It was afternoon and he had not eaten. The day was gray, sunless; the air was damp, cold. He passed men and women whose faces expressed the intensity of their personal concerns. His eyes drifted distractedly over drugstore windows, the façades of stone and brick houses, the long green buses pulling through icy streets, and now and then idly up at some tall apartment-hotel building. He longed suddenly to be near Eva; but that, too, was a dubious thing. Why not flee now and start afresh? But he had done that once and it had led to nothing, to the nowhere in which he now lived. Running off was no solution, for he would simply take his problems with him. In any new place he would be worse off, for Eva wouldn't be there.

He entered a drugstore and ate a ham sandwich and drank a cup of hot coffee, neither of which he tasted. Had he gotten himself into such an emotional state that nothing meant anything any more, or had *too* much meaning now entered his life, more meaning than he could handle? On the streets again he came to a tavern and went in and drank a glass of beer. He saw a pinball machine in a corner; he dropped a coin into the slot, thumped the tiny shining balls with a lever and watched them veer and jump and bounce amid the flickering lights; he heard the excited clatter of machinery as the scores flashed in yellow numbers on a glass screen in front of him and there was a girl in a scanty red bathing suit who danced and leaped and romped on a gleaming, curving sandy beach under tall palm trees. . . . He played twice and did not win. What the hell was he doing? Was he so lost that he had to resort to this for distraction? Disgust drove him at last out into the streets again.

Hilton lay like a coiled threat deep in his mind. He had condemned Bob to ten years of suffering and Cross was now trying to find some way of getting at him. . . . His anger kept rising. Only the presence of Eva could make him try to forget himself. Yes, he would make of that girl his life's project, his life's aim; he would take her hand and lead her and, in leading her, he would be leading himself out of despair toward some kind of hope. . . . Suppose Hilton tried to take Eva from him; Hilton had the authority of the Party and could make endless trouble. . . . He had to have it out with that man, *now*—

He turned and made his way back to the Edward Hotel and entered. But why ask for Hilton, he told himself. Just go up and knock on the door of his room. Sure. . . . He crossed the lobby and stood in front of the elevator, waiting. Naw; walk up. . . . He turned and saw that no one was observing him and he took the stairs to the right. Yes; Room 342 would be on the third floor. . . . When he reached the third-floor corridor, he looked for the number. He came to the door of Hilton's room and paused; the door stood open and he could hear the whirr of a vacuum cleaner. He stepped to one side and waited. Was Hilton married? Or living with some girl? Strangely, he'd never considered that Hilton might not be alone. . . . He peered into the doorway for an instant and saw the white uniform and the bare, dark brown arm of a Negro maid. Then he stiffened as he heard footsteps and he walked quickly away, looking over his shoulder. The Negro maid came out with a pile of dirty linen over her arm and headed down the hallway, leaving the door open. She was no doubt going to dump the soiled linen into some receptacle. Cross thought quickly; there might be a bare chance of hiding in the room. . . . The maid went out of sight and he ducked through the door and looked about frantically. Yes; the clothes closet. He opened it, slid in, and crouched in a corner, smelling the sweet-sour odor of stale sweat. He pulled the door shut. Footsteps sounded again and he heard the maid humming a spiritual. Then the low whine of the vacuum cleaner came to his ears, and when it stopped there was the musical flow of water in the bathroom. More footsteps, silence. Had she gone? He heard the door slam and all was quiet. A moment later he emerged and looked about; the room was empty. A grayish light seeped in through half-closed Venetian blinds. He looked in the bathroom to make sure that he was alone, then turned to the top of the dresser and studied the comb, brush, and tube of shaving soap. He began pulling out dresser drawers. Clothing, pamphlets, a scrapbook, a flashlight . . .

His breath caught in his throat. *What!* Good God in Heaven! What was this? That *Hilton!* What a tricky bastard . . . On top of a pair of pajamas lay the balled and bloody handkerchief which he thought he had burnt by dropping it into the incinerator! The crumpled handkerchief showed burnt spots where it had lain on a pile of hot ashes; in fact, one corner was charred black. . . . He stood without moving a muscle, unable to believe what his eyes saw so plainly. So Hilton had known all along! But why hadn't he said anything? Why had Hilton defended him so ardently before the police?

Then he understood. . . . Hilton was saving this handkerchief as his trump card; he was trying to *own* him morally. . . . Hilton had seen him drop that handkerchief into the incinerator and had pretended that he had noticed nothing; and when he had gone back to his room, Hilton had gone downstairs and had gotten it . . . had bribed the cop at the door, perhaps. . . . Or he had gone down to the basement this morning on leaving the apartment and had raked it out of the ashes. The fact was: Hilton had

294

proof of his guilt! Eva had been in his room last night and maybe Hilton had eavesdropped at his door . . . ? Of course! That was the meaning of that last crack that Hilton had made just before he had left the apartment. Hilton had asked him to look after Eva and when he had said that he would do so, Hilton had said, "I *know* you will."

Gingerly, he stuffed the handkerchief into his pocket, then paused. No; it was not safe to put the handkerchief in his pocket like that. He withdrew the spotted handkerchief and then pulled out his clean, freshly laundered one. He wrapped the spotted handkerchief in the clean one; if he happened to pull out his handkerchief, he wouldn't run the risk of dangling the bloody one carelessly in the face of some stranger.

He rummaged further in the dresser drawers. A gun! A .32 and fully loaded . . . He took it and broke it and emptied the bullets into his palm and pocketed them. Now he was ready to face Hilton. Where was he? Had he gone to the headquarters of the Communist Party? If he had, why hadn't he taken the handkerchief with him? Or did he have some other idea in mind? Anyway, it seemed that Hilton had not acted against him yet. Well, he'd had his chance; he wouldn't act, not *now*. What a fool he'd been! These Communists were so tricky that it was hard to cope with them. When Hilton came, he would have to be on his guard each second, for the man was dangerous. How calm he had acted this morning! A disciplined man, cold, precise, farseeing, ruthless. Hilton was after power and keeping his mouth shut about Cross's guilt was but one more step in getting hold of a bright young man whose life he would own and whose talents would serve him in his struggle for power. . . .

Cross saw a little radio on the night table at the bedside. He looked at his wrist watch; it was nearing five o'clock. Where was Hilton? Had he gone to the police? No; if he had, he certainly would have taken the handkerchief with him as evidence. . . . He sat in a chair near the bed and turned on the radio, softly, and listened to the low, surging beat of jazz music. He kept his hand in his pocket on his gun and waited. . . .

Half an hour later he jerked alert. A key turned with a

click in the lock of the door. Cross quickly twirled the knob on the radio, leaving the radio still turned on, going in a soft hum. His hand was on his gun and the gun was jammed deep in his overcoat pocket. The door swung in and Hilton, with a toothpick slanting downward from one corner of his thin lips, came into the room and stopped short, blinking his eyes at the sight of Cross. Hilton's body twitched as from an electric shock; then he rushed to the dresser and yanked open the drawer that had held his .32. . . . He's quick, Cross thought. He smiled at Hilton, stepped past him and shut the door to the corridor. Hilton was pawing frantically in the dresser drawer, then he was still for a second. He spun around and faced Cross, his eyes bulging, his hands empty and trembling.

"I've got your gun, Hilton," Cross told him matter-of-factly.

Cross pulled out the .32 with his left hand and at the same time he drew his .38 with his right.

"Say," Hilton began in a whisper. "What's wrong?"

"Are you asking me?" Cross mocked him.

Hilton's face was gray, his eyes like flat discs of metal. He moved nervously, backing away from Cross one moment and advancing the next, his mouth working spasmodically.

"If you shout, Hilton, I'll just have to shoot you," Cross told him, gravely. "Have some sense. I'm in danger, and I won't hesitate to shoot, see? I was a fool to underestimate you once, but I won't do it twice."

Cross could almost see the rapid calculations spinning around in Hilton's brain. He had backed off to a wall now.

"What do you want, Lane?" he asked.

"Why didn't you tell me you knew what I'd done?" Cross asked.

"What you'd done?" Hilton pretended amazement. "What are you talking about?"

"Quit stalling, Hilton," Cross said. "Look, I found the handkerchief. . . . You got it out of the incinerator—"

"Oh," Hilton said, turning pale.

"You knew what I'd done. Why didn't you tell the cops?"

"Because I was glad that you'd done it," Hilton said
296

promptly, simply. "It solved a multitude of problems for me. Gil stood between me and one of the most important assignments on the Central Committee. Gil is gone and I've already got the job. I've wanted Eva for a long time; you freed her. . . . Gil's death was like a gift dropped from the sky."

Cross recalled how Hilton had spoken of Gil last night. . . . But he hadn't thought that much hate and cupidity had been behind those casual words!

"And when did you know I'd done it?"

"Your coolness made me suspect you right off," Hilton said without a trace of emotion. "I'm not so stupid a white man that I can't tell the difference between fear and self-possession in a Negro. You were self-possessed. The cops thought you were just another scared darky. Okay, Lane. You got the handkerchief. Let's make a deal. Let's be reasonable. You wanted Eva. Well, you got her. . . . Okay. Take off and let's call it quits—"

"So you think it was to get Eva that I did it?"

"Hell, yes. She's nuts about you and you're in love with her," Hilton said.

"It wasn't because of Eva," Cross told him.

"Then what was it?"

"You'll never know."

"Another revolutionary group?"

"No."

"You're with the police, then?"

"Hell, no."

"Then why did you do it?"

Cross laughed. Just as every man, perhaps, has his price, so every man, it seems, has a limit to his intelligence. Hilton knew that Cross was sincere and it bewildered him.

"I'll trade with you," Hilton urged him. "I don't know what your angle is, but shooting's not going to help anybody. . . ."

"It's not that easy," Cross told him. "You and your crowd are smart. I trust *nobody* now."

Hilton's voice came in a low, urgent stream of words, all precise and straight to the point.

"I won't tell anybody, the Party or the police," he swore. "Look, I just left Party headquarters. I'm taking Gil's place, in addition to my other assignment. So everything's settled. I wanted to get my hands on a quick boy like you, but you got away. Okay. No hard feelings. You go your way and I'll go mine. To hell with Gil. I don't care. I know you'll never speak of it, and God knows I won't. After all, I helped you with the D.A., didn't I? I kept making a racket about how Herndon was the murderer, didn't I? And Eva worships you. . . . You got what you want, huh? Things went your way."

"What about Bob?"

"Bob?" Hilton blinked. "What the hell do you care?" His eyes were round with surprise. "Was he your brother or something?"

"No. You sent Bob to Trinidad, to his death—"

"So what? There are a million Bob Hunters. What do they mean? They don't count. . . ."

Cross smiled bitterly. How those quiet words riled him! He had to deal with this man in a way that would make him feel what he felt.

"Sit down, Hilton."

Hilton hesitated; he did not know what was coming; his eyes darted.

"Make no mistake, Hilton," Cross warned him. "I'd kill you in a minute. If you've got any tricks in mind, forget 'em."

"I've no tricks, Lane. I want to live. . . ."

"So did Bob," Cross said. "Now, sit down. . . . In that chair there, where I can see you."

Hilton sat down and Cross sat on the edge of the bed and held his gun on Hilton.

"I want to know some things, Hilton," he began.

"Let's be reasonable," Hilton said. "Let's not be foolish about this. There's no sense in being drastic. . . ."

The man had begun to plead for his life.

"How is it that you care so much for your life and nothing for Bob's?" Cross demanded.

"And what in hell do *you* care for life?" Hilton asked.

Cross smiled bitterly. It was a fair question.

"Who do you think *you* are to kill as *you* did?" Hilton demanded. "Herndon's no loss. But Gil was helping you, wasn't he? He took you into his home, trusted you, didn't he? And I shielded you from the cops, didn't I? What are you kicking about, Lane? Let's call it quits."

"No," Cross said thoughtfully. "There's something here I want to understand. . . . I'm caught in these compulsions, just like you are. But, Hilton, I'm reluctantly in it. I don't like it. I want to get out of it."

"But killing me isn't going to get you out of it," Hilton reminded him eagerly. "The only way out is to *stop*."

"I won't stop; I can't stop as long as men like you keep playing your dirty games," Cross said; and there was a genuine despair in his voice. "I won't ever feel free as long as you exist, even if you aren't hunting me down. You and men like you are my enemies. Bob Hunters will go on being shipped to their deaths as long as you live. . . . And don't give me this goddamn argument about your helping me. You help others when it *suits* you, and when it doesn't, you *don't!*"

"That's the law of life," Hilton stated simply.

"It isn't," Cross contradicted him in a frenzy that made Hilton's face turn still whiter. "Maybe you're trying to *make* it into a law—"

"It's what I've found, Lane; and it's what you'll find too."

"I don't believe it," Cross said, knowing what Hilton had said was true. "And even if it's true now, we can change it. We can make it different; it *must* be different. . . ."

"Why?" Hilton asked mockingly.

"Because—because—"

"You're looking for paradise on earth," Hilton told him, managing a soft smile. "You're confused, Lane. You're seeking for something that doesn't exist. You want to redeem life on this earth with so-called meaning— But what you see before your eyes is all there is. Get all that idealistic rot out of your head, boy—"

"I'm *not* idealistic," Cross insisted.

"You are!" Hilton swore. "You're an inverted idealist. You're groping for some over-all concept to tie all life together. There is none, Lane." Hilton was struggling to master his fear; he was trying to get at Cross's feelings, trying to make him feel that he was his older brother, that they shared basically the same views of life, and that Cross

299

should accept his guidance. "Living in this world, Lane, is what we make it, and we make what there is of it. Beyond that there's nothing, nothing at all. . . . To think that there's something is foolish; to act as if there is something is mad. . . . Now, let's do business like rational men. Let's make a deal. You do what you want to do, and I'll do what I want. We'll leave each other alone. I don't give a *damn* what you do. . . ."

But Cross was not moved. He still held the gun on Hilton, smiling a little, appreciating Hilton's tactics. Then he shook his head; he could not accept what he had heard. Somewhere there was an anchorage to be found. The logic of Hilton reduced all actions of life to a kind of trading in death. And that was not his sense of it; he had killed, but not to exalt that. He had been trying to find a way out, to test himself, to see, to know; but not killing just to live. . . .

"You don't feel that there is any real justification for anything, hunh, Hilton?"

"No! I am here, alive, real. That's all the justification there is and will ever be, Lane," Hilton spoke earnestly. "Let's start from that. I let you live and you let me live. . . ."

"Why should I, if there's no justification? And suppose we break our contract?"

"Then one of us dies, that's all. What the hell is there so important about men dying? Tell me. We're not like the goddamn bourgeois, Lane. We don't make deals in shoes, cotton, iron, and wool. We make deals in human lives. Those are the good deals, the important deals, the history-making deals when they are made in a big way. Sweep your illusions aside, Lane. Get down to what is left, and that is: life, life; bare, naked, unjustifiable life; just life existing there and for no reason and no end. The end and the reason are for us to say, to project. That's all. My wanting to live even in this reasonless way is the only check and guarantee you have that I'll keep my promise."

"That's not *enough!*" Cross shouted.

"You're a romantic fool!" Hilton shouted in turn. "You're a kid! An idiot! You're just going about spilling blood for no reason at all, looking for what doesn't exist!"

"And what do *you* kill for?" Cross asked tauntingly.

"Practical reasons."

"And Bob was betrayed to death for practical reasons?"

"Yes. For practical reasons."

"But they were such trivial practical reasons," Cross protested, remembering the agony on Bob's face. "Couldn't there be—?"

"A pretense? Why? Look at it simply, Lane. Why fool yourself? You know and understand too much to go about looking for rainbows. Let's trade. I've no proof against you. If anything ever happens to you, I'll help you; I'll remember and will stand by you. After all, Lane, no matter what plan I had in mind, I wasn't going to kill you—"

"That's just it!" Cross burst out. "I might forgive you if you had been going to kill me. But, no; you were going to make me a slave. I would never have been able to draw a free breath as long as I lived if you had had your way. I'd have suffered, night and day. You would have dominated my consciousness. No, no, Hilton, there's more here than you say. Goddammit, there *is!* If not, then why all this meaningless suffering? If you had killed me, that would have been a simple act. Killing Bob might have been in a way merciful. He wasn't happy. But to make him suffer ten long years! Hell, *no!* You say life is just life, a simple act of accidental possession in the hands of him who happens to have it. But what's *suffering?* That rests in the senses. . . . You might argue that you could snatch a life, blot out a consciousness and get away with it because you're strong and free enough to do it; but why turn a consciousness into a flame of suffering and let it lie, squirming . . . ? No!" Cross's eyes were unblinking, seeing not Hilton sitting there staring at him, but Eva's diary, those pages telling of deception, of shame, of fear; and, too, he was remembering his own agonies in Chicago. He rose from the bed and looked wildly about the room.

"No, Lane," Hilton was saying. "What are you going to do?"

Yes, he would turn up the radio, good and loud; it would help drown out the pistol shot. He turned the knob up and a leaping flood of jazz music filled the room. Hilton rose slowly, sensing that Cross was preparing to act. Cross

301

kept the gun on him, then he saw the bed. Yes, make him get down there on the mattress, and the sound of the shot would not be heard.

"Lane, Lane, you're crazy!" Hilton was saying, his head shaking.

"Take it easy, Hilton," Cross told him.

"You can't get away with it, Lane!" Hilton begged. "They'll hear the shot—somebody will know—they'll catch you. Listen, you want money? I got a few thousand—I'll give you anything—but *don't* do this. . . ."

Cross was possessed. He was crouching a little and his finger was conscious of the trigger. No, not yet; load the .32 and use it. . . . That was better. . . . He backed off from Hilton, pulled out the .32, and, aiming his own gun with his right hand, he awkwardly took one bullet from his pocket, wiped it clean of his fingerprints and slipped it into a chamber of Hilton's gun, his eyes hard on Hilton's face. His fingers fumbled as he worked.

Trusting, hoping for luck, Hilton rushed at him and Cross met the attack with a sharp blow from the butt of his gun across Hilton's forehead. The man slumped to the floor, still conscious, his eyes filmed with fear.

"No, Lane; no, no!"

Hilton was weeping now, suffering. Cross knew that he had to do it quickly or he could not do it at all. He grabbed Hilton by the collar, and yanked him toward the bed. He was surprised at how light the man was. Hilton, in his fear, offered little resistance, as though he thought that being pliable might make Cross compassionate enough to spare his life.

"No, no, no . . . for God's sake, Lane, don't kill me!"

He put his gun in his pocket and held the .32 in his right hand. He kicked Hilton and muttered: "Get on the bed!"

He had to act quickly, or this man's wild face would make him stop. Hilton, with glazed eyes, scrambled obediently upon the bed.

"Lane, Lane, listen—*please!*" he sobbed.

Cross grabbed Hilton's head and, pulling one corner of the mattress up, he forced it over Hilton's head. Quick, quick, or he could not do it. Hilton's fingers were now clawing at his hand. Cross placed the .32 at Hilton's temple and squeezed the trigger; there was a click. Oh, God, five of the chambers were empty; only one chamber was filled. Hilton's mouth was moving, but terror robbed him of speech. Cross squeezed the trigger again and another empty click sounded, then again and then there was a spurt of blue flame and a gaping hole showed in Hilton's temple. Cross became aware of the dancing waves of jazz music that swirled around the room. He saw the black powder burns circling the bloody bullet hole in Hilton's temple.

He dropped the corner of the mattress and lowered the volume of the radio. Hilton's hands still moved; a labored breathing went in and out of the thin lips; there was a groan and the form on the bed was quiet. Cross strained, listening. There were no sounds in the corridor. He had to get out of here. . . . The .32 . . . Yes . . . He wiped it clean of fingerprints on the sheet of the bed and tossed it beside Hilton's hand. He paused, then forced the gun into Hilton's fingers.

He looked about. His fingerprints— Suddenly he did not want to try to save himself. What was the use? But he had to. He took a dirty shirt of Hilton's and wiped wherever he thought he had touched. He had to go, had to get out of this room. He was more concerned with getting away from the sight of that grotesquely gray face with its gaping mouth than with saving himself. He went to the door, opened it slowly and looked into the corridor. He saw the retreating back of a man. He waited until the man had turned a corner, then he went out of the room, drawing the door to, and walked toward the elevator. He seemed to be floating along without effort; he was never able to remember afterward making any attempt to run or hide. But when he got to the elevator, he pushed a button and then seemed to realize that he mustn't be seen by the elevator boy. The shadow of the car heaved into view through the glass door of the elevator and he ducked away. He saw a flight of steps leading down; he took them, running, then slowed and walked on down to the lobby. Act natural, he told himself. He walked across the lobby, passing one or two people who glanced casually at him. He came to the newsstand and stopped.

"A *Daily News*," he said.

He paid for the paper and, as he turned to walk to the door, a way to establish a partial alibi for himself came to him. . . . Ought he try it? Why not? Holding the paper before his eyes and pretending to scan the headlines, he glanced quickly about. No one seemed to be aware of him. Yes, he would do it.

He went casually to the desk and asked the clerk: "Is Mr. Hilton in?"

"Oh, yes; I think he's in now, sir," the clerk replied; he evidently remembered that Cross had asked for Hilton before. Turning, he examined the board holding the keys, then spoke to a brunette girl who sat facing a switchboard. "Will you ring Mr. Hilton, please . . . ? Room 342."

"Okay," the girl said.

"Whom shall we tell him is calling?" the clerk asked.

"Lionel Lane."

"Tell him Mr. Lane is calling," the clerk told the girl.

Cross watched the girl plug in on Room 342 and jiggle a tiny lever. A young woman with a suitcase came to the desk and Cross stepped to one side and listened as she inquired for a room. . . .

"There's no answer from Mr. Hilton," the girl at the switchboard told the clerk.

"But I saw him go up a few minutes ago," the clerk said.

"I'll try again," the girl said.

"Did you have an appointment with him?"

"Well, yes. He asked me to come and see him as soon as possible. No time was specified," Cross explained.

"She's ringing him again," the clerk said, giving the woman with the suitcase the hotel register to sign.

Cross sat down. He hoped that his present actions would indicate in any future inquiry that he had not been upstairs. Would a murderer act as calm and polite as he was acting now?

"There's no response at all from Mr. Hilton's room," Cross heard the girl say.

"I'm sorry, sir," the clerk said, "but we don't seem to be able to locate Mr. Hilton."

"That's all right," Cross said, rising.

"Would you like to leave a message?"

"All right," Cross said.

On a pad of paper supplied by the clerk, Cross wrote:

Dear Hilton: I was by to see you twice this afternoon. I'll try again tomorrow morning. Everything's fine. Hope you got some sleep after that session last night.

LANE

P.S. Don't worry about anything. Eva's doing wonderfully well.
P.P.S. Since you're so busy, why don't you phone me instead and let's fix a time?

He folded the note and handed it to the clerk, who pushed it into the letter slot, numbered 342, of the keyboard behind him.

"Thank you," Cross said.

"You're welcome, sir."

It was not until Cross had gone out into the cold streets that the full reaction to what he had done began to set in. He trembled as he walked. Had he acted normal enough? Wasn't it in favor of his innocence that he had asked for Jack Hilton *twice?* As his mind grasped more fully the folly of his having killed Hilton, a sense of nauseous depression seized him. He had killed Jack Hilton for many reasons: to redeem Bob's betrayal, for the sake of Sarah's indignation, for Eva's deceived heart; but mainly it had been to rid himself of that sense of outrage that Hilton's attitude had evoked in him, Hilton's assumption that he could have made a slave of him. He was deeper now than ever in the consequences flowing from his compulsive acts. He would be caught. . . . Surely they would come at him now. To be found on the fringes of *two* crimes would certainly make the police think something was wrong. . . . All right, so what? He was already lost anyway. . . .

But was it as bad as all that? Didn't he have an ironical array of invisible allies on his side? Wouldn't the police have a rather difficult job proving his guilt in terms of motives? What motives could they impute to him? The police would first have to prove that he had killed Gil and Herndon before they could get near his motive for having killed Hilton. . . . Lacking concrete evidence, the police would have to fall back on psychological motives. And in that realm he was certain that even Houston, that old outlaw who had trapped himself with the law, that outsider

305

who was privy to the secrets of the moon's dark side, would find it well-nigh impossible to bring himself to the point of believing him guilty. . . . Even if Houston should actually believe him guilty, would he dare express his theories about it publicly? Houston had a passion for toying with daring ideas, but juggling with possibilities and saying definitely that a man committed a particular crime because of those possibilities were two wholly different things. And especially when the crime stemmed from such a ghostly set of reasons. . . .

He turned off Eighth Street and walked toward home. As he neared Herndon's apartment building he became aware that a police car was pulling slowly into Charles Street at the opposite end of the block. He panicked. Did they know already? He had to act natural, keep his wits about him. A confrontation regarding the death of Hilton would be far more serious than the questions he had answered about Gil and Herndon.

Yes, the occupants of the police car had evidently spotted him, for the car slowed and he arrived at the entrance to Herndon's building at the same time that the car did. He paid no attention to the car and turned to mount the steps of the stoop. The door of the car flew open and a cop leaped to the sidewalk, ran, grabbed his arm, and spun him around.

"Just a minute!"

Cross gaped at the cop a moment in simulated surprise.

"What's the matter? What do you want?"

"We want to talk to you!"

Two more policemen came running from the car and the three of them surrounded him in the growing darkness. Several people paused and stared. One of the cops barked roughly:

"Get going. This is none of your business!"

The passers-by moved reluctantly on.

"What do you want?" Cross asked.

"You're Lionel Lane?"

"That's right."

"You'd better come with us."

"I'll come willingly, but why?"

"You'll know soon enough."

He allowed himself to be led, looking in alarm from one face to the other. He would pretend to be stunned; he would not talk. As they pushed him into the car, he glanced up at the lighted windows of Eva's apartment and wondered if she knew. He was sitting jammed between the policemen when the car jerked into motion and the siren rose to a wail as the car picked up speed. Then his breath was knocked out of him as the cops seized him from both left and right and patted his pockets. They found his gun and snatched it.

"Ah, a Colt .38 . . . so you carry a gun, hunh?"

"Of course . . ."

"What the hell do you mean, 'Of course?'"

The cop broke the gun and extracted the bullets.

"I've a permit to carry a gun," he told them.

There was a moment's silence. Cross took his wallet from his inside coat pocket and tendered the permit.

"Jesus! It was issued yesterday," a cop exclaimed.

"Has the gun been fired?"

"Doesn't look or smell like it. . . ."

Three minutes later the siren died and the car pulled to a screeching stop and the doors were yanked open. Cross was pushed out and hustled into the interior of a police station and made to sit facing a tough, wide-mouthed, gray-haired policeman who sat behind a desk. A plaque on the desk identified the man as Captain Ross.

"We picked him up in front of where he lives," a cop reported to the captain. "We grabbed him about two minutes after we got the call. He had this. . . ." The cop put Cross's gun on the desk. "Here's his permit."

The captain quickly examined the gun, then eyed Cross intently. He rose and stood over Cross.

"Frisk him," the captain ordered.

One policeman held him while another swiftly emptied his pockets and piled his package of cigarettes, his ring of keys, his wallet, his lighter, his loose coins, and his folded newspaper upon the desk. He had a moment of wild panic when the policeman pulled the balled handkerchief from his pocket. . . . But the policeman handled it gingerly, as though he was afraid of germs.

"Okay," the captain said. "Take your stuff. What do you do for a living?"

"I'm a student."

"Where?"

"Well, I haven't enrolled yet—"

"Where were you going when the officer met you?"

"Home. I was in front of the house where I live."

"Why do you carry a gun?"

"My life has been threatened."

"By whom?"

"My landlord, who was—"

"When was this?"

"Yesterday. You see—"

"Have you used this gun recently?"

"No. I haven't fired the gun in over five years."

"Do you know John Hilton?"

"Of course. I just left his hotel—"

"You had an appointment with him?"

"That's right. But why are you asking me all this—?"

"We'll do the questioning. Now, what was the purpose of your visit to Mr. Hilton?"

"He invited me to see him."

"What did you say to him?"

The police had not mentioned that Hilton was dead, and Cross knew that they were trying to trap him into some inadvertent admission that he knew that Hilton was dead or that he had recently seen him.

"Nothing. He wasn't in."

"But you *saw* him?"

"No, I didn't."

"Did you have a quarrel with him?"

"No. I've never quarreled with him."

"You were good friends?"

"I wouldn't quite say that."

"Why?"

"I just met the man two nights ago—"

"And when you saw him just a few minutes ago—"

"I haven't seen Mr. Hilton since ten o'clock this morning."

"Did he give you an appointment to see him another time?"

"What do you mean?"

"I mean, when you left him this afternoon, when did he tell you that you could see him?"

"But I didn't *see* him this afternoon, I tell you."

"What did he want to see you about?"

"Well," Cross allowed himself to relax a little. "He wanted to talk politics. . . . Look, you know as well as I that Hilton's a Communist. But I thought it was legal to talk to him."

The captain sat down and pulled from the desk drawer the note which he had given to the clerk in the hotel.

"Did you write this?"

Cross acted astonished as he examined the note.

"Yes. I wrote this this afternoon, about forty-five minutes ago; or maybe half an hour. . . . But how did you get this? I left it for Mr. Hilton. . . ."

"Did you push it under the door of his room?"

"No. I left it at the desk. But where did you get it?"

"We found it," the captain said vaguely.

"Then Hilton must have dropped it out of his pocket, or something like that. Or maybe the hotel clerk dropped it, lost it. . . . But I could swear I left it at the desk with the clerk." Cross allowed himself to be confused, bewildered. He looked nonplused from one face to another. The policemen were puzzled. "What's this all about? What do you want with me? Did Mr. Hilton say something to you?"

"Mr. Hilton had an accident—"

"Oh," Cross said in surprise. "Not serious, I hope—— An automobile accident?"

"You tried to see Hilton earlier today?" the captain asked, ignoring the question.

"Yes."

"And he wasn't in?"

"That's right."

"Did you see Hilton at any time today?"

"Yes. It was this morning when he left the apartment where I live. But what's this all about? What has that got to do with his being hurt? If you told me what you wanted, maybe I could help you," Cross said.

"When did you see Hilton *after* he left you this

morning?" the captain continued to ignore his request for more information. "You saw him?"

"No."

"Did Hilton ever threaten you?"

"No; why should he? Look, let me explain. . . . Hilton came last night—"

"We're doing the questioning. You just answer!" the captain reminded him. "Do you know anyone who'd want to harm Hilton?"

Cross gaped and let his eyes assume a roundness of understanding. This was the closest the captain had come to saying that some *person* had hurt Hilton. Should he try to confuse them by telling them about Bob and Sarah? Bob and Sarah had real, ordinary motives for wanting to kill Hilton and both of them had airtight alibis. . . . So what harm would it do to tell of the row that Bob had had with Gil and Hilton? It would give their literal minds something to chew upon for a few minutes.

"Well, look now . . . let me think—"

"Don't think! Talk! Tell what you know. This is serious."

"Well, it's kind of complicated and I'm rather a stranger to all of them, you see. These people, you know, are Communists, all of them. They had a hot argument the other night about Party matters. . . ."

"What people and where was the argument?"

"Bob Hunter and Hilton— It was at Bob's place—"

"Go on; get to the point!"

His eyes roved from face to face. Yes, they were eager to hear the story. Bob was on Ellis Island and had the best of all possible alibis. And no doubt Sarah could prove that she had been with Eva at the time that Hilton was killed. He told them the tale of Bob's illegal entry into the country, of how Hilton had—according to Bob's way of explaining it—threatened to have him deported to Trinidad, if he did not obey the Party. . . .

"You see, according to Bob, Hilton was going to tip off the Immigration authorities and have him picked up," Cross said.

"Where's this Bob Hunter now?" the captain demanded.

310

"He was at Ellis Island the last I heard," Cross said. "They picked him up for deportation."

The faces of the policemen showed keen disappointment.

"And his wife, Sarah? Where's she now?"

"At my house, maybe. That is, if she's not gone to her own home by now—"

"Where does she live?"

He gave them the information. He was sure that Sarah could readily account for herself.

"Lane, did you go up to Hilton's room?" the captain asked suddenly, softly.

"No; I told you he wasn't in."

"Did you ever fire a .32?"

"No. I own a .38. You see my gun—"

"Aren't you associated with Hilton in some way?"

"No. Why do you ask?"

"You could have walked up the stairs, you know," the captain suggested.

"What stairs?" Cross asked.

"The hotel stairs. Didn't you walk up to Hilton's room?"

"Good God, no! I told you I didn't *see* Hilton!"

There was silence. The captain turned to his desk and wrote something hurriedly upon a pad, tore off the sheet and handed it to a policeman.

"Check at Ellis Island about this Bob Hunter. Make sure he's still there and hasn't been out. . . . And send out a radio call for this Sarah, his wife—"

"Say!" Cross exclaimed. "Look, here—" He pretended to be overcome with contrition. "I didn't mean to get Sarah in trouble. . . . She's all upset about her husband. I'm sure that she hasn't done anything to anybody. She'll hate me for making people think that she's done something. . . ."

"We'll take good care and keep what you've told us strictly confidential, Mr. Lane," the captain said. "Now, let me tell you that Hilton was found dead a few minutes ago in his hotel room. . . ."

Cross lifted his head with a jerk and stared at the captain.

"*Dead?*" he echoed.

"Yeah."

He kept his eyes intently upon the captain's face, then took a deep breath; he looked disbelievingly around the room at the faces and leaned weakly forward and rested his hands on the edge of the captain's desk, as though for support.

"God," he sighed. "And I was trying to see him all afternoon."

"You did not go to his room?"

"Of course not. He wasn't in. . . ." He paused. "God, he might've been dead when I was asking for him."

"That's possible," the captain said.

"And only last night his friend, Mr. Blount, was killed— What's happening—?"

"Blount? Gilbert Blount?" the captain asked.

"Yes. That was Hilton's friend. I'm living in Mr. Blount's apartment. I just spoke to the District Attorney this morning about all of that—"

The policemen were astonished. He knew that their minds were wandering far from him now.

"Get the District Attorney's office on the telephone," the captain ordered. "We'll see what this is all about."

"Yes, sir," a policeman answered and left the room.

Cross sat and waited.

"How deep are you in this Communist business?" the captain asked.

Cross relaxed a bit; their minds were now working normally, leading them into paths where they could find nothing against him.

"I'm not in it at all," he answered. "I don't belong to any political organizations."

"How long have you known Blount?"

"Two days."

"How did you come to meet him?"

"At Bob Hunter's place."

"How did you meet Bob Hunter?"

"On a train."

"And Hilton? How long have you known him?"

"Two days. I met them both the same night."

"Did you ever hear anybody threaten either of them?"

"No."

312

"Did Bob Hunter or his wife ever threaten them?"

"They had a hot argument, but nobody threatened anybody."

"By the way, let me see your draft card."

Cross handed him his draft card; the captain examined it, copied down some information and gave it back to him.

"Where were you born?"

"In Newark, New Jersey."

"Where did you go to school?"

"In Newark."

The captain's manner made Cross feel that he had given up any hope of linking him with the killing of Hilton.

"Now, Lane, account for your movements during the afternoon."

Cross sighed, looked at the ceiling, then at the faces around him. He laughed and said:

"You'll have to let me think a minute—"

"Take your time," the captain said.

He told them of his movements in complete detail, leaving out only the half hour he had been in Hilton's room. He was deliberately shrewd enough to get the sequence of his actions twisted, and several times he had to interrupt himself and reorder the chronology of events. He told them of his visit to the drugstore, the bar, of his two visits to the hotel, the newspaper he had bought. He told of waiting in the lobby while the girl at the switchboard tried to ring Hilton. When he was pressed to give a conception of how much time he had spent in each place, he grew vague in a helpless sort of way and would not commit himself. Instead he tried to recall in concrete detail all the many tiny things he had done or seen. He even told them of his playing the pinball machine and he extended the number of times he had tried to win. . . .

"We'll check on all of this," the captain told him. "Lane, you can go now. But don't change your address. And say nothing about this to anyone."

"Just as you say, Captain. And if I can help you in any way, I'd be glad to do so. I didn't know Hilton very well, but I'd do what I could—"

The telephone rang and the captain picked up the receiver and listened.

"Okay," he said, hanging up. "Lane, I'm afraid that you'll have to stick around. The D.A.'s coming over."

"You mean Mr. Houston?"

"Yes."

"Sure. He's a swell guy. I've got a date to have dinner with him Sunday evening. . . ."

The policemen looked at one another.

He sat alone in an anteroom waiting for the arrival of Houston. What would the old hunchback think now? Even if he *thought* him guilty, what could he do? Would Houston want to hold him for investigation? But wouldn't he need real evidence to do that? Houston could, of course, put him in the Tombs and then carry on his investigation. But would he? Wouldn't he be thrown off and think that these two crimes were of a political nature? That some Communist had become disgruntled and had killed Gil and had to kill Herndon to silence him? And that maybe the same disgruntled Communist had had to kill Hilton to silence him also? While he waited, one of the cops came to him and gave him his gun and the permit.

"The D.A.'s on his way over," the cop said.

"Thanks," Cross said, pocketing his gun.

Cross saw Houston arrive; a policeman escorted him into the captain's office. They're giving me a going-over in there, Cross thought. Half an hour later Cross was taken into the captain's office to confront Houston. They were alone. Houston was grim, tense. He moved lightly and nervously about the room, more stooped and humped than ever, throwing a darting glance at Cross from time to time. Finally he stopped in front of Cross and said: "You seem to be getting to know the police pretty well."

"Looks like it, doesn't it?" Cross said.

"Is there anything you want to add to what you've told the captain?" Houston asked.

"No; not that I can think of."

"You were *not* in Hilton's room today?"

"Absolutely not."

"And you are *not* in the Party?" Houston asked.

"No. I'm not a member of the Party and I never have been."

"Had they asked you to join?"

314

"Of course."

"And what did you say?"

"I stalled. I talked with them about general subjects—"

"And you did *not* see Hilton?"

"I did not."

"When did you last see him?"

"When he left Blount's apartment this morning."

"Were you in communication with him by phone or in any other way since then?"

"No. There'd be no reason for me to be."

Houston paused and brought his fist down on the edge of the captain's desk.

"I wonder what these damned totalitarians are killing each other about!"

"That would be hard to tell," Cross said softly.

"Lane, you know something about how men's minds work. Now, do you think that what we were discussing this morning could have any relation or bearing on these killings?"

Cross felt dread enter him. Houston was again sniffing around on that highly dangerous ground.

"I don't know, Mr. Houston," he said. "It's all fantastic."

"And nothing like it *could* happen." Houston spoke as though he was protesting against something in his own mind. "It's these Communists. . . . They're involved in something. Maybe Blount and Hilton were mixed up in spying. . . ."

"And Herndon?" Cross felt compelled to ask.

"Goddammit, it doesn't make sense," Houston spluttered, planting himself in front of Cross. "There *must* be a *third* man involved in this."

"It's beginning to appear like it," Cross said, looking Houston straight in the eyes.

Again Houston was wading in his direction. But could Houston permit himself to accept what he was undoubtedly thinking? Could he bring himself to admit that he was standing and looking at a man who acknowledged no laws? Didn't the very thought create a dizzy kind of guilt? He saw the hunchback blink his eyes and shake his head. . . . Yes; he's backing off from it; he's scared. . . .

"There's absolutely nothing concrete to go on in all of this," Houston said, as though he was talking to Cross directly for the first time. "I have to keep fighting myself to reject the one and only theory that could tie all of this together. . . ."

"What theory is that?"

Cross held his body so tense that he feared that Houston would notice it.

"Could there be a man in whose mind and consciousness all the hopes and inhibitions of the last two thousand years have died? A man whose consciousness has not been conditioned by our culture? A man speaking our language, dressing and behaving as we do, and yet living on a completely different plane? A man who would be the return of ancient man, pre-Christian man? Do you know what I mean?"

Cross felt his body grow hot. His judgment told him to keep quiet, to pretend ignorance; but his emotions clamored to enter this discussion, to tell what he knew. He drew his breath, pushed his personal feelings aside, and when he spoke he was discussing himself in terms that were displaced and projected:

"He's a man living in our modern industrial cities, but he is devoid of all the moral influences of Christianity. He has all the unique advantages of being privy to our knowledge, but he has either rejected it or has somehow escaped its influence. That he's an atheist goes without saying, but he'd be something more than an atheist. He'd be something like a pagan, but a pagan who feels no need to worship. . . . And, by the nature of things, such a man sooner or later is bound to appear. Modern man sleeps in the myths of the Greeks and the Jews. Those myths are now dying in his head and in his heart. They can no longer serve him. When they are really gone, those myths, *man* returns. Ancient man . . . And what's there to guide him? Nothing at all but his own desires, which would be his only values."

Cross confessed his crime as much as he dared. Houston stood looking moodily out of a dingy window.

"I don't believe it," Houston muttered at last. "It's the Communists. They know something of this. I'm sure of that." But there was no conviction in his voice. He turned

316

to Cross and spoke without looking at him. "All right, Lane. That's all."

"I'll be seeing you Sunday night at Frank's, huh?"

"What?" Houston asked; he seemed preoccupied. "Oh, yes. Of course. And keep away from those Communists, boy."

"I shall."

Houston's eyes still avoided him. He was rigid a moment, then he turned and strode out of the captain's office, leaving the door ajar. Cross watched his humped back disappear down a dim corridor. He didn't dare. . . . The hunchback had looked right at it and had turned his face away! The captain entered.

"That's all, Lane."

"Good evening, sir."

He went out into the street. Yes, he was going to Eva. . . . Out of the corner of his eye he was vaguely conscious of a man leaning against the wall of a building and reading a newspaper. I wonder if they are trailing me . . . ? He'd see. He was spent; he needed a drink. He headed toward Sixth Avenue, saw a bar; he paused and looked over his shoulder. Yes; the man was following him. . . . He went into the bar and had a whisky. God, how could he get out of this? He wanted to rise and yell for help. Would it not be better to see Houston and tell him that he had gotten in too deep, that he was afraid of himself? His head felt hot; his fingers were trembling. He yearned for the sight of Eva. If only he could talk to somebody! To wander always alone was too much. . . . Once again he had killed and he feared that this time he would be caught. Maybe I *want* to be caught, he told himself. Is that it? He didn't care. . . . He had done what he wanted to do, hadn't he? Then why worry. . . . He paid for his drink and went out into the streets again. The man with the newspaper fell in slowly behind him. He had to see Eva, yet he feared seeing her. He knew that he had to tell her everything now; he *had* to tell. . . .

He walked aimlessly, turning corners. He glanced over his shoulder; the man was still trailing him. The street lamps came on, gleaming through the misty winter night.

317

The traffic was heavy. Eva would be worrying, wondering what had happened to him. . . . Yes; go to her, get it over with, tell her. . . . He'd throw himself upon her mercy.

He turned toward Charles Street and as he neared the apartment he knew that the man was still following him. To hell with him . . . His hands felt like ice, but his body and his face were burning. God, I must have a fever. . . . He shivered. He came to the building and stared at the windows of Herndon's apartment. That fool! How much of the world's suffering had been inflicted on men by Herndon and his kind? He was not sorry that he had killed him. He would do it again, if need be. . . . He shook his head, realizing that Herndon had felt the same about him. How bewilderingly tangled it all was. . . .

He went up the steps and entered the downstairs hallway; he paused, full of contrition at the thought of Eva. Could he face her? He had to; to keep alive he had to face her. He pulled up the stairs and stood uncertainly before the door. He pushed the bell; the door swung open and Eva was looking at him.

"Lionel, where on earth have you been?" she asked him.

He did not answer; he pushed past her and went stumbling into the living room. She followed him and he did not want to look into her face. He glared about nervously, then turned and went into the hallway again, heading for his room.

"Lionel, what's the matter?"

He flopped on his bed and closed his eyes. He felt her fingers on his face.

"You have a fever," she said in alarm. "You silly boy; why did you tramp about so long in the cold? Listen, the police came here asking for Sarah. . . . They wouldn't tell me why. What do you suppose they want with her? Do you hear me? Darling, what's the matter? Sarah fixed some food for us. Are you hungry? Oh, God, you must be ill. . . . Open your eyes and look at me! Oh, Lionel, you're *really* ill! Here, let me help get you out of your clothes. You must rest. You're under too great a strain. Lord, what have we done to you—poor boy— I'll get you some hot tea."

318

He felt he wanted to die. What was he worth in the presence of this girl? He was ill, but not with the kind of illness she thought. He felt her pulling off his shoes; then when she tried to get his coat off, he opened his eyes and looked at her.

"Eva," he whispered.

"Darling, you're exhausted," she said. "Where were you and what were you doing?"

"I don't know," he answered.

"Did someone bother you?"

He did not answer. She helped him to undress and he lay under the covers quietly, keeping his eyes closed. Eva pulled down the shades and he could feel that the room had grown dark. She cradled his head in her arms and whispered to him: "Can I get you something?"

"No."

He was fighting the fight of his life. His lips were tightly clamped, his eyes closed. He knew that he wanted to spill it all out, everything. Yet he held still, hoping that it would not come. It no longer now depended upon his debating if he should tell or not, but upon how much strength he had. He opened his eyes and looked at her. Oh, God, such trust in that face . . . How could he tell her? He pulled himself free and stood up in the darkness of the room, his back to her.

"Lionel, get back in bed! You have a temperature," she wailed.

She caught his arm and led him back to the bed; he allowed himself to be guided by her, his eyes glazed and unseeing. She placed her cool palm on his forehead.

"You're burning with fever. . . ."

"Naw," he groaned.

"You haven't eaten—"

"I don't care."

"You've got to take care of yourself. . . . You're worried, that's all. Listen, tramping about the streets in the cold and brooding, what's the good of it? You stood up to those cops fine, you talked wonderfully. . . . Then afterward you start fretting and you break down. . . . You mustn't let them get you like that, Lionel. Now, more than ever, you've got to be strong. We have no gang with us now. No Party . . . We're alone, and that means we've got to fight, fight, and be careful. . . ."

He stiffened. He'd scream if she kept expressing her faith and belief in him. He tried to pull away from the tug of her hand.

"Lionel, look at me—look at me— I love you," she whispered.

He shot from the bed and stood up in the darkness of the room, trembling; his body was hot, yet he felt cold.

"Lionel, what's wrong?"

"Everything," he breathed.

"Can't you tell me? Did somebody bother you?"

"No."

"Then what is it?"

He was still, his body rigid. Then he felt his lips forming sounds, heard words issuing from his mouth.

"Eva, I killed Hilton—"

"What?"

"I killed Hilton. . . ."

"Lionel, get to bed," she said sternly. "You've got a fever."

"No; listen—" He still did not turn around. "My name's not Lionel Lane. It's Cross Damon. Oh, God, what have I done? I've killed and killed and killed. . . . Eva, save me; help to save me—"

He felt her arms about him, tugging at him.

"Get in bed, darling," she begged. "You're sick."

She pushed him back to the bed and held him again in her arms.

"Eva, you must listen—"

"No; don't think, don't talk," she cautioned. "Lie still! Be quiet, honey."

"I *must* talk," he said. "I must tell you— Darling, I killed your husband— I killed Gil and Herndon too—"

"Oh, *God,* Lionel," she cried. "You're delirious!"

"No, no; I'm not," he cried to her. "I killed Gil—I, I killed him, Eva. And Herndon, too. And Hilton—just now. I did. And in Chicago, I killed a man— Oh, God—Eva, don't leave me now. I need you, I need somebody—"

He clutched at her arms and she held him tightly, like one holding a child.

320

"Don't leave me, Eva— Never leave me— Promise me you won't— Promise me," he begged.

"I promise," she whispered.

"If you leave me, it's all over."

"I'll never leave you, Lionel."

What was this? She was not listening to what he was telling her. She thought him delirious. Mad. Wild.

"Eva, don't you realize what I've been telling you? I, *I* killed Gil, Herndon, Hilton, and another man. . . . My hands are wet with blood. . . ."

She stopped his mouth with her hand, and then he felt tears, hot and copious, falling onto his face.

"Hush, darling," she said. "You're sick."

She pulled away from him and he lay there, his eyes closed, trying to realize that she did not believe him. He heard her moving softly about behind him, and then he was paralyzed with surprise when he felt her soft, naked body coming into bed and nestling close to him. Her warm arms went about his neck and she pulled his face to hers and he felt her lips clinging to his. Good God, he had told her his horror and had expected to hear her scream and run from him; and now she was surrendering herself, giving her gift to the man she loved, hoping to cure the distraction of his mind by placing a benediction upon his senses. For a moment he was rigid, not knowing what to do. Then the warmth of her reached him, stole into his blood; and he was still, tasting the sweet pull of her clinging lips on his. He sighed, lay still for a moment, then caught her face in his hands and kissed her. She had thought his confession was an eruption of delirium; she had been moved to pity by his state of wild anxiousness. What he had tried to tell her had sounded so fantastic that she had with swift instinct rejected it as unreal, the irresponsible babblings of a sick man. She would never be able to comprehend that he was a lost soul, spinning like a stray atom far beyond the ken of her mind. The extremity of his state had unveiled Eva, had made hope and trust rise in her for the first time since her deception. She was with him, close to him, mingling the warmth of her flesh with his, but she did not understand who or what he was or what he had done, could not believe it when she heard it.

Yet he needed her. And then he turned to her and took her in his arms and had her so slowly and so intensely and with such a mounting frenzy of sensual greed that they both died the little death together and he lay staring into the dark with wide, vacant eyes, afraid even to think. And then, quietly, as his sense of reality returned, as he felt himself again in the room on the bed with her, something close to a prayer rose up from his heart. . . . Show me a way not to hurt her . . . not to let her know. . . . I don't want to kill this sweet girl clinging to me. . . . I should not have let it happen. . . . And his despair seeped from his hot and tired eyes in large, salty tears. . . .

Cross now groped his way through uneasy hours under the protection of Eva's colossal illusion. His happiness was a kind of terror and he strove in vain to banish from his consciousness the realization that he was the quintessence of all that Eva most deeply loathed and would flee to avoid. Eva was his kind of woman, but he was not her kind of man nor would he ever be. But he begged the grace of nameless powers to let him linger with her for yet awhile before he went to grapple with the dark tides of his destiny. During the next few hours they moved around each other with slow and muted tenderness. He ached with anxiety as he watched the flame of love and trust glowing in her eyes, for it was he who had lit that fire with his unintentional deception, and he knew that when she finally gained a knowledge of what he was, it would be snuffed out; and his heart shuddered in fear of her going back into her feminine house and slamming the door on life forever.

Early that evening an official showed up with a summons demanding their presence the following morning at the hearing to be held over the bodies of Gil and Herndon at the office of the Chief Medical Examiner.

"Will it be awful, Lionel?" she asked.

"I'm afraid so, darling. But you must brace yourself for it."

"Lionel." Tenderly she caught hold of his hand, turned his face to her, and smiled faintly.

"Tell me, darling," she inquired in a whisper, "is it wrong to love so soon like this?"

322

Dismay made his lips tremble. "Trust is the heart of life," he whispered, and felt he wanted something to strike him dead. "How can one's trusting another be bad?"

She opened her hazel eyes full on him. "I trust you," she said simply. "I wanted to help you and I saw a way to do it. . . ."

"Bless you, Eva," he said, averting his face, feeling a constriction in his throat.

"Sarah'll be here in the morning to help me. I must find a black dress—"

"Will you need to buy any clothes?"

"No, honey. I've plenty. You must rest. I'll handle this," she smiled.

How wrapped up she was in her love! How demurely happy! He wandered into the living room. Could he let her go on like that? But how could he undo it? He sat, his mind roving back over the deaths of Gil and Herndon and Hilton, his feelings protesting against the whole, wild nightmare; but he could think of no concrete move to make. He recalled having bought a newspaper. Had there been anything in it about the deaths of Gil and Herndon? He found the folded copy of the tabloid jammed into his overcoat pocket. When he had bought it in the lobby of the Edward Hotel right after leaving Hilton sprawled and bloody on the bed, he had been too harassed and frightened to read it. He opened it and was amazed to see an artist's pen-and-ink drawing covering the entire front page under a tall, black headline:

DOUBLE TOTALITARIAN MURDER

The picture showed two tall, popeyed, hawk-faced young men in their shirt sleeves—in truth, both men had worn coats and Herndon had been fifty-eight and Gil thirty-six—attacking each other in a savage rage; one was flailing a fire poker and the other was wielding a huge table leg which he was about to crash down on the head of the other. Cross's lips twitched in a smile at the expressions of exaggerated hatred which the artist had injected into the facial features of both men; their long, unruly hair was matted and falling almost into their eyes; they were unshaven and their skins were pimply; their teeth were bared, long, and pointed; and the fingers of their hands were gnarled, lumpy, with long, curving nails suggestive of animal claws. The background depicted by the artist was not the Fascist Herndon's chastely furnished study, but a filthy den whose ceiling was cracking and peeling, showing the laths. The corners of the room revealed dense spiderwebs; several empty whisky bottles lay on the floor. Tacked to the torn wallpaper were several photographs of nude women in erotic poses, with legends like: FREE LOVE—JOY AND MADNESS—NIGHT OF ABANDON.

Cross didn't know whether to laugh or curse. He read the long caption running beneath the drawing:

Hardened Metropolitan police circles were stunned late yesterday by the freakish Greenwich Village double murder of a Communist by a Fascist and of a Fascist by a Communist. The Medical Examiner has technically dubbed the crime double manslaughter. It was learned through unusually reliable sources that these men's brains had been poisoned by the dangerous doctrines of communal property advocated in the writings of the notorious German author Karl Marx, and the Superman ideas sponsored by the syphilis-infected German philosopher Friedrich Nietzsche. These two agitators, Gilbert Blount and Langley Herndon, clashed in a bloody quarrel regarding racial amalgamation theories and both died of their mutually inflicted wounds. (See page 3 for further details.)

Cross tossed the paper aside in disgust; then he remembered that Eva might get hold of it and become upset. He took it into the kitchen and dropped it into the incinerator. He paused; oh, God, that goddamned handkerchief that had brought so much trouble! It was *still* in his pocket! He looked around; he was alone. He took the balled, reddish handkerchief from his pocket and stared at the burns; then once again he dropped it into the incinerator, hoping that this would be the last time he saw it.

Still brooding over the garbled newspaper story, he went back into the living room. What protection did men have against the Blounts and the Herndons of this world if newspapers could give no better interpretation of what they were after than what he had read? Both Gil and Herndon were so much more intelligent than the men who had writ-

324

ten the news story that it was pathetic. Did that mean that the future was in the hands of totalitarians? And that the shape of that future would be determined by which of these monsters was triumphant . . . ? Did the arrogant confidence of these two monsters stem from their secret knowledge that they knew that those who sought to defeat them would have to become like them, have to turn into the very kind of monsters they wanted to destroy? Was it that the totalitarians *knew* that, historically, no matter if they won or lost battles, the war against individuality and for the subjugation of freedom was bound to be won by their side? Cross shook his head in wonder.

Could they eventually trace Hilton's death to him? Now that he longed to plot out a future with Eva, he could not let his mind stray too far into the realms of hope; he might be accused at any time. . . .

He sighed, rose, strode restlessly about. Eva came in and looked anxiously at him.

"How are you, darling?"

"I'm fine," he lied.

She sat at Gil's desk and began sorting papers.

"You have no more fever?"

"None at all. I'm all right."

She rose and went to him; he knew that she had not come into the room to look for papers, but to be near him, to see that he was not fretting.

"Why don't you relax? It's better for you."

"I'll try, Eva," he said and stretched out on the sofa.

He lay with closed eyes, but relaxation was impossible. Eva knelt at the side of the sofa.

"Come to bed, darling. You need sleep. . . ."

"Let me just lie here and think a little. . . ."

"You're not worrying? Tell me the truth."

"I'm not worrying, Eva," he lied despairingly.

She kissed him, gazed long into his dark, brooding eyes.

"Everything'll be all right," she said cheerfully. "You'll see."

"As long as you are there, I'll be all right," he told her.

"I'm all in; I'm going to bed."

"Do that, Eva. I'll be along in a little while—"

"And don't go out into that cold again. We'll soon be

325

free from this. . . . We'll be where a big, blue sky stretches over our heads, with the wind blowing through the high pine trees. . . . They tell me that the lakes in the Gatineau are blue and deep and clear. . . ."

"Yes."

"And all this deception'll be at an end. Things'll be as clear, as sharp as mountains. . . ." She sighed. "I want to paint again. . . . This time I want to create images common to everybody, symbols that can link men together. . . . Rest now, Lionel."

She was gone. He closed his eyes. What could he do for Eva? His obsession was with him again. How much time did he have before his foolish world caved in?

He turned the dial on the radio, keeping the tone barely audible, and listened to the impish notes of blue-jazz leaping in freedom. . . . At ten-thirty there was a pause and a sonorously masculine voice recited a medley of political news items, and then:

The second Communist leader in twenty-four hours has been found shot to death by a .32-caliber revolver under baffling circumstances in a Greenwich Village hotel room late today. The body, that of John Hilton, 32, ex-schoolteacher, a militant Communist leader, was discovered early this evening.

John Hilton died as a result of a fatal bullet wound in his left temple. Death, according to the Medical Examiner, was instantaneous. The death scene showed no signs of violence or physical struggle save for a slight abrasion on the forehead of Hilton.

Though all present indications point to suicide, police are continuing their investigation. Murder has not been ruled out.

Hilton's death comes a few hours after that of Gilbert Blount, member of the Central Committee of the Communist Party. Speculation is rife as to whether Hilton was killed by some recently expelled member of the Communist Party.

That was all; Cross switched off the radio and stood up. He had not been mentioned, and whether the police would find some trail leading to him was problematical. He went to the window and stared into the winter night; traces of snow and ice showed on the pavements. A heavy mist hung over the city, and the houses on the opposite side of the street were dim and ghostly. Occasionally a man or a woman hurried past.

Now that the news of Hilton's death was public, what would Eva think when she heard it? Would she still believe that he had been babbling senselessly when he had come in earlier that evening? Or would the news of Hilton's death plant a tiny seed of doubt in her mind, a doubt that would grow until she regarded him with fearfully questioning eyes? Though Eva was sleeping, he felt driven to know what she would say; it was much better to learn her reaction now than later.

He walked slowly toward Eva's bedroom and stood hesitantly in the partially opened doorway, listening to her quiet, regular breathing in the dark. Would it not be better for her to die now and be spared the pain and shock which he knew he had yet to bring her? Hadn't he told Hilton that death was better than prolonged suffering? Didn't he owe it to her to kill her and thereby guard her from the monstrousness of himself? He advanced to the bed and his right hand lifted itself above her head and hovered there. God, no; no more of this killing whose logic led on and on into the gray, deadening reaches of inhuman meaning . . . ! His damned habit of relentless thinking was mangling the very tendons and nerves of the flesh of life! Eva stirred uneasily on the bed and gave a profound sigh, a sigh that told him that the destiny of the soul from which it came could not be encompassed by his mental processes alone. As he stood there in the dark straining at a decision, he could see that the grinding mechanisms of man's thought could destroy all life on earth and leave this watery globe bare of the human beings who had produced the thinking. . . .

To slay Gil and Herndon and Hilton in a fit of cold rage because they had outraged his sense of existence was one thing; but only if he were *outside* of life itself, beyond existence, could he make such a judgment about Eva whom he loved. How would he ever be able to tell, after killing Eva, that his judgment had been a correct one? Hate yearned to destroy and sought to forget, but love could not. Love strove creatively toward days yet to come. If he killed himself, his processes of thought stopped. Or did they? How could he ever tell after having killed himself that his judgment-act had been the right one?

His hand was still trembling in the air; he was not feeling, just thinking. . . . Logic sustained by love could lift future suffering from her, but love informed by hope could keep her with him to live out the unpredictable chances of life. For life's sake, he would spare Eva. For Eva's sake, he would spare her life. Time alone made this teeming world gush and roar like a Niagara with its richness of unforeseeable events; it was only by plunging rashly onward that one could see at all. And even if a god could exist he would have to be bound to some extent by that. . . .

Eva turned over and mumbled something in her sleep and he could see the faint sheen of her soft white cheeks glowing like a half-perceived image in the dark. His breath went from his lungs in a long, despairing sigh; he reached out his hand, the fingers still shaking from the throes of indecision, touched her shoulder tenderly, and whispered: "Eva, darling . . ."

He felt her warm body give a slight start, and then her face turned toward him.

"Yes, Lionel."

"Listen, darling. I've something to tell you. . . ."

"Yes?"

"I was listening to the radio and some news about Hilton just came over."

"What is it?"

"He's been killed, shot in his hotel room," he said quietly.

Eva was still as stone for a moment; then she stared at him with wildness in her eyes. Did she think he was guilty? He held his breath and waited. Was she linking up his gibberish with what he was now telling her? She gasped and her hand went to her mouth.

"Oh, God . . . *Why?* Who did it?"

"I don't know," he whispered.

She was silent. Did she know? Why didn't she speak? What was the meaning of that fixed, bleak stare? Yes; her hand was moving now; he could hear the whispering rustle of the bed covers. Then he felt as though he would fall to the floor as her fingers touched his hand.

"I feel awful," she whispered in horror. "Only today I said he should be killed. . . ." Her wide eyes glistened in the shadows. "Do you think it's the Party? Has he disobeyed them?"

His forehead rested on the edge of the bed and he knelt to her, as though mutely appealing against her judgment.

"I don't know," he breathed.

Couldn't she tell? He heard her breath catching in her throat; then the sound of soft crying came to him.

"Why, why, Lionel, is life like this?" she begged of him. "I feel darkness closing in all around me. . . . I'm afraid. . . . Hold me. . . ."

Her trembling arms groped for him and he held her.

"I'm sorry," he mumbled.

"Hilton always frightened me," Eva whispered. "I never liked him. I don't know why. And he had just turned poor Bob over to the authorities. . . . It's *wrong* to kill like that, Lionel. . . ."

Cross bowed his head; he knew that those words, though she did not know it, were really directed at him. . . .

"I'm sorry I had to tell you like this. But try to sleep now," he said. "Try and forget it. . . ."

He still held her. Her sobs grew less and finally, as though overwhelmed by too much horror, she slept once more. Cross rose and went into the living room and stood at the front window. Eva's own sense of guilt had protected her from suspecting him; she too had had the impulse to kill Hilton. Eva was *too* good, believed *too* strongly in life. Maybe this belief in goodness was her life, and once it was gone, what then?

Should he vanish into the winter night and leave her forever? He had a chance to make a clean run for it before suspicion pointed in his direction. In deserting her like that she wouldn't know what he had done; there would be a hurt in her heart for a while, but in the end she would get over it and there would always remain a spot of tenderness in her memory for him. And if he stayed, he would surely have to face the shock of her learning of his monstrous deeds. Was there the remotest hope of her still loving him

329

after she had discovered the reaches and depths of his problem? Again the pages of her diary stood before his eyes and his question answered itself. But where could he run to? And what was he running from? He knew that in any hiding place, under whatever guise he chose to conceal himself, he would be alone with himself to meditate in dismay the ungovernable compulsiveness of himself and the loss of his sense of direction in life.

No . . . He had to remain. If he ran off, Houston would then be certain of his guilt. He cocked his head, listening; from far off came the wail of a siren so faint that it seemed that he was imagining it. Would those sirens sound for him soon? And if they caught him, what would he do? The shame of having to tell, to explain to strangers, would be overpowering. That could not happen; he would make use of his gun on himself first. . . .

It was only in relation to Eva that his thoughts could shape themselves with any meaning. Wasn't there some way of telling her and stealing the horror from it as he did so? He would go to bed. Half an hour later he lay down by the sleeping form of Eva, but he did not close his eyes. He knew her hurt, but could she ever know his? Was there really no direct bridge between the subjective worlds of people? Was the possibility of communication only a kind of pretense, an arrangement assumed to exist but which really did not? Was the core of the subjective life of each person sealed off absolutely from that of another? Eva had not responded to him as he really was; his life had represented for her something which she had yearned to embrace. He lay here now, knowing from a stolen, lawless glimpse into her diary what she felt, her deception, her shame, but unable really to touch her heart, feeling that she was forever beyond his reach. Were we really that much alone in this life? Were all human hearts encased in this irredeemable isolation and had we only the satisfaction of fooling ourselves that we were together? He groaned softly and did not close his eyes in sleep until dawn.

A little after eight o'clock he was awakened by the ringing of the doorbell. Eva was still sleeping. He put on his
330

robe and went to the door. It was Sarah.

"Good morning, Sarah," Cross said casually, braced to hear her tell of her experience with the police.

"God, Lionel, did you know that Hilton's dead?"

"Yes; I heard about it on the radio."

"Do you know where I slept last night?"

"No. What do you mean?"

"In the police station," Sarah said indignantly. "I've been in jail, you hear? When I got home last night, the cops were waiting for me at the door of my apartment. . . . They hauled me to jail and grilled me for four hours. . . . I'm so glad Bob's in Ellis Island, or they'd have him now, for sure."

"But why did they take you to jail?" Cross asked.

"They had the idea that I killed Hilton because Hilton told on Bob—"

"But how did they find out about that?"

"I don't know. Lionel, what's *happening?*"

"God only knows, Sarah."

Sarah was hanging up her overcoat in the hallway.

"You think it was the Party?" she asked in a whisper.

"I don't know. . . ." Cross knew now that she didn't suspect him. "When I came in last night, Eva told me the cops had been here asking for you."

"Here?" Sarah echoed.

"Yes."

"How's Eva?"

"She's sleeping," Cross told her.

He told Sarah to wait while he dressed, and then he brewed a pot of coffee.

"I know it's wrong," Sarah began, drinking her coffee, "but I can't say I'm sorry about Hilton. . . . But that can't help poor Bob now. He's gone." She set down her cup and wept. "Lionel, I still hate Hilton. He's dead and I still hate 'im. . . ." She shook her head. "There was something cold about Hilton."

"I think Hilton would have agreed with you," Cross said.

"Lionel, what do you suppose he got out of sending Bob to his death?"

"Nothing."

"Then why did he take such drastic action for such a little offense against the Party?"

"Hilton was obeying orders, and he believed in the orders."

"But Bob's *human*," Sarah protested.

"To Hilton, Bob was only something to be sacrificed in the interests of a vast design," Cross explained.

"To make a better world?" Sarah asked; her voice was strangely hopeful.

Cross knew that she was now seeking for something to redeem the suffering and death that Bob would inherit.

"No, Sarah. To Hilton and men like him the world is perfect just like it is. They just want a chance to rule that world."

"I don't understand," Sarah sighed.

"It's better maybe not to understand," Cross told her.

They fell silent. An idea came to Cross. Eva was deeply attached to Sarah, and wouldn't his case be stronger if he threw the two women together? He felt he needed the strength and help of a woman whose reactions were as straightforward as those of Sarah.

"What are you going to do now, Sarah?" he asked her. "Bob's gone and you're alone."

"I don't know," she mumbled.

"Look, after the hearing with the Medical Examiner, suppose Eva and I moved up to Harlem with you for a while?"

Sarah's eyes brightened.

"I'd like that—I'm so alone up there. . . . But what would Eva think of it?"

"I don't know. I haven't asked her yet, but I will."

Sarah's feminine instinct for matchmaking came to the fore.

"Eva likes you," she said in a tone of voice indicating she approved. "What's she going to do now that Gil's dead?"

"She wants to be with me—"

"Oh!" Sarah pondered a moment, then she smiled. "Old Funny Face . . ." She was moody again, thinking of her own lonely life. "Some people have all the luck."

332

The official aspects of the Medical Examiner's hearing did not prove to be as much of an ordeal as either Cross or Eva had feared. Cross gave the longest and most detailed testimony of all the witnesses, for the Communist Party's able and noisy lawyer strove tenaciously to obtain a verdict branding Langley Herndon as the murderer of Gil. Cross, knowing that the Party, in its own interests, would leap to protect him if the police turned on him, answered repeatedly and emphatically that he had seen Herndon beating Gil with the fire poker and he even went so far as to testify that Gil had not seemed to be in a condition to defend himself.

Eva testified to having seen Herndon with his gun on the stairs; she told of running back into the apartment and of Lionel Lane's bolting the door against him. But Eva's and Cross's testimony was not strong enough to influence the studied, scientific opinion of the cool Medical Examiner, who contended that both men died so close together that he could not honorably or justifiably entertain any verdict save that of double manslaughter. In so far as Cross was personally concerned, the hearing was a success; he had managed to deflect all suspicions from himself.

The most frightening phase of the hearing came after the verdict had been rendered, for newsmen crowded around to get photographs of Eva. Cross was glad that he was forgotten, for he dreaded having his face appear in the papers under the false name of Lionel Lane. Sarah hurried Eva to a waiting car provided by the Party and they managed to get away with but a few flashbulbs exploding in Eva's anxious, drawn, and veiled face. Menti had been assigned by the Party to accompany them, and he drove the car. Back in Charles Street, in the lower hallway of the building, they ran into another battery of newsmen and Cross's admiration for Menti rose as he watched the man unhesitatingly and ruthlessly dispatch the reporters and photographers. At last they were in the shelter of the apartment and Cross fastened the night-chain on the door. Sarah took Eva to her room and Cross paced to and fro, preoccupied, conscious of Menti hanging on for no apparent reason. Menti's presence irked Cross; he had nothing in common with this lackey and wished that he would make himself absent. Menti was a hireling, an errand boy, a white-collar by-product of the American industrial world who had offered his meaningless, self-despised existence to the Party to be used, ravaged, dominated, and filled with a purpose, any purpose as long as the burden of the responsibility for his own life was lifted from his shoulders.

"You seem nervous, Lane," Menti commented, smiling and sucking at his cigarette. "What's the matter?"

"Just restless," Cross answered.

"You know, the Party's interested in you," Menti said in a voice that carried a multiplicity of meanings: ironical, teasing, threatening, warning. . . .

Cross paused and studied the servile mask of geniality that always served to hide Menti's real motives. Was Menti spying on him for the Party?

"Why?" Cross asked.

"The Party's interested in intelligent men, and you are intelligent," Menti said in tones of flattery, as though bound to give even Cross, an outsider, his due.

"But I know so little about these matters, Menti," Cross protested, knowing that he knew more than Menti would believe.

"Too bad Gil couldn't've lived to coach you until you were seasoned," Menti said in a tone of wistful regret. "Gil told Hilton before he died that you had the makings of a real Bolshevik: outlook, temperament, and all. . . . You liked Gil, didn't you?"

"Of course, Menti," Cross lied. "Gil was my friend."

"And I reckon you liked Hilton too, didn't you?" Menti asked slowly, watching Cross's face.

"Of course," Cross answered. "But I didn't know poor Hilton very well. . . ."

"Too bad. He was a brilliant guy. He could have been a damn good friend of yours if they hadn't killed 'im. . . ."

"Has the Party got any line on who did it?" Cross asked.

"No," Menti said. "But they'll find out. The Party never sleeps. Once they get an idea into their heads, they *never* give up."

"What idea have they got?"

"How do I know?" Menti said, smiling and studying Cross.

Cross restrained a chuckle, then resumed his striding to and fro. He could handle this Menti. He was certain that Hilton had not taken Menti into his confidence. But did Menti himself suspect him? The hell with Menti . . . But in his heart he hoped fervently that no other fool would threaten him; he was sick of the thought of murder.

"Say, Menti, have the police found any clues as to who killed Hilton?" he asked.

"Nothing. But we know he didn't kill himself," Menti said.

"Really? How do you know?"

"We just know. He didn't have any reason. Say, Lane, could I ask you a question?"

Cross turned and stood in front of Menti, his hands deep in his pockets. Just try to figure me out, boy, Cross mused.

"Sure. What is it?"

"What school did you say you came from?"

"I didn't say," Cross told him; yes, Menti was digging at him now.

"But you told the D.A. that you came from Fisk. . . ."

So this clown was not so dumb after all. The Party had checked with Houston and Menti had been informed. Cross's eyes narrowed.

"Why are you asking me this, Menti?" he countered softly.

"To find out the truth, of course," Menti said.

"Did the Party ask you to?"

"Yes," Menti answered honestly, looking boldly at Cross.

For the first time the reality of Menti broke through to Cross. There was a shy fanaticism in the man's deep, brown eyes, an apologetic inferiority in his demeanor, an ingratiating humility even in the way he talked—all of which hid something that Cross could not fathom. What was this man up to? That the Party trusted Menti was obvious. But how far would Menti go? Cross blamed himself for not having sized up Menti better.

"You knew Hilton well, didn't you?" Cross asked him.

"Better than he knew himself." Menti smiled and hung his head, a sheepish look coming into his eyes.

Then Cross knew. Menti had been spying on Hilton! And Hilton had suspected it, but had not been certain of it. That was why Hilton hadn't told Menti about finding the bloody handkerchief. How complicated it was! Spies spying upon spies who were being spied upon. Imagine a society like that! It would be an elaborate kind of transparent ant heap in which the most intimate feelings of all the men and women in it would be known, a glass jailhouse in which the subjective existence of each man and woman would be public each living moment. . . . And if an alien happened to show up in that ant heap, it would at once become evident because that alien would be opaque and, hence, known as alien. And for his spying in this ant heap, each spy would derive, as his reward, a satisfaction from the godlike position which he could assume in relation to his neighbor. This spy would not be a complete god, of course; that would be reserved for the distant dictator. But being a little god was better than being no god at all. . . . It was perfect, giving each spy something for his pains and hopes, and supplying each with an explanation for his suffering should he fail. . . .

Cross admitted that he had made a psychological mistake; he should have observed Menti more closely. Intuitively he sensed an almost organic servility that would make this man lend himself to any use by those whom he respected and loved. He had now to try to get to this man, for he felt that the influence of the Party on Menti's mind now caused Menti to regard him as an opaque object that had to be accounted for. He studied Menti's too white, sensitive face, almost a woman's face; he looked wonderingly at the deep, brooding eyes that never let you hold their gaze for long; at the bluish tint that always showed just beneath his dead-white, close-shaven skin; at those long and tapering fingers that were sensitive without being in any way delicate. . . . The man seemed like an empty, waiting vessel that could be easily filled with either a frightened acquiescence or a strident brutality; or, if necessary, a combination of both.

Cross sat next to Menti and asked him:

"Menti, what have you got against me?"

"Personally, nothing." Menti's voice was affable.

"What do you think I'm up to?"

"I don't know."

"Have you seen me do anything that would make you suspicious of me?"

"No."

"Then why are you prying into me?"

"We don't know you," Menti said without anger.

"What do you want to know about me?"

"Everything."

"What do you call 'knowing' somebody, Menti?"

Menti smiled, crushed out a cigarette, and lit another one.

"It's possible to know enough about a man to know when he would or wouldn't do certain things," Menti said.

"You talk about people as if they were machines, something *made*," Cross protested. "How can you predict behavior?"

"By a man's convictions," Menti said. "By where he stands in the context of a concrete situation."

"So the Party can tell in *advance* if a man will be guilty or not in any given instance?" Cross asked. "You mean to say that?"

"Just that," Menti said. "The logic of a position will make a man act in a certain way. Given a man with a given set of convictions, and given a situation, the Party can tell what that man would do."

"And you could condemn him in advance of his deed?"

"Certainly. It's logical, isn't it?" Menti asked.

"What are you trying to find out about me?"

"Who you are and what you're doing."

Menti was fluent in his answers and Cross knew that the Party would soon know that he had asked these questions. He would try to send back a human answer.

"I'm a Negro, Menti; I'm trying to learn," Cross lied.

"Learn *what?*"

"How to live."

"Hunh. You mean how the *Party* lives?"

"Hell, no. Have I ever asked you anything about the Party?"

"No. But you got Eva—"

337

"But Eva's not a political person, Menti. You know that."

"She was Gil's wife."

"So what? Are you moral?"

"The Party is not moral," Menti answered, declining to assert his personal opinion. "You love Eva, don't you?"

"Yes, I do."

"Why?"

"She's a woman, one I've been seeking all my life."

"And she happened to be a wife of a member of the Central Committee—"

"She knows nothing about politics," Cross protested.

"You found that out, didn't you?" Menti demanded.

"Yes."

"Why?"

It was hopeless. Goddamn this dirty spoon in the hands of the Party! Cross rose. This man would not, could not believe that men existed who could, at some moments of their lives, be honest as Cross was now honest about Eva. Indeed, Cross could feel that his love of Eva would assume baffling guises in the Party's mind. The simpler and more human a thing was, the more the Party feared it. . . .

"Listen, Menti, if the Party wants to know anything about me, let 'em come and ask me," Cross said. "They don't have to go licking around the District Attorney. . . ."

"They'll come to you, don't worry," Menti assured him. "They went to the D.A. because you know him."

And what would Houston think of their asking? Cross felt that he was in danger, but it was not acute yet. Yes, he would move Eva out of this apartment tonight. His real hope was that he could get Eva to trust him and run off somewhere with him. But what explanations could he give her for such a drastic move? The only reasons he could give would guarantee her not coming. . . . Menti stood and put on his overcoat; he paused, a cigarette smoldering in his lips.

"The Party's checked at Fisk University and has found that you never went to school there." Menti came to the point at last.

"So?"

"Then why did you tell the D.A. that you went there?"

338

"Must I tell the D.A. the truth?" Cross hedged.

"Tell me, what do you plan to do now?"

"Nothing."

"You got any money?"

"Not much."

"You're staying with Eva here?"

"If she lets me," he said.

"She'll let you," Menti said.

Cross was angry, but he knew that he had invited that crack. He held his peace. But it was clear that the crux of the Party's attitude was his relationship with Eva.

"I'm blowing, guy," Menti said suddenly. "I'll be seeing you." He got up and left.

Cross sat and brooded. If the Party checked up on him, they would run into a blank wall, and then what would they do? Just because his life was not transparent, would they get suspicious? The secret side of him was a handicap in the Party's eyes. . . . The more they probed into his background to uncover his identity, the more inflamed their suspicions would become. But what would they be suspicious of? And suspicion was not proof of murder. They would have to peel off layer after layer of pretense, uncover front after front of make-believe and where would it lead them in the end?

Eventually, of course, the police could trace him by his fingerprints back to his Post Office identity in Chicago. But what would that really prove? They would run into a truly bewildering set of facts. . . .

Sarah came out of Eva's room.

"She wants to see you, Funny Face," Sarah said.

Sarah looked lost, peaked. And Eva's happiness was exciting her jealousy.

"I'm going to ask Eva to come to your place," he told her. "We'll all chip in together on the expenses, hunh?"

"I could use some money," Sarah told him flatly. "I've no work now. I got to look for something."

"Don't worry," Cross told her.

He went in to Eva, who lay pale and limp on the bed. She summoned a smile for him. He took her hand and they were silent for a long time.

"Eva, I've got an idea. . . . Until Gil is buried, let's go

339

and live with Sarah in Harlem. It'll take you away from this apartment, those reporters, and you'll be in different surroundings," he explained.

She was thoughtful for a moment, then nodded her head in assent.

"That would be nice. I've always wanted to live there. Is it all right with Sarah?"

"She loves it."

"And we can be alone there, Lionel," Eva said with a sense of relief.

Life in Sarah's sixth-floor walk-up apartment eased the sense of strain in Cross, but it did not free him from the probing presence of Menti, who came the next morning, expressing great astonishment at the fact that they had moved. He had gone to the Charles Street apartment, he said, and rung and rung and no one had answered the door.

"Then I knew that if anyone would know where Eva was, it would be Sarah," Menti explained.

He had come, he told them unctuously, to bring Eva news of the Party's elaborate arrangements for Gil's funeral. All Sunday morning Gil's body would lie in state in a union hall, guarded by Communist militants, and in the afternoon it would be taken to Gil's family in the Bronx for burial. As Menti described the reaction of the Party to Gil's death, Cross could see that Gil's dying was being used to excite admiration for Party leaders in general. Gil had already, in Party circles, been deified as a kind of god who had laid down his only life as a sacrifice on the altar of freedom. Menti then, with measured movements which were supposed to be consonant with death and grief, hauled from his pockets a huge batch of messages of condolences which had come from as far away as Moscow. But Cross observed that Communists were not good when it came to paying respects to the dead; there was something embarrassingly self-conscious about Menti's manner as he sought to convince Eva of the touching solicitude of the Party for her in her bereavement. It's hard to pretend something about death that you really don't feel, Cross thought.

"Now, Eva," Menti went on, smiling slightly. "Don't
340

think the Party has forgotten you. The Party never forgets its own." He drew forth from an inner coat pocket a big envelope and handed it to Eva.

"What's this?" she asked.

"It's for you. Look at it and see," Menti urged.

Cross was standing behind Eva when she tore open the envelope; it was filled with greenbacks.

"But why?" Eva asked, her eyes round with surprise.

"It's yours," Menti said. "You're Gil's widow. The Party will look after you. . . ."

"But I can work," Eva's voice faltered. "I'm an artist—"

"Don't you want the sympathy of the Party?" Menti asked.

"Oh, no . . . It's not that, Menti," Eva said. "But I've never worked for the Party. I was only Gil's wife. . . ."

"You helped Gil, you comforted him; you enabled him to keep up his hard pace of work for the Party. . . ."

Eva's eyes filled with a look of terror and she sank to the floor and sobbed, shaking her head. Cross knew what was going through her mind. All that Menti had just said about Eva's relationship to Gil was blatantly untrue; Eva had not helped him because she felt she had been deceived and turned into an object, a means. . . . Then what was the meaning of this gesture of the Party? It was a threat wrapped in kindness. They were seeking a way to keep a hold over Eva, trying to buy her loyalty, laying the basis for future demands. Cross could feel that the Party was delicately making its first moves against him. He felt alarm, but he knew that he had some time yet before things would become serious enough to warrant his taking action.

"But why are you crying so, Eva?" Menti asked. "Are you surprised?"

"But I shouldn't take it," Eva evaded his question. "I've no right to it."

"The Party is loyal to you," Menti pointed out.

"Yes," Eva gulped.

"And don't you want to be loyal to the Party?"

Eva did not reply; she turned her fear-filled eyes questioningly on Cross's face, seeking his guidance. And Cross noticed that Eva's appeal for his advice was not lost upon

341

Menti's smilingly observant eyes, eyes that traveled cryptically from Eva's face to Cross's, and then back to Eva's again. . . .

Cross found himself paraphrasing a Biblical passage:

"Thou shalt not depend upon others, nor trust them: for this your Party is a jealous Party, visiting the suspicions of the leaders upon the members unto the third and fourth friends of the friends around the Party. . . ."

He was now sure that Menti was reporting back to the Party every nuance which he could observe between him and Eva. He hated the money that the Party was offering, but he could not afford to tell Eva not to accept it. He must make them guess at what he knew and felt.

"Why not, honey? It's for you. . . ."

"But I don't *want* it, Lionel," she whispered; she was still afraid that the Party would try to dictate her life.

Cross cursed himself. Each step he took carried him deeper into a morass of lies and deceit.

"The Party feels an obligation," Cross said, trying to make his lie sound genuine. "If you refuse, they'll wonder what reasons you could have."

"Exactly," Menti said.

Cross did not believe what Menti had said, and he knew that Menti knew that he did not believe it.

"Oh, all right," Eva sighed. "But I'm young and I have my painting!"

"As soon as you're rested and settled, the Party wants you to paint," Menti told her hurriedly. "Now, tomorrow's Sunday. I'll pick you up in the morning at nine and take you to the union hall."

Eva nodded her head. Menti shook hands with her and left. Sarah, who had overhead it all from the back of the room, came forward with a tight and angry face.

"Well, I'll be goddamned," she swore.

"What's the matter?" Eva asked.

"They pay you, but *me* . . . ? I lost Bob, but do they give me one red cent? They took Bob from me, but do they *care?*" Bitter tears welled in her eyes.

"Oh, Sarah," Eva protested guiltily. "Here, you take this money. You need it." She held out the envelope with childish generosity.

342

"I don't want it!" Sarah shouted.

"But, Sarah," Eva wept, "I didn't *ask* the Party for it. . . ."

"I ain't mad at you," Sarah stormed. "I'm mad at them! There's something fishy behind this. They don't give a good goddamn what happens to you. They're trying to buy your loyalty for some reason." Sarah turned to Cross. "What do you think, Lionel?"

"I don't know, Sarah," he lied helplessly; he agreed with Sarah, but he could not tell her so, at least not yet.

Cross wondered if he was underestimating the Party. Though the Party was certainly not an official adjunct of the police department, it did have wide powers of an effective and peculiar nature; it had its own underground apparatus and special methods of investigation. But what could they do with their findings? And he was convinced that he would have more than ample warning of their movements before they got too close to him.

Late that evening, immediately following dinner, Cross knew that the Party was adamantly on his trail, for Menti showed up accompanied by a short, dark Negro who hovered silently behind him, keeping on his hat and overcoat. This man, known as Hank, had a black, blank mask for a face, a grayish scar that went diagonally across his lips and chin, eyes that held a look of chronic hate whose origin seemed to go back to some inaccessible past. Cross knew that the Party had given Menti assistance in the form of this thug to help in spying upon him and Eva. This meant that the Party had not acted because it had not quite made up its mind. But what were the leaders thinking? Did they regard him as a spy? If so, for whom? And would they ever be able to fathom his motive in killing Gil? Or would they in the end just create some imaginary crime and try to brand him with its guilt? He knew that they were fully capable of that. . . .

Menti pretended that the Party had asked for papers of an urgent political nature that Gil had left behind in his desk. Eva willingly surrendered to Menti the keys of the apartment on Charles Street. Cross had no fear of the Party finding anything incriminating in Eva's apartment, for he had brought his only suitcase with him. Before leaving, Menti lingered at the door, smiling, looking thoughtfully off into space. Hank stood behind Menti, morose, his eyes darting about.

"How are you getting on, Lane?" Menti asked.

"Oh, so-so," Cross said.

"Only so-so?" Menti asked. "You need money?"

"No."

Hank was listening so intently that his eyes glittered.

"The Party's curious about you," Menti said.

"You've told me I'm under suspicion," Cross said. "But you haven't told me why."

"Say, where were you born?" Menti asked suddenly. "I want to know."

"You mean the Party wants to know— Tell the Party folks to come and ask me what they want to hear—"

"I'm the Party; I'm asking—"

"You think I'm with the police, don't you?" Cross evaded him.

Menti laughed, then playfully slapped Cross on the shoulder.

"Hell, Lane, we're not children," Menti said. "You don't have connections with the police; we've investigated and we know. . . . Say, tell me, when did you last see Hilton?"

"I tried to see him yesterday afternoon. But he wasn't in."

"What time was that?"

"Gosh, I don't know," Cross smiled. "Is it important?"

"Could be." Menti was baffled at Cross's casual manner. "Can you *prove* you didn't see him?"

"I haven't bothered to think about that," Cross said.

"The hotel clerk said a guy of your description asked for Hilton around four o'clock," Menti told him. "That must have been you, huh?"

"Maybe. There are plenty of Negroes who look like me," Cross said.

"Not likely," Menti said. "At least they don't act like you. The hotel clerk remembers you because you acted self-assured, like a man who knows his way around."

"I know my way around," Cross laughed.

"Good-by," Menti said suddenly.

They left. Cross shut the door and at once Sarah came out of the living room and Cross could see that she had overheard the conversation.

"What are they after you for?" she asked.

"They're crazy," Cross told her, laughing. "You know, they're trying to build up a case. . . . They want to accuse me of killing Hilton. . . ."

"Good God!" Sarah looked stunned. "Because you're living with Eva? But the Party isn't interested in things like that. They're trying to put their finger on you for something and they're going about it slow and easy. They know you're here with Eva and won't run off—"

"You think so?" Cross asked to test her intuitions.

"I *know* it; I can feel it. . . ."

Cross forced a laugh and shrugged his shoulders.

Just before going to bed that night, when they were alone together, Eva came demurely to him with a package wrapped up in heavy brown paper. He saw a look of devotion and trust in her tranquil, hazel eyes. She knelt at his feet and caught hold of his hand.

"Lionel," she whispered.

"Yes, darling."

In her attitude was a mute giving of her life to him that sprang from a sense of her newly gained freedom.

"Lionel," she began, "I'm going to let you know something that I once swore that I'd never divulge to anyone on earth. I want you to know the Party you're dealing with. . . . They deceived me with Gil. Darling, here in this package are my diaries. They contain my hope and my despair. . . . You must not let them make you a victim too. . . . They're clever. Menti's hounding you for something. . . . Read these diaries and know the world in which I once lived. . . ."

Cross's eyes fell; he tried to keep his sense of shame from showing.

"You must know the kind of woman with whom you've elected to go through life," Eva continued bravely, her eyes full upon his face. "Life has made me like you. The world has treated me as it has treated you. You'll see that when you read this. . . ."

Cross was a riot of impulses; he wanted to tell her that

345

he had already read them; that he was not worthy of what she was doing; that he too had a past to tell of; that it was to her that he ought to kneel and not she to him. . . . One impulse canceled the other and he said nothing; then he seized her and crushed her to him in an outburst of despair that was so deep and sharp that it seemed to stop his breath.

"Until death, Lionel," she whispered.

"Yes; until death." He clung to her and hid his face; he did not want her to see the tears that stung his eyes. When she pulled herself free, she laughed and wiped his eyes with the tips of her fingers.

"You silly-billy," she said.

"You make me feel that way," he told her truthfully.

"Look, let's go to a midnight movie," she suggested. "I'm tired of being cooped up."

"Okay."

No sooner was he upon the street with Eva than he saw Menti and Hank in a shadowy doorway near a corner. And he knew that Menti had seen him, for the man lowered his head and walked off quickly, pulling Hank after him. He did not call Eva's attention to Menti, feeling that it would only worry her. With Eva clinging to his arm, he moved on over patches of snow and ice, wondering what the Party knew and when it planned to act.

He was now under twenty-four-hour surveillance. Did they think he was going to run off? Were they working with the District Attorney? He felt that he could handle the Party, but Houston was another matter. He damned the day he had met the man who knew so well the spiritual malady that had plagued and undone him—the dilemma of the ethical criminal, the millions of men who lived in the tiny crevices of industrial society completely cut off from humanity, the multitudes of little gods who ruled their own private worlds and acknowledged no outside authority. Hating that part of himself that he could not manage, Cross had to fear and hate Houston, who knew how close to crime men of his kind had by necessity to live.

After the movie they returned to the apartment to find that Sarah was not in. Eva was worried; it was past two o'clock in the morning and she lamented that they hadn't invited Sarah along with them, and Cross agreed with her, but for reasons of his own. He suspected that Sarah was with Menti. . . .

Sarah arrived around three o'clock, accompanied by Menti, Hank, and an elderly, portly, white-haired, well-dressed man. Sarah, slightly tipsy, came straight to Cross with a knowing look in her eyes. They've been pumping her, Cross thought.

"Lionel, I want you to meet Menti's friend, Mr. Blimin," Sarah said.

"How are you?" Cross said.

"I'm glad to meet you, Lane," Blimin said.

They shook hands. Menti at once went to Blimin and Hank and took both of them by their arms.

"Say, you two wanted to find that little room, didn't you?"

"Oh, yes," Blimin said, looking around the room at Cross, Eva, and Sarah. "Will you excuse me?"

Menti herded the two of them into the hallway. It did not look natural. Cross knew that Menti had gotten Blimin and Hank out of the room in order to say something to them of a confidential nature. The moment Menti's footsteps had ceased to sound in the hallway, Sarah rushed to Cross and Eva and burst out in a loud whisper: "You should have heard what they were asking me about you—"

"Yes? Tell me," Cross urged her.

"Blimin wanted to know your age, your background, how you spoke, who your mother was, who your father was, what school you came from, what organizations you belonged to. . . ."

"Good God!" Cross forced himself to laugh.

"But, why?" Eva stood and indignation blazed in her eyes.

"I don't know," Sarah said.

Eva turned to Cross and said: "What do they mean? You've got to tell them off, Lionel."

"I will," he said.

"If you don't tell them off, I will," Eva swore with anger.

"But this just started today, honey," he reminded her.

347

He had to keep this thing to normal proportions in her mind. "I'll see them as soon as the ceremony for Gil's over."

"And tell them to keep out of our life," Eva demanded.

"But wait—I haven't told you everything yet," Sarah said. "That Blimin wanted to know what kind of books you read, what kind of mail you received, if you spoke any foreign languages, if you had any secret appointments, if a lot of telephone calls came for you, how large were the bills you spent, what kind of people came to see you, if I could hear you typing late at night, if you mailed any big envelopes. . . . Lord, he was like a lawyer."

"Don't worry, Sarah," Cross told her. "They're worried about Gil and Hilton and they're trying to find out who killed them."

"But why are they snooping around *us?*" Eva demanded.

"Listen, Lionel," Sarah said with deep care. "I hope to God that you're not like Bob. Don't have a past for them to dig into. This is exactly how they were acting before they turned Bob over to the Immigration authorities. . . . Oh, God, I hate those people, I *hate* 'em!" Tears of rage blinded Sarah.

"But there are others who are worse than Communists," Cross told Sarah. "The Communists are kittens; but there are tigers in the jungle."

"What do you mean?" Sarah asked.

"Communists are trained and organized; but there are men, their equals, who have never been broken. *They* are more dangerous than Communists."

"Well, I hate 'em, *hate* 'em *all!*" Sarah hissed.

"If you hate them, then you'll never understand them," Cross said.

"Why in hell would I want to understand them?" Sarah demanded.

The doorknob turned and Menti, Blimin, and Hank re-entered the room. Blimin came straight to Cross and went to work.

"Say, they tell me you were a friend of Gil," Blimin said.

"That's right," Cross answered.

"And you knew Hilton?"

348

"Not as well as I knew Gil."

"Is this your first contact with the Party?"

"That's it."

"What do you think of our Party?"

"Well, I doubt if I know it well enough to form a worth-while opinion," Cross hedged.

"Could I ask you a direct question?"

"Of course."

"Lane, are you now, directly or indirectly, verbally or organizationally, by proxy or on your own behalf engaged in anti-Party activity?" Blimin let the words roll neatly off the tip of his tongue.

Cross rose from Eva's side and faced Blimin. How could he tell this man something that would set his mind at rest, and yet not leave the impression that he was evading anything?

"You don't have to answer unless you want to, Lane," Blimin said.

"I'm hesitating in order to give full weight to what you've asked me," Cross said.

The Communists were at last boldly leaping into an area where the police had feared to tread. His relation to the Party was the reverse of his relation to Houston. The essence of the Party was an open lawlessness and it could smell lawlessness in others even when it could not identify it correctly. What tactic could he use here? His first move should be to find out how much they suspected and the degree and intensity of their seriousness.

"Mr. Blimin, I suppose this is as good a time as any for us to have a showdown," Cross began. "What are you suspecting me of? Why are you posing all these vague and roundabout questions?"

"Blimin's not a man to play with," Menti reminded Cross.

"We're careful in the Party, Lane," Blimin said. "And we don't know who you are. You are a close friend of Eva; Eva is close to us, and so you are close to us, but we don't know you. I'd like to see you account for yourself, to put it frankly. We've been trying to get a line on you, and the more we try, the less we find. You don't add up. What do you think of things? How do you feel? To our Party, these

349

questions are of paramount importance. Our Party is under attack from many quarters. You show up suddenly on the scene, and two of our best leaders die under questionable circumstances and you are nearby. . . . Naturally the question arises: *Who is Lionel Lane?* What organization does he belong to? What are his interests? Who are his friends? What ideas does he hold? Now, Lane, I'm here to listen to you. I'm an old man and I'm a pretty good judge of men. If you're honest and on the up and up, I'll be able to tell it, feel it. If you're hiding something, I can tell that too. Is what I'm asking fair?"

"It's fair," Cross conceded.

"Are you willing to talk?"

"Of course," Cross laughed. He knew that Blimin could not drag his secret from him; his past was safe; his past was himself. "I know nothing of the ideology of the Party."

Blimin's face changed; he stood; his eyes grew hard; when he spoke his words were strident and underlined with a tinge of viciousness.

"I'm not talking about ideology. You're a man with the ability to grasp situations. I know that. . . . You know goddamn well what I'm wondering about you."

"Well," Cross drawled, "I know you know I'm a stranger—"

"No; no!" Blimin slapped his hand through the air with a gesture of disdain. "I mean this— Your appearance in our midst coincides with death and violence! I'm talking to the point now. . . . In the eyes of the Party you are under *suspicion*."

"You suspect me of what?" Cross asked boldly.

"Of almost anything and everything," Blimin stated his case.

"And what do you expect me to do about that?" Cross egged him on.

"Clear yourself of suspicion, or we will take measures to see that you don't remain in our midst," Blimin said.

"This is vague," Cross argued. "I'm guilty, you say; but you don't say what I'm supposed to be guilty of—"

"You're dodging, Lane! Right now you're guilty of evading my questions— Look, you can't play possum with us.

You're dealing with experienced men. You are supposed to have a background that would make you acceptable to us, but you haven't revealed it. We don't understand you, and we don't like to be with people we don't understand. The world in which we live is much too dangerous for us to tolerate you a moment longer."

"Look, for Christ's sake," Cross begged. "I haven't had a chance to say anything to anybody yet. . . . Gil died suddenly; he was the only high-ranking member of the Party I'd talked to."

"Lane, stop trying to make me believe that you're naïve!" Blimin shouted. "I'm *serious!*"

Eva rose; anger shone in her eyes.

"Comrade Blimin—"

"You keep quiet!" Blimin ordered. "This is no time for you to speak!"

"But—" Eva protested.

"You'll get your chance to speak to the Party later about all this," Blimin said, waving a fat forefinger at her.

"Mr. Blimin, what do you want to know?" Cross demanded of him. "You must tell me, for I refuse to relate my entire life to you and let you pick out what part you want and then brand me with it."

"I don't understand all this," Sarah mumbled uneasily.

"This is no concern of yours!" Blimin snapped at Sarah. His anger fully roused, he whirled on Cross. "Lane, what the hell ghastly joke is this you're pulling? Who the god-damn hell do you think you *are?* What are you doing here? When we try to check on you, we run into a maze that leads nowhere. That's no *accident.* Are you a spy? Frankly, we doubt it; we thought so at first, but you haven't been close enough to us to get hold of any information. Don't you think, now, that we are scared of you. If we were, you wouldn't be breathing now. . . . But we want to know. . . ."

"Know *what?*"

"Are you a *killer?*"

"No!" Eva screamed.

"God in Heaven," Sarah gasped.

The room was silent. He had at last been accused. Now, he had to act. First, he'd let the Party know that he knew

351

what the score was in the world. He'd make them feel that maybe they could use him despite all the vague clouds of suspicion around him. He would make use of Blimin's urging him to talk to make a bid to them.

"We've no evidence, you might say," Blimin went on with his charge. "That's right; we haven't. But *you* are evidence. You come—death! *Why?* Lane, I'm accusing you of EVERYTHING! Now talk for your life." Blimin pronounced a provisional death sentence.

Cross laughed softly, went to the sofa and sat down, lit a cigarette, lifted smiling eyes to Blimin as he drew smoke deep into his lungs.

"Do you think I'm crazy enough to try to defend myself against a charge about which I know nothing? You say you don't understand me. Well, I'm going to talk, and *you're* going to listen. I'm not the kind of fool who'd let you push him into a position of defending himself against a charge of something he's never even dreamed of doing— If you make me do that, why, I'd really be somehow guilty—"

Cross rose, went to the center table and poured out a glass of water; he acted slowly, methodically, taking his time. I'm acting as Gil acted when he was trying to impress me, he told himself. He drained the glass, turned to Blimin, and he confessed not as Blimin wanted him to, but as he felt it. It was as though he was not only speaking to Blimin but to and for himself, trying to clarify his predicament in his own eyes.

"Now, Mr. Blimin, I take it for granted that you are a member of the Central Committee of the Communist Party, or you wouldn't be here talking to me tonight, or rather this morning. It's half-past three. . . . Oh, no; you needn't bother to affirm or deny it. I assume you're here for your Party. Let's let it go at that. I'd like for you to take back a straight message to them. They may not like my answer, but I'm not going to try to couch it in terms that will please them. My answer is just simply my way of looking at things, my slant, if you want to call it that.

"One way, among a variety of others, of looking at what is happening in this world today is to view all modern history as being tied together by one over-all meaning. And that meaning is this: to a greater or lesser degree, all hu-

352

man life on this earth today *can* be described as moving away from traditional, agrarian, simple handicraft ways of life toward modern industrialization. Some nations, owing mainly to their historical backgrounds, have already made this journey, have already, so to speak, exhausted their industrial potentials of development and are industrially overripe. I'm referring to nations like England, Japan, Germany, etc. In these nations the problem of the future structure of society and the question of what kind of faith will sustain the individual in his daily life constitute a kind of chronic spiritual terror."

"Lane," Blimin accused him, "you're evading my question—"

"You asked me what I thought and felt about things," Cross shot at him. "Do you want to hear it or not?"

"But get to the point," Blimin insisted.

"Are you in a hurry?" Cross asked. "If so, I'll talk to you some other time—"

"Get to the point, Lane," Blimin said.

"This *is* my point," Cross said. "Now, Mr. Blimin, as I said, other nations, such as China, India, and the vast stretches of Africa have hardly begun this journey toward industrialization. The human and physical resources of these huge nations, comprising as they do more than half the human race and more than half the territory of the earth, have been stimulated as much as retarded by the impact of Western imperialism; they were retarded inasmuch as they were captive peoples in the hands of the industrialists of the West who needed their physical labor and the natural riches of their soil to keep the giant industrial machines of the West going. . . . They were stimulated to leave their tribal, ancestral anchorages of living by being sucked into the orbit of industrial enterprises operating under the management of whites in their homelands under their own eyes. . . . The hands of the West reached out greedily for the natural resources of these peoples; but, in reaching, they awakened black, red, brown, and yellow men from their long slumber and sent them, willy-nilly, hurtling down the road of industrialization. . . .

"During the past seventy years, America, under the ideological banner of free enterprise, fought a bloody civil war and defeated its agrarian provinces and launched itself, with no prehistory and practically no traditions to check it, upon a program of industrialization the equal of which, in terms of speed and magnitude, the world has never seen. From my point of view, this industrial program could have been accomplished under any of a dozen different ideological banners. The ideas were not so important as people thought they were; the important thing was the fact of industrialization. Of course, and it is understandable, the defenders of this industrial program justified their dazzling progress by claiming that an organic relationship obtained between their ideas and industrialization. But, really, there was none. . . .

"Now, during the past thirty-five years, under the ideological banner of dialectical materialism, a small group of ruthless men in Russia seized political power and the entire state apparatus and established a dictatorship. Rationalizing human life to the last degree, they launched a vast, well-disciplined program of industrialization which now rivals that of the United States of America in pretentiousness and power. . . . Again I say that what happened in Russia, just as with what happened in America, could have happened under a dozen different ideological banners. . . . If you lived in Russia and made such a statement, they'd shoot you; and if you lived in America and made such a statement, they'd blacklist you and starve you to death. . . . Modern man still believes in magic; he lives in a rational world but insists on interpreting the events of the world in terms of mystical forces. The simple fact is, the social cat can be skinned in many different ways. The coming history of the many new nations now launching their industrial programs will prove this to be true. . . ."

"So!" Blimin exploded. "You sneer at our ideology? You ignore the role of the working class? You see no difference between Russia and the imperialist powers?"

"Mr. Blimin," Cross said patiently, "I'm talking to you as one man to another. I'm propaganda-proof. Communism has two truths, two faces. The face you're talking about now is for the workers, for the public, not for me. I look at facts, processes—"

"You're slandering—"

"Don't impute motives to me," Cross insisted. "Am I

condemning you and men like you for what you've done? You did what you did because you had to! Anybody who launches himself on the road to naked power is caught in a trap. . . . You use idealistic words as your smoke screen, but behind that screen you *rule.* . . . It's a question of *power!*"

"I'll not tolerate your reducing the noble aims of Lenin to a power-hungry man," Blimin raged.

"But Lenin admitted it," Cross told him. "Lenin repeatedly chided his comrades for lacking the will-to-power. . . . Again, Mr. Blimin, if you want to talk to me, please understand that I'm not naïve. Your propaganda is *not* for me. Do you get that? Now, let me get back to my point. . . .

"You may like industrialization or you may hate it. You may think that the process of industrialization ought to be stopped, that it has done great harm to mankind. Or you may feel that it is best to flee from this industrial machine and find haven in some tropical island. (Those little islands, too, are being caught up in the global tide of industrialization and soon there will be no hideaways.) Neither attitude really has anything to do with the basic reality of industrialization itself, which is a neutral process. Industrialization is simply an efficient way of making and doing things, a labor-saving, a life-saving way of living. Industrialization is simply a hammer or a saw which has grown infinitely complex and, in itself, is not evil and cannot be evil. . . . We can either find ways of controlling this complex hammer or saw and make it serve us, or we can simply drift, let industrial life bog us down, as we have already done. In any case, the sweep of industrialization has gone so far, its spirit has entered so deep in the hearts and habits of men, that we cannot stop it now even if we wanted to. It is a part of us and we are a part of it; if we go on, it goes on, so organically it is a part of our living. . . . It cannot be stopped unless we all die or revert to a manner of living that would reduce our lives to a kind of Old Testament simplicity, which is highly unlikely.

"Quickening the process of industrialization was the marriage of scientific knowledge and industry. The interaction between the two progressed like a game of leapfrog. The more society became industrialized, the more men learned about the nature of the world in which they lived, and the more knowledge they gained from that world, the more skill they had in applying their knowledge to the methods of industry.

"Now, had this global tide of industrialization consisted only of this, we'd have no problem at all. Indeed, the world would be piled high with products and this earth would be the long-dreamed-of goal of mankind.

"What I've described becomes interesting only in the light of one question: What kind of a queer animal is this being called man who embarked—and without quite knowing it!—upon this program of industrialization? Well, his most dominant characteristic is an enormous propensity toward fear. He is the most scared and trembling of all the animals, and I'm not forgetting those wild ones who live in jungles. . . . Learned men have long declaimed upon the thinking and loving capacities of man, but we have yet to hear of man's fears. It might well be that the most important part of human existence is fear itself.

"Primitive man, naked and afraid, found that only *one* thing could really quiet his terrors: that is, *Untruth*. He stuffed his head full of myths, and if he had not, he might well have died from fear itself. How many people on this earth die from fear is something we've yet to find out; but that is another story. . . .

"The degree and quality of man's fears can be gauged by the scope and density of his myths; that is, by the ingenious manner in which he disguised the world about him. Man was afraid of the clamoring world of storms, volcanoes, and heaving waves and he wanted to change that world. His myths sought to recast that world, tame it, make it more humanly meaningful and endurable. The more abjectly frightened the nation or race of men, the more their myths and religions projected out upon the world another world in *front* of the real world, or, in another way of speaking, they projected another world *behind* the real world they saw, lived, suffered, and died in. Until today almost all of man's worlds have been either pre-worlds or back-worlds, *never* the real world. . . . (The ancient nations today we call great are the ones who

356

left behind them those towering monuments of fear in the forms of their so-called cultures!)

"That real world man did not want; he was not stout-hearted enough to endure its dangers and uncertainties. . . . In making his pre-worlds, he always saw reality as a wonderful drama enacted for his special benefit; there were gods and counter-gods locked in deadly conflict, the outcome of which spelled good or evil for him, all shaping his destiny. In making his back-worlds man was vain enough to believe that this real world could not be all, that there was another world into which he could somehow escape when he died. Entrance into that back-world depended upon how faithfully he observed certain compulsive rituals which he, in his fear and anxiety, had created over aeons of time to placate his sense of dread.

"Man cringed even before the ordinary workings of his own mind; he would not even dare admit the authorship of his own fantasies. He found himself so complex that he fled from himself. That which transpired in his heart he projected out into the skies, or else he would not have been able to sleep at night. . . .

"War, famines, earthquakes, epidemics, and social upheavals made no impact upon man's myth worlds; indeed, calamities served but to strengthen them, for man felt that he was somehow guilty when he was overwhelmed with disaster, had somehow failed to pronounce the magic talisman correctly when catastrophe descended upon him. One thing, however, did get at those myth worlds, did gnaw at them until they fell from man's eyes and left him staring in dismay at the real, natural, workaday world from which he had for millions of years tried to hide.

"The ravaging scourge that tore away the veil of myth worlds was science and industry; science slowly painting another world, the real one; and industry uprooting man from his ancestral, ritualized existence and casting him into rational schemes of living in vast, impersonal cities. A split took place in man's consciousness; he began living in the real world by the totems and taboos that had guided him in the world of myths. But that could not last for long. Today we are in the midst of that crisis. . . . The real world stands at last before our eyes and we don't want to look at

it, don't know how to live in it; it terrifies us. All of the
vast dramas which man once thought took place in the
skies now transpire in our hearts and we quake and are
moved compulsively to do what we know not. . . ."

"You deliberately and consistently omit to mention the
role of the working class," Blimin pointed out, smiling. "It
was oppression that awakened man from his slumber—"

"Oppression was simply an added irritant," Cross said.
"Even if man had not been oppressed, this crisis would
have taken place, and you know it. Oppression was a part
of the process of industrialization—"

"And wars? You omit war altogether," Blimin said.

"When used as it is used," Cross told him, "industrialization is a kind of war against mankind. That same war is
going on in Russia today, for all I know. . . . But let me
get on.

"Now, this real world in which we live today has a
strange tone and aspect. We twentieth-century Westerners
have outlived the faith of our fathers; our minds have
grown so skeptical that we cannot accept the old scheme of
moral precepts which once guided man's life. In our modern industrial society we try to steer our hearts by impro-
vised, pragmatic rules which are, in the end, no rules at all.
If there are people who tell you that they live by traditional values and precepts—as the English sometimes pretend—then they are either lying to you or to themselves;
maybe they are lying both ways. . . . There is no modern
industrial nation on earth today that makes decisions based
upon anything remotely resembling the injunctions of the
Old or New Testament; this holds true in their domestic as
well as in their foreign policies.

"Of course, the historical transition from the unreal
myth worlds of yesterday to the bleak, terrifying world of
today was not sudden, did not take place all at once. Acting as a brake upon the hot winds of scientific knowledge
and the tidal waves of industrial erosion was a group of
wonderful people, unhappily now extinct, called liberals.
Full of the juices of human kindness, these people decided
that they were going to be good, honest Christians without
believing in Christianity, which their logical minds found
offensive. Let reason prevail, they declared. But these kind-

hearted atheists got scared. They went so far down the godless road that they could see a black nothingness looming as its final end. They retreated in fear. They helped to undermine the old world, but they discovered that the building of a new world was much harder than they had suspected. They called for new systems of ideas, and when no valid ones were forthcoming, they demanded new myths that would not insult the intelligence of man. For their pains they got programs for wars and revolutions. . . .

"But one must not overlook the fact that, had it not been for these liberals, the full flood of a senseless existence would have long since broken through the myths of progress which have sustained modern man so far. They did an impossible job with great skill, those liberals. Future history will regard the liberals as the last great defenders of that which really could not be defended, as the last spokesmen of historical man as we've known him for the past two thousand years.

"All of this brings us to one central, decisive fact: the consequences of the atheistic position of modern man, for most men today are atheists, even though they don't know it or won't admit it. They live, dream, and plan on the assumption that there is no God. The full implications of this are enormous. It means that God no longer really concerns us as a reality beyond life, but simply as something projected compulsively from men's minds in answer to their chronic need to be rid of fear, something to meet the obscure needs of daily lives lived amidst strange and threatening facts."

"At least we agree on *something*," Blimin muttered, eying Cross askance. "You see the central fact, so why don't you admit the rest? Only the Party can save this world, give it guidance, direction—"

"Mr. Blimin," Cross overrode him, "since religion is dead, religion is everywhere. . . . Religion was once an affair of the church; it is now in the streets in each man's heart. Once there were priests; now every man's a priest. Religion's a compulsion, and a compulsion seems to spring from something total in us, catching up in its mighty grip all the other forces of life—sex, intellect, will, physical

359

strength, and carrying them forward toward—what goals? We wish we knew. . . . Compulsions exist as much in the individual as in society. Lucky is the man who can share his neighbor's religion! Damned is the man who must invent his own god! Shun that man, for he is a part of the vast cosmos; he is akin to it and he can no more know himself than he can know the world of which he is in some mysterious way a part. . . . Blessed is the artificial man, the determined man, the social man. . . .

"Mr. Blimin, I'm not even an atheist. To me it's just too bad that some people must lean on imagined gods, that's all. Yet I'd not have it otherwise. They need religion. All right; let them have it. What harm does it do? And it does make for a greater measure of social stability. But I object if somebody grabs me when I'm a defenseless child and injects into me a sedative—the power of which lasts for a lifetime!—which no one would ever be able to tell if I'd ever need it or not!

"Now, what does this mean—that I don't believe in God? It means that I, and you too, can do what we damn well please on this earth. Many men have been doing just that, of course, for a long time, but they didn't have the courage to admit it. They pretended that they were following higher laws, practicing virtue, etc. But such clumsy games exposed themselves before long. Naïve governments allowed historical records to be kept! Imagine the British, past masters of exploitation and duplicity, allowing a Karl Marx into their British Museum to pore over and unravel the pretensions and self-deceptions of British banditry! Such records of blatant chicanery served thoughtful and astute men as guides in the building of new, scientific, and more efficient methods of deception!

"Today governments, democratic or totalitarian, are much wiser. It is better, they feel, for mankind to be unconscious—or ignorant, which is the same thing—than knowing. They regard the writing of history as the most supremely important of all tasks. Modern governments today watch their history and, since men seem to have developed a habit of wanting to know what has happened, they doctor up events, rewrite the past, improvise limited myths and give those myths to the masses of men. But this history is a simple, inspected history, fumigated, purged, and sterilized of all contagious ideas that might lead to the illnesses of independence, freedom, and individuality. Mankind is coming of age. . . .

"Those few strong men who do not want to be duped, and who are stout enough in their hearts to accept a godless world, are quite willing, aye, anxious to let the masses of men rest comfortably in their warm cocoons of traditional illusions. Men are more easily and cheaply governed when they fear ghosts more than guns! The real slaves of the twentieth century are not those sharecroppers who wince at the stinging swish of a riding boss's whip; the slaves of today are those who are congenitally afraid of the new and the untried, who fall on their knees and break into a deep sweat when confronted with the horrible truth of the uncertain and enigmatic nature of life. . . .

"It is the strong at the top, however, who represent modern man. Beyond themselves, their dreams, their hopes, their plans, they know that there is nothing. . . .

"Now, the next point, Mr. Blimin. Most of the decisive historic events that happen in this world are not known until *after* they have happened. Few are the people who know the meaning of what they are living through, who even have an inkling of what is happening to them. That's the big trouble with history. . . .

"Keep that point in mind while I remind you of what is happening in the great cities of the earth today—Chicago, Detroit, Pittsburgh, London, Manchester, Paris, Tokyo, Hong Kong, and the rest. These cities are, for the most part, vast pools of human misery, networks of raw human nerves exposed without benefit of illusion or hope to the new, godless world wrought by industrial man. Industrial life plus a rampant capitalism have blasted the lives of men in these cities; those who are lucky enough not to be hungry are ridden with exquisite psychological sufferings. The people of these cities are lost; some of them are so lost that they no longer even know it, and they are the real lost ones. They haunt the movies for distraction; they gamble; they depress their sensibilities with alcohol; or they seek strong sensations to dull their sense of a meaningless existence. . . .

"Now, Mr. Blimin, above these so-called toiling masses, for whom I have some sympathy but not as much as you'd expect, are the few industrialists and politicians who yell night and day about freedom, democracy, high wages, etc. These are the exploiters of the millions of rats caught in the industrial trap. That they make great profits out of the exercise of their lordship is perhaps the least of their crimes—"

"Oh, you're showing your true colors," Blimin snorted. "Are you defending *exploitation* now? Next you're going to tell me what wonderful philanthropists these capitalists are—"

"Not at all. It just so happens, Mr. Blimin," Cross explained, "that I think their crime is a blacker one than mere exploitation. The end results of their rule is that they keep the lives of their rats pitched to a mean, sordid level of consciousness. It's right here where you and I disagree deeply. Your wonderful trade unions for a quarter of a century have been fighting for so-called standards of living for workers, fighting for higher wages. Had I had anything to say about the goals of those trade unions, I'd have insisted that their fight be to escape completely the domination of the capitalists. Not that the workers become richer, but that they become more human, freer. You don't want that, Mr. Blimin, and the capitalists don't want it. Why? Because you cannot dupe free men who can think and know.

"Now back to my theme. . . . The point is not so much that these capitalists despise their rats, but that they despise themselves and all mankind. To keep their rats contented, they strive to convince them that their rats' lives are more glorious, better, richer than at any time in history, and, in the end, they come to believe in their own lies. Consequently, today the content of human life on earth is what these cheap-minded men say it is. They are jealous and uneasy, these men, of anyone who tries to lure their rats away. They preach to their rats that their nation is the best of any of the nations, and that as rats they are the very best of all possible rats. They even have I-Am-a-Rat days. As long as this works, it's wonderful. The only real enemies of this system are not the rats themselves, but those outsiders who are conscious of what is happening and who seek to change the consciousness of the rats who are being controlled. In situations like this, public consciousness is the key to political power. . . . The essence of life today is psychological; men may take power with arms, but their keeping of it is by other means. Get me so far, Mr. Blimin?

"Now, rising up from time to time from the pools of restless millions in these vast cities are men who seek to head new movements. Their appearance is much rarer than is popularly supposed, just as genuine revolutions on this earth are rare, few and far between. . . . These men who rise to challenge the rulers are jealous men. They feel that they are just as good as the men who rule; indeed, they suspect that they are better. They see the countless mistakes that are being made by the men who rule and they think that they could do a more honest, a much cleaner job, a more efficient job. For simplicity's sake, let's call them the Jealous Rebels—"

"Lane!" Blimin thundered, rising in anger. "You *are* cynical, that's all! How can you say Lenin was jealous? He had the fate of mankind close to his heart! We love people—"

Cross was tempted to tell of what Hilton had told him just before he had shot him; but no, he couldn't do that.

"Mr. Blimin, *please*, be honest," Cross begged. "You must assume that I know what this is all about. Don't tell me about the nobility of labor, the glorious future. *You* don't believe in that. That's for others, and you damn well know it. You and men of your type are convinced that you know how the game goes and you've thrown down the gauntlet to the capitalists, conservatives, socialists. You Jealous Rebels are intellectuals who know your history and you are anxious not to make the mistakes of your predecessors in rebellious undertakings. You feel that life has become crummy and meaningless and you feel you can give it more meaning than the clumsy men who now rule.

"The thinking of the revolutionary is a cold kind of thinking; he has a realistic insight into history; he has, above all, a sense of what power is, what it's for, both as a means of governing other men and as a means of personal expression. That absolute power is corrupting, à la Lord Acton, is something revolutionaries laugh at. These Jealous Rebels would much rather be corrupted with absolute power than live under the heels of men whom they despise.

"In order to test themselves, to make life a meaningful game, these Jealous Rebels proceed to organize political parties, Communist parties, Nazi parties, Fascist parties, all kinds of parties—"

"No!" Blimin roared. "You cannot equate or confound communism with fascism! They are *different!*"

"I admit they are different," Cross conceded. "But the degree of the difference is not worth arguing about. Fascists operate from a narrow, limited basis; they preach nationality, race, soil, blood, folk feeling and other rot to capture men's hearts. What makes one man a Fascist and another a Communist might be found in the degree in which they are integrated with their culture. The more alienated a man is, the more he'd lean toward communism. . . ."

"Toward rationality," Blimin stated.

"No," Cross corrected him, "Communists *use* rationality. I admit that the Communists are more intelligent, more general in their approach, but the same power-hungry heart beats behind the desire to rule! I'm on prepolitical ground here, Mr. Blimin. And you know I'm speaking the truth.

"Now, where do these Jealous Rebels get their programs . . . ? Out of books? From Plato's *Republic?* No! Their programs are but the crude translations of the daydreams of the man in the street, daydreams in which the Jealous Rebels do *not* believe!

"In order to catch their prey, they deliberately spin vast spiderwebs of ideology, the glittering strands of which are designed to appeal to the hopes of hopeful men. Yes, there are men who think that ideas will lead them to freedom and a fuller life, and these are the natural victims of the Jealous Rebels, who do not feel that to dupe others in this way is immoral; it is their conviction that this is the way life is and only the naïve think to the contrary.

"Their aims? Direct and naked power! They know as few others that there is no valid, functioning religion to
364

take the place of the values and creeds of yesterday; and they know that political power, if it is to perform in the minds and emotions of men the role that the idea of God once performed, must be total and absolute. These Jealous Rebels are sustained by a sense of the total meaning—or lack of meaning!—of human life on this earth. Their courage is derived from the fact that, win or lose, they are making history, that what they do is decisive for mankind. Caught up passionately in such a realistic myth, what will not an ardent man do?

"These men are free from petty prejudices. They have to be free from such, for it is precisely the prejudices of *others* that they seek to manipulate for their own uses. They will commit any crime, but never in passion. They work slowly, deliberately, with refinement even. And whatever natural terrors of life there are in the hearts of man, whatever stupid prejudices they harbor in their damp souls, they know how to rouse and sustain those terrors and prejudices and mobilize them for *their* ends. The mere act of hoping, believing, of being alive makes you a prospective victim for these knowing men! Modern life is a kind of confidence game; if you dream, you can be defeated unless you are careful that you do not dream a dream that has been set up for you!

"I'm not so naïve as to believe that these men want to *change* the world! Why, they love human nature just as it is! They simply want their chance to show what they can do with that world and the people in it. To their minds human life on this earth is a process that is transparently *known!* They are out to grab the entire body of mankind and they will replace faith and habit with organization and discipline. *And they feel that they have a chance to do it!*

"Since God as functioning reality in men's minds and hearts has gone, since the death of the gallant liberal, every event of the modern world feeds the growing movement toward the total and absolute, making the Jealous Rebels believe that they have allies everywhere. Wars, by mobilizing men into vast armies to fight and die for ideals that are transparently fraudulent, justify this drift toward the total and absolute in modern life. Industrialism, whether it operates for profit or not, herds men around assembly lines to perform senseless tasks—all of which conditions men toward the acceptance of the total and absolute in modern life. Implicit in all political and speculative thought are the germs of ideas that prefigure the triumph of the total and absolute attitudes in modern life. Communication, inventions, radio, television, movies, atomic energy, by annihilating distance and space and the atmosphere of mystery and romance, create the conditions for the creation of organizations reflecting the total and absolute in modern life. Commercial advertising, cheapening and devaluing our notions of human personality, develops and perfects techniques which can be used by political leaders who want to enthrone the total and absolute in modern life. Even anti-Communists and anti-Fascists must, by fighting the totalitarian threat by using the methods of the totalitarians—and there are no other methods, it seems, to use—guarantee and make inevitable this surge toward the total and absolute in modern life.

"There is no escaping what the future holds. We are going back, *back* to something earlier, maybe better, maybe worse, maybe something more terrifyingly human! These few hundred years of freedom, empire building, voting, liberty, democracy—these will be regarded as the *romantic* centuries in human history. There will be in that future no trial by jury, no writs of habeas corpus, no freedom of speech, of religion—all of this is being buried and not by Communists or Fascists alone, but by their opponents as well. All hands are shoveling clay onto the body of freedom before it even dies, while it lies breathing its last. . . .

"There are some people today who sincerely but mistakenly believe that by going to war against a totalitarian nation they can save the past of which they are so deeply fond. Unwilling or unable to believe that the crisis is as serious and deep as it really is, these people want to launch vast armies and smash the evildoers and reestablish a reign of peace and good will!—the right to exploit others without interference!—on earth. What these sincere people do not realize is that communism and fascism are but the political expressions of the twentieth century's atheistic way of life, and that the future will reveal many, many

366

more of these absolutistic systems, whose brutality and rigor will make the present-day systems seem like summer outings. The most ludicrous and tragic spectacle on earth is to see a powerful nation bleeding itself white to build up vast heaps of armaments to put down a menace that cannot be put down by military means at all. . . . Wars will but tear away the last shreds of belief, leaving man's heart more naked and compulsive than ever before. Can atom bombs correct a man's sense of life? Can ultimatums alter the basic beliefs or nonbeliefs of millions of men? Can you shoot attitudes?

"Mr. Blimin, if you believe that I believe what I've told you, how do you think I'm a menace to your Party? True, I may not believe your Party's aims, but I know enough about politics to know that I could not change your Party, or, as an individual, fight it. So what are you scared of in me? I give you my word that I do not belong to any political party on this earth, and I don't think I will ever join one.

"Now, you asked me what I am doing. Knowing and seeing what is happening in the world today, I don't think that there is much of anything that one can do about it. But there is one little thing, it seems to me, that a man owes to himself. He can look bravely at this horrible totalitarian reptile and, while doing so, discipline his dread, his fear, and study it coolly, observe every slither and convolution of its sensuous movements and note down with calmness the pertinent facts. In the face of the totalitarian danger, these facts can help a man to save himself; and he may then be able to call the attention of others around him to the presence and meaning of this reptile and its multitudinous writhings. . . .

"That's all, Mr. Blimin. I'm not really anti anything."

There was a long silence. Blimin sat looking at the floor, lifting his eyes now and then to Cross's face. Blimin's eyes were serious; he seemed not to know if he should believe Cross or not; or, if he did believe Cross, then in what way . . . ? Finally Blimin rose, laughed, stared at Cross and said: "You've answered my question, but I'm afraid that you've raised more questions than you've answered. Frankly, Lane, it's dangerous for a man knowing and feeling what you know and feel to hang around loosely on the peripheries of our Party. . . ."

"I came in contact with the Party in quite a natural manner, Mr. Blimin," Cross told him. "I was eating in a dining car one morning and met the late Mr. Bob Hunter. . . ."

Blimin reddened. Bob was en route to Trinidad and the Party had helped to speed him on his way. Blimin covered his embarrassment by shrugging and laughing.

"Well, I won't bother you any more tonight, Lane," he said.

"It's no bother," Cross said.

Hank still stood in the back of the room, his hat and coat still on, his eyes intent upon the face of Cross. Menti had been impressed by what Cross had said; he stared, grinned, winked, and said: "With a gift of gab like that, you ought to be on the Central Committee."

"No," Cross said. "You don't want men in your Party who can think."

"It all depends," Blimin mumbled; he was leaving the door open.

Yet, Blimin was worried. Cross had tempted him, made him feel that maybe he would work with them, that maybe he could be persuaded. . . . *Maybe* . . . Blimin and Menti left with cryptic smiles, but Hank was not moved; his face still held that blank, stolid expression as he went from sight.

"Lionel, I'm worried," Eva confessed. "How could they think that you, knowing what you know, would stoop to killing . . . ?"

"They can't find who killed Gil and Hilton, so they've got to get a scapegoat," Cross said in a cool, level tone.

He watched her closely, wondering if she remembered his confessional babblings. For a moment her stare was full on him, then she looked at the floor. Suddenly she reached for his hand and squeezed it tightly.

"These Communists are mad!" Sarah exclaimed. "I think some spy with a grudge against the Party killed Gil and Hilton."

"If they really knew Lionel, they'd never think he would do anything like that," Eva said.

368

Cross was numb in his heart. Couldn't they tell he was guilty? Yes, it was their own innocence that kept them from seeing his guilt; they identified themselves with what they hoped he was, and, since they were innocent, he *must* be innocent.

"Now, don't go worrying about foolishness like this," he gently chided the two women, forcing a smile.

Back in the bedroom, he pondered and weighed his chances. Had he spoken too much to Blimin? But how else could he have behaved? He had given some vent to his feelings in a way that he hoped would take some of the pressure of the Party off him. Would a normally guilty man have spoken like that? No. The Party knew now that he was not with the police; they knew also that he was not spying for another political party. What motive, then, could he have had, from their point of view, for killing . . . ? They'll think I did it because of Eva! No; Communists were not unintelligent; they could not seriously think that. There was one thing of which he was certain: they would never credit him with as much freedom to act as they had. A certain psychological blindness seemed to be the hallmark of all men who had to create their own worlds. . . . All other men were mere material for them; they could admit no rivals, no equals; other men were either above them or below them.

Long after Eva had gone to sleep in his arms, he lay awake wondering if he could ride out this trouble and keep her with him. He was suffering this torturing surveillance of the Party only to keep near her. It was dawn before he managed to sleep.

The next morning Cross searched the Sunday papers in vain for further mention of Hilton. Nor was there any news on the radio. Maybe things would quiet down for a while. But he knew that the Party and the police were still hunting, probing, observing. Dread was still with him; he lived in anticipation of another sudden confrontation that would send him hurtling down the path of blood again. . . .

After breakfast Menti and Hank came with a car and took them to the union hall. Long queues of workers were

369

entering the doors and filing slowly past the dark, shining coffin in which Gil lay with ashen and upturned face. Huge wreaths of flowers were banked about the coffin, which was surrounded by Communist militants standing stiffly at attention. Cross was impressed by the soberness of the shabby men and women who had come to pay their tribute to Gil.

Eva was sobbing quietly as he led her by the arm to the coffin. Why's she weeping? he wondered. Was it for grief over Gil? That could hardly be, for she had hated him. Was it because her life had been blasted? Or was it because she was on the verge of freedom?

Cross stood looking at Gil's cold and tired face, which seemed now somewhat shrunken, but still retained its lines of rigidity of character. There lies a modern man, Cross said to himself sadly. He lived as reasonlessly as he died. . . . Life, to him, was a game devoid of all significance except that which he put into it. Life was a game and he played it with all of his skill to the bitter end. Cross was convinced that Gil, in an abstract sense, could not have disagreed with the manner in which he had met his death. Gil just experienced a sudden, transitional leap in the dialectical materialistic development of life, that's all. . . . Cross repressed a wry smile as he gently led Eva from the side of the coffin.

After the Party had had its last say over the body of Gil, Gil's sister, Blanche, a graying woman of forty-odd from the Bronx, deeply religious and sharply color-conscious, took charge and began to make arrangements for taking Gil's remains to the Bronx for proper religious ceremonies and burial. Cross kept discreetly in the background while Eva and Blanche, who were strained, cold, and distant toward each other, discussed the disposition of Gil's books, furniture, and other personal belongings.

Blimin accosted Cross cordially at the back of the union hall.

"I've been thinking over your analysis of last night," Blimin said. "With a little discipline, we could do something with you."

"And?" Cross prompted.

"Why do you shun us when you understand so much?"

"I'm not shunning anybody," Cross told him.

370

"I can see why Gil wanted to train you," Blimin said. "Why have you changed your mind? You accepted Gil's offer—"

"I've been so busy coping with suspicions that I've had no chance to think of anything," Cross said.

"Lane, is there anything you *want?*" Blimin asked.

"What do you mean?"

"For a man of your ability, the Party can make exceptions," Blimin explained. "Or maybe you've *got* what you want already?"

Cross stared. This was the nearest the Party had come to hinting that he had perhaps killed Gil to get Eva! And Blimin had implied that if he would surrender, the Party would consider forgiving him for even that! But that meant giving up Eva . . . !

"Blimin, I don't like talk like this," Cross said.

"It's easier and simpler when we know what a man wants," Blimin went relentlessly on. "But with you, we don't know what you want. Well, good-by." Blimin turned and walked off briskly.

Menti, still accompanied by the sullen Hank, was restrained, cordial, and noncommittal as he drove them back to Harlem. The nervous tension of the ceremony had given Eva a headache for which she took some aspirins and went to bed. Cross loitered in the living room, mulling over his dinner engagement with Houston. What had the Party said to him? And how much weight would Houston give to what the Party had said? He knew that the best proof of Houston's suspiciousness would be for Houston to begin straightaway prying into his past. And it was too late now for him to fabricate a new past for himself. Every lie he told now would only increase his difficulties.

He left the apartment early to keep his dinner appointment; he wanted a chance to breathe some fresh air and organize his thoughts before confronting a man whose mind he feared. Houston knew what power was and loved it, or else he would not have stood to be elected to a public office. Would he, if he had Cross dead-to-rights, ravage him as he had seen Gil ravage Bob and Eva? It was possible. . . Cross knew in his heart that the first man, from the police or from the Party, who could sense intuitively

371

what his psychological state was would know that he was guilty. But in order to know that they would have to have courage enough to admit the character of the world in which he and they both lived; and he seriously doubted if Houston really had that much courage.

Reluctantly he made his way through the cold wintry air toward Frank's Restaurant on 125th Street. About him neon lights shimmered in red and blue and green and rose. For the first time in months Cross could see the sky stretching above the tenement roofs. A few clusters of brittle stars winked in a blue-black luminosity. Cars whirred over the icy asphalt pavement with sticky whines. He tramped grimly past towering Negro churches from whose doorways rolled softly, almost apologetically, the plaintive spirituals of his people. How lucky they were, those black worshipers, to be able to feel lonely together! What fantastic blessings were theirs to be able to express their sense of abandonment in a manner that bound them in unison! But with whom could he join in howling his loneliness?

When he came in view of Frank's Restaurant, he paused, dropped his cigarette and stomped out its glow with his heel. Then his body tensed; out of a corner of his eye he saw two white men approaching. He lifted his head and looked at them. His lips parted slowly.

"Are you Lionel Lane?" one of the men asked.

"That's right," he answered.

One of the men pulled his right hand from his coat pocket and pushed his outstretched palm under Cross's nose; in that palm gleamed a police badge.

"I'm Detective Hornsby, attached to the District Attorney's office," he said.

"Yes?" he said and waited.

"You had an appointment, I believe, with the District Attorney here at eight o'clock?"

"That's right."

"The District Attorney can't make it. We tried to see you at your apartment, but you had gone," Hornsby said.

"I'm sorry," Cross mumbled and waited; there was something else he knew that these men had to tell him.

"The District Attorney asked us to bring you to him," Hornsby said.

372

Cross noticed that the other detective had his hands jammed into his overcoat pockets and he had not spoken a word or moved.

"Am I being arrested?" Cross asked softly.

"We can't answer any questions, I'm afraid. Will you come along with us?" Hornsby asked.

So this was it at last. The dinner engagement was resolving itself into an official confrontation. What did they know? Should he make a dash for it? No; he couldn't get away; they might have other armed, plain-clothesmen nearby. He did not move and they had not moved. He was suddenly tired. The face of Eva flashed through his mind; he would lose her. And if he lost her, what else mattered? He sighed, nodded his head.

"All right," he said quietly.

"Are you armed?" Hornsby asked.

He hesitated, then smiled. "Yes."

"Where's the gun? Don't move. Just tell us and we'll take it from you."

"It's on my right hip," he said.

They were efficient; they relieved him of his gun without attracting the attention of a single passer-by.

"The car is that black sedan at the curb. Walk toward it between us and get in," Hornsby said.

Cross did as he was told; when seated in the car he leaned back and sighed. His despair drained off in one second and he felt that he wanted to sleep. And in the next instant he knew exactly what he had to do. He would do nothing, say nothing; there was nothing that he could really say. Let them make their case; he would not help or hinder them. He would bear it as though it was not he himself who was undergoing it. The car moved off into the night, heading downtown, and he lay back, his heart locked against the world. I'll see what they can make out of me, he said to himself.

BOOK 5

Decision

> . . . Man is the only being who makes
> promises.
>
> — FRIEDRICH NIETZSCHE

Cross found himself in the uniquely ironic position of comprehending far more keenly than his captors the nature and meaning of the situation confronting him. Even while the car in which he sat huddled between the two detectives bore him toward the office of the District Attorney, he could anticipate the general methods and approach of the police. They had first to prove who he was. Well, let them; that was their business, not his. . . . He wondered how much of his path of blood and deception they had uncovered; but his wonderment was devoid of any desire to erect a strategy of legal defense for himself. That did not concern him at all; his preoccupations were more basic and recondite.

He knew that he had cynically scorned, wantonly violated, every commitment that civilized men owe, in terms of common honesty and sacred honor, to those with whom they live. That, in essence, was his crime. The rest of his brutal and bloody thrashings about were the mere offshoots of that one central, cardinal fact. And for the crime of his contemptuous repudiation of all the fundamental promises that men live by he intended to make no legal defense, for the good and ample reason that he knew no such defense was possible. And he was staunchly resolved to face his would-be judgers with a tight mouth from which not one word to help clarify his emotions or motives would issue. He would compel them, by a challenging silence, to identify his attitude.

And Houston . . . ? Was he still juggling ideas or had he found the courage to put two and two together? Houston, of all the officers of the law, could put the "finger" on him, could brand him guilty in a psychological sense. But had he dug up enough proof to make a legal charge stick? And would Houston dare explain his conception of this guilt to his colleagues? Wouldn't a man in so responsible a position run the risk of losing public confidence by merely putting such notions into words . . . ? Cross barely suppressed a smile as he glanced furtively at the stolid faces of the two detectives who sat on either side of him.

The moment he entered the police car he knew that his search was over. There were to be no more of those torrid promptings of his heart to make him confess his horrible deeds and then wrestle and sweat to restrain his urge to kill the recipient of his confession. The burden of what was to be proved would fall upon those who had brought him to heel. His crimes had carried a stamp of the absolute and if they wanted to nail him down, their actions and attitudes would have to carry a stamp of the absolute against him. Let them haul up all of his bloody doings and turn them this way and that and see what conclusions they could come to. . . .

There were two immediate dangers threatening him. The District Attorney could, if he were so minded, remand him for psychological observation at Bellevue; all right, he was confident of being declared sane. The other danger was more indirect, more difficult. Suppose the police had unraveled all that he had done and suppose the general public felt so revolted that they would want to drag him into some dirty alley and take his life and be done with it. He understood that reaction and feared it; it was the same cold fury he had felt against Herndon and Gil and Hilton. . . . Should such now fall to him, he would be watching his own compulsions in reverse! If he could avoid those two pitfalls, he was prepared, willing even, to undergo whatever inquisitions they could serve up.

At some point in his past life, while living the normal ritual of days allotted to us all, he had come to a consciousness of having somehow fallen into a vast web of pledges and promises which he had not intended to make and whose implied obligations had been slowly smothering his spirit; and, by a stroke of freakish good luck, he had been able to rip the viscous strands of that web and fling them behind him. As always he was honest with himself; he knew, of course, that his commitments had been no more galling or burdensome than those which other millions of men and women about him shouldered so uncomplainingly every day; yet he knew that deep in the hearts of many of those millions was the same desire—shamefaced, inarticulate, and impotent—to have done with them as he had. It was not because he was a Negro that he had found his obligations intolerable; it was because there resided in his heart a sharp sense of freedom that had somehow escaped being dulled by intimidating conditions. Cross had never really been tamed. . . .

He felt that at the time he made his promises—it had started in his childhood, before he had even been able to talk!—his true and free consent had not been asked or given and he had not been in a condition to understand the far-reaching nature of what he had been asked to pledge.

What was the question with which he, in his silence, would confront them? It was this: If he was to be loyal, to love, to show pity, mercy, forgiveness; if he was to abstain from cruelty, to be mindful of the rights of others, to live and let live, to believe in such resounding words as glory, culture, civilization, and progress, then let them demonstrate how it was to be done so that the carrying out of these duties and the practicing of these virtues in the modern world would not reduce a healthy, hungry man to a creature of nervous dread and paint that man's look of the world in the black hues of meaninglessness.

To be sure, accident had made possible his decision to dishonor those unwritten vows that he had been made to promise, but his eagerness in embracing the opportunities presented by that subway accident had robbed that accident of its element of contingency, and the rest had flowed naturally and inevitably.

The assumptive promises he had welshed on were not materially anchored, yet they were indubitably the things of this world, the axis of daily existence. He, like Gil and

Hilton, but for radically divergent reasons, had not been concerned with the buying and selling of corn, bonds, machines, paper, or steel. It had been the naked, irreducible facts of sentient life itself that he had tried to grapple with in snapping the ties that bound him. It was the restrictions of marriage, the duties to children, obligations to friends, to sweethearts, and to blood kin that he had struck at so blindly and—gallantly? For Cross had had no party, no myths, no tradition, no race, no soil, no culture, and no ideas—except perhaps the idea that ideas in themselves were, at best, dubious!

What made him wonder so anxiously about how much they knew of his past was that he wanted to be at once in the center of what was about to happen to him. He detested surprises. To be confronted continuously with the unforeseen when his movements were restricted would deprive him of coherence and balance, and it was an evenness of deportment that he wanted now above all. For Cross was proud and was proud of his pride and knew it.

And Eva—? His memory of her made a dart of wincing pain go through him. He had at last found a recollection which he could not reduce to some impulse projected out of his hungry heart, for Eva's loneliness as expressed in her life and in her painting had become identified with the deepest regions of his being. He could have shared so much with her; they could have walked together through life; he could have been an anchor to her and she to him. But all chance of that was now gone. . . .

The police car pulled to a stop and Cross looked curiously at the entrance of a huge building.

"Is this the District Attorney's office?" he asked.

"Yep," Hornsby said.

The detectives guided Cross out and escorted him through a wide door, across a deserted, spacious lobby, and stood on either side of him as they were lifted up in an elevator to the tenth floor. He was marched down a white-tiled corridor and into the anteroom of an ornately furnished office where two uniformed policemen stood guard. Hornsby pushed open a door and Cross was ushered into the presence of Houston who, flanked by two

377

other men, sat behind a large desk staring solemnly at him.

"Here's your man, sir," Hornsby said, saluting, turning, and leaving with the other officer.

Cross stared at the three men wordlessly. He was not going to say anything. Theirs was the burden. Houston, leaning back in a swivel chair, both watchful and relaxed, stroked his chin. Cross knew that he was in the presence of men sworn to punish those who did not obey the law, and toward them he felt no bitterness, no hate; he did not regard them as his enemies. He understood the origin of their power and authority and the scope of their duties, and he did not look upon his being hauled here as an act of injustice. Had the situation been different, he wouldn't have hesitated to sit down and talk with them, try to show them that really his so-called crime was derived basically from the fact that he saw and felt the world differently than they did; he would even have tried, had he had the chance, to make them see and feel it as he did. But he knew that was useless now; it was too late. . . . But he would not help or hinder them; theirs was the power, theirs the initiative.

Houston finally pulled himself erect and came from behind his desk on those softly padding feet of his, his body moving slowly and stiffly, his hump seemingly more prominent than Cross could ever remember having seen it. Houston's face was tensely concentrated, his eyes absorbed with inner considerations. His long, dangling arms and his pointed, strong fingers swung grotesquely at his sides. He turned and studied a pile of papers on his desk for a moment, then whirled to Cross and said:

"I hardly know where to begin with you. I wish to God I hadn't met you on that train, or hadn't talked to you. It would make my task easier. . . ."

"I'm sorry if I'm embarrassing you, Mr. Houston." Cross smiled as he spoke.

Houston stared, then glanced at his two aides and again at Cross.

"Do you know what this is all about?" Houston asked; he acted as though he was puzzled as to what line to take.

"I know nothing whatsoever," Cross replied affably.

"I'd been looking forward to having dinner with you,

then these reports began to flood in here," Houston sighed.

The other two men, both standing, were youngish. One, the younger, looked like a lawyer. The other was tall, gray at the temples, and had the air of being a high-ranking police official, though he was dressed in plain clothes.

"Is there anything you want to say before we begin questioning you, Lane or Damon or whatever the hell your name is?"

So they had found out who he was! Well, good . . . but what else did they know?

"I have nothing whatever to say," Cross answered.

"Do you acknowledge the name of Cross Damon to be your real, your own, your true name?" Houston asked.

"I acknowledge nothing," Cross replied.

The three men looked at one another.

"Listen, you're intelligent enough, of course, to realize that I cannot force you to answer my questions. You also know that you have the right to counsel. You know too that what you tell me I can use against you in court. I can't force you to incriminate youurself. But whatever it is you're hiding, it would be better if you told me; it would be easier for you in the long run."

Cross smiled. He would at once set Houston straight about that.

"You may question me, sir," he said, hoping that Houston would question him, for that was the only way in which he could tell how much Houston knew, "but I reserve the right to answer what questions of yours I please. I might as well tell you that I'm not concerned with incriminating myself. I'm a perfectly free agent and if I elect to remain silent to some of your questions, it is for reasons of my own."

"Right," Houston said, staring thoughtfully at Cross. He then went back to his desk and sat. "Sit down."

"I prefer standing for a while, if you don't mind," Cross said; he felt better on his feet to face what was coming. He was alert, tense, but free of all dread and compulsions. He was focused to a point of supreme self-defense.

"If you like," Houston muttered. "Now, let's start at the beginning. You worked until about a month and a half ago as a clerk in the Post Office in Chicago, did you not?"

"I don't affirm it or deny it," Cross said.

"But, Damon, we've *proof* of who you are," Houston said. "We got your fingerprints out of Mrs. Blount's apartment and the FBI has at last identified you."

Cross didn't answer; his facial expression didn't change.

"Do you now persist in denying your identity?"

"I affirm or deny nothing," Cross repeated.

Houston frowned, then turned to the older of his two aides. "Bring in that secretary of the Postal Union, Neil," Houston ordered.

"Right, sir," Neil answered, going to a door and beckoning.

Finch, with whom Cross had negotiated his eight-hundred-dollar loan, walked slowly into the room. He stopped and stared at Cross; Cross returned Finch's gaze with level eyes.

"Is this man known to you as Cross Damon?" Houston asked.

"Yes, sir. That's him all right. I'd know him in a million," Finch said eagerly. "Hello, Damon."

Cross kept his eyes steadily on Finch's face and did not answer.

"Are you in trouble, boy?" Finch asked cordially.

Cross was silent, but his lips twitched in a slight smile.

"You'd swear to this identification in court?" Houston asked.

"Of course I would," Finch said.

"Well, that's all, Mr. Finch. Thanks for your co-operation."

"Not at all. Are you through with me, sir?" Finch asked.

"Yes, for the time being."

Finch started out, turning and straining his neck, his baffled eyes remaining on Cross's face until he collided with the edge of the opened door. Neil had to grab Finch's arm to keep him from falling. Cross's face broke into a wide grin; he watched Finch vanish down the hallway, holding his hand to his forehead where he had bumped it against the door.

"Are you crazy?" Houston's voice came to him.

"I'm sorry, sir," Cross said.

"What are you laughing at?"

"Finch was so amazed he didn't see the door," Cross explained soberly.

"*You* may be the amazed one before I'm through with you," Houston snapped. "You are presumed to be dead; you know that?"

"I know nothing," Cross said.

"You were in a subway accident. Do you acknowledge that?"

"I acknowledge nothing, sir."

"Good God, man!" Houston exploded. "Maybe you're an amnesia victim. Do you recall being injured in the subway accident?"

"I've nothing to say."

"You say you *don't* remember?"

"I say *nothing,* sir."

"If you say you don't remember, it simplifies things—"

"I say nothing," he repeated.

He doubted now if Houston knew of the hotel in which he had met Jenny and had killed Joe Thomas. So far, nothing of a damaging nature had come to light. Some of his past was known. So what?

"We'll see about that," Houston said; he was plainly annoyed. "It's just possible you're telling the truth. You may have been injured and don't recall anything. . . ."

Cross knew that Houston was now toying with the idea that he *was* perhaps an amnesia victim; but no one knew for sure that he had been in the subway accident and he loathed anybody's thinking that his conduct had been influenced by any injury.

"May I state quite clearly and plainly, Mr. Houston, that I've never at any time in my life sustained any injuries that would cause me any lapse of memory," Cross said.

Houston was momentarily rattled. Yeah; they'd been planning to bait me with that amnesia approach, Cross told himself.

"What is this, a game?" Houston demanded.

"That depends upon your interpretation, sir."

"What are you hiding, Damon?"

"Nothing."

"You know of that accident." Houston spoke in a puzzled tone of voice. "You admitted it by implication. But you don't want to take advantage of that accident to justify anything you've done." Houston spoke in a tone of voice that showed that he was thinking out loud, trying to find a way to get at Cross. He rose and walked close to Cross and stared into his face and said in a low, charged voice: "Damon, I've some very bad news for you."

"Yes," Cross said, holding tense and ready for surprises.

"Damon, your mother died in Chicago yesterday. She was astonished that you were still alive. It is believed that she died of shock, the shock of what you had done to her. . . ."

He held still. Was this true? Or was Houston lying, trying to break him down? He was aware that Houston was watching every flicker of his eyelids. His mother was over sixty; she had been in frail health for a long time, and he was inclined to believe that what Houston had said was true. . . . And the shock of what he had done had killed her? A churning wave went through his stomach, but he steeled himself against emotion. Well, he had already grieved over her once, and so it made no real difference now. A slow sigh went from him. He saw again his mother as he had seen her that last time, walking with faltering steps over the snow in front of the church, going to get into the car that was to bear his supposed body to the cemetery for burial. . . . How bent and frail she had looked! How lost, uncomprehending, and weak. . . . But not a facial muscle moved as he gazed into the eyes of Houston. Houston turned and walked slowly back to his desk, glancing at his aides as he did so. He sat and resumed his watching of Cross's face. He's waiting for the news to sink in, Cross thought. He felt that he ought to be sorry, but he could not summon the necessary degree of emotion. Had she suffered much? Then the truth of it dawned upon him; his mother had been dead for him for years, and that was why he had been able to reflect on her so coldly and analytically while she had still been living. . . . To him his mother's reality was that she had taught him to feel what he was now feeling. He was at this moment living out the sense of life that she had conferred upon him, a sense of life which, in the end, he had accepted as his own. It had been her moral strictures that had made him a criminal in a deeper sense than Houston's questions so far could admit.

"Did you hear what I said, Damon?" Houston asked softly.

"Certainly."

"And what's your reaction?"

"Nothing."

"You're not even curious as to how she died?"

Cross struggled with himself; yes, Houston was using the tactics of Gil and Hilton. Houston was attempting to bring him repentantly to his knees, trying to rule him through the deep feeling that all men had in common for their parents.

"No," he said, the word coming softly from his lips.

Houston shook his head in disbelief.

"Damon, do you deny meeting me in the dining car of a train on the eighth of February last?"

"I affirm or deny nothing."

"Do you belong to any organizations whatsoever?"

"I belong to nothing."

"Do you subscribe to any political philosophy?"

"I subscribe to nothing."

"Are you working for any foreign government?"

"No."

"Have you ever made any public speeches?"

"No."

"Did you ever write under your own or an assumed name in any periodical or newspaper?"

"No."

"Have you ever been in jail?"

"I've nothing to say."

"Did you ever commit a felony?"

"I admit nothing."

Houston leaped to his feet and walked with long strides toward Cross.

"Damon, did you kill Gilbert Blount?" Houston thundered.

"I've nothing to say."

"Did you kill Langley Herndon?"

"I affirm or deny nothing."

"Did you kill Jack Hilton?"

"I affirm or deny nothing."

Houston had reached the important questions, but he had not mentioned Joe Thomas yet. Did that mean that he did not have to worry about Joe? Surely, Houston would have thrown it at him if he had known. . . . He was not absolutely certain about Joe Thomas, but he was reasonably sure. . . . What could have happened there? Perhaps the Chicago police had marked it "Unsolved"? Now, what evidence did they have against him in relation to Gil and Herndon and Hilton? Houston's eyes were wide and intent as they stared at his face, but Cross knew that those eyes were reflecting processes of thought far removed from the questions that Houston had asked so far.

"Do you hate communism, Damon?" Houston asked softly, suddenly.

Now, Houston had gotten to the point. This is where I must be careful. . . . Houston had now entered territory known well to both of them.

"What a strange question to ask me," Cross stalled.

"I'm asking you do you hate communism?" Houston insisted.

"How can one *hate* communism?" he asked, smiling.

"Then you love communism?"

"No."

"Are you a member of any so-called revolutionary party?"

"No."

"Were you *ever* a member of the Communist Party?"

"No. And I've never been a Fascist either."

"I know that—"

"How *could* you know that?" Cross asked.

Houston blinked, pulled down the corners of his mouth. "You're a Negro—"

"Negroes can be Fascists too," Cross told him.

"Are you a Fascist then?"

"No."

"The Fascist angle is not important; they wouldn't take you in anyhow," Houston said with a tinge of satisfaction.

"Fundamentally, fascism has nothing to do with race," Cross told him.

"Are you bragging about that?"

384

"I'm stating facts to you, sir."

"Do you believe in communism?"

"How can one believe in communism?" Cross countered again.

He saw that Houston resented his question; he knew that Houston was seeking for a motive for the deaths of Gil and Hilton, and Houston knew that he knew it.

"Isn't communism something one believes in?" Houston asked.

Cross drew a deep breath. Should he wade out into this? Why not? If he did, he would isolate himself so sharply in a psychological sense that Houston would be bound to get a faint clue, but a psychological clue only. And there was a vast distance between psychological clues and concrete proof.

"Some people believe in the ideology of communism," Cross said. "But real Communist leaders don't. Ideology is simply in their hands and minds an instrument for organizing people. The real heart of communism, Mr. Houston, is the will to power. And you know that, sir, as well as I do."

"Would you use such an instrument in organizing people?"

"I wouldn't touch such an instrument with a ten-foot pole," Cross said earnestly.

"Why?"

"I think such an instrument is an insult to human life and intelligence," Cross said.

"Well, what kind of instrument would you use in organizing people?"

"I don't know, sir."

"But you agree that people ought to be organized?"

"Certainly."

"Why?"

"Human life on this earth must proceed on some rational basis."

"Then, what organizational instrument would you advocate?"

"None. I haven't discovered any to my liking, sir."

"And still you feel that human society needs organization? That it stands in urgent need of such, in your opinion?"

385

"Yes; of course. It's self-evident."

"You feel that the inability of men to form stable governments in the nations of the world proves that, don't you?"

"It's self-evident, sir."

"You know that if America pulled its support from Europe, Europe would collapse?"

"Yes."

"Are you willing to see that support pulled out?"

"No."

"You agree with that support?"

"No."

"You think it's bad?"

"Yes; it is very bad."

"But you do not advocate its being pulled out?"

"No."

"Why?"

"It's better than nothing, sir."

"But it's bad?"

"Yes."

"Why?"

"It doesn't answer their needs, sir. It's a stopgap."

"Would communism answer their needs?"

"No. Of course not."

"What, then, would answer their needs, in your opinion?"

"Really, Mr. Houston— You are aware as well as I am of the complex nature of human needs, especially the needs of modern man. . . . We've been over this ground once. Maybe there's no answer to their needs—"

"Do you support the Red Chinese?"

"I don't support 'em or fight 'em; they're just Red Chinese, sir. It's the way they've organized themselves."

"Don't you think they could have organized themselves our way?"

"Why should they?"

"I'm asking you do you think they ought to have done it our way?"

"I could not say yes to that unless, first, I felt that ours was the system that they should have, sir. Second, I'm the kind of man who simply cannot feel that kind of godlike imperiousness to impose my will on others."

386

"But you feel that all of this unrest on earth today is because man is seeking for an organization of his social life?"

"He urgently needs one," Cross said stoutly. "I'm guilty of thinking and believing that."

Houston's eyes roved restlessly about the room.

"Yes, you told me that on the train when I first met you. But I'm not accusing you of any such—"

"I know it, sir," Cross said jovially. "I was just making a little confession to you."

"It's no crime under our laws to believe that something or other ought to be done in society—"

"I beg your pardon, sir. In my opinion, it is right *there* where the real crime is," Cross maintained. "A man today who believes that he cannot live by the articles of faith of his society is a criminal and you know it, even though Congress has not got around to making such into law. You know that as well as I do, sir. We've talked about that."

Houston threw up his hands. Cross was amused. Houston was looking right at his guilt, and would not admit it. Houston stared at him with wide, startled eyes, then, glancing at his aides, sat again at his desk and pored over his stack of papers. Cross wanted to laugh. What did papers have to do with this? Houston looked at Neil, nodded to him, and Neil hurriedly left the room. He's executing something previously agreed upon, Cross said to himself. He waited. Houston looked up suddenly.

"Damon, suppose you come upon a man attempting to organize human society in a way that was supremely offensive to you, what would you do?" he asked in a slow, loud voice.

He was asking indirectly if he had killed Gil and Herndon and Hilton.

"I decline to say."

"You don't like Communists, do you?"

"No."

"Which do you hate more? Communists or Fascists?"

"Well, I'm afraid I hate the Fascists more, sir."

"Why?"

387

"Well, they've more real support. Maybe I feel like that because I'm a Negro and Fascists are dead against us."

"If you saw an opportunity to send two of them to their graves in one blow, would you do it?"

Cross looked at Houston and laughed.

"Would *you?*" he countered.

"Will you answer the question?" Houston demanded.

"I decline to answer, sir," Cross said.

"Why?"

"Because you know the answer."

"You would kill them, wouldn't you?"

"I decline to answer."

"Goddammit, I'll break your spirit yet!" Houston raged.

The next face that appeared in the doorway made Cross feel that he should have been sitting down, because, for a moment, he felt like falling. It was Gladys. She was smartly dressed. Her face was pale with apprehension and her movements stiff with shock. She was clutching a pocketbook and staring at Cross. Houston looked quickly from Gladys to Cross. Gladys reached out a trembling hand and caught hold of the edge of the desk for support. Cross was furious; he gritted his teeth. What point was there in Houston's dragging Gladys into this? Yes; Houston, too, liked to play at being a little god, liked to ravage the souls of others. That was why he was District Attorney. . . . And Cross vowed that Houston would never see him humbled, unnerved, or weeping. Houston had thought the sight of Gladys would make him break down and talk. Well, he would not react. He would show Houston that he had miscalculated. Then Cross sucked his breath in sharply; from the open door behind Gladys, being led by Neil, came his three sons, Cross Junior, Robert, and Peter. He whirled to Houston and saw an expression of sensual excitement upon the hunchback's lean face. That sonofabitch . . . Cross Junior, his eyes wide and his lips parted, stared at his father, then clutched his mother's hand, whimpering:

"Mummy, is he *Daddy* for real?"

Cross felt the muscles in his calves aching. Robert and Peter stood close to Gladys, staring; then they, too, began

388

weeping, more from fear and uneasiness than any understanding.

"Why did Daddy come back, Mummy?" Peter asked.

"It's *not* Daddy," Robert said emphatically, indignantly,
still crying.

Keep still, Cross told himself. His body was rigid. He
had often imagined many kinds of confrontations, but he
had never dreamed of this. To let his sons see him standing
mute, stony . . . ! He could *kill* Houston!

Gladys, blinded by tears, her mouth distorted with silent
weeping, groped for her children and huddled them
clumsily about her, trying to keep her face averted. Cross
returned the stares of everyone in the room, not allowing
his face to betray any expression. Then he could hold it in
no longer.

"Why are you doing this?" The words broke from him in
a spasm of rage.

"At last I got a rise out of you, hunh?" Houston asked,
wetting his lips with his tongue, reveling in deep satisfaction.
"I had your wife and children flown here this morning
from Chicago. . . ."

Cross could tell that Houston was trying to justify his
actions.

"I didn't want to make any mistake about identifying
you, Damon," Houston said.

But Cross wasn't fooled; he knew that Houston loved
this. But that look of sensual triumph on Houston's face
had already sent Cross scuttling back to his shell of iron
reserve, to his stance of defense. All right, suppose they
were his sons? He had given them up, hadn't he? He would
make a supreme effort and remain cold, hard. Sentiment
must not subvert him now. He was lost, that much was
true; but he must not let human claims drag him into a
position where Houston could crow over him. . . . Nothing could undo him so easily now as Houston's gloating or
bragging. Those frightened, little brown-faced boys were
his sons, flesh of his flesh; they were the future of himself
and he had rejected that self.

"Damon, I realize that you and your wife did not get
along together," Houston said. "She told me that. But,

man, here are your children. . . . They need you. Go to them."

Cross made his face a mask.

"Damon, can you stand there and look at the bewildered faces of those children and say nothing?" Houston demanded.

Cross shut out the sight of the world and tried not to hear.

"You can redeem yourself with them, Damon," Houston was saying. "Are you going to let them remember you all of their lives like *this?* Boys love to think of their fathers as strong, wise men," Houston went implacably on. "To many a son the image of his father is what lifts him up in life. A father can make a boy feel that he has a sure foundation under him, can give him confidence. . . ."

Cross summoned all his control and pushed Houston's words away; he would not react; he would not be human; he was shut of these claims and he would die shut of them. . . .

Houston turned and looked at Gladys, whose face was hidden by her crumpled handkerchief; the woman's body seemed so rigid that if one touched her ever so lightly she would fall.

"Mrs. Damon," Houston began in a loud, clear voice, "do you recognize this man standing there?" Houston pointed at Cross.

Gladys slowly turned her face and stared at Cross with wet, red eyes. Then she quickly bowed her head; both of her hands convulsively covered her face in one shuddering motion and her chest heaved as she wept. Houston gently grasped her shoulder and led her to a chair.

"I'm asking you: Do you recognize this man as your husband, Mrs. Damon?" Houston demanded.

Gladys was still, then she shook her head with a slow, dreamy movement, shook it negatively, and at once Cross knew that Gladys was not shaking her head in answer to Houston's question, but was asserting her right to reject him as he had once rejected her! Gladys was protesting his presence on earth. Houston's face showed astonishment; he did not understand what was transpiring in the woman. He had thought that a storm of words would have poured out of Gladys, and that Cross would have been moved to pity. Cross knew that Gladys would rather have had him dead.

"Mrs. Damon, I *asked* you if that is your *husband?*"

Her cheeks wet with tears as far down as her chin, Gladys finally nodded her head affirmatively. Houston blinked in bewilderment.

"Now, *which* answer is it, Mrs. Damon?" Houston demanded. "Is he your *husband,* or is he *not?*"

Cross burst into a gale of laughter that made the bodies of everyone in the room stiffen. Houston gaped at Cross, then his face settled into a mold of anger. Cross knew that there was a conflict in Gladys. Her first reaction had been to say that she did not know him; then she had wanted to be honest with the District Attorney and had said yes. And now she was more confused than ever and she shook her head again, negatively. It was an identity deeper than that which Houston was asking for that Gladys was denying.

"Mrs. Damon, again I ask you, is this your husband, Cross Damon?"

Gladys rose, turned her back on Cross, nodded affirmatively to Houston and murmured brokenly: "Yes, it's he—"

She ran to the door, turned, snatched wildly at her children, grabbing them by their clothes, and pulled them into the other room.

"But, Mrs. Damon, you—" Houston was trying to speak.

"No, no, no!" Gladys screamed and wept and the little boys joined her in crying, crying because they saw their mother unnerved and bitterly hysterical.

"Help her, Neil," Houston said; comprehension was now in his eyes.

The two men assisted Gladys into the next room and finally the door closed. Cross still stood, his face impassive.

"You are the lowest sonofabitch I've ever seen in all of my life," Houston said savagely.

"I return the compliment," Cross said. "What on earth did you gain by dragging her in here?"

Houston did not answer and Cross knew that he could not. Houston ran his spread fingers through his hair and sat again behind his desk, glaring at Cross.

"Damon, I'll get to the point. The Communists have been badgering me night and day to take action against you. They are charging that you killed Blount, Hilton, and Herndon," Houston told him.

"And what are *you* charging me with?" Cross asked.

Houston did not reply.

"How can you charge me merely on the insistence of Communists who are suspicious and frightened of me?" Cross demanded.

"*Why* are they frightened of you?"

"Ask them."

"Are you a member of any anti-Communist group?"

"I'm not a member of *anything*, Mr. Houston."

"Are you anti-Communist even as an individual?"

"I'll tell you as I told them: I'm not anti anything."

"But you don't support them, do you?"

"Hell, no. And millions of other men don't either—"

"But you're like them in your reactions. That much I know," Houston said. "And the motive is right here."

"You think so?"

"The strongest motive on earth—"

"There are millions of men with the same motive—"

"I've no evidence against you, Damon, or Lane; if I had, I'd tell you so. I'm straight in this office. But I had a right to find out who you are," Houston explained in a tired voice. "There's another motive you could have had—"

"Yes?"

"You wanted Mrs. Blount. Men have killed for women before—"

"Mr. Houston, I don't believe that you really believe that," Cross told him. "Before Gil died, I never touched his wife, never so much as looked at her with desire in my eyes. Now, for the rest of this mess, you will have to prove your case against me."

"You started living with Mrs. Blount right off, before her husband was even buried," Houston charged.

"What law did I violate in doing that?" Cross countered. "And don't forget that I was living in the apartment *when* he died."

"You took her to Harlem—"

"That was to get her away from the press."

Cross was now convinced that Houston had no evidence; he had thought that Cross would collapse at the sight of Gladys and his sons and would make some fatal mistake, some slip that would have helped him to build his case.

"The Communist case against you is as follows," Houston told him. "They claim that you went downstairs that night to see if Blount was all right. You saw him wounded. You finished him off. Then Herndon came upon you and you had to kill him. Hilton found out about it in some way, and you had to kill him to keep him silent."

"I've no comment to make on that."

Houston stood again and Neil and the other assistant re-entered the room.

"I was thinking of remanding you for a psychiatric examination," Houston said.

"What purpose would that serve?" asked the youngish man who had stood silent through all of this.

"Sending me for psychiatric observation would be as good an excuse as any to hold me on," Cross told him placidly.

Houston sat down heavily in his chair.

"Hell, *no!*" He turned and stared exasperatedly at the youngish man who had spoken. "I'm not going to play games with this man. I've run this office straight so far, and I'll continue. If the police and the Medical Examiner cannot dig up enough evidence, I'll be damned if I'll hold him till they cook up something."

Cross realized that the youngish man was no doubt a psychiatrist.

"No opinion that we could give you from the hospital would be of any legal use in relation to what I've heard so far. The man seems to be orientated and is defending himself," the young man said.

Houston stood and smiled at Cross.

"That's all for tonight, Lane," he said.

"You mean you are through with me for the time being?" Cross asked.

"For the time being, yes. You may go."

Neil held open the door for him and Cross slowly walked toward it; then he paused, his mind filled with an impish notion. He turned to Houston.

"The best way to get a victim is to find an innocent man," he told the District Attorney. "An *absolutely* innocent man. Such a man is *free* to be charged with anything. An innocent man is overwhelmed when he is falsely accused and he is at a loss for words. He doesn't know how to defend himself," Cross went on, teasing the District Attorney. "You don't really need much evidence at all to charge an innocent man. The bigger the charge, the more likely people are to think that that man *must* have done something, or else no one would have charged him. The way to make a man guilty is to attack him without cause, without reason. The logic there is: if he was not guilty, no one would have dared to charge him. I was innocent to the extent that I didn't have a good name that would stand up under investigation. I had a secret name and you found it, *ergo*, I'm guilty of something. Good night, sir."

He walked down the corridor to the elevator and dropped to the street, thinking, I've got to see Eva. . . . He grabbed a taxi and shot uptown. He knew that Houston was not through with him yet. But I *dare* him to admit what he knows. . . . He already knows, but what use is his knowledge? But the Party . . . ? That was another thing. They did not have to be certain to brand you guilty. If they could not *understand* you, then you were guilty! Yes; he'd have to take Eva away at once, take her out of New York. He'd ask her to come away tonight. . . .

He paid the taxi and looked up at the windows of Sarah's apartment. Lights were blazing through the curtains. Were Menti and Hank up there? He grew hot with hate. He'd send them packing, those fools! He'd take Eva with him right now. . . .

He bounded up the steps and pushed the bell of the door. Sarah opened it almost at once. Her face was tense with fear and curiosity.

"Did the police find you?"

"Yes. Where's Eva?"

"But what have you done, Lionel? What did they want?"

"Nothing. But where's Eva?"

"She's gone. With Menti and Blimin— But what are the cops after you for?"

"It's nothing— Where did Menti and Blimin take Eva?"

394

"I don't know. They just asked her to come with them. But are you in some kind of trouble?"

He sighed, then whirled as the doorbell rang.

"Maybe that's Eva now," Sarah said, hurrying.

It was Eva. She came quickly and excitedly into the hallway. She was a little stooped, as though bent with dread; she stopped at the sight of Cross. Her face went white and her eyes held a wild, scared look. *She knows something. . . . The Party had told her; he could feel it.* He ran toward her.

"God, Eva, what's the matter?"

She backed away from him, stumbling against a wall, her eyes transfixed with terror.

"Eva, let me tell you everything!" he cried.

She looked at him with an opened mouth and shook her head.

"Darling, listen. I've been wanting to tell you—"

"Your name's not Lionel. . . . You're married, aren't you?"

"Yes," he sighed.

"Why didn't you tell me?" she demanded in helpless despair.

"I'll explain everything. . . ."

"Oh, God, the Party's accusing you of *everything*. All night I've battled and fought and wept and screamed to save you—to protect you— And they say I'm wrong; they say you're guilty of something— Why didn't you tell me this? Where's your wife?"

"She's here in the city somewhere; but you and I are together—"

"Does she love you?"

How like a woman to think of those little things first!

"No."

"Do you love her?"

"No."

"You have three small sons—?"

"Yes."

"You deserted them?"

"Yes, Eva."

"And you know that your mother died yesterday?"

"Yes."

"Then you're really the man who ran off from Chicago, leaving his family—?"

"Yes."

"You don't love your family?"

"No."

His answers had come automatically; he was staring at the floor, waiting for her to question him further. Eva covered her eyes with her hands and leaned against the wall.

"What kind of a man are you?" she asked in a whisper.

He had confessed a part of it; now he had to tell her all. She had to believe in him, help him, understand him. . . .

"Eva, come into the room," he begged her. "I must talk to you—"

"I feel dead. *Why* did you fool me?" She choked and wept for a moment. "Nothing you ever told me was true. . . . And Lionel's not your name! Oh, God!"

Sarah was staring from one to the other with an open mouth.

"What's happened?" she asked.

"His name's not Lionel Lane," Eva sobbed.

Sarah backed away from Cross as though he had become a leper.

"You mean you gave us *another* false name?" she demanded indignantly. "You gave Bob a false name the first time you met him. . . ."

"I must talk to you, Eva," he said. "Come into the room. I love you. This *can't* break us up. It *mustn't*. I'll explain everything. You'll see."

Sarah stepped between him and Eva.

"What are you doing to her? Leave her alone. She's scared to death—"

"I've *got* to talk to her, Sarah. I'll explain everything to you later," he said, taking Sarah's arm and pushing her to one side.

He was clinging to a thread of hope. He knew that in spite of all, she still believed in him. But what was he to tell her? Her staunch confidence in him had helped her to weather the storm she had met at the Party headquarters, and now she had come meekly to him for confirmation of what she had fought for, and he could not give it to her. He took her gently by the arm and led her down the hallway and into their bedroom. He could feel the tension in her body as she moved, pulling jerkily but feebly against his hand. He wanted more than anything on earth to keep her, and yet he did not know how; he had no notion of what to say. He closed the bedroom door and turned to her.

"*What's* your name?" she asked him softly.

"Cross Damon," he answered, but he could not look her in the eye.

"*Why* didn't you tell me this before?"

"I was afraid to, and I was ashamed," he told her truthfully.

He glanced at her now and what he saw filled him with frenzy. There were other and bigger questions looming behind those clear, hazel eyes, and those questions condemned him more crushingly than anything that Houston could have said to him. He saw her lips move several times, but no words came from her. She turned from him and leaned against the wall, sobbing softly.

"I gave you my diary to read," she whimpered. "I thought you'd be honest with me. . . . *You've* deceived me too!"

"I was frightened of telling you everything, of telling you the truth," he said. "I was afraid that you'd run off from me."

"Lionel—" She paused and cried afresh. "I don't even know what to call you now. . . ." She went to the bed and sank upon it, staring before her.

Yes, she wants to ask me about Gil. . . . She wants to know. . . . Oh, God! He went to his knees and clutched his arms about her legs. He would beg and plead for his life. He waited in agony for her to ask, and he felt that he could scarcely draw his breath into his lungs.

"Eva," he begged. "It's not too late. If you love me, it's never too late. Remember that. You told me you loved me, and I need you now. If you turn from me, the world collapses. . . ."

"So—s-s-so it w-was *true.* . . . What you told me that night? When you came in?"

He hung his head and could not answer.

"You were trying to tell me something— You were all mixed up and you spoke of killing men— Oh, God—! I thought you were delirious, ill. I thought you were talking out of your mind because of fever and worry. . . ."

She had asked him directly at last! And he could not lift his eyes to look her in the face. He tightened his arms about her legs, afraid to let go of her.

"Eva, I love you; I love you," he mumbled frantically. "You must remember that. I'm crazy with fear and worry now. Don't leave me. . . ."

"You *did* it, then? What the Party said?"

"What did they say?"

"They said you killed Gil to get me. . . ."

He was tempted. Ought he tell her a lie and let her think that? Would it touch her heart and make the look of the world seem less strange and hostile to her? Would it make her love him more? But he'd be locking himself up again behind the wall of himself if he lied to her again. What would lying solve now? Nothing . . . And what made it so horrible was that when he lifted his eyes he could see in her face that she was expecting to hear him say that he had killed Gil for her, to get her, out of his love for her.

"No," he breathed. "I killed Gil . . . but it was not for you—"

"Oh, God in Heaven! Why *did* you kill him, Lionel?"

"I don't know," he whispered.

"*Why?* There must be some *reason*. . . ."

He shook his head; his body was trembling all over.

"You *must* know; you *say* you did it," she said.

Could he ever tell her? He had to try. He had to talk or he could not go on living. He had to try to get for once in his life from behind himself, to walk out of his house as she had once walked out of her house to meet him.

"Eva," he whispered hoarsely, still clutching her legs. "It goes way back. . . . God, help me to explain. . . . I *want* to explain. . . ." He felt hot tears rolling down his cheeks. "You see, Eva, I don't *believe* in anything. . . ." He spoke in a tone of voice that he knew sounded unreal, not convincing. But how could he make it sound otherwise? How did one *tell* these things?

398

"What had Gil done to you?" she asked in a whisper that carried an overtone of hope.

"Nothing," he sighed and felt that he would choke. "Oh, God, he did nothing to me. . . . Eva, I'm praying to you to try to understand me. . . . *Somebody* must understand me. . . . I'll die if you don't understand. . . . Look, when you can't believe in anything, when you're just here on this earth and there's nothing, *nothing* else. . . . Oh, Christ, I can't explain it! You have to *feel* it! You have to *live* it! It has to be in your blood before it can become real to you. . . . I feel like I'm talking to you from another world . . . trying to talk to you through a glass wall. . . . I know you can't understand. . . . But, Eva, you must love me and trust me!" He shook his head in bewilderment. "If you understand, you'd suffer, too, like I did. . . . Oh, no; you'll never understand this. . . ." Despair was full in him. "I didn't ever want to tell you like this. . . ." All of his hope had gone and he was talking to her out of a sense of futility.

"When did you kill him?"

"When I went down to see what had happened. They were fighting. God, I can't explain how I felt. . . . When I looked at them, I suddenly hated them both. . . . They'd done nothing to me. . . . They weren't even paying any attention to me; they were fighting so hard that they didn't even know I was in the room. . . ." He knew that what he was saying did not reach her. And the knowledge of it maddened him; he stood and began shouting: "Don't you *understand?* You've been scared, haven't you? You know what it means to live senselessly? When every day is a foolish day? And when I stood in that room I saw more senselessness and foolishness right before my eyes and I felt a way to stop it! I hated what I saw! And I hated myself because all my life I was unable to do anything about it. . . . I tell you, I *hated* it. It insulted me. . . . I wanted to blot it out, wipe it from the face of the earth. . . ." It seemed that he had forgotten that he was speaking to her; his hands and arms made gestures as he stood in the dim room before her and re-enacted his crime. "I took the table leg and battered Herndon down, killed him. . . . I did it; yes. . . . I wasn't angry with him per-

399

sonally; not then. I'd been angry with him before, but I felt
no anger then. I killed him because I didn't think he had a
right to live. . . . Did you ever feel like that about anybody? No; you couldn't feel that. . . ." He paused and
rubbed his eyes; then he seemed to remember that he was
telling her about what had happened. "Then I hit Gil.
. . . He wasn't expecting it. . . . I was mad with them.
. . . No; not personally mad. Don't you know what I
mean?. I can't say it right, goddammit, I *can't*. . . . I
wanted to live so badly; I wanted a good life so terribly
much that what I saw made me mad, *mad*. . . . And I
killed them. . . . Eva, *believe me*. . . . It was that that
made me kill them. . . ." He looked at her and there was
no light of comprehension in her eyes. "Oh, God, you
don't *believe* me. . . . You *can't* believe me. . . . But
you *must*, Eva; you *can*; you of all the people in the world
can understand. . . . I *know* it. . . ." His voice died
away in a whisper. Then he resumed, reciting his words as
though he was reliving the scene of the murder and blood
again. "I kept hitting them until they were dead. . . . I
wasn't sorry. . . . I knew I was right. . . . Then I
wiped off all the fingerprints. . . . I didn't want to be
caught; I didn't want to be punished. . . . Then I came
up to you. . . . That's what I did, Eva. Now, can you
understand that?"

She was white as a sheet; she seemed not to breathe.

"And Hilton *too*?" she asked in a whisper.

"Yes," he sighed.

"Because he knew?"

"No; not exactly. No."

"Then *why*?"

"Mainly because of what he did to Bob. . . . And because of what he wanted to do to me," he said, speaking
mechanically.

She was still as a block of ice. Her eyes stared unseeingly into the shadows of the room.

"That night when you were trying to tell me," she began
in a whisper, "you spoke of Chicago. . . ." She shook her
head helplessly, then bit her pale lips. "You said you killed
somebody else. . . ."

"Eva, Eva . . . please, I need help. . . . If ever a man

400

needed your love, I need it. . . . I've killed and killed. . . . Have mercy on me. . . . Pity me, but not for what has been done to me, but for what I've done to others and myself. . . . You be my judge; you tell me if I'm to live now. . . . Can you tell me . . . ?"

She was edging away from him; her eyes reflected horror.

"But I thought you were against brutality— I thought you were going to tell me what Gil had done to you— I thought you hated suffering—"

"I do!" he shouted. "That's why I did it! I couldn't stand the thought of it, the sight of it . . . !"

She did not believe him; she could not believe him. She was a reluctant victim and he was a willing one. . . . He stared fully at her and reached out his hand to touch her. She leaped away from him, gasping, and scrambled to her feet.

"Eva," he pleaded.

She ran from him to the door. He started after her, frantic, his bloodshot eyes glistening.

"Eva, please try to understand. . . . It's hard, I know. But try, try. . . . I can redeem myself. . . . Let me be with you. . . ." He was praying to her.

She gave a short scream and ran out of the room. He followed her out the door. Sarah came rushing down the hall.

"What's the matter?"

"Sarah, Sarah, help me," Eva wailed.

"Lionel, leave her alone!" Sarah yelled.

Eva clutched Sarah and clung to her, her body shaking.

"Lionel, what have you done to her?"

Then, abruptly, Eva twisted around in the arms of Sarah and looked at Cross and while she was looking he saw the light go out of her eyes. She seemed stricken, not knowing where she was; she pulled away from Sarah and ran on down the hall until she came to the door of the living room. She paused, looked wildly about her, then ran into the living room and slammed the door. He rushed to the door and heard the lock click.

"Eva, for God's sake, listen. . . ."

"What did you do to her?" Sarah wailed.

"Leave me alone, will you!" he told her savagely.

"But, Lionel, you're driving her crazy."

The front doorbell pealed and Cross stood wondering who it was. The hell with them. . . . He pounded on the door of the living room with his fists as Sarah went down the hall to the front door.

"Eva, let me come in and talk to you," he begged her, but deep in him he felt that she never would.

Menti came through the front door; Sarah was holding the door open for him. Behind Menti was Hank, sullen, his hands thrust deep in his overcoat pockets. Menti paused, sensing that something was happening.

"What's the matter here?" he asked.

"Eva's locked herself inside and won't come out," Sarah said.

"What are you doing here?" Menti asked Cross.

"The hell with you," Cross snapped at him. "I've got a right to be here."

"I thought the D.A. grabbed you," Menti said.

"He did, but I'm free now," Cross told him. "Your Party's trick didn't work, Menti."

"Be careful of what you say about the Party—"

"Oh, God, don't fight in here," Sarah begged.

"Eva," Cross called through the door. "Open the door, honey!"

Cross felt his legs trembling. What could he do? If he could only talk to her, quiet her down, he might make her see what had happened to him.

"Eva!" he called again.

Cross turned and looked appealingly at Sarah.

"Don't you have a key to this door?"

"No," she said, shaking her head.

Cross put his ear to the panel of the door; he could hear no sounds. God, what could she be doing?

"Eva! Eva!" He took hold of the doorknob and rattled it furiously.

He was conscious that Menti was looking at him with a sardonic smile. That sonofabitch . . . ! But maybe Menti could help make Eva open the door.

"Menti, call her. Tell her to open the door."

402

"Why? Leave her alone. What can I do if she runs away from you?" Menti said, chuckling.

"Damn you!" Cross growled. He saw Hank staring at him with tense hatred. "And you too!" Cross spat at him. He turned to the door again. "Eva!"

There came a loud, heavy pounding upon the front hall door. Sarah started toward it, then paused, looking at Cross. The pounding came again. Then a hoarse voice yelled:

"Say, open up in there!"

Sarah opened the door and backed away as a tall, black man rushed into the hallway, his eyes wide with excitement.

"Say, wasn't it from this apartment that a woman jumped from a window?" he asked, looking from one to the other of them.

Sarah, Hank, Menti, and Cross—all of them were silent, staring at the black man's face. Cross, for a moment, could not think; his feelings froze; he was not even aware of his surroundings. Then a realization of what the man had said came to him in the form of a flashing image of Eva's frail body hurtling through the icy air of the night outside. The words clanged in his mind as though someone were shouting in his ears: *Oh, God, it's Eva!* For a split second the world was blotted out; then he was running and stumbling through the doorway, falling and sliding down the dark, winding flights of rickety stairs. He reached the street panting and aching from where he had knocked himself against the walls and banisters. He leaped clear of the steps of the stoop and saw a crowd of Negroes gathering in a knot near the edge of the sidewalk. He sprinted to them, plowing them aside. Yes . . . there was Eva. . . . She was lying half on her stomach with her face to the pavement, her body twisted so that the toes of her shoes were pointing upward and her face was hidden in the snow. Already blobs of blood had seeped from her head and Cross could see where someone had stepped on a loosened lock of her blonde hair, crunching and burying it in the dirty snow. *Eva!* the word rang so loud in his mind that he was not

403

conscious of what went on about him. He had lost. She had fled him forever; she had taken one swift look into the black depths of his heart, into the horror of his deeds, and had been so revolted that she had chosen this way out, had slammed her door on life.

He knelt, turned her gently over, stared at the bruised and shattered face, the defenseless mouth, the flattened nostrils from which blood streaked and stained his trembling hands.

"Eva, Eva," he cried and cradled her head in his arms.

He looked up at the looming circle of dark faces for the first time, his eyes pleading for help.

"Get a doctor," he begged.

"Better get the police," someone said roughly.

"Did he *kill* her?"

"Maybe a car ran over her. . . ."

"Naw; somebody pushed her out of a window. . . ."

"I heard her hit the sidewalk; it was like a pistol shot!"

"Look, she's a *white* gal!"

"What she doing up here in Harlem?"

"Get some help, please," Cross pleaded. "Somebody— somebody *do* something— She's hurt!"

An elderly Negro with white hair bent to him and whispered: "I sent in an alarm for the police."

"Did she jump outta a window?"

"It was from up there—one, two, three, four— Lord, she fell *six* floors— She's dead or she'll die—"

Cross held his breath and stared directly in front of him, holding Eva against his chest. She was limp in his arms and her body felt terribly light, as though her substance was dwindling as her life ebbed. He bent closer and saw that under the waving, tumbling coils of her blonde hair the top of her skull was bashed in. His lips trembled as he realized that it was hopeless. Gently, he eased her body back to the snow-packed pavement and felt for her pulse; she had none. He hardly knew what happened after that. He kept kneeling, staring at her, repeating softly:

"Eva, Eva . . ."

At last Menti was at his side, and there was the dark form of Hank looming menacingly in the background Sarah, her eyes bulging, her fingers twisting nervously,

404

stood whimpering. And he heard the distant sound of sirens, the sirens he had so long feared, sirens that rose to a hysterical scream on the winter air. They were not sounding for him, those sirens, but for the only woman he had ever loved. He was now locked in loneliness.

"Why did she do it?" Menti asked.

Cross glanced at him and did not answer. He saw that Menti's face was calm, alert, devoid of grief or shock, his eyes glowing with the intense, detached curiosity of a man long schooled in disaster. To those hard, disciplined eyes the sight of Eva's crumpled body was a thing to be expected, was something that fitted inevitably into life's cryptic design.

"Did somebody push her out?" a man's voice asked.

"No, no," Sarah said. "She jumped. I was there. . . ."

"*Why* did she do it, Lane?" Menti asked again, softly, insistently, into Cross's ear.

Cross looked into Menti's eyes without making any sign that he had heard him. The sirens were wailing closer now; then he saw the police cars screech around the corner; there was a swish of tires on ice and snow as the cars skidded to a stop. Blue-coated officers leaped out and ran forward. Cross saw Menti rise, detach himself stealthily from the crowd, walk down the sidewalk and go into a candy store. Menti was going to call the Party and report.

"My God," a young white cop said as he bent forward, "what's she doing in Harlem?"

Another cop felt for Eva's pulse.

"Call for an ambulance, *quick!*" he said.

"Now, what happened?" another cop demanded.

"She jumped from the window of my apartment," Sarah managed to say.

"Who are you?"

"Sarah Hunter. I live up there on the sixth floor—where you see the lights in the window," Sarah said haltingly, pointing. "I don't know what made her do it. . . . Her husband was killed two days ago. Maybe that's why— But she didn't seem worried or anything— It was suddenlike—"

"What's her name?"

"Mrs. Eva Blount."

"Where did she live?"

"In the Village, but she was staying with me. . . ."

The cop grunted, looking at Cross, then at Menti, who had come back. He turned and addressed a young cop. "You better get hold of the Medical Examiner's office." The young cop rushed off to the police car.

Cross stood up. He could feel Menti's elbow touching him. The cops were now asking the names and addresses of those who had seen Eva fall, what time she had fallen, and who had seen her in the neighborhood before. Cross gave his name and address, so did Menti and Sarah.

"You three," the cop said, indicating Cross, Menti, and Sarah, "will have to come to the station with us."

Cross did not care; it was over for him. Eva was gone; she had slipped through his clutching, clumsy fingers. He had botched it and Eva's crushed, mute face told him that this was hell: this swooping sense of meaninglessness, this having done what could never be undone. . . . He had in him to the full the feeling that had sent him on this long, bloody, twisting road: self-loathing. . . .

"She's gone," he heard a cop say.

"Really?"

"Yep."

From the throat of the night another siren screamed. That must be the ambulance. . . . Eva was dead and now in recollection he knew her for what she had meant to him; already he was feeling what he had been grasping for in loving her. That capacity in him to suffer had seized upon this lovely, frail girl as the representation and appearance in life of what he felt had to be protected and defended. To that frightened heart he had made, out of his compulsive need for companionship, out of his hunger for solace, a promise that he had not been able to keep, that he had *known* he could not keep, and, as the intensity of his lying promise had swollen, so had her distance from him widened until at last she was forever beyond his reach. Self-love as well as self-hate had dogged him to the end and he had not been able to outwit the predetermined mold of his destiny. And his too keen habit of self-reflection would not permit him to hide from himself what he had done. Between him and Eva a mutual selfishness had entwined itself, and, in that reciprocally devouring passion, his falsely pledged promise had been the single element that had broken the unity, smashing it beyond all mending, all recall, for eternity.

Two internes pushed past Cross. A chill seized him as he saw them lift Eva's limp body and place it on a stretcher and march with it to the ambulance and shove it in the rear door. The motor roared; the ambulance started off and the siren rose to a screaming pitch. . . . Eva . . . Eva . . . He was alone.

"All right, folks. Break it up, now. Move along. Get going—" the police were saying.

Cross, Sarah, and Menti were jammed into the back seat of a police car and driven to a nearby station where they had to wait in a dirty anteroom for hours. It was the Party again that tried unwittingly to come to Cross's assistance, for Menti, bending to him and whispering, said: "Tell 'em nothing. Just say she jumped, but nobody saw her, see? But nothing else. We don't talk to cops."

Cross and Sarah nodded. He saw a look of wonder in Sarah's eyes as she stared at him. Yes, Sarah was silently asking what it was that he had said to Eva that had made her lock herself in the room and jump. . . . And Cross was aware that Menti now regarded him with mounting hatred; his eyes were harder than agate as they rested on Cross's face. I'm glad that Sarah was there when Eva jumped, he told himself. Menti would like to accuse me of pushing her out the window. . . . The Party would be more suspicious of him than ever. The hour was approaching when he would have to flee New York and try his luckless fortune elsewhere; that is, if Houston did not first point a fatal finger at him.

They were questioned in relays, and when Cross's turn came, he obeyed Menti's injunction to the extent that he told a simple story of a girl whose husband had just been killed; he said that grief, maybe, had made her jump out of the window. But he thought better of Menti's advice and felt that he ought to tell the impersonal captain who was questioning him that he had just been interviewed by the District Attorney, for they would most surely discover it

407

after he had gone and they would come rushing to question him again, thinking that he had for some reason tried to conceal it.

Complications arose at once; the puzzled captain telephoned Houston and Cross was instructed to go back home and remain there until further notice, and he was informed that a police guard would be placed at the front and back doors of the apartment.

When he emerged from the police station, Sarah and Menti had gone. He walked back to the apartment alone, climbed the steps and found a cop on guard in the hallway.

"You live here?" the cop asked.

"Yeah."

"If you go in, you can't come out till the D.A. says so," the cop informed him.

"I know that," Cross said.

The cop let him pass. He let himself in and went straight to the room he had shared with Eva and stood staring at her comb and lipstick on the cluttered top of the dresser. A few strands of her blonde hair still clung to the bristles of the hairbrush. There was her purse, an ashtray of cigarette stubs whose tips showed the rouge she had worn, a delicately scented handkerchief, a crumpled wad of face tissue. . . . His throat ached and he fell upon the bed, burying his face in the pillow, and lay as still as death, longing for oblivion, for the world to close in on him and swallow him forever.

He started when the door opened. It was Menti; he had not bothered to knock. Resentment flooded Cross and he didn't rise to receive him. Menti left the door ajar and came to the bed and sat upon it, a few inches from Cross. These sonsofbitches! They presumed they owned him, that they could come upon him when they liked, that he had no inviolate, private world of his own into which they could not penetrate at will. He clenched his teeth and kept his eyes averted and waited for Menti to speak. Then he was forced to look at Menti, for Menti gave a series of low, contented chuckles.

"You *are* an important man," Menti said.

"What the hell are you talking about?" Cross demanded

"The whole Central Committee is meeting just about

you," Menti informed him. "You sure bring trouble. You've been in this city just a few days, but wherever you show your face, death's not far behind. . . ." Menti rubbed his chin meditatively and continued: "Why did Eva jump?"

"You ought to be telling me," Cross hedged; he wanted to know what had been said when the Party questioned Eva. "She was terribly upset when she came in. She said she'd been to a Party meeting—"

"Did she tell *you* that?" Menti asked.

"Sure. Why not?"

"She was instructed not to."

"By whom?"

"The Party—"

"But why?"

"Well," Menti said, ignoring Cross's question, "she was never really a Bolshevik, you know." Menti shook his head in wonder. "She was a self-centered bourgeois artist. . . . Say, do you know that the Party estimates that only about thirteen per cent of all artists and intellectuals ever make the grade with us?" Menti smiled, indicating that Eva was no great loss. He continued: "Eva broke a decision when she talked to you. But what did she say?"

Cross saw an opportunity to sow confusion in Menti's mind by interpreting Eva's words to his advantage.

"She was horrified," he said. "She said that the Party was trying to convince her that I'd killed Gil to get her— But she knew that that wasn't true. I'd never said a word to Eva until after Herndon had killed Gil— It was Eva who made the advances. She came to my room that very night—"

Menti was impressed; he nodded his head.

"Hilton told the Party that," he admitted. "I don't get this."

"I didn't kill Gil to get Eva," Cross went on. "Anybody who thinks that is crazy. You and your Party are looking for the wrong motives, Menti. . . . I ought to smash you and your comrades for putting the D.A. on me. But he's no fool. Do you think a guy walks into a man's apartment and that very night kills him to take his wife? Good Lord, Menti, *think* a little. Do you think I'd risk my neck doing a

409

thing like that? All right, maybe someone *did* go in there
and kill the two of them. But how do you know they did it
just to get Eva? Think of the many people the Party has
wronged. . . . They might have had a motive. . . . A
woman could have done it. . . ."

"What woman?" Menti asked slyly.

"Look, Menti," Cross said shrewdly, "don't think everybody's naïve. Eva was a victim. . . ."

"How do you know that?" Menti demanded. "What kind
of a victim?"

"The Party tricked her into marrying Gil—"

"Who told you that?"

"Eva did," Cross said. "Even Eva had a motive for
killing Gil. . . . But, of course, she was with me when
Herndon killed Gil—"

"And you were with her when Hilton was killed?" Menti
asked, fishing.

"No."

"Where were you then?" Menti tried to tie him down.

"In a bar. I've accounted for myself with the police,"
Cross maintained. "Look, I'm just as worried about the
motive that could have made anybody go in there and kill
Gil and Herndon as you are. But to say that getting Eva
was the motive—why, that's underestimating people, Menti.
. . . Maybe Gil had enemies with strange motives, motives which only the Party can understand. Did you ever
think of that?"

Before Menti could answer, Cross saw Blimin come
through the door and head for the bed. He understood
why Menti had left the door ajar; it was to give Blimin a
chance to eavesdrop on their conversation.

"I see I won't have to repeat what I've said," Cross said
to Blimin.

Blimin smiled coldly, planted himself in front of Cross
and studied him for some time. Cross met the stare calmly,
waiting.

"Well, at last we know *who* you are, Damon," Blimin
said.

"So?"

"What are you up to? What's your game?"

410

"I'm trying to live, Mr. Blimin—"

"Do you want to join our Party?"

"Frankly, no."

"Menti says you promised Hilton that you would."

"That was before I'd met you," Cross said.

"What did you tell Mrs. Blount?"

"Nothing," Cross said, looking Blimin straight in the eyes.

"Tell me, have you ever been outside the United States?" Blimin asked.

"No. I haven't been to Russia, Italy, Germany, Mexico, Argentina, or Spain. . . ."

"Now that Mrs. Blount's dead, what do you intend to do?"

"I don't know."

"May I ask what arrangements you made with the District Attorney?"

"None. He put me through the paces, but he had no evidence to hold me," Cross explained.

"Don't you consider it an honor to be asked to join the Party?" Blimin was smiling now.

Cross had watched Blimin's mood change; the man had assumed a debonair attitude, as though all of his previous questions had not been as important as he had pretended. But Cross wasn't taken in by this belated pretense of cordiality; he knew that it meant simply that the Party was more baffled about him and his motives than ever; and they were trying to get closer in order to learn more about him. How free these men were! How they could turn, change; how they played make-believe with human emotions! They sensed, as Houston had, that in some as yet unknown and oblique way he was related to them and, being of their moods and temperament, he could sense this in them. He had to act in a way that wouldn't completely kill their trust, yet, at the same time, not let them make him pledge more than he was willing to yield. If he refused to promise to join the Party now they might suspect that his finality and abruptness had back of them something fatally serious; yes, he would make his attitude more equivocal. . . .

"If you're not anti-Party, then why do you so flatly refuse to consider the Party's invitation to become a member?" Blimin asked.

"Look, man," Cross protested. "I've just undergone a prolonged grilling at the hands of the District Attorney. And it was you and your friends who egged the D.A. to pin something on me. . . . Now, I ask you: don't you think I'm right when I hesitate to join? Haven't you a sense of balance?"

"Come now, Lane or Damon," Blimin chided him unctuously. "We admit we put you through the paces. But we were trying to protect ourselves. Can you really blame us for that?"

Cross bowed his head in thought. He wondered why Menti and Blimin had been allowed to enter the apartment and talk to him? They must be trying to get information from me for the police, he reasoned. He could not trust anyone now. . . .

"I can't give you an answer now," he hedged, leaving the door open. "I'm just too tired and upset. I've got to get my bearings— Look, as soon as I hit this city and touched the Party, my life's turned upside down—"

"I understand," Blimin said softly.

Cross did not believe that Blimin understood, and he knew that Blimin knew that he did not believe it; they had reached that point where mutual lies made further communication impossible. But at least they had arrived at a truce. Cross smiled and said: "Can't we talk about this later?"

"Of course," Blimin agreed readily, his mind busy elsewhere. "You're staying here?"

"Yes."

"Then we'll see you?"

"Of course."

Menti and Blimin left. They've gone straight to the police to report, he assured himself. They had been gone barely two minutes when Sarah came to him.

"I know there ain't no use asking you what it's all about, 'cause you ain't gonna tell me," she protested tearfully.

"Sarah, I'm tired; sit down, though," he said, lying back on the bed.

"What happened to Eva? And what is your name? You make me scared. . . ." She let her voice trail off in confusion. Then, as though she did not expect him to answer, she said: "I'm sick of all this. I'm alone. I'm thirty-five years old. And what have I got? Nothing. Bob's gone; they took 'im from me. The Party? The hell with it. I'll never work with them again. Listen, Lionel, you know what I'm gonna do? I'm gonna do what my mother told me to do when I was sick and tired and didn't know where I was going—"

"What are you going to do?"

"I'm going to confession."

"Are you Catholic?"

"Yes," she said. "I ditched the church 'cause I felt they were doping me. But, now—I give up. . . . I'm lost; I don't know if I'm going or coming. . . . Bob and Gil and Hilton and now Eva. . . . Why? It scares me. . . . Only God can answer all this. Don't you think so?"

Her eyes had that restless, desperate look of one tired and confused and unable to support the feeling any longer.

"What are you talking about, Sarah? Only God can answer what?"

"These killings . . ." She groped for words. "Life doesn't make sense any more; it's crazy. . . . People getting killed and nobody even sorry about it . . . it ain't *right*. . . . I can't understand it. You know, Menti really laughed about Eva?" she stated in a half-questioning tone.

Poor Sarah . . . she was crushed and scared. She had to rest, to find support, a master; she was yearning to submit.

"What are you going to do, Lionel?" She paused, shook her head and looked at him with wonder. "Your name's Cross; that's what Menti said. I don't like it; I like Lionel better. . . ."

She was reacting to him now as woman; she knew that he was alone and she was wondering if she, maybe, could somehow team up with him. How movingly simple this woman was! She, like Eva, would recoil in horror (or maybe laughter; who knows?) if she knew the kind of man she was letting her dreams mull over.

"Forget me, Sarah," he told her directly.

413

"But what can I do?"

"What do you want to do?" he asked her.

"You asked Bob that question just before they took him away. You told him to do what he wanted. . . . No; no; I don't want to do that. Look what it brings!"

She did not want the responsibility of her life any longer. Why was life given to man if man could not handle it?

"Sarah, what I'm trying to ask you is this: What helps you most? What makes you feel better, good?" he asked her gently.

She brooded a bit, her face soft with memory.

"When I was a child I was happy," she mused. "At least, I thought I was. . . ."

Cross wanted to dispute that; he was convinced that there were no happy childhoods, that the myth of the happy childhood had been invented by middle-class people to show that their parents had had money when they were children, or by people whose memories of unpleasant days were so defective that they could delude themselves into believing that they had come into this world trailing clouds of glory.

But why argue with Sarah about all this? Her case was urgent and truths of this nature would only make her more unhappy.

"And what do you think made you happy when you were a child, Sarah?"

"I don't know for sure," Sarah sighed. "But I didn't keep wondering about things like this. . . . I believed in God. . . . I went to Mass. . . . Everything was simple. . . ."

"And you want it to be simple again," he said. "I know. . . . Well, do what you were doing when you were a child and see if it makes life simple again. Now, what do you really want to do? Look at me and tell me."

"I want to find a man. . . ."

"Can you? Be honest."

"I'm pretty old for that," she sighed, biting her lips. "I'm fat now. And I've no confidence in myself any more." She let her voice die in her throat and tears began to well into her eyes. She bent forward and cried: "I'm going to confession."

414

Well; why not? All the church had to do was predict that life would be terrible, that man would become overwhelmed with contradictory experiences. They could drill this simple, elementary truth of life into the hearts of impressionable children. Then the fathers of the church could sit back and watch the generations of the sons and daughters of men grow up and go forth on their little voyages of proud, vain desire, could watch them with soft, ironic smiles, for they knew that sooner or later they would come crawling back to the faith of their childhood, seeking solace, wanting mercy, forgiveness. Cross rose and paced the room, looking at Sarah now and then, smiling compassionately at her. Sarah leaped to her feet, her face wet with tears and her eyes hard with outrage.

"Are you laughing at me?" she demanded. "Then you *must* be crazy, like Menti said."

"So, Menti said that, hunh?"

"And, by God, now I'm beginning to believe he's right!"

Cross went to her and placed his hand tenderly on top of her head.

"It might be better for you if you did believe that," he said.

She stopped crying and stared at him, not understanding. "Why do you say that?"

"You need rest, Sarah," he said. "Take your burden to God and lay it down. . . . Remember, He said: *'Come unto me, all ye that labour and are heavy laden, and I will give you rest'?*"

"But you don't *believe* that," she protested, baffled, half-scared. "I know you don't. *Do* you?"

"No." He could not resist telling her the truth.

"Then why do you tell *me* that?"

"Perhaps God uses the Devil to guide people home," he told her.

Sarah blinked, then she ran to him, her lips curling with hate and scorn; she began hitting him with her doubled fists. Cross ducked his head and burst into prolonged laughter.

"Don't, Sarah," he protested good-naturedly.

"You *bastard!* You're making *fun* of me! I could kill you, kill you. . . . I swear, I could! You hear, I could kill

415

you. . . ." She paused, thinking. "Maybe you *did* kill
them like Menti said. . . ."

"It's you who're talking about killing me," he reminded
her. "When did I ever say I wanted to kill somebody?"

"You're laughing, but you can't fool me," she said, her
eyes lit with intuition. "I saw something crazy in you the
first time. . . ."

"Oh, no!" Cross protested, chuckling. "You laughed at
me. Remember how you laughed?"

"I didn't know you then—"

"You don't know me now," Cross told her. "But look, in
all seriousness, I tell you that you ought to go back to your
church. You *need* it."

She did not know what to think. She saw that Cross was
both serious and amused. The expression on her face told
him that thoughts were clashing violently in her mind.

"You are a *devil!*" she burst out bitterly. "You're making fun of me and it ain't *right!* It ain't *good* to laugh at
people for things like that. You like to see suffering. . . ."

"I don't," he said.

"You do; I see it in you—"

"Sarah, what I feel doesn't concern you; forget it," he
told her. "You asked my advice; I say you ought to go
back to God."

"And what are you going to do?"

"Nothing," he said simply, quietly.

She gazed at him, then looked away. She went to the
door, pivoted; her mind was made up.

"*I don't like you!*" she shouted in a sudden rage and
went out, slamming the door.

Yes, Sarah was going back to the church. What did it
matter that the church had no answer for the ills of this
earth? The priests could at least tell her to stop hoping for
anything in this life, to curb and deny her desires, to forget
her humiliating color-consciousness, her poverty, that all of
that was as nothing in the eyes of an eternal God. And for
those who were weak, was that not right, fitting, necessary?
Was it such a bad world, after all? The only trouble was
that he and his kind were restlessly envious of the priests,
the churches, the Communists, the Fascists, the men of
power. . . . That was it. He would have to live without

416

that jealousy blinding him to how weak he was in relation to their organized strength. Render unto the church that which is the church's, and render unto the Party that which is the Party's. . . . But where would *he* stand? Was there no neutral ground?

He sat on the bed, looking at his suitcase. He ought to pack his things. Yes . . . He moved about listlessly, absent-mindedly, slowly filling the suitcase without conviction that he would ever have the right to move about again in freedom. There was something he really wanted to do; he would take Eva's diaries with him, keep them as a memento. . . . He pulled out the dresser drawer and saw that they weren't there. He looked through all the drawers, under the bed, in the clothes closet. Now, where had he put them? Maybe Eva had taken them back when she'd heard the Party's suspicions? But she wouldn't have done that without first telling him; it was not like her. Then where *were* they? *The Party!* He'd bet his life that Menti had them. . . . Goddamn him! He had wanted those diaries. . . . Well, if Menti had stolen them, they were gone. To argue with the Party about them was useless.

Through the closed door of his room came the faint tinkling of the front doorbell. He stood still, waiting, wondering. Was it Menti again with his everlasting Hank? He placed his ear to the door panel and listened.

"Is Lane, or Damon, in?"

It was Houston's voice. Had he dug up any new evidence against him? Was he coming finally to arrest him?

Sarah's voice sounded cold and clipped: "He's in his room. There . . ."

Footsteps echoed down the hallway and died in front of his door. Cross sank onto the bed. He would let Houston take the initiative. Eva was dead and there was no fight in him. A series of sharp knocks sounded on the door.

"Come in," he called.

The door swung open and there was Houston and behind him loomed a tall, blue-coated officer. Under Houston's arm was a package wrapped in brown paper. Houston turned to the officer and said: "Wait down the hall."

"Yes, sir."

The officer left and Houston came in and closed the

417

door softly behind him. He approached Cross, smiling vaguely. Houston had a relaxed, confident air and Cross felt that his time had come. He *knows* now. . . . All right; if this was the end, then he didn't care. . . . Houston looked around, found a chair, dragged it to the bed and eased his deformed body onto it, some two feet from Cross. Cross felt sweat breaking out over his chest and he cursed himself for being unable to control his physical reactions. Well, why didn't the hunchback sonofabitch speak? Why did he sit there with that goddamn gloating smirk on his face? He longed for his gun; if he had it in his hands he would shoot the hell out of that little triumphant god even if he burned for it. . . . All right; he had lost, but Houston would see that he could take his defeat without flinching.

"Damon, I've solved it. You're guilty. You killed Blount, Herndon, and Hilton. . . ."

Houston's voice rang with finality. Cross waited. Slowly Houston unwrapped the brown package and there lay the set of thin angular notebooks: the diaries of Eva. . . .

"You're a lucky, blundering fool," Houston spat at him. "The only witness I could have put in the box against you was Eva Blount, and she's dead. If she hadn't leaped from that window, you'd be on your way to the electric chair. . . . If she had lived, she would have told me what you told her, and what you *told* her made her kill herself. I've found out that much, Damon." Houston rubbed his hands nervously across his eyes. "Goddammit, I was your unwitting accomplice for seventy-two hours! I just couldn't bring myself to admit what I knew in my heart to be true! And no doubt you were banking on just that. What made that girl kill herself was what made me unable to admit that you were guilty. I wonder if you planned it like that? No; I don't think you did. It was too perfect to be planned. You depended upon the human heart rejecting a horror of that magnitude and you were almost right, almost successful. . . ."

"How did you get those diaries?" Cross asked him. "From the Party?"

"No. An officer took them from this room when you

and the others were in the police station," Houston said. "I've read them and I understand it *all* now."

"Did she mention me in there?" he asked, feeling that he had to know at once.

"Only a little, toward the end— What she said didn't matter. It was what she *was* that mattered," Houston told him. "She said that she loved you, but that was all."

Houston carelessly tossed the notebooks on the bed, at Cross's side. Cross was surprised, wondering why Houston was returning the books to him.

"It was all very simple when at last I'd found the key," Houston began in a slow, measured tone. "And the key was this deceived woman, Eva Blount. . . . Look, Damon, I'm an honest man; I'm not going to brag or lie to you. Right off I want to confess that I was haywire in the beginning. That damned Communist Party pushed me off on the wrong track. That paranoiac Blimin was at my office day and night, demanding action, yelling that you had killed Blount and Herndon because of Eva. . . . The Party claimed at first that you were a Trotskyite; then they swore that you were a government spy. In the end they screamed that you saw an opportunity to kill Blount and take his wife and you took it. . . . Funny, isn't it, how they misread things? Every man interprets the world in the light of his habits and desires. The Party shouted at me: 'He sold out to get the girl!' Their own slogans blinded them. They argued that you had to kill Herndon because Herndon had seen you kill Blount; further, they claimed that Hilton had found out somehow and that you then had to kill him. Despite the fact that they could not offer any evidence in support of this, I, at first, felt that it did sound rather plausible. But deep down I was worried; it was *too* pat; it didn't suit your character, didn't fit what you told me that morning on the train. Remember? 'Man's nothing in particular. . . .'

"What a baffling chase you gave us! In the first place, you seemed so innocent, *too* innocent; we made only the most perfunctory investigations. . . . When we began to feel that you *must* know something, we checked your draft card and found a fire had destroyed the records! I wonder

419

if you could have had anything to do with that? You won't answer? All right; it ,isn't important. . . . Then, for twenty-four hours, we made no new moves against you. But Hilton's death told us that we were up against something sinister. We decided to track down every lead, no matter how trivial. . . .

"It was not until we, almost as an afterthought, tried to verify your birth certificate that we began to think of you seriously as a possible murderer. What a joke that certificate was! In Newark the clerks in the Bureau of Vital Statistics remembered you, but we thought that we were surely on the wrong track when we heard their description of you. You're a good actor. You should have been on the stage. . . . When we were certain that you were Lionel Lane and that Lionel Lane was dead, we were back where we started from. We decided that you had assumed this man's name, and we swung then toward thinking that you were in some Communist opposition group. But that fizzled. No political group in America had ever heard of you. . . .

"Then we began checking your fingerprints and we ran into another stone wall. For the second time we discovered that you were dead. Cross Damon, Negro postal clerk of Chicago: *dead* . . . killed in a subway accident. The FBI flew to Chicago to make sure. They reported to me that you were no more. They even exhumed the other Negro's body, but that didn't tell us anything. Then the police started checking with the Missing Persons Bureau. We found that a man of your height and description had been reported missing the day after you were *supposed* to have been killed. Who was this man? He cleaned and dressed chickens in a meat market. . . .

"Finally we had to rely on comparing descriptions of you that we got from Chicago with what we could observe of you here in New York, then we knew that we had the right man. We knew you were Cross Damon, no matter how many dead men you were hiding behind.

"But was it possible that Cross Damon was doing all of this killing? But why? That was the most baffling aspect of all. You'll never know how I struggled against accepting
420

your guilt. *I didn't want to believe it.* After having isolated you, identified you, we faced a riddle. Nothing in your entire background had touched politics. Then I had a brainstorm. I wired Chicago to send me a list of the titles of the books you'd left behind in your room and when they wired back a long list I was delighted. . . . That was the first real clue. Your Nietzsche, your Hegel, your Jaspers, your Heidegger, your Husserl, your Kierkegaard, and your Dostoevski were the clues. . . . I said to myself that we were dealing with a man who had wallowed in guilty thought. But the more I pondered this thing, the sorrier I felt for you. I began to feel as though I'd killed Blount, Herndon, and Hilton myself.

"And when I read those diaries and saw into the deceived heart of this Eva, I knew damn well that you didn't kill to get her. She was hysterically waiting for some man to ask her to run off from that impossible Blount and his Party. . . . I visited her studio and looked at those projections of nonobjective horror she had painted; then I read her diaries and I knew you'd love her, understand her; she was a sensitive artist and represented in her life and work a quality of suffering that would move a heart like yours. In spirit, Eva was your sister. Both of you were abandoned, fearful, without a form or discipline for living; and, therefore, you were both a prey to compulsions. In the face of life, she shrank, but you advanced. But here, attack or retreat is a form of fear. No; you didn't kill to get her; you didn't have to. You'd want to lead her, remake her, save her, and at bottom you'd be wanting, in doing this, to save yourself. . . . And she was ripe to respond on the same basis; she wanted to *help* you. . . .

"Damon, last night you said something that hurt me. When I had the cops pick you up and bring you to my office, when I was putting the heat on you, you told me—well, you implied that I was a kind of monster for confronting you with your wife and children. No, Damon, I'm not that kind of a man. If I were a sadist, I could have had you locked up in the Tombs days ago for investigation, but I didn't." Houston smiled ironically. "I wouldn't deliberately torture anything or anybody on this earth. But, of course, I do so live that I find myself in situations where people are suffering. After all, why did I become District Attorney? But, hell, that's another story.

"No; I wasn't torturing you last night. I was trying to identify you; I had to be absolutely certain that you were Cross Damon, postal clerk of Chicago, supposedly dead, married, and so on. But there was another thing I wanted to know. I had to see how you would react when I told you of your mother's death, how you would react when you saw your sons. . . . I'm a District Attorney, Damon; I was tracking down emotional clues; I was doing my police work . . .

"You were so inhuman that I wouldn't have believed it unless I'd seen it. Many sociologists say that the American Negro hasn't had time to become completely adjusted to our mores, that the life of the family of the Western world hasn't had time to sink in. But with you, you're adjusted and more. You've grown up and gone beyond our rituals. I knew you were beyond organized religion, but I didn't suspect that you were already beyond the family. Last night you stood there in my office and committed the greatest and last crime of all. You didn't bat your eye when I told you that your mother was dead. It hurt you, yes; I could see it, but you rode it out. Boy, you killed your mother long, long ago. . . . You must have known your mother well, understood her both emotionally and intellectually; and when one can see and weigh one's mother like that, well, she's dead to one. . . . And when you saw those three fine sons of yours! They tugged at your heart and memory and you were wildly angry and ashamed; but you rode out that too; you overcame it. And I said to myself: 'This man *could* have killed Blount, Herndon, and Hilton. Only *he* could have done it. He has the emotional capacity—or *lack* of it!—to do it.'

"Then I sat down and thought. After all, Damon, as I told you, I'm close enough to you, being a hunchback, being an outsider, to know how some of your feelings and thought processes *must* go. In a sense, I'm your brother. . . . We men are not complete strangers on this earth. The world changes, but men are always the same. And

422

especially the various basic types of men—and you are an ancient, fundamental type—run the same.

"When I first talked to you in the Blount apartment, how you must have laughed at me! I walked all around you and couldn't see you! And then Hilton started his crazy, class-conscious pressure. Strange, the Communists had access to this insight as well as I and they didn't want to see. . . ."

Cross was still. Yes; he was caught. But where was the *proof*? Eva couldn't witness against him. Had Houston, then, some hidden evidence? If this was the best that Houston could do, why, he would simply walk into court and keep his damned mouth shut and let him see if he could convict him.

"Damon, you're an atheist," Houston resumed, "and that is the heart of this matter. You know what convinced me that you were guilty? No; I didn't find any clues you'd left behind. . . . It was in a realm far afield that I found conclusive proof. Where?" Houston lifted his arm toward the window. "Right out there in those teeming streets. . . . Damon, you act individually just as modern man lives in the mass each day.

"You see, hopeful men seize upon every tiny incident and read the dreams of their hearts into them. Each hour of the day men are asking: 'Do you think we'll have peace? Don't you think what General So-and-So said means we'll have war? Don't you think that the White House pronouncement means that prices will be lower?' Or maybe he observes that his neighbor is reading a radical book and comes to the conclusion that he is a spy and ought to be killed? And, Damon, that was the way you were living. The only difference was that your compulsions were negative, had no direction. . . .

"In the old days we were concerned with mobs, with thousands of men running amuck in the streets. The mob has conquered completely. When the mob has grown so vast that you cannot see it, then it is everywhere. Today the compulsive acts of the lynching mobs have become enthroned in each individual heart. Every man now acts as a criminal, a policeman, a judge, and an executioner. . . .

"But to come back to this individual mob-you who is called Cross Damon. What an atheist you are! You know, real atheists are rare, really. A genuine atheist is a real Christian turned upside down; God descends from the sky and takes up abode, so to speak, behind the fleshy bars of his heart! Men argue about not believing in God and the mere act of doing so makes them believers. It is only when they don't feel the need to deny Him that they really don't believe in Him." Houston rose in his excitement and paced the floor, as though he had forgotten the existence of Cross. "*You went all the way!* You have drawn all the conclusions and deductions that could be drawn from the atheistic position and you have inherited the feelings that only real atheists can have. At first I didn't believe it, but when you stared so unfeelingly at your sons, when you laughed when your poor wife could not summon enough strength to identify you, I knew that you were beyond the pale of all the *little* feelings, the *humble* feelings, the *human* feelings. . . . *I knew that you could do anything!* Not in a towering rage, not to save falling mankind, not to establish social justice, not for glory. . . . But just because you happen to feel like that one day.

"You are a free man. Ideas don't knock you off your feet, make you dizzy, make you fall down and serve others. You always suspect that ideas are in the service of other people. . . . Oh, I *know* you, boy!"

Cross hovered over a vast void. Was this man making fun of him or was he sympathizing with him? What he had feared most had come; there was nothing he could hide from Houston. He kept his eyes on the floor, afraid to look up at Houston's passion-inflamed face.

"You felt that you were right, but not in the sense that you had to insist upon it. No! Does one explain when he says he wants three teaspoons of sugar in his coffee instead of two? You don't have to justify that, do you? You had risen—or sunk!—to that attitude toward the lives of those about you. . . .

"But, Damon, you made one fatal mistake. You saw through all the ideologies, pretenses, frauds, but you did not see through *yourself*. How magnificently you tossed away this God who plagues and helps man so much! But you did not and could not toss out of your heart that part of you from which the God notion had come. And what part of a man is that? It is desire. . . . Don't you know it? Why didn't you just live a quiet life like all other men? That's the correct way of being godless. Why be restless? Why let desire plague you? Why not conquer it too?"

· Houston was questioning Cross in a kind manner, as a brother would question him.

"Desire? Why does man desire? It's crazy, for it's almost certain that he'll never get what he desires. . . . Isn't desire a kind of warning in man to let him know that he is limited? A danger signal of man to himself? Desire is the mad thing, the irrational thing. Damon, you peeled off layer after layer of illusion and make-believe and stripped yourself down to just simply naked desire and you thought that you had gotten hold of the core of reality. And, in a sense, you had. But what does one *do* with desire? Man desires ultimately to be a god. Man desires *everything*. . . . Why not? Desire is a restless, floating demon. . . . Desire tries to seize itself and never can. . . . It's an illusion, but the most solid one! Desire is what snared you, my boy. You felt that what obstructed desire could be killed; what annoyed, could be gotten rid of. . . .

"Only a man feeling like that could have gone down into that room and seen those two men fighting it out, and then killed *both* of them! Not taking sides . . . Not preferring the lesser evil . . . Just a sweeping and supreme gesture of disdain and disgust for both of them! And only a man akin to them could have hated them that much, and you know it, Damon! You slew them just because they offended you. It was just like taking a cinder out of your eye because it stings a bit. . . ."

Houston paused in front of Cross and chuckled. Cross looked at him and said to himself: That must have been how I looked when Sarah saw me laughing at her! Sarah had leaped to her feet and had tried to beat him with her doubled fists, had shouted and cursed him; but he could not afford to act that way with Houston. Pride held him still. To show resentment would give the game away. No; he would sit and take it all.

"How you must have felt in that awful room! I wish

you'd tell me. Did you calculate every movement? Or did you act without knowing it? Did you realize what you were doing, or did you invent the idea of it afterward? How did those two men look to you? And which one did you kill first? I'll bet a million dollars that, even though you're a free man, you killed Herndon first, eh? You're a Negro and you know what fascism means to you and your people. Even a man like you cannot be as indifferent as he would like. . . . Your feet, Damon, I'll bet, were of earthy clay and you killed Herndon first. . . . Won't you tell me? No? All right . . . I won't press you; these are unimportant details. . . .

"Of course, I don't believe that Eva Blount saw Herndon on those stairs. I can't *prove* that she didn't, but I don't believe it. She was wrought up; she wished Blount out of her life, wanted him dead. She imagined she saw Herndon. And I'll bet you seized upon her fantasy and tried to fool us all with it. . . .

"I know that Blount wouldn't have touched you. He thought he had snared you into his ideological spiderweb and that you were his slave, his moral slave, the slave who believes in the ideas that are given to him. . . . But, if you killed Blount first, Herndon would have killed you the next instant, wouldn't he? I'm right, hunh? And you must certainly have gotten a rich, deep satisfaction out of killing that nigger-hater, Herndon. And Blount's face must have been a study in amazement when you suddenly turned on him. . . .

"Then you wiped off all the fingerprints; there were none of yours in the room except on the door. And they had a right to be there, for you had been in the room talking to Herndon that afternoon, hadn't you?

"All right . . . Now comes a gap that I can't fill— I don't know how Hilton found out that you had killed the two of them. . . . Did you tell him? No; you don't want to answer? All right. You can tell me. . . . No; you must not. Then I'd be bound by my oath of office and I'd have to use it against you. . . . Get the point, Damon?

"But I don't think you told Hilton anything. You're much too clever for that. Anyhow, he found out some way. These Communists eat and breathe suspicion. He had his
426

eyes on you from the beginning, according to the Party, but not for any reason, just in general. And he caught you in your little godly game. . . .

"You went to see him. You must have known that he knew. I must admit that I'm a bit foggy about this part of it. He had asked you to come and talk to him about joining the Party. But I can't believe that you went there for that. *That* might have been your excuse. But that was not your purpose. After all, Damon, I'm only human. I can't know all. I'm not a god and do not claim to be one, or want to be onè. I curb my desires, you see?

"But, if I know the Hilton type, and I do to some extent, I'd expect a deal to be made. Damon, why wasn't there a deal, an understanding arrived at between you and Hilton? Maybe the reality of this beautiful Eva had begun to enter the picture to some extent then? Maybe you two just hated each other naturally because you were so much alike? You little gods who traffic in human life, who buy and sell the souls of men, why couldn't you have made a trade?

"Maybe you couldn't trust each other, huh? That's the big trouble with gods when they get together. Gods cannot share power; each god must have all the power or he's no god. For what's a god if he has a rival? Look at Hitler and Stalin. . . . Boy, if they could have been reasonable, they could have divided this whole earth up between them. But, no; each felt that he and he alone had to have the whole earth. So they chewed each other up. When gods fall out, little worms can live. . . .

"But joking aside . . . You killed Hilton with his own gun and you didn't leave a clue. How did you get into the hotel? You were at the hotel desk early that afternoon, but no one remembers seeing you there after that, either entering or leaving. Of course, they have a liberal policy at the Edward Hotel and Negroes leaving or entering wouldn't be the occasion for anybody's noticing, would they? And sometimes I suppose all things work together for the loves and desires of little gods?"

Cross felt dead. How could this man lay open his life with such decisive strokes? With such mocking cynicism? Goddamn him to hell!

"Now, these diaries . . . this girl deceived by the Party

427

. . . this naïve child made the mistake of thinking that she had found in you something clean, pure, something her heart had dreamed of. In *you*, of all the men on earth! She looked upon you and your people as her brothers and sisters in suffering. . . . What irony! Hurt, deceived, she projected her desires on you. Afraid of deception, she embraced a fount of deception! Full of timid, feminine desire, she flings her arms about a furnace of desire and is consumed in it. . . . Then you, in your desert of loneliness, must have told her what you had done. She'd fought the Party for you, told them on her life that you were an innocent man. . . . And, in a sense, she was right; you were innocent of what the Party was charging. But, for a reason I do not know, you told her and she leaped. . . . That's how I figure it. What you told her was too much for her. You made her feel that she could no longer trust any person on this earth. She leaped from that window to escape the kind of a world you showed her! You *drove* her out of life. What you told her was the crowning horror of all the horrors! The apex of deception. . . . And you *had* to tell her; you wanted her help. But did you tell her that Gil had not done anything to you? Did you tell her that you killed Gil for *nothing?* Did you, could you go that far? I wonder. . . .

"Damon, those diaries told me that you were guilty, and that girl's leaping from that window was proof of it. Will you admit it? No? Your silence is a confession! Your inability to challenge me is proof! I'm waiting. . . . *Speak!* Tell me I'm wrong. . . . You *can't!*"

Houston turned, opened the door of the room and went out. Cross lay watching the door swing a little to and fro on a squeaky hinge. Well, Houston was going to get the cops and they were going to take him to the station now. . . . This was the end. But what evidence did Houston have? What facts to buttress all of this? So far he had cited nothing but psychological facts. Come to think of it, they were not even psychological facts. They were feelings, lightning-like intuitions which only a man who had lived long on that lower (or was it a higher?) level of life could know. He heard Houston's footsteps coming back. He braced himself.

428

Houston entered the room with a glass of water in his right hand. He stood looking at Cross a solemn moment, then he lifted the glass to his lips and drained it thirstily, his humped body resembling that of a huge, waiting spider.

"I was thirsty," Houston confessed in the voice of a man who had satisfied a physical need. He sighed. "I haven't spoken so much since I was facing a jury a month ago."

Cross could bear it no longer; his lips trembled.

"Get it over with! If you think you'll drag one word from me, you're crazy!" he shouted.

"Now," Houston spoke in a soothing tone, "don't spoil it all. You were playing your role so well. . . ."

"You're gloating over me! Okay, start your damned wheels turning!"

"Hold on. I'm not through yet," Houston said, with a feeling of deep relish in his voice. "You'll be punished, but not in the way you think. Ah, I know. . . . You have visions of lashes, third-degree sessions, blinding spotlights in your eyes, questions popping at you for hours on end. You may even think of mobs, for all I know. And all of this because the cops want you to confess. But, Damon, you've confessed already. . . ."

Hot tension leaped in Cross. Had he overlooked something silly that would send him to the chair? Had he left some foolish thing undone that would make him look like an adolescent boy stealing apples from a neighbor's orchard?

"Confession?" he stammered. "What do you mean?"

Houston threw back his head and laughed. "You confessed to *me*, just to *me*, to *me* alone. See? I've no concrete evidence to use in court against you."

Was the man crazy? What was he getting at?

"Listen, Damon, you made your own law," Houston pronounced. "And, by God, I, for one, am going to let you live by it. I'm pretty certain you're finished with this killing phase. . . . So, I'm going to let you go. See? Yes; just go! *You're free!* Just like that." Houston snapped his fingers in Cross's face. "I'm going to let you keep this in your heart until the end of your days! Sleep with it, eat with it, brood over it, make love with it. . . . You are going to punish yourself, see? You are your own law, so you'll be your own judge. . . . I wouldn't *help* you by taking you to jail. I've very little concrete evidence to haul you into court on anyhow; it's likely I couldn't convict you. And I won't give you the satisfaction of sitting in a court of law with those tight lips of yours and gloating at me or any jury while we tried to prove the impossible. What the hell could a jury of housewives make out of a guy like you? I won't give you the chance to make that kind of a fool out of me, Damon. I'm much too smart for that.

"These killings will be marked unsolved. And, in a sense, they are. Even now I cannot say why you killed in a rational manner, in a manner that would persuade others . . . I haven't told anyone of what I've found out about you." Houston tapped his head. "It's all right here. And it'll stay there. You're trembling. . . . Oh, yes; I understand now. You thought that I was going to get the cop to arrest you when I went out for that glass of water. You're sweating. Boy, you'll sweat tears of terror, night and day. That's the lot of a little god. Didn't you know that gods were lonely? When you eat, a part of you will stand back, shy and embarrassed. When you make love, a part of you will turn away in shame. From now on, there will be a dead hand holding life back from you. . . . Will you find your way back? I doubt it. To whom could you tell your story, Damon? Who will listen? A psychoanalyst? You have no respect for them, and what the hell could they do for you? They'd be frightened of you; they'd rush out of their consulting rooms, their hair standing on end, screaming with terror. No; they are not for you, my boy. It's between *you* and *you*, you and yourself."

Houston stood looking down with musing eyes at Cross. And Cross felt sweat running down his face; it was on his chest, seeping down his arms. Even his legs were wet. Suddenly he wanted to beg this man not to leave him. He could not believe that it was like this that it was to end. . . . But he could make no move.

"That's all," Houston said. "Whatever nameless powers that be, may they have something like mercy on your tormented soul."

He turned and strode out of the room. Cross could hear him speaking in low tones to Sarah; then he heard the echo
430

of his footsteps along the hallway, the front door open and close. He was alone. He felt like screaming for Houston to come back, to talk to him, to tell him what to do. But he clamped his teeth and held still. I'm alone, he said to himself. He felt dizzy. Terror wrapped him around in a sheet of flame and his body wept tears. . . . The prop had gone; Houston had gone; the world against which he had pitched his rebellion had pitied him, almost forgiven him. . . . The thing he had been fighting had turned its face from him as though he was no longer worthy of having an opponent and this rejection was a judgment so inhuman that he could not bear to think of it.

He had broken all of his promises to the world and the people in it, but he had never reckoned on that world turning on him and breaking its promise to him too! He was not to be punished! Men would not give meaning to what he had done! Society would not even look at it, recognize it! That was not fair, wasn't right, just. . . . The ludicrous nature of his protest came to him and he smiled wryly at his own self-deception. Always back deep in his mind, he had counted on their railing at him, storming, cursing, condemning. Instead, nothing, silence, the silence that roars like an indifferent cataract, the silence that reaches like a casual clap of thunder to the end of space and time. . . .

He had to talk to somebody! But to whom? No; he had to keep this crime choked in his throat. He, like others, had to pretend that nothing like this could ever happen; he had to collaborate and help keep the secret. He had to go forward into the future and pretend that the world was as tradition said it was. . . .

His head dropped senselessly to the bed cover and he drifted off into that state of bleak relaxation that comes after an exhausting strain. He was not sleeping, not fully awake; he was existing, with an alien world looming implacably over and against him. But all of his compulsions were gone, leaving him empty of even desire. . . .

He did not stir from his room until late the next morning, and when he did emerge, it was to go into the kitchen with Eva's diary. Since Houston had laid his self-hate and his self-love so mockingly naked, he felt that he no longer had any right to keep the diary and he was resolved to burn it. He opened one of the notebooks and tore out a sheet; just before touching the page to the flame of his lighter, he let his eyes stray listlessly over the lines, reading:

March 3rd

Last night was in Harlem and had dinner with Bob and Sarah Hunter. A tall, sensitive young Negro, Lionel Lane, was there; he was tense and seemed to be seeking for something in life. He struck me as one who would leave no stone unturned to find his destiny. Gil was taken with him and asked him to come and live with us awhile. Will he too be "used" as I have been? How can I warn him? I dreamed of him after going to bed— I thought he asked me to come and see him and I was afraid because he lived in Harlem— Then I became so ashamed of my fear that I decided to go anyhow. I dreamed that when I got to Harlem there was, for some reason, a huge crowd of people waiting to see me and I felt quite embarrassed and lost. I was trembling, fearing to be asked to explain why I was in Harlem. Lionel came and rescued me; he was so magnificently himself, so self-assured among his own people who loved and respected him. The moment he arrived the crowd changed its attitude toward me. Then he took my arm and led me down the street; he was smiling as we passed in front of the masses of strange people. A wave of happiness flooded me and I fainted. Is not all virtue with the oppressed who are not corrupted? I must find some way of saving this boy from the muck in which my life has become bogged. But how can I do it?

March 4th

Lionel is now in the apartment and I'm filled with a sense of dread. I'd planned to remain in all day, but since he is here, I've decided to go out. I'll go to a concert in the afternoon. That is as good an excuse as any to get away. But I must try to save him from his own naïveté. He is so quiet, trusting, sensitive. What is he thinking all the time? I see him sitting and brooding and his eyes hold the most self-absorbed look I've ever seen in a human being. God, he must be suffering. Is he mulling over

432

the past wrongs done to him and his people? I wish I could help someone like that.

Cross crumpled the sheet, held it to the flame, and watched it burn. Once he turned his head sharply, feeling that Eva was standing near, watching him. . . . Slowly he burned the pages, dropped the charred remains in the sink, ran water over them and flushed them down the drain. When he finished he lifted his eyes and looked out the window.

Bright sunshine was flooding the world with warm, yellow light and he became aware of the soft, faint sounds of water dripping. Yes, a thaw had set in. The ice was melting; the snow was dissolving and flowing from the roofs. . . .

He heard the front door of the apartment open and close; a moment later Sarah came into the kitchen. She had been out into the streets and was still wearing her overcoat.

"I knew you were tired and I didn't want to awaken you," she began without ceremony. "But now you are up and I can talk to you."

"Yes, Sarah. What is it?"

"I want you to move." She did not look at him as she spoke.

"Of course. What do I owe you for our staying here?"

"Nothing." Her voice was bitter.

"I can pay my way." He wanted to help her, but he did not know how.

"I don't want your money," she said. "I'm starting a new life. . . . I went to confession this morning." Her voice was metallic, cold.

"I'm glad for you," Cross said. He was suddenly resentful of the fact that Sarah had failed to see that he, of his own accord, was about to move. "Is your telling me to move so bluntly your first act of Christian charity?"

Sarah's eyes hardened.

"This is *my* apartment—" she began.

"I don't dispute that," Cross told her. "But I thought religion would make you a little kind. . . . I'm all packed to go. I've enough money to take care of myself for a bit.

433

. . . And for that, I'm damned lucky. I'm glad that I'm not at your mercy. . . ."

"I don't want to argue with you—"

"You won't. I'll get out in five minutes."

There was no communication between them. Couldn't they part as friends who had a little sympathy for each other? Cross looked at her and knew at once that there was no way. Sarah desired too much. Only a great promise could lift her up and help her to live again. Promises . . . ? Could he ever make promises again? And he could not promise anything to Sarah; she had already received from her church a promise covering the whole of her life on this earth and the life to come. . . . He turned from her, entered his room, picked up his suitcase, and went into the hall. Sarah stood in the kitchen doorway, looking at him.

"Good-by, Sarah."

She didn't answer; he saw her face reflect a struggle. He started toward her and she burst into tears, whirled, turned into the kitchen and slammed the door. He pivoted on his heels and walked on down the hall, opened the door and went out.

The streets were wet under the glare of a bright sun. He paused on the stoop; he had no notion where he was going. He heard water gurgling in the gutters, running toward the conduits of the sewers. He walked toward Seventh Avenue, thinking: Was it possible that all he had learned in the last few weeks would remain locked forever in his heart? Would he ever be able to say anything about it? And Eva . . . ?

He became aware of someone following him and he turned. It was Menti, and behind Menti was the sullen, inexpressive Hank, whose hands were jammed as always in his overcoat pockets, his eyes staring hard at Cross from beneath the brim of a dirty hat.

Cross stopped and waited for Menti to catch up with him. "Are you following me, Menti?"

"Where are you going?" Menti asked, grinning.

"I don't know. Tell the Party that I said I didn't know."

"Leaving town?"

"I don't know."

434

"How can one get in touch with you?"

"You can't."

"You won't have an address?"

"Maybe not."

"Well, I'll be seeing you," Menti said. "Don't forget the Party."

"How could I ever forget the Party?"

Menti grinned and turned away. Cross kept on to the end of the block. He was moving again among people. But how could he ever make a bridge from him to them? To live with them again would mean making promises, commitments. But he had strayed so far that little commitments were now of no avail. He would have to start all over again. And it was impossible to do that *alone*. . . .

He checked his suitcase and went into a movie and sat looking at the gliding shadows on the screen without understanding their import. Two hours later he came out and had lunch. Once again he stood on the sidewalk, will-less, aimless. Then he was agitated. There was Menti down at the far end of the block, and Hank was behind him. They were watching him. Goddamn them . . .

He came to Lenox Avenue and headed downtown. He saw another movie house. He looked over his shoulder; Menti and Hank were moving toward him. . . . Quickly he paid his admission and ducked into the sheltering darkness, looking now and then to see if Menti or his man was near. . . . He could not find them.

When he emerged three hours later, stiff and thirsty, Menti and Hank were not to be seen. Had he ditched them? Maybe . . . Dusk was falling on Harlem. Neon lights gleamed in the deepening mists. He went into a bar and sat in the rear, facing the door, keeping watch. He downed several whiskies which he could not feel or taste. What was he going to do? Find another room or leave town . . . ?

Once more on the sidewalk, he looked for Menti. Suddenly he longed for the shelter of a well-lighted place, something like a huge hotel lobby with throngs of people and hard, g̱̱ ᵻing electric bulbs shedding clarity and safety upon everything. . . . He found himself facing Central

Park. He paused at a street corner till the red traffic light turned green, then he crossed and walked alongside Central Park, heading downtown.

He glanced over his shoulder, feeling that he was being followed; but there was no one to be seen on the night streets behind him. An occasional car whizzed past, its headlights illuminating the foggy night about him for a moment, then leaving him alone in the dark once more. Ahead he saw a young couple coming toward him, engrossed in each other. . . . A sense of Eva flashed through him and he knew that the bleakness he was now feeling came from the desire he had had of having her with him. . . . This homelessness would not have been so difficult to bear if he had not based his hopes on being with her.

Again he paused and glanced over his shoulder. Yes; there were two dark forms lurking in the shadows about a block away. Menti and Hank were after him. . . . And he was in a bad spot here next to Central Park. He was in danger; he looked around him in panic. He had to hide somewhere, quickly. . . . If he could dodge them tonight, he would leave the city first thing tomorrow morning. . . . A taxi? But there was none in sight. If only he had the shelter of the home of a friend in which to hide. . . . There's a taxi. . . .

"Taxi!" he bellowed.

The taxi slowed and pulled to a curb half a block away alongside the park. He broke into a wild run, waving his hand to assure the driver that he was coming. He ran with the park flanking him. He was lucky, after all. . . .

A second later he heard a snapping sound, like a twig being broken, and then a faint footfall; there was a shower of something like loose gravel and in the same instant he felt tearing through his chest a searing streak of fire; a loud, sharp report smote his ears, and his body jerked. The next moment he was sprawled flat on his back, staring toward a sky he could not see. Pain ripped at his chest. He had been shot. He heard footsteps running. The Party . . . Then his inner world began to turn as dark as that world around him. He heard vague voices.

436